A COURT FOR OWLS

A COURT FOR OWLS

A NOVEL BY
RICHARD ADICKS

PINEAPPLE PRESS, INC.
SARASOTA, FLORIDA

PUBLISHED BY
PINEAPPLE PRESS, INC.
POST OFFICE DRAWER 16008
SARASOTA, FLORIDA 34239

PRINTED IN THE UNITED STATES OF AMERICA

LIBRARY OF CONGRESS CATALOGING-IN-PUBLICATION DATA
ADICKS,RICHARD, 1932–
A COURT FOR OWLS / RICHARD ADICKS. — 1ST ED.
P. CM.
ISBN 0-910923-65-5
1. PAYNE, LEWIS, 1845–1865 — FICTION.
2. LINCOLN, ABRAHAM, 1809–1865 — ASSASSINATION — FICTION.
3. UNITED STATES — HISTORY — CIVIL WAR, 1861–1865 — FICTION.
I. TITLE.
PS3551.D435C6 1989   813'.54 — DC19   89-3466   CIP

FIRST EDITION
10 9 8 7 6 5 4 3 2 1

FOR MILDRED AND JENNIFER

And thorns shall come up in her palaces, nettles and
brambles in the fortresses thereof: and it shall be an
habitation of dragons, and a court for owls.
Isaiah 34:13

A COURT FOR OWLS

PROLOGUE

WASHINGTON CITY
MAY 21, 1865

D<small>AYLIGHT MADE ITS WAY</small> unwelcome through the barred window at
the end of the corridor and forced itself onto the damp wall. It spent
nearly all of itself in the four empty cells before crawling into the
gloom of the fifth, where, on the cot against the back wall, sat a man,
his head bowed and his hands resting on his knees. His feet were side
by side and his knees apart, his arms held rigidly separate by an iron
bar between iron wristbands. He wore a dingy, collarless sailor's shirt
and loose pants held at the waist by a thin cotton drawstring. Covering
his head was a yellow canvas bag with a hole about where his mouth
and nose should be, as if cut by a careless child. Out of it came a
muttering that might have been a prayer or a curse.

Far away a metal door clanged, and footsteps sounded on the
wooden stairway at the other end of the cell block. Three soldiers in
blue stalked down the short corridor, the one in front a sergeant rattling
a chain in his hands, and the others carrying rifles diagonally across
their chests. The riflemen stood at either side of the cell door while
the sergeant fumbled a large key into the lock. He turned the key and
pulled the door open.

"Come on, Paine."

The prisoner stood, a six-foot docile giant beside the three soldiers, ducking his head to pass through the door of the cell. The
sergeant squatted and slid either end of the chain through loops on the
prisoner's iron anklebands, brought both ends up to the manacle, and

wrapped the ends loosely around the iron bar. He lifted a padlock from his belt, thrust its curved bar through the end links, and snapped the lock.

~ The sergeant stepped back so that the other two soldiers could take hold of the prisoner's arms. Steadily they guided him along the corridor, his feet shuffling, toward the wooden stairway. The sergeant strode behind them to the stairway, which was so narrow that one soldier had to go ahead, pulling the prisoner behind him while the other soldier held him back from pitching headlong down the stairs.

At the bottom of the stairs, the first soldier flung open a metal door and drew the prisoner into a long corridor that permitted, through two high windows, a hint of dawn. He let go of the prisoner's arm and rifle-saluted an officer who was facing the door. The other private and the sergeant followed through the door and saluted.

"Take Paine to the courtroom," the officer told them. "His lawyer's got permission to talk to him. Post a guard on the room, Sergeant."

"Yes, sir," responded the sergeant, saluting again. The uneven quartet made its way along the corridor to a wooden door, the prisoner's chains rattling rhythmically. The door was ajar, and the sergeant shoved it open. It swung into one corner of a large, silent room, about twenty paces wide and slightly longer. To the left of the door, running nearly the full width of the room, was a raised dock fenced by a sturdy wooden railing. Three stout pillars supported a high ceiling, and meager light filtered through three crossbarred windows. It was a stern, forbidding room, a place of judgment, but with no single seat of authority for a presiding judge, as in civilian courts. Instead there were two large, long tables, one on either side of the room, two smaller tables in front of the prisoner's dock, and two other small tables near the central pillars. In the middle of the room was a waist-high box, evidently for witnesses.

A man in a black suit sat at one of the tables in front of the prisoner's dock. He was about thirty-five years old, slightly less than six feet tall, with light brown hair and a thick moustache and goatee.

"Here's Paine, Colonel Doster," the sergeant announced.

"Take off that hood, Sergeant—that wretched replica of an iron mask," the man replied. "And don't call me Colonel. I'm not in the army anymore."

The sergeant reached up and almost compassionately lifted the canvas bag from the prisoner's head. A square-jawed, clean-shaven man of twenty-one with tousled black hair stood blinking in the unfamiliar light. His blue eyes looked dull and weary.

"I'll be right outside."

"I'll call you when I'm done, Sergeant."

The sergeant hesitated and glanced at the prisoner before pulling the door shut.

"Sit down, Paine." The lawyer motioned to a chair beside the table. With a rattle of chains, the prisoner sat. "What do you want to tell me, Paine?"

"Today's Sunday, ain't it, Captain?"

"That's right—the twenty-first of May. We're two weeks into the trial."

"Captain, when I was a little chap I always dreaded Sundays like a dose of tonic. My pa's a preacher, and he always made us fancy up and go to meeting. Sometimes near about all day. I hated it. And it always seemed like God slowed the sun down on Sundays." He looked at the floor. "Now every day is Sunday."

He looked up at Doster. "That old man, Seward—the one in Lincoln's government. They say I cut him up real bad, but I don't recollect that. I was just carrying out my orders. But the young man, his son—the one that they say I busted his head open. He going to live?"

"They don't know. He's bad off."

"I'm mighty sorry about it, Captain. Will you tell him for me that I owe it to him to apologize?"

"Yes, I will tell him, Paine."

"I sure wish they would have took this here bar off, Captain. I was glad they taken it off the other day whenever they went to try that hat and coat on me in here."

"Do you have something to tell me, Paine?" Doster asked again.

"Captain, am I going to hang?"

"I'm doing my best to prevent that. But I can defend you only if I know more about you. Who are you? You are called Paine, but the government has learned that you called yourself Powell in Baltimore."

The young man reached his manacled hands toward a glass of water on the table, took hold of it with his right hand, and raised the glass shakily to his lips. He drank with loud gulps. When he set the glass down, Doster filled it again from a pitcher.

"Yes, that's it. My name is Powell. Lewis Powell. Captain Booth, he give me that name, Paine. That was even before I come to know the Paines in Virginia. Them and Clara Meredith. He was a powerful man, Captain Booth was. Why, he . . . he was fit to be a general, maybe a president." He seemed to think about his words. "Maybe even a king." He was silent for a moment, looking at the floor, and he sucked in a breath with a sob. "I am a soldier in General Lee's army—Perry's Brigade, from Florida. I rode with Mosby's Rangers too, back last year in Fauquier County, and Captain Dolly Richards can vouch for me there. That was before I joined up with Captain John Wilkes Booth." He said "John Wilkes Booth" evenly, punctuating each syllable as though the name spoke for itself. "We would have captured old Abe Lincoln if we could have, and there would not have been none of this stabbing and skull-busting that I got sent to do." He cleared his throat. "And Mary Surratt—is she going to hang?"

Doster looked at him.

"She didn't have no part in this." He gritted his teeth and shook his head. "If I had not have gone there to her house that night while I was trying to run away, she would not have to be here. If she hangs, it will be my fault." Lewis Powell stared at one of the barred windows, his mouth agape, as if he saw something there that the lawyer could not see. "Captain," he asked, "do you believe in the signs?"

"What do you mean, Paine?"

"She seen it in the signs, and she told me I would hang."

"Who did?"

"Aunt Sarah. She is an old slave woman on our farm in Florida. She reads signs. Signs in chicken guts, signs in the stars, signs in the way bones fall when you throw them. Pa used to say it was devil-worship, but he give up on beating it out of her. I think he half believed it hisself." He shifted in his chair, and his chains rattled. "I was seventeen then," he said, "and I reckon I was always a bit scared of her, because she is one-eyed and wears a patch over the blind eye. But whenever any of us boys set out to go anywheres, we would ask her what the signs said about the trip."

"Was that when you joined the Rebel army—when you were seventeen?"

"Me and Riley Green—he was from Jasper, in Florida—we joined the Jasper Blues together. Ready to lick the whole Yank nation, we was then."

Outside the window thudded the tread of a company of guards, and a man shouted "Attention!" Lewis Powell drank again. "Her and her boy Martin come from Georgia to Florida with us, and before that from Alabama. That's where I was born, in Alabama, twenty-one years ago last month. We lived in Georgia till I was fifteen years old, and then Pa bought a farm out of Live Oak Station in East Florida. That's where we was at when Florida seceded and the war started.

"I got it set in my head that I wanted to be a soldier soon as I seen the other boys getting into the militia, but Pa, he didn't hold much with secession, and it looked to me for a long time like he weren't going to let me go." Like a man raising a floodgate to release waters long pent, Lewis Powell let loose the words that carried his story, haltingly and then with more assurance, with all the release of the confessional.

1

LIVE OAK, EAST FLORIDA
JUNE 1861

It was so hot and so dry in Florida that summer folks were saying it would take three men and a catfish to work up a good spit. When they could find the chance to go to the settlement for supplies, boys would hang around the general store at Live Oak Station, watching flies circle the sugar barrel and listening to farmers who suddenly knew more about politics and strategy than about hay-making. The boys wanted something to happen, something desperate and critical—a flood, or a hurricane, or a war. They listened to the men because they thought the men could tell them what would happen, but all they learned was what the men thought was the right and the wrong of what was going to happen.

Whatever was coming, it was going to have something to do with somebody called Abraham Lincoln. The men said the election of Lincoln was reason enough for Florida to become the third state to leave the Union, after only sixteen years of statehood. Lincoln, the men said, was getting ready to send troops to Fort Pickens at Pensacola, and how much further, they asked, would he go? One plantation owner, a Mr. Watts, was even heard to say that this Lincoln was going to personally lead an army of free slaves into Florida.

On a day in the second week of June, Lewis Powell was one of the boys who listened to that plantation owner. Lewis could tell that Mr. Watts was an important man. He wore a hat of fine gray felt, a white broadcloth shirt, and a string bow tie, instead of the homespun shirt and floppy straw hat other men wore. The other men sat or stood around him and murmured "That's right" to everything he said.

"Why, my field hands have a better life with me than they would have on their own," Mr. Watts said, "and you can be damn sure a better life than they could have under any abolitionist like Abe Lincoln."

His listeners nodded.

Mr. Watts went on. "I let them have their hootch and women every Saturday night, I doctor them when they are sick, I punish them when they don't do right, and I see that they never go hungry and always have a roof over their heads."

"That's right," grunted the other men.

"Now that boy yonder." Lewis suddenly realized that Mr. Watts was pointing his way, and that every man in the store was looking at him. "That boy and boys like him are going to keep Abe Lincoln and them other Yankees from taking our property and running us off our land." Lewis felt hot, and he stared at the floor and shuffled his feet.

Later, driving the wagon back to his father's farm, Lewis kept hearing over and over what Mr. Watts had said about him. When Mr. Watts and the other men had found out that he was leaving the next day to muster with the Jasper Blues, they had praised him and slapped him on the back, and every man had lined up to shake his hand and to tell him that he would show the Yanks a thing or two. Lewis felt proud.

It was nearly dark when Lewis drove the mule through the gate. As soon as he had unhitched the mule and led her into the lot, he went to Aunt Sarah's cabin. Her son Martin was sitting on a stump in front of the door.

"Where's Aunt Sarah at, Martin?" Lewis asked. "I got to talk to her."

"Mama in the cabin, Doc, but she say what she got to tell you, you don't want to hear."

If Lewis's brothers, Oliver and Wash, had been there, they would have cussed Martin out for not putting "Mister" in front of the name that everybody had called Lewis for nearly all his life, and they would have cussed Lewis out for letting him get away with it. "You are too easy on that nigger," they would say. "Make him do what you say,

7

and make him say 'Mister Doc.' " Lewis would nod, but never do as they said. They would surely have laughed at him if he had told them that Martin was his friend. After all, they had grown up together. But Oliver and Wash were gone now, serving in the state militia ahead of Lewis.

Lewis edged past Martin and stepped through the door. The old woman sat in front of the sparse cooking fire, mixing stew in a black hanging pot. Her head wrapped in a white cloth, she stared at the fire as if she drew some knowledge out of it. Martin followed Lewis into the cabin and squatted next to his mother's straight-back chair.

Lewis looked down at Aunt Sarah. When she glanced up at him, the fire reflected in her one good eye, making it look like a knothole that you could try and try but never see anything through.

"Tell me what the signs say, Aunt Sarah. I asked you last week, and you ain't told me yet."

She turned away from him and talked in the direction of the fire. "I know I ain't told you yet. The signs say don't go. That's all." Her voice made her words sound like sticks being dragged out of a pile of dead brush.

Lewis snorted. "But I got to go. I done give my word on it."

"If you go, you ain't going to come back. The signs say you will hang."

Lewis shivered in spite of the fire and the hot night air. "You are wrong, Aunt Sarah," he said. "I might get shot, but I ain't going to hang. Besides, the war ain't going to last long. Hanging is for treason. I ain't going as no traitor. I am going to serve my state. That's loyalty, not treason."

"You will hang," she rasped again.

Lewis looked at Martin, who rolled his eyes at Lewis as though he only half-believed his mother.

"Martin," Lewis said, "I will be gone for a while. I reckon I won't be in on the bear-hunting this year."

"I'll miss you," Martin said. "Won't seem right, you not being there. Don't walk on top of no rattlesnakes."

"I'll try not to. I won't forget you saving my life that time I got snake-bit down in the river bottom." Lewis looked at Aunt Sarah, who was silently stirring the rabbit stew. "Anyways, your ma says I'm going to hang. Guess I'm safe from rattlesnakes."

"Wish I could come with you."

"Hmm. First sight of you, them Yanks would try to free you and haul you out of state, and you'd have to shoot them just so you could stay where you are."

"Some of the soldiers are taking servants with them."

"The rich ones, maybe. But Pa needs you here. He can't afford to let you go with me. Martin, I mean what I already told you. When I get to be twenty-one, I'm going to buy you from Pa, and I'm going to free you. Soon as I am twenty-one, you'll be free. So you can't go with me, but I'm counting on you to take me as far as Jasper tomorrow morning."

"I'll be hitched up and ready before your feet hits the floor."

"I knowed you wouldn't miss out on driving the mule and wagon through the middle of Jasper." Lewis laid his hand on Aunt Sarah's bony shoulder. "Aunt Sarah, you come on out to see me off in the morning."

She did not turn. "You stay out of the devil's way."

"The devil, he ain't got enough iron bars in hell to hold me," Lewis said.

He left the cabin, ducking his head to clear the low lintel. His foot sank in soft sand, and the still night air felt heavy on his face. He did not go to the house right away. Instead, he went to the horse lot and leaned against the rail fence. The mule was feeding, and Lewis saw the dim outline of her head raised toward him, then bent again to the trough. He listened to the steady crunch of the mule feeding, and he gazed beyond the lot to the dark fringe of woods lined against the fragile blue remaining in the evening sky. Crickets had begun to sing, and on the pond frogs croaked. From the edge of the woods, close by, a chuck-will's-widow shrilled. Farther away a dog barked, and then was answered by a nearer one.

"Hang?" he asked aloud. Crazy old woman, with all that devil-talk. He was a fool to listen to her. "Do you think I'm going to hang, Jenny?" he asked the mule. The mule went on eating. "Reckon not," Lewis said. Maybe it was like Oliver said. Ask Aunt Sarah one day, and she will say you are going to drown. Ask her the next day, and she will say that you are going to come home rich.

*   *   *

Back in February, when the governor of Florida called for militia volunteers, Lewis's father had refused to allow any of his three sons to go into the army. There was the spring planting to be done, he said. But the sons knew that was just an excuse, because the state was not going to call anybody into service until after the crop was in the ground. On the new moon in March, Lewis worked with Oliver and Wash to plow the land and to sow forty acres of corn. They borrowed two mules, and finished the work in three days. While they worked, Wash's wife Susan would come with the children to the cornfield, bringing cornbread and cool well water. She carried the baby, and three-year-old Benjamin ran along beside her. Lewis would pick up the baby and swing him in the air. The child had his name, and when Lewis held him he felt that a life had been lent him to protect.

"Say 'Lewis,' " Susan would coo, without any effect, and Lewis would say, "I reckon he don't know his name yet."

Once the crop was sown, his father kept thinking of one excuse after another. A new barn had to be built, Wash would need a house, new land had to be cleared. It was Oliver, the grumbler, resentful of the old man's high-handed way, who talked Wash into enlisting. Finally, their father let them go—not because they wanted to, but because he knew that if he did not let them go, every Sunday he would have to stare back from his pulpit at the hard-eyed blame of his congregation: Our sons have shouldered their muskets and answered the call of their state—what about yours? So Oliver and Wash had joined Bragg's army at Pensacola.

But Lewis was a different case. "Wait till you're eighteen," George Powell told him. "You're needed here on the farm. With you gone, I ain't going to have nobody but Martin. Maybe he'll be good help some day, but he ain't but sixteen now, and I can't count on him now to show much gumption."

He was standing in the door of the barn while Lewis unbuckled the harness from the mule and lifted the collar over the mule's head. "From the way a lot of chaps is talking, they'll have the war over and done with without you, anyhow. You don't know nothing about soldiering, but you're starting to learn about farming. You might as well do your marching behind old Jenny instead of behind some prancing general. So you can just get that notion out of your head right now about joining up. We'll talk about it when we got a full corn crib."

"Pa, the war will be over and done with, with me missing my chance to be in it."

His father put his hands behind his back and spat, then ground the spittle under the heel of his boot. "Look here, son. I done lost one farm in Georgia on account of a sneaky, double-dealing partner that left me holding the bills. Took me every slave I owned to settle the debts. Now we ain't made no more than two crops since we come to Suwannee County, and they start talking this secession, which ain't nothing but a scheme to make the poor man give everything he's got to keep the rich man's field hands for him. I ain't got nothing left now but this here farm, and without you and Wash and Oliver to help me work it, I'll have to give it back to the bank in Live Oak."

Lewis hung the collar over a peg on the barn wall, then gathered the loose reins and draped them over another peg. He was not used to arguing with his father, and he could see the justice in what his father had said. He had heard it all before, he and his brothers. George Powell never spoke about the war and secession to anybody but his family. In the sermons he preached every Sunday, he stirred his listeners to quake for their sins and thirst after salvation, but he always stood silent about the political quarrels that were dividing state from state.

"I don't want to hear nothing about it," Lewis's mother had told him when he had mentioned to her that he wanted to join. And there was his eight-year-old sister Annie, who would jump on his broad back and ride around the yard, just as she had done since she was a baby. "Doc, don't go and be a soldier. But if you do, will you bring your horse back and give me a ride?"

Finally his chance came on a day and in a place where he had not expected it. In early May, old man Witherspoon across the Suwannee in Hamilton County had hired several boys to ride through the woods on the north bank of the river and round up range cattle for a drive to Jasper, where he had a buyer. Before sunrise Lewis rode his father's horse across the river at the ford and then on along the narrow trail through the pine woods to Witherspoon's farmhouse. Four boys were already there—brothers or cousins Lewis had seen in Live Oak. The youngest, Adam, had sat against a pine tree in a bed of ants, and he was dancing and flapping his hat at the ants that covered his legs while

Luke, Tom, and Jake circled him, pointing and laughing. They did not pay any attention to Lewis when he rode up and swung down from his horse. Lewis was watching the four of them when old Witherspoon came from the house, leading his horse.

"Ain't they but five of you? Where the hell's the other one I hired?" He was a small, wiry man with a quick step and sharp, mean eyes.

"Well," said one of the early arrivals, "Riley said he'd be here, but I ain't seen him this morning."

They heard a whoop from the woods.

"That would be him now."

They all looked in the direction of the whoop. Out of the pine thicket came a cow pony with a shouting, skinny figure on his back. Lewis looked on curiously while the other four boys laughed and hooted. The boy riding toward them whooped again and chanted:

> My name's Riley Green,
> And I'm the best cowboy you ever seen.
> My daddy's a cyclone
> And my mama's a pine tree,
> So get out of the way. Look out for me.

Witherspoon's jaw dropped. "Well, I be damned."

"Howdy, Captain. You ain't going to need none of these Crackers here. Because Riley Green's here, and you got any jobs you want done, I can handle them."

Riley was taller than Lewis, about six-four, but his lanky frame made him seem even taller, with legs that stretched his stirrups almost to the ground and a long neck topped by a narrow face with a long chin and high forehead. His ears stuck out like pump handles, and his pointed nose punctuated his broad grin.

"Just you make sure you don't fall off that there pony while you performing all them jobs, Riley," said one of the four. The others laughed again and jeered at the newcomer.

"You look ahere now," Witherspoon said. "I ain't paying you all seventy-five cents a day just for a lot of jawing and bragging. I got to have fifty head rounded up and penned up over yonder and we're gonna get it done today. You'll sleep here tonight, and we'll drive them to Jasper tomorrow. You all four ride east—Luke knows how far—and

I'll go west with this new feller and this flop-eared jay-bird that's doing so much yelling and bragging. I don't want him meddling with what the rest of you are doing.''

Witherspoon mounted his horse and led Lewis and Riley Green to the crest of a low ridge that ran parallel to the river. They rode along the ridge for half an hour before turning toward the bottomland beside the river. Along the way, Riley tried without success to start up a conversation with Witherspoon while Lewis rode behind in silence.

"Mr. Witherspoon, I bet you got a lot of cows in here."

"Mr. Witherspoon, I hear they're paying near about ten dollars a head now. It's the war coming on, you know."

"Mr. Witherspoon, I seen a hound dog get et by a 'gator in here one time."

Riley finally gave up and dropped back to talk with Lewis. When he found out who Lewis was, Riley told him that he had heard his daddy preach one time at a revival in White Springs, and that it fairly made the goosebumps crawl all up and down his back to hear the scary things he told the people about hell and the devil. "It sure made me want to stay out of hell," he said. "Right there and then I accepted the Lord Jesus as my personal savior, and ever since I been reading my Bible and praying without ceasing."

He asked Lewis if he was saved, and Lewis said that he was, and Riley said that he was mighty glad to hear it, because a man that was not saved was in the devil's clutches for sure.

Witherspoon reined in his horse on the edge of a slough that bit off the end of the ridge. Staying on the ridge, he sent Lewis and Riley down toward the river, where they found a small bunch of cows. They were able to turn the cows back toward the east, while Witherspoon herded them between the ridge and the river. All morning the boys zigzagged through the dense river swamp driving strays into the herd. Riley tried to keep up with Lewis, but his little pony always struck off in the wrong direction. "You wall-eyed gopher!" Witherspoon yelled at him again and again. "Git on over yonder after that there steer!" Riley would grin and try to chase the stray, whooping at the top of his lungs. After a while, Lewis learned to circle ahead of a steer that Riley had startled so that he could drive the animal back toward the herd. Witherspoon would yell at them because they were letting bunches of cattle slip behind them, but it would have taken more experienced cowboys than the ones he had hired to make a clean sweep of the woods.

By late afternoon they had circled back to the flatwoods near the farmhouse where they could turn their horses more easily. Witherspoon uncoiled a bullwhip and rode back and forth behind the cattle, popping the whip and sending the cattle toward the pens. They heard the yells of the other boys coming from the east, driving another small herd ahead of them. Now and then a yearling would get away, but Witherspoon could scare it back with his bullwhip. If the roundup had been more thorough and the cowboys more experienced, they would have sorted out calves for branding and bull yearlings for castration, but as it was, the boys had rounded up barely the fifty head that Witherspoon wanted to sell, and all they could do was herd them into a holding pen to await the drive.

When the last cow was in the pen, Luke slid two rails across the gap in the fence. The other boys dropped wearily off their horses and unsaddled them. Jake nursed a bruised shoulder from his horse having scraped him against a tree, and Lewis's face was scratched from thrashing in the underbrush. Tom had been dragged through a patch of prickly pears and was still pulling thorns out of his body.

Mrs. Witherspoon, a drawn, bony, nervous woman, had supper ready, baked ham with sweet potatoes, black-eyed peas, and cornbread. The boys ate hungrily and noisily, swapping stories about the roundup. When Mrs. Witherspoon set a big dish of cassava pudding in the middle of the table, all of them forgot everything else as they spooned the steaming pudding into their bowls. Luke gulped down his bowlful, then pointed toward the bare rafters and yelled, "Look out, Riley, what's about to drop on you!" Just as Riley looked up, Luke grabbed the bowl of pudding from in front of him and jumped from the table. He jerked Riley's hat off the rack by the door and dumped the pudding into it. While Riley stumbled away from his chair like a bear caught in a trap, Tom, Jake, and Adam danced around the room, jeering. Luke clattered the wooden bowl back onto the table and held the hatful of pudding in front of him like a surprise Christmas gift.

Witherspoon sprang to his feet, his head lowered like an angry bull's, while his wife groped the air with a sign language all her own.

"Damn it," Witherspoon rasped, "take your fights outside! I ain't having none of this in this here house!"

Luke ran out the door. "You all come on and let's have some fun."

Riley kicked his chair across the room and chased after Luke with Tom, Jake, and Adam close behind him. Lewis stopped to grab his own hat before walking outside and leaning against the porch railing. The four boys circled Riley, tossing his dishonored hat from one to another, while he spun dizzily and grabbed at air. It was not until Adam feinted to his left, then tossed the hat over Riley's head toward Jake, that Riley leaped up and caught it. In the same movement he threw himself toward Luke and smashed the soggy hat into his face. They rolled in the dirt, punching and grabbing at each other's wrists.

Lewis wanted to be in on the fun, and his chance came when Jake moved into the fight. Riley was sitting on Luke's chest, trying to hold his wrists against the ground, when Jake slipped behind him and dropped a loop of rope over his shoulders. When he jerked the rope tight, Riley looked up, startled. Lewis jumped off the porch and ran at them. He seized Jake by one shoulder, spun him, and drove his fist into his face. Jake crashed backward, stumbling into a washpot, while Tom grabbed Lewis from behind, pinning his arms to his side as Adam began to pummel him in the stomach, chest, and face. Lewis kicked Adam in the groin, doubling him up in pain. Then he twisted his body, loosening Tom's grip, and smashed him in the stomach. Catching him off balance, Lewis fell on him, his knee in Tom's chest and his left hand pushing into his face.

"Let go of Tom, Doc, and I'll let go of this one." Lewis looked around. Luke, who had thrown Riley and pinned him to the ground, grimaced at Lewis through a layer of the pudding that Riley had ground into his face, and Lewis broke into laughter. He let go of Tom and moved away from him to kneel on one knee. Adam was rolling on the ground, moaning and holding his crotch, and Jake dragged himself from the washpot, spitting out blood. Luke stood and let Riley up. Luke laughed too, and sucked in a big breath of air.

"Whoo-ee, that sure was a full dinner, weren't it?" They all laughed then, even Adam, who was able to stand, though doubled over.

"Hey, let's go for a swim," Riley said. Tom reached Jake a hand, and helped him to his feet, and Riley picked up his hat, gummy with the remains of pudding and caked with dirt, and looked at it forlornly. He slapped it against his britches leg twice, then let it droop from his hand like the flag of a fallen legion as he limped beside Lewis to the spring.

There was not much daylight left when they stripped off their clothes and jumped into the chilly spring water. Adam was the first one in. He ducked under and came up blubbering and shaking water from his hair. They all splashed and shivered, and Luke climbed onto an oak limb over the water and dropped in.

"Oh, Lord! This is cold!"

"One thing for sure. I'll have the cleanest hat in town."

Lewis felt the warm air on his body, washed clean of the sweat and the fight. Even the scratches of the day's work had stopped stinging, and he felt comfortable and at ease with the world as he slipped into his long suit of underwear and pulled on his boots. Coming back to the clear field beside the house, the boys spread their bedrolls, pulling the blankets around their ears against the mosquitoes that swarmed around them.

The talk was all of the coming war.

"My daddy says that anybody that is against see-cession is a low-down abolitionist," Luke said. "Why, there was one of them over in Lake City, and they say the Regulators got after him and beat him good."

Lewis thought of his own father and wondered if anybody suspected that he opposed secession. "Is your daddy a Regulator?" he asked Luke.

"No, but he says they been a-doing a lot of good work around here, making sure the niggers ain't giving nobody no trouble, and looking out for abolitionists and that sort of trash and beating them up or running them out of the country."

"Well," Tom put in, "what I mean to do is join the militia and go off and shoot Yankees."

"Me, too," said Riley. "One of my schoolteachers is helping to get a company up, and I'm gonna join."

"Who's that?"

"Moses Duncan."

"Oh, him. He sure can hit hard with a hickory paddle. I hope he don't do no switching in the army."

"Godamighty," Jake said, "I ain't taking no whipping off nobody, teacher or lieutenant. He better do his whipping on the Yankees."

"Hey, Riley, would you know a Yank if you seen one?" Adam asked.

"I sure would. They're powerful little fellows, with little black, beady eyes, and they liable to run like jackrabbits when a Southerner gets after them."

"Well, if that's so, there must be a swarm of Yanks whining and buzzing around my head, except they don't run when I tell them to."

It was still dark the next morning when they began stirring. Witherspoon growled at them to get moving, and they groped their way to the house, doused their heads in a bucket of water from the well, and went inside, where Mrs. Witherspoon had already set out cold cornbread and cane syrup. There was a pot of strong coffee on the stove, and they drank the coffee out of tin cups. Then they went outside, saddled their ponies, and turned out the cattle that Witherspoon wanted to drive to Jasper.

Lewis had heard of drives where hundreds, even thousands of cattle had been moved through the Florida woods to Tampa to be loaded on flatboats to Cuba, and now he imagined that he was part of one of those adventures. He rode beside the herd of fifty cattle, with Luke behind him, and from time to time he would have to leave the trail to turn a steer back toward the herd. But the day went without any trouble, and in the middle of the afternoon they drove the cattle into the stockyard at Jasper. While Witherspoon went to look for his buyer, the boys unsaddled their horses.

Luke, Adam, Jake, and Tom huddled together like conspirators, then slipped away from Riley and Lewis as soon as they could leave their horses at the stable.

"Come on, Doc," Riley said. He led Lewis down the dirt street and around a corner to a clapboard shack under some oak trees. Crossing a narrow yard of white sand, Riley tiptoed onto the porch and, pulling Lewis by the shirt, slipped into the cool breezeway that ran through the middle of the house. Riley put his finger to his lips and pointed at a short, lean man sitting at a plank table, his back toward them, bent over something he was writing. Riley drew himself fully erect, puffed out his chest, and squeaked, "Private Green reporting for duty, Lieutenant!"

The man at the table dipped his pen in an ink bottle and spoke without turning around. "About time you got here, Green. Thought you would let the war get over and done with before we saw you." Then he rose from his chair, laughed, and shook Riley's hand. "Riley, I'm mighty glad to see you. So you decided to join up with us after all."

"Mr. Duncan, you knowed all along I couldn't stay away. I brung another man, too. This here's Doc Powell. I been talking to him about the Jasper Blues, and I think he's about ready to sign on with us."

"Riley," Duncan said, "I always knew you were my star pupil, but now I see you're a star recruiting sergeant as well. Both of you sit down and have some coffee and biscuits. I was just making a roster for the company. We'll soon be at full strength."

Riley and Lewis took off their hats and sat at the table while Moses Duncan paced around the room, talking about his hopes for the company, about Judge Stewart, who would be the captain, and most of all about the readiness of men all over Hamilton County to rally to the cause. "Why, some days as many as ten men have come in to sign up, and sometimes brothers will come together. We'll have the best-spirited company in the whole state. We're going to give the folks in this county good reason to be proud of the Jasper Blues."

While Lewis listened, he thought about his brother Wash leaving Susan and the children and going to the war, about all the men who were volunteering to defend their homeland from the hostile North. His skin felt so tight that he shivered, as if he could not hold in the hope and pride that were building in him. What did it matter if his father would not let him join in Suwannee County? Here across the river he could go with his friend, fight by his side, begin as an outsider but win his way by his courage and his service to his state. He would become one with these men ready to defend their homeland. Some day his father would admit that Lewis was doing a noble thing for his home, his family, his country, and would be proud.

That night, in his bedroll at the stockyard, Lewis could not sleep. He lay awake, listening to Riley snoring, and saw himself as part of a great and powerful force that would smite its enemies with the terrible swift sword of God, sweeping those enemies before it like dry leaves and leaving their homeland free. When he felt afraid to tell his father about the oath he had taken, he was able to chase away his fears with thoughts of the deeds it would be his honor to perform, and by which his name would become known. Some day he would surely stand beside his brothers, basking in the pride of his mother and his father.

The next day the ride back to his father's farm seemed short, and Lewis was even disappointed when he learned that his father had gone into Live Oak on business. He had to wait until night to tell him about his enlistment, but Lewis was surprised to find that his father had somehow expected the news, that he had resigned himself to the departure of all his sons. Perhaps seeing the joyous arming that was afoot in Live Oak had served to prepare George Powell, but Lewis discovered that even his mother had prepared herself to let him go. She knelt beside him and prayed, and then his father called in the servants to pray with them. He called on the Lord to bless and preserve his son and to guard him from all the snares that the devil would set in his path. In response Lewis murmured, "Oh, yes, Lord, amen," and felt strength surge within him, confident that he could stand against either the devil or the Yankees—and he had by now been led to believe there was no more difference between them than between two fence posts.

A month had passed since Lewis had enlisted. He had laid the last rail on the last fence and had dug the last stump out of the new ground that he had helped his brothers to clear. Tonight, with the well-wishing of the men in the store at Live Oak fresh in his memory, he had listened to Aunt Sarah's dark prophecy. Lewis fanned his hand at the mosquitoes whining around his ears, turned away from the horse lot, and started toward the dim rectangle of light that told him where the house was. As he neared the porch, he saw his mother silhouetted in the door. A small shadow pulled away from the larger one and drifted toward him. It was his sister Annie, who threw her arms around him, sobbing and begging him not to go.

2

FLORIDA
JULY 1861

THE BAND KNEW only two pieces — "Suwannee River" and "Home Sweet Home" — and they had been playing them over and over all morning. There were two trumpet players, three fiddlers, and one drummer, a fat man with a grinning red face who wore a blue coat with gold epaulets. He pounded on the bass drum like a man driving nails, stopping now and then to mop the sweat from his forehead.

Moses Duncan adjusted his freshly blocked wide-brimmed hat before twisting his neck and rolling his eyes toward first his left shoulder and then his right to make sure that the silver bars that proclaimed him a first lieutenant were still attached. He had made the bars himself a month before, immediately after being elected to the rank, staying up all one night to melt silver coins and then hammer and polish the metal into what he thought would be regulation size. Sewn onto his tunic, they made him feel more like a military leader, even though he had to admit to himself that his only qualifications as an officer were that he had taught lessons on the Napoleonic Wars to most of the boys in the company, and that he was over twenty-one — by less than a year, to be sure, but those few months made a difference.

Duncan scanned the ranks of the ninety-six men who made up the company, a mere handful of them freshly suited in blue uniforms befitting the company name. He had put those few in front, with swapped or borrowed deer rifles on their shoulders. The rest of the company wore civilian clothes and carried shotguns or nothing. Most were boys he had taught algebra and history, grinding the lessons into them until he had learned more about the subjects than they would ever care to learn. School days were behind them all now—even the days of mustering and drilling were behind—and he thrilled at the thought that soon he would have the chance to taste of the battle that he had read about in stories of Alexander the Great, Julius Caesar, and Napoleon.

Moses Duncan turned slowly to look over the crowd gathering at the edge of the parade ground. Mattie and her family had not come into town yet. "I could not love thee, dear, so much, loved I not glory more," he whispered to himself. *Glory?* No. The word was *honor*. He said the line again, this time with *honor* in it. No matter. *Glory* was a good word too, and it would fit just as well. But the best thing he had for her was the poem, which had taken him half the night to write. He mouthed the words again to himself, words already set down in neat script on the paper trimly folded and tucked into the sweatband of his hat.

> A silver moon through the pines I see,
> As battle trumpets sound afar,
> And these arms of thine I pain to flee,
> To heed the call of thund'ring war.

Battle-trumpets. He especially liked that, and he thought she would like it too.

A loud, braying laugh distracted him, and he looked over at Judge Henry Stewart, the captain, standing by the speaker's platform talking with the senator, who was Moses' brother Will. Will's jackass laugh had made him famous all over Hamilton County. Will laughed again and clapped Henry Stewart on the back, then mounted the platform.

Henry walked toward the front of the company, stood waiting while two privates ran to join ranks, and commanded, "Comp-nee!"—his voice always broke on the second syllable—"Ten-shun!" Behind him, Moses Duncan heard the rattle and shuffle as the men tried to look like a military unit. The crowd, seated on wagons or leaning against them, hushed their talk enough to strand one small boy in the middle of a yell. Here and there a baby cried. A sudden loud crack from one end of the parade ground made everybody turn in time to see a boy desperately swinging from a broken branch high in a dead tree. Two boys on a lower limb grabbed him and eased him to the ground. Laughter rippled through the crowd, and boys in another tree applauded. The breeze quickened, and the Stars and Bars popped against its halyards, extending three broad stripes from the union of a cross and stars.

The clerk of court looked right and left, half stood, and started to sit down again. Will Duncan leaned toward him and said something, and the clerk stood again. "Ladies and gentlemen— " he began.

"Louder, Jehu," somebody in the crowd yelled. The clerk spat and started again. The wind carried most of his words away, but not until he had managed to announce that he was calling on Elder Peacock for a prayer.

While the black-coated old man was intoning his prayer, Moses Duncan watched three or four wagons pull to the edge of the parade ground, the drivers reverently pulling off their hats and tugging reins to keep the mules still.

When Elder Peacock uttered "Amen," there was a rustle in the crowd as men put their hats on and the talking started again. Then Moses saw Milton Bryan's wagon, with Mattie sitting beside her father, and her brothers and younger sisters in the bed of the wagon. Moses Duncan knew that she saw him, but he stood more stiffly and kept his eyes straight ahead, except when he would dart a glance toward where she sat, holding her bonnet on her head against the wind.

By now his brother Will was on his feet, and the clerk was introducing him, making him out to be a blend of Thomas Jefferson and Pericles. Moses Duncan was proud that his brother Will had gone to Tallahassee and voted for secession, but he did not care to hear what he had to say about it.

While Will talked about secession, about the founding of the Confederate States of America, and most of all about his archenemies, Floridians like ex-Governor Call who opposed secession, Moses Duncan was thinking about what he would say to Mattie. At the frolic last month, when he had a chance to dance with her, he asked her to wait for him to return from the war, but she would not give him an answer.

The crowd cheered. Will Duncan had started talking about the Jasper Blues. "Man by man, arm in arm," he was saying, "they have lifted their hands from the plow and answered the call of their state. Many are beardless youths who have never tasted the bitter flavor of battle. But like those who followed Washington at Valley Forge, like those who stood with Andrew Jackson at New Orleans, they have stretched their hands toward their mother state and said, 'Take them. They are yours.' And she has replied, 'Here is a sword for those hands. Bear it with pride and vanquish your country's enemies.' With such men marching under the banner of Florida, of the Confederacy, of God Himself, how can we fail?"

Amid the clapping and cheering of the crowd, Moses Duncan thought of the men who did not have uniforms or weapons, and he wondered what kind of sword his brother Will thought the state would give them. But when he heard the cheers spread to the men behind him, he felt in his throat a lump of pride and sentiment, and he looked again at Mattie in her flowered frock and white bonnet. Even before Henry Stewart could dismiss the company, they were swarmed by mothers, fathers, sisters, brothers, sweethearts. Moses Duncan hugged his mother and shook his father's hand. Then he left them to go to Mattie.

She was talking to Bessie Freeman, who kept trilling that giggle that he would know with his back turned, and squint-eyed Mary Phillips.

"I thought you would not get here," he said to Mattie.

"The axle broke on the wagon just when we left home, and Papa and the boys had to fix it. But we got here in time for the senator's speech. My, it was a good one."

"Well, that's not what I wanted to talk to you about." He looked at Bessie and Mary.

"Well, Mary," Bessie said, "I can see we are not wanted here. Let's go and find my brother." She giggled again, shoved Moses on the shoulder, and pulled Mary by the arm. Mary squinted at Moses and Mattie, then followed.

"Come on," he laughed, taking Mattie's hand. "Let's go over yonder by that pecan tree and talk before they come back."

"They won't be back in a hurry. Who's that big soldier they found to talk to?"

Moses Duncan looked back toward the parade ground. "Oh, that's Doc Powell. Friend of Riley Green's. He's so big the other fellows say when they get into a shooting match with the Yankees, they'll shoot from behind him."

"Well, if he can stand Bessie Freeman's giggling, he ought to be able to stand up to the Yankees."

Moses pulled off his tunic and spread it on the ground under a pecan tree for her to sit on, while he leaned against the tree, fanning himself with his hat.

"It's so thrilling," Mattie said. "I wish I was a man, so I could be going off to war like this."

"You? Why your papa won't even let your brothers go. He plumb near ran me off the place when I came out to talk to them about joining. He wouldn't let you go, if you was a man."

She jumped up, laughing, and snatched his hat from his hand. She pulled it down on top of her bonnet, its brim to her eyebrows, and saluted. "I would change his mind, and I would march off like this and fight the Yankees anyway."

Moses Duncan looked down at her body, tight against the figured dress, and remembered her breasts against him when he had swung her in the square dance.

"I'm sorry that this month's frolic got rained out," he told her. "You said you would dance with me again then."

"I'm sorry, too. But I made you something." She reached into a pocket of her skirt, pulled out a red-checked piece of cloth, and un-folded it to show "Moses Duncan, Jasper Blues" stitched in blue letters like the writing in a child's copybook.

"Why, that is a mighty fine gift," he told her. "A lot of fellows carry things with their names on them, and I didn't have anything until now." He folded it into a triangle and tied it around his neck. "I will bring it back, though. The Yanks can't shoot very straight."

"I am so proud of you—of all of you. Everybody says this war has got to be fought if our state is to be free. I want you to give those low-down abolitionists what they've got coming to them, then come back home in time for school to start."

Moses smiled. "Well, it just might last longer than that. We have enlisted for a whole year."

"If it lasts into the cold weather, I'll knit you a sweater. All the ladies are starting to sew and send you all the things you need."

"The ladies are doing their part. That's for sure."

Blee-ahp!

They looked around at the drill field, where one of the young boys had taken possession of the company bugle and was showing off. Moses and Mattie turned back toward each other and laughed.

"Oh," he said, "I plumb forgot. Let me have the hat. I have something for you." When she took off the hat and handed it back to him, he pulled the folded paper from under the hatband. "It's something I wrote."

"You wrote something for me? Let me see it."

"Not so fast now." He pulled his hand away and held the paper straight up while Mattie reached for it. "I'll read it to you myself."

"I'm all ears."

"That's what the cornfield said to the crow."

Fwa-a-ahp! Two boys were tussling over the bugle, and one had just snatched it from the self-appointed herald.

Moses Duncan glared at them, and started reading, trying to give his voice the mellowness that he thought the poem deserved.

A silver moon through the pines I see
As battle-trumpets sound afar—

Blaa-a-aht!

He looked around, annoyed, but when he looked back at Mattie she was standing with her eyes closed, her hands folded in front of her, her nose wrinkled in an anguished way.

And these arms of thine I pain to flee,
To heed the call of thund'ring war.
Thy voice, raised in some sweet hymn,
So like unto an angel's song
Will echo in my memory dim
Through times I hope will not be long.

Ah-choo! The sneeze that had been building in her gave way, rustling the paper in his hand.

He read on:

And so, my tender thoughts of thee,
Will guide me through the cannon's roar,
Filling my grieving heart with glee,
Till back again with thee once more.

He looked at Mattie, who appeared to be waiting to find out if there was more to the poem. "The end," he said.

"It's—it's such a lovely poem," she said, her eyes rimmed with tears. "I've never heard a prettier poem than that." She laid her hand on his. "I like where you said, 'back again with thee once more.' "

"Well, I hope it won't be long." He looked into her eyes, until she blushed and looked down. She stooped and picked up his tunic. She looked up with a sad smile as she rubbed her sleeve on the shiny silver bars, then handed him the tunic. When he put it on and started to button it, she reached to fasten a button. Their fingers touched, and his blood raced. Then she took his arm, and they walked together toward the company.

The men were falling into formation, and the time would soon be gone for the words that he had searched a book of poems to find and now held ready on his tongue. Taking her hand, he said, "I could not love thee, dear, so much—"

Pwoo-ah-oot! Somebody tooted a wavering note on the bugle not ten feet from them.

—"loved I not glory more."

Mattie was so startled by the bugle that he was never sure that she heard the second line—and he realized that he had said *glory* again instead of *honor*—but he set his hat on his head, turned, and walked toward the company. The other men were running from all corners of the parade ground. Some stuffed small parcels—shirts, scarves, food—into knapsacks, and one man was even carrying a cake. There was nowhere for him to put it, and he cradled it in his left arm while he stood at attention. The men were laughing at Riley Green, who had a live chicken tied by the feet and slung over his shoulder.

Henry and John Stewart, the only officers who had horses, led the company while Moses Duncan and the other lieutenants marched beside the men. The band rushed to the front of the column and started to play "Suwannee River" again. Three girls ran forward and kissed some of the soldiers while their comrades hooted, and a troop of small boys and dogs skipped behind the company as far as the edge of town, where the six musicians drifted to the side of the road and wiped their sweaty faces while the company marched past them. By the time the Jasper Blues had gone a mile, they could look back and see the last well-wishers turning their wagons around.

* * *

The thirty-mile march to Lake City took two days. Lewis was as excited as a young plowhorse just out of the traces. This was nothing like the month he had spent in Jasper while the company was being formed. There he had to drill every day, marching up and down a parade ground, with the sergeant yelling at him for being out of line or out of step. He had joined to fight the Yankees, not to wear out good shoe leather marching. But the most stupid thing of all was guard duty. Once a week he had to walk around the camp with a musket on his shoulder when there was not a Yankee within a thousand miles. What he was guarding or who he was guarding it from, nobody could tell him, least of all the officers. They were the most useless plunder in the army. Captain Stewart spent most of his time back at his plantation, and the lieutenants sat around and told lies to one another. You never caught any of them walking guard duty. That young officer, Riley's schoolteacher, Duncan, did not do anything but watch for the girls to come to the camp. Then he would strut around with his saber and his hat guiding the ladies. Riley would just laugh and say that was the way the army was.

But now Lewis felt like he was part of a real army. Everybody was talking about where they were going. Most of the talk was about a great army gathering in Virginia, to march on Washington City itself. Riley would say that he and Lewis were going to capture Abe Lincoln by themselves. Sergeant Willis said the company would sure take Riley and Lewis when they went to arrest old Abe, because they said that Abe Lincoln was as tall and as thin as a pine tree, and it would take somebody just as tall to look him in the eye.

Sometimes, when they would pass a farm, the farmer and his wife would come out and give them milk and eggs, and small boys would walk along with them until they got tired and turned back home.

At night they camped at White Springs, by the Suwannee, spreading their bedrolls close to the campfires in hopes of driving off the mosquitoes. One of the men had brought a fiddle, and he could do wonderful things with it. Lewis liked to sing "Lorena" and "Home Sweet Home" with the men, but the songs made him feel sad. He had always liked to sing, and his family and neighbors always called on him at home and at church to sing hymns, but this was the first time

27

that he had ever sung with men beside a fire at night. Some songs were lively and full of forbidden words, like the version of "The Girl I Left Behind Me" that one of the men sang until Captain Stewart told him that he ought not to sing that kind of song around the younger soldiers. Then late in the evening they softly sang "Juanita" and some old hymns.

Lewis liked to sing his favorite:

> Farewell, farewell to all below,
> My Jesus calls and I must go;
> I launch my boat upon the sea,
> This land is not for me.

The words were not just about heaven. They described anybody who was having to go from one place to another. Still, Lewis had never felt more at peace with the world than he felt on this march, among these men. If this land was not for him, surely no land on earth could be. Was there anything even in heaven to equal the feeling of lying on his blanket, his stomach full, the stars above him, listening to the wind in the pines and the laughter of comrades?

The rain started when they were still a half-day's march out of Lake City. At first it was a slow drizzle, but it had turned into a cloudburst by the time they reached the edge of town. Lieutenant Stewart rode ahead and came back to say that there were no cars to carry them to Jacksonville. Some men wearing new boots were suffering sore feet, and they complained that it sure seemed like the army would have known they were coming and got ready for them. Lewis's tunic was too small for him, and the collar chafed his neck even after he loosened it. Walking in the rain had done nothing to help the ill fit, and the heaviness of the water-soaked tunic was like an extra burden.

So the Jasper Blues, hungry and weary, walked into Lake City under a heavy rain, in ranks the officers no longer tried to keep straight. They trudged past scattered houses shuttered against the wet gloom of the afternoon; the only sound of their passing was the sucking of their boots as they drew them out of the mud. As the day waned, the officers and the few men who had tents set them up on a muddy field between the courthouse and a lake, on a ground trodden for three days by the other companies that had passed through the town and travelled on to Jacksonville. The mess tent that had served the earlier arrivals now stood empty, and the men ate a cold supper of fatback and cornbread out of their knapsacks.

Toward sundown some townspeople came to the campsite and offered the soldiers lodging in their houses and barns. Lewis, Riley, and a man named Coalson shared the planks of an empty smokehouse that smelled of the hams that had been hanging in it, and they fell asleep listening to the rain drumming on the cypress shingles.

Lewis woke in the night to the sound of sobbing. "Riley? You all right?" But Riley was snoring. The stifled sobs came from Coalson.

"Something the matter?"

"N-no."

Coalson was moody, always staying apart when the other men would join in games or song. At Jasper, his family came to visit him every day, and with them came a large, strong-looking girl who would sit on a rail fence by Coalson for an hour at a time, sometimes talking and most of the time staring with him in silence at the grass in front of them. After she left, Coalson would lie alone, brooding, in his tent. He's just homesick, Lewis thought, bawling like a calf at weaning time. The calf gets over it, and he will, too. Lewis thought about his own home. Sometimes he missed them—Pa, Ma, his sisters, Wash and Susan and their children, even Oliver—but back there it meant getting up and doing the same dull work over and over every day. Maybe it would be better someday when he had his own farm, but his father was a hard man to work for, and this soldier life had farm life beat. No, he would not get homesick, and neither would Riley, who knew how to make the best of things wherever he was.

When Riley shook Lewis awake the next morning, Coalson was gone. "Likely gone to look for something to eat," Riley suggested. But he was not present at roll call, and later in the day Lewis heard that Coalson was being reported absent without leave. The men spoke about it in low tones, as if they had heard that a man had stolen money from a church. Lewis felt as though something had been taken away from him.

The Jasper Blues waited in Lake City for another day before the locomotive and a string of cars arrived. The soldiers boarded the boxcars and left Lake City with only a handful of people to wave

29

goodbye to them. One old man stood in his buggy and waved his hat. "Hoorah for Florida and the Confederacy!" The cars started with a jolt, and Lewis, standing in the door behind a fence of cypress rails, lost his balance and crashed to the floor. When he was getting onto his feet, another soldier told him, "I do declare, Doc, if an old man hoorahing is going to knock you over, you better watch out for them Yanks."

Lewis had never been on the cars before, although he had watched them pass through Live Oak. The locomotive was only three cars ahead of the one that he was riding in, and on the curves he could lean out and watch it, black smoke puffing out of the stack, and listen to the joyful hoots of its whistle as they passed through town after town. At Olustee, at Sanderson, at Baldwin, the locomotive announced, "Hoot! Hoot! I am carrying soldiers to defend our country." And people stood by the tracks, old men and children waving, ragged slaves watching curiously, small boys who tried to race the train on foot. Lewis felt proud to be part of this great movement of the army, proud that these strangers approved of what they were doing. The joy of their greeting went into his blood and filled the empty place Coalson had made there by his desertion.

"Make way, Lieutenant!" Moses Duncan looked behind him to see a major on horseback riding ahead of a train of ammunition wagons. He hopped aside as the wagons clattered by, leaving a choking cloud of dust behind them. This time he kept to the side of the road, watching warily for horsemen and wagons, realizing that he had been too absorbed in the news that he was bringing from regimental headquarters. The companies that he passed hardly looked as if they were part of the same army. Not all of the men in any company had uniforms. Some uniforms were gray, others blue, and a few even green or red. Many men, however, still were dressed as they had dressed as farmers, and some brought shotguns, muskets and rifles with them. One company was drilling, the men carrying sticks. In other companies, displaying placards and pennants with names like "Bartow Yankee Killers" and "South Florida Bull Dogs," the clusters of men loafing about looked more like civilians at a camp meeting than like soldiers in a military regiment.

When he came to the clump of oaks where his company was camped, Riley Green came out to meet him, holding a piece of cloth. "Look a here, Lieutenant," he boasted. "Doc and me done made us a new company flag." He held up a pennant with a blue border bearing the letters "CO. I" in red.

"The men won't have any trouble following that flag, Riley," Moses Duncan told him.

Another private was sitting on the ground, trying to patch a pair of britches. "Hey, Mose—I mean Lieutenant—when do we leave?"

"Tell you later, but you're going to like what you hear."

"Did you hear that?" the private said to Riley Green and Lewis Powell as Duncan walked away from them. The three men ran to spread the word.

Henry Stewart was sitting on the edge of a chair in front of his tent, writing on papers strewn on a box in front of him. He looked up. "There. That's the last of those requisitions. I doubt whether they'll do much good, but maybe we can get a few blankets and a couple of guns out of them. What did you find out at headquarters, Mose?"

"It's for sure and for certain this time, Captain. We won't be staying at Jacksonville another day. They've ordered the regiment to Virginia. There's a big army getting together under General Johnston, and the Yanks are putting up another big army at Washington City. It looks like we're going to get into the fighting right off."

"We leave tomorrow?"

"First light."

"Well, I sure hope we can pick up a bunch of rocks on the way to Virginia, because we're going to need them to chunk at the Yanks. Did Colonel Ward say anything about us getting any guns?"

"Not a word. I heard him tell Colonel Rogers that this is what comes of Governor Perry being in such a rush to put the regiment under Confederate command. And Colonel Rogers said he expects the Governor got more than he bargained for and that—"

"Well, Governor Milton won't take office till later in the year, and he won't take too kindly to swearing to defend a state that has given away its regiments to fight someplace else." Stewart sighed. "Mose, I don't know what he would do if the Yankees stir up a slave uprising. A lot of us were hoping they would leave us here at least long enough to get some weapons, anyway."

"Reckon we'll have to wait till we get to Virginia for that," Duncan said. He tried to hold back his excitement, but he was so glad about the news that he wanted to run out and yell it to all the winds. Stewart could not have been less pleased if he had heard that his best mule had dropped dead. Duncan wondered if Stewart was just a cautious old soldier or if he wanted to stay closer to his plantation. He was forty years old and had to leave his wife to run the plantation by herself, something he had not counted on when he organized the company.

Henry Stewart told him, "Go call in the other officers, and we'll let them know. And give these requisitions to somebody to run over to the quartermaster."

But when Moses Duncan turned around, the other three lieutenants—Hall, Stewart, and De Loach—were already running toward Henry Stewart's tent, laughing in anticipation.

Lewis Powell was too excited to sleep. Some men lay under a shelter of thatched palmettos, but he and Riley had spread their bedrolls close to the trunk of a big oak, and they laughed at the jokes the men were telling until the talk subsided into sleep.

"Riley," Lewis asked, "what are you going to do when we get done with the fighting?"

"Well, my uncle wants me to come live with him and farm, and I expect to have my own farm one day. Grow me a lot of corn and collards. I like collards."

Lewis said, "My pa wants me to be a preacher, and I think I might do that. But I want to have a farm, too."

"Doc, are you called to be a preacher? If you ain't heard the call, it won't be no use in preaching."

Lewis was silent. "I don't rightly know, Riley. I've got the feeling that God has meant me for something. Something big. But I'm not sure what."

"Well, Doc, if the Lord calls you, you've got to be sure the call is meant for you. We had a preacher at our church one time that my pa said he had overheard somebody else's call."

Lewis laughed, and they were both quiet for a long time. A whippoorwill whistled deep in the woods, and they lay listening to it.

"Doc, you think we'll get into that big fight in Virginia? I would sure hate to miss out on it."

"Me too."

Riley dropped his voice to a whisper. "Doc, sometimes I wonder if I'll get scared. I don't want to run. If I do, you'll stop me, won't you, Doc?"

Lewis swallowed hard. "Sure I will, Riley. I won't let you do that."

They did not say anymore to each other that night, and Lewis drifted to sleep listening to the whippoorwill and to a hoot-owl deep in the woods. In a dream he saw his father, taller than in life, clad all in black with a wide-brimmed black hat, stalking through the tents of the company, looking for his son. But Lewis was always farther and farther away. And there were fierce, foreign soldiers pointing spears at the people in his father's church, until he and Riley rode at them with raised swords, scattering them to the winds.

3

RICHMOND, VIRGINIA
AUGUST 1861

As THE SUMMER WORE ON, Virginia was heavy with blackflies and dysentery. The men were restless, dissatisfied. They had come all this way for a war, and what were they doing? Nothing but guarding prisoners from Manassas—and marching, marching, marching. There were guns enough now, captured from the Yankees who threw them down and ran at Manassas, but when would they get to shoot them at the enemy? When the men asked him this, Moses Duncan could not tell them.

Today was the day of the big match. All week the men of the Second Florida had been laying their bets. Duncan himself had bet a whole dollar. It had all started with the turkey. Some of the boys in the Jasper Blues had pooled their money and bought a turkey from a farmer. As the turkey stewed over a fire, the cooks happened to leave the pot unattended, and when they came back, the turkey was gone. They accused a nearby company of Alabamians of stealing the bird, and a fight broke out. Once the officers had broken it up, the argument spread to everybody in the two companies, until it was finally decided to settle the dispute with a free-for-all wrestling match. Each company was to put up its ten best men.

The Jasper Blues had chosen their ten champions, but the one who carried their best hopes was Lewis Powell, who had earned a reputation as the best wrestler in the company. In match after match,

34

he had stayed in the ring longest, and he had earned the right to choose the other nine to defend the honor of the Jasper Blues.

Stripped to the waist, the champions were being rubbed down with pork fat. Riley Green, who had appointed himself Lewis's manager, was coaching him: "Now, Doc, get on the inside of them fellows, you hear, so you can shove them on out."

Duncan heard a voice behind him.

"Lieutenant, do you mind if I observe the engagement?"

Duncan turned to see a smartly dressed civilian standing next to a major from brigade headquarters. The major returned Duncan's salute and told him, "Lieutenant, this is Mr. John Wilkes Booth. He's an actor out of Richmond, and he wanted to see the camp. Seeing as we're a bit shy of Yankees to fight, he wants to watch the boys scrapping among themselves."

Moses Duncan looked at Booth. He saw a man of average height, not much older than Duncan himself, with dark eyes and a full moustache. A fringe of coal-black curly hair showed underneath his broad-brimmed straw hat. He wore a tan waistcoat over gray trousers, and he stood in highly polished, expensive boots. In spite of the heat of the day, he wore a chestnut-red frock coat with a velvet collar.

Booth leaned with his left hand on his walking stick as he shook hands with Duncan. "Delighted to meet you, Lieutenant. Are your men prepared for the skirmish that lies before them?"

"Couldn't be readier, Mr. Booth. Do you want to lay a bet with the sergeant major?"

"Indeed I do. Send a man with this." He handed Duncan a ten-dollar piece, at which the lieutenant blinked before calling a private to take it to the sergeant major.

"Are you playing in Richmond now, Mr. Booth?" Duncan asked.

"I perform tomorrow night in Macbeth, in a benefit performance for the cause of Southron independence." He lingered on "Southron" as though he loved its sound.

"That's a fine thing to do, sir."

Booth bowed slightly. "I am but a humble player, Lieutenant, while it is you and your stalwart men who bear the hopes, as they bear the arms, of the South. I draw a sword of lath against an enemy in greasepaint, but it is you who strike the decisive blow. Though I admit that sometimes I am inspired to don actual armor and to sally forth with martial comrades, as I did nearly two years ago in the John Brown affair."

"John Brown?"

"Yes, I was with the Richmond Grays when they guarded the wretch and oversaw his deserved execution." A look of pain came into his eyes, as though he had surprised himself into recalling an unpleasant scene. "But, behold! The dogged adversaries draw nigh."

Along the street, raising a cloud of dust like a pack of hunting dogs on the trail of a bear, came the Alabamians, stripped to the waist and smeared with grease, surrounded by a throng of jeering and taunting comrades.

"You ready to git whipped?"

"If I was, it'd take more than you to do it."

One short, muscular man danced about, throwing punches at the air. "I'm taller than a mountain," he sang, "and I weigh a ton."

"And I wring the necks off little banty roosters like you, just for fun," hooted one of the Jasper boys.

Riley clapped one hand on Lewis's shoulder and yelled, "My man here is meaner than a hurricane and can lick ten 'gators at a time." Lewis grinned and scraped his feet in the dust.

With Lewis towering in their midst, the ten Florida champions swaggered toward the challengers. The sergeant major stood between the adversaries, sometimes pushing a pair of eager combatants apart, while he steered them toward a circle he had drawn in the sand.

The sergeant major had to shout in his deep voice over and over again to quiet the two companies.

"Let me see your thumbs! Come on! Up with 'em!" He walked around the circle to inspect the length of the nails. "You know the rules. Colonel says no gouging, 'cause you all need your eyeballs to shoot Yanks with. No hitting, neither."

Booth turned to Duncan. "Lieutenant, who is that powerful man, the tallest one?"

"That's Lewis Powell, Mr. Booth. The boys call him Doc."

Booth turned to the staff officer. "Major, I'll place a side bet of a dollar on Powell against any two men you choose."

"I'm from Alabama, Mr. Booth, and I'll have to take your wager. I'll put my money on that big redheaded fellow and the one with the brown beard."

36

"Good choices, Major."

The sergeant major gave the signal, and the two gangs, splitting the air with yells, crashed into each other with slaps, grunts, and thuds. In less than a minute five or six men were lying outside the ring, and before a man could draw a bucket of water only five were left. The crowd outside had grown to several hundred, and men in back were climbing onto others' shoulders. Shouts encouraged one champion or another, and groans of disappointment would rise from the crowd as this one or that one was hurled sprawling and dazed outside the ring. One man rolled across the line, rubbing a shoulder and wailing over and over that it was broken. In the middle, blood streaming into his eyes from a broad gash across his forehead, stood the red-haired Alabamian, whirling in circles until he caught one of the Jasper boys and thudded to the ground with him.

The Banty Rooster had endured by catching bigger men off balance, then crowing as he would twist an arm or a leg and send the opponent sprawling. Lewis lowered his head, caught him around the middle, lifted him, spun around, and hurled him into the sand outside the circle, where he rolled and lay still.

There were three Alabamians left now, and two Jasper Blues, Lewis and a man named Daniel. All breathed heavily and circled like cats waiting for a chance to pounce. Lewis wrapped the crook of his arm around the redhead's neck and tried to throw him, but Brown Beard grabbed him from behind and tore him away. Then Daniel seized Red Hair, and locked together, the two crashed into Lewis and Brown Beard. Lewis jumped to his feet, cheered on by his comrades in the crowd, whose voices melted into a solid roar. While Red Hair was still on his hands and knees, Lewis grabbed his right foot and dragged him toward the edge of the circle.

"Shove him, Dan'l!" he yelled.

Daniel, on his knees, heaved into Red Hair and fell on top of him outside the circle, pushed by Brown Beard. Then, while Brown Beard was off balance, Lewis grabbed his right leg and twisted it from under him, sending the big man thudding senseless to the ground, his torso outside the ring.

The men of the Jasper Blues, roaring their approval, rushed toward Lewis, who lay half crumpled, his head down, at the edge of the circle. As the men rushed around, jostling him, Booth was waving his hat and cane in the air, shouting to the major, "Aha, Major! I win! Pay up! Pay up!" Lewis's comrades hoisted him to their shoulders, nearly trampling the vanquished wrestlers who were being hauled out of the way by anxious friends. Now Lewis and the few of his fellow combatants who still had their senses about them were being carried through the camp to the chant of "Jasper Blues! Jasper Blues!"

The sergeant major approached the jubilant, laughing actor, holding out money. "Your winnings, Mr. Booth."

"Give it all to the Cause, Sergeant Major," Booth replied, with a grand sweep of his hand. He turned toward the capering, exultant men who were bringing the victors back to the company tents after their circuit of the regimental camp. Booth and Duncan watched as they set Lewis and the other wrestlers down and sloshed water on them.

Booth walked toward the milling company, with Moses Duncan behind him. The circle of men parted, and Booth moved toward Lewis Powell, who was sitting on a split-rail bench shaking his dripping head. Booth's lone shadow fell on Lewis's feet before the soldier looked up. Moses Duncan would later remember that look of rapt wonder on Lewis's face. His jaw dropped, and he stared in awe at Booth, at the apparition of this splendid man looking down on Lewis and blocking out the sun.

"You're a splendid wrestler, Powell," John Wilkes Booth said. "The Cause needs strong men like you."

"Much obliged, Captain."

"Powell, you and your comrades will be my guests at the Richmond Theater tomorrow night. The lieutenant, I am sure, will make the necessary arrangements."

"I'll talk to the captain about it soon as he gets back from headquarters," Duncan said. Suddenly he envied and disliked this peacock of a man, who spoke of "the Cause" as if he relished it as the only thing big enough to hold Booth's grand, theatrical conception of himself.

"Very good," Booth replied. He touched his cane to the brim of his hat and swept his eyes commandingly around the company. "Boys, my compliments on your victory today, and my best wishes for your greater victory over our country's enemies." He walked away as though he were leaving an applauding audience behind.

"My oh my," came a voice from the crowd. "Ain't we a jack-a-dandy?"

Lewis glared in the direction from which the voice had come, but all the faces looked innocent. Then Riley came with liniment and started to rub Lewis down while others went to attend to the knocked heads and bruises of the other wrestlers.

"Lieutenant, who did you say that fellow is?" Lewis asked Moses Duncan.

"His name is John Wilkes Booth, Powell."

"Just think. A gentleman like that wanting to talk to me. Riley, you ever been to a theater before? Me neither. Ain't that something?" He looked again in the direction where Booth had gone, but the actor was out of sight.

"Riley, it would be mighty dreadful if that there lamp was to fall down." Lewis pointed up to the chandelier, glowing with a hundred candles and reflecting like jewels the countless pieces of faceted glass that hung from every tier. They cast around the lobby shades of emerald, scarlet, and violet, gently lighting the frieze that encircled the room with its pudgy cupids, woodlands, and shepherds. Lewis looked down at his boots, freshly blacked to cover the scuffs, and saw how they sank into the crimson carpet.

"S-s-t, Doc, looky there!" Riley whispered. The picture on the wall was the most fascinating sight of all. It was a large, somber painting of the inside of a tomb, with skulls and bones lying around; sprawled on a slab, one arm hanging down, was a man. Kneeling beside him was a woman holding a dagger pointed to her breast. She was half turned toward the front, and her shoulders were uncovered down to the filmy gown she held over her bosom.

"Now, ain't that something?" Riley asked, and Lewis nodded. Playgoers were streaming through the lobby now. Most were gray-uniformed officers, wearing the yellow sashes of cavalry, the blue of infantry, or the red of artillery, escorting beautiful ladies dressed in hoop skirts, with their hair in tidy ringlets brushing their bare white shoulders. Some men were older, their white hair set off against black evening wear, in the company of smiling elderly ladies greeting one another with elaborate gestures. Everybody spoke to the soldiers, even to the privates, and each lady beamed smiles and encouragement upon Lewis, Riley, and their comrades.

When somebody said, "We better go in so the play can start," they filed through narrow portals with red curtains trimmed in gold braid and tassels, and Lewis saw around him the splendor of the ivory theater, three tiers of boxes rising above him, decorated with golden scrolls and paintings and graceful lamps softly glowing, placing every gentleman, every lady, in an enchanting light. In front, flanked by white columns, hung a curtain that displayed a forest scene complete with crags and a majestic stag.

Chatter and laughter died as soon as the curtain rose. There was another behind that one, this one of rich scarlet and gold that parted and flowed to either side, revealing a bleak stage setting of scattered rocks and a background streaked in ominous blacks and reds.

Lewis could not understand much of what the players said, and it was not until later that the play became exciting. When the dark witches appeared, he and Riley leaned forward, absorbed in the rhythmic chanting and awed by the terrible warnings. Suddenly the audience was galvanized as Booth exploded onto the stage as if by magic, appearing high on an outcropping of rocks from where he leaped into the midst of the witches. From then on he was a tormented man, at times driven by his wife, at times defiant of all fate. In some parts of the play the people on the stage talked too much, and what they said did not make sense. But Booth made up for that. One time a glowing dagger hung in the air in front of him, and he seemed afraid to take hold of it but tried to catch it anyway. Lewis shivered when the ghost of Macbeth's murdered friend appeared. But nothing else in the tragedy could equal the final scene where, surrounded by his enemies and his cause lost, Booth shot forth a glow from his eyes that penetrated all the theater as he defied his opponent: "Lay on, Macduff! And damned be him that first cries, 'Hold, enough!' " The stage echoed with clash of swords as Booth and the other player fought back and forth. Once Booth even climbed onto a parapet and leaped again into the fight. For a while it seemed that he would win, but in one last encounter, Booth fell, his body jerking in mock death throes. When his head was lifted exultantly in the last scene, justice resided with lesser men, and Lewis felt torn between two kinds of right. Enthralled and marvelling, he stood and applauded as the curtain fell. But there was more. In front of the curtain, one by one, the actors reappeared, the victors sweeping their arms outward to honor Booth himself, who bowed and took as his due the cheers and the applause. The man who had gone down in defeat against overwhelming numbers now stood approved by all, his arms extended in a triumphant gesture of sovereign possession.

The wide door of the Swan Tavern yawned open to the steamy night, sucking in the swarm of men, then chewing and spitting them out like spent plugs of tobacco. The boisterous laughter and shouts seemed enough to raise the dust in the street where Lewis Powell and Riley Green stood gawking. A dozen or so men crossed the street to encircle two women in red satin dresses and black-feathered hats. Gray-uniformed soldiers staggered out of the tavern, some of them arm-in-arm with loud, hearty laboring men of the city. A wedge of five soldiers, yelling Rebel battle cries, shoved their way through the crowd toward the bar inside. Four gentlemen in brown frock coats quarreled with two soldiers, then discreetly retreated when the soldiers' reinforcements appeared.

"Doc, are you sure this is the place that darky told us to meet Mr. Booth?" Riley rolled his eyes and stared toward the saloon as if he expected Booth to leap out over the heads of the crowd, escorted by the witches of the play.

"Well, this here's the Broad Street Hotel, ain't it? That's what he said. But I don't see no better than you how we are going to find him in this here herd of folks."

"Wait a minute, Doc. Look yonder."

From the Richmond Theater, a block up Broad Street, appeared a cheering crowd of about thirty men, carrying flambeaux. Riley and Lewis watched the mob flow out of the theater, their torches swaying against the night as their voices broke into "The Bonnie Blue Flag." In front of the crowd pranced John Wilkes Booth, a sable cape draped across his shoulders. Booth was joyfully leading the song, beating time with his walking stick.

Hurrah, hurrah, for Southern rights hurrah!
Hurrah for the Bonnie Blue Flag that bears a single star!

At the saloon door, Booth stopped in front of Lewis and Riley, letting the crowd flow past him into the tavern.

"Aha!" Booth exclaimed. "It is the dauntless gladiator of yesterday, and a gallant comrade. Welcome, sirs, to the Swan. Come within, and join me in a flagon of ale."

Booth threaded his way into the saloon ahead of Lewis and Riley and was greeted by cries of welcome from townsmen at the bar. "Johnny, it's good to see you back among us," hailed the saloonkeeper. "Here's your brandy all ready for you." He set a squat glass in front of Booth and turned to Lewis and Riley.

"What'll it be, soldiers?"

Lewis glanced at Riley and back at the bartender.

"Uh—same as Mr. Booth," Riley said, trying to sound sure of himself.

"Me too," Lewis joined in.

Booth dropped some coins on the bar and motioned for Lewis and Riley to follow him. They made their way through the crowd and the haze of tobacco smoke toward a corner table where some laborers cried greetings to Booth and made room for him. Lewis and Riley squeezed onto a bench near the table.

Later Lewis tried to remember all that Booth said that night, but his mind was so clouded with one brandy after another that he was aware only of the grandiloquent actor giving words to the high spirit of the Cause which had inspired Lewis and Riley to join the militia and led them to this distant state. For the first time since leaving Florida, Lewis began to stir again with zeal for the South, and he was lifted by the pride of being part of a great movement for the defense of his home and his family, and of the soil that fed them.

The night was still full of magic for Lewis when he left the tavern with Riley and Booth hours later. The stars were dimming, and a first faint whiteness was reflected in the river. As Riley lagged silently, heavy with drink, the man who had been Macbeth linked his arm in Lewis's and walked with him past the columned state capitol and the ghostly warehouse with its sweet, pungent smell of tobacco toward the depot at the head of Mayo's Bridge.

Outside the depot, they stopped and looked down at the dark river while they waited for Riley to stagger up to them. Booth reached up and clasped a hand tightly on Lewis's shoulder. "Powell," Booth said, "we have committed ourselves to a great Cause. I hope we shall meet again, for I feel that we are destined for a great venture, you and I. Whatever it may be, I shall serve the Cause until my dying breath. No enemy can conquer men who have the will to fight on to victory. Go now, and smite the enemy and hasten the day when Abe Lincoln and his minions lie vanquished at our feet."

Booth turned and walked away, alone on the Richmond street. Lewis watched him pass from one circle of light to the next until he was lost in the shadows left over from the night.

4

JASPER, FLORIDA
JUNE 1863

"Powell and Green were a sight after they saw that play in Richmond. They would pick up sticks and charge at one another, yelling, 'Lay on, Macduff!' The first time or two the other men would laugh at it, and then they got sick of watching it."

Captain Moses Duncan, late of the Second Florida Infantry, leaned back in his chair and stared up through the oak leaves, his eyes half shut against the sun. He waved a feeble hand through a cloud of gnats. The dizziness was on him again, and he craved shade. In the east, thunder rolled. He dozed for a while, and dreamed that he was lying on a field, with the awful quiet around him. It was not until George Powell spoke to him that he remembered where he was.

"That boy always could play the jackass when he got it in his head to do it." Powell had pulled his hat off and dropped it onto the ground. Moses Duncan looked at the thick gray hair hanging over a stick the old man was whittling.

"He wasn't the only play-actor. There was the general, too. It wasn't too long before we were ordered out, to Yorktown. Camped about a rifle-shot from the monument they put up to show where the British surrendered to George Washington. The boys had to dig trenches there, with the Yanks building up in front of us. There wasn't much time for horsing around playing Macbeth and Macduff. Anyway, it was the general's chance to make play-actors out of us all. Marching out of the woods, across the road, into the woods, across the road, into the woods, and back around the town. It was the second time around before we caught on to what he was up to. That way he had the Yanks thinking there were ten times as many of us as there were."

"Captain, I just hope that is not what all the generals have been up to for the last two years—marching you in circles."

Moses Duncan looked up to meet the old man's gaze. In the two months since he had come back from the war, he had told the same story over and over to the families of every man in the company. At first he had not been able to talk. After three days of bouncing in a railroad car with sick, groaning men and another three days in his brother's wagon from Savannah, he had wanted only to sleep, while the chills and fever shook him and forced the sweat out of him. A dozen times every night he would wake, thinking that he was lying in blood, then discovering that it was his own sweat. A month passed before he started answering questions from anxious fathers, crying mothers and sweethearts, angry brothers, always telling them what he knew they wanted to hear—stories of gallantry and devotion to duty and country. Now here was the last of them, the father of Lewis Powell, who was no better and no worse than any of the others, and Moses Duncan was doing his last duty to the Jasper Blues, stuffing the ears of the last one with confirmation of the patriotic slogans. Return with your shield or on it. *Dulce et decorum est pro patria mori.* Mattie ought to be here by now, he thought. He looked at the road, then across the field next to the courthouse, at the dogwood tree where he had stood with her two years before. Half the tree was dead now, its withered brown leaves holding out of habit onto the branches, while the other half was as green as the one he lay under now, shading his eyes from the sun. Behind the half- dead tree boiled dark storm clouds. He pulled off his hat and mopped his brow with the cloth that lay in his lap, then set the hat back on his head, pulling the brim low over his eyes. Again the thunder sounded.

"Well, it worked, the general's play-acting did. The Yanks stayed back where they were. Not that we wanted them to, in those days. The boys had been in garrison for two months, and so full of piss and vinegar that they wanted to get into a scrap with the Yanks right off and send them packing.

"It was not long before they got their chance. One morning we looked up to see a regiment in blue forming in front of us. By then it was one of those cool fall days that they call Indian summer up yonder. Fog was clearing, and the blue was taking over the sky. The sun was reflecting off the brass on the officers' badges and on the horses' harnesses. It was infantry, but we thought at first it was cavalry because all the staff officers came out front. One of the officers was wearing a hat with a plume, and he gave the signal. It was the first charge we had ever faced, and we brought all of our regiment up behind the parapet of logs that we had built in front of our trenches. The Yankee officer turned his horse, with that plume waving, brandished his saber, and led the men toward us. We were all quiet, watching them come. Powell was kneeling right next to me, with his musket on the log, and he said to me, 'Lieutenant, I aim to knock that hat off that officer's head.' He said it kind of low and reverent, like he was talking in church. It was a mighty pretty sight. They had a drummer boy beating a cadence, and we could hear the commands of the officers keeping them in line. The color-bearer was stepping out, and the breeze picked up the flag and stretched it out against the sky. It looked so much like a military review that I almost forgot to look at the captain for orders. When I turned, he was just bringing his saber down as a signal to fire, and I relayed the command to the men. When they all fired together, at first there was so much smoke that we couldn't tell what had happened, but when it cleared, there were soldiers in blue lying on the field in front of us, and what was left of the regiment was running back toward their lines, and that officer's horse was running with an empty saddle ahead of them.''

A mule and wagon pulled a dust swirl past them along the road, and the old Negro driver tipped his hat to them. George Powell picked up another stick and started to whittle.

"The boys jumped up on the logs after that and yelled at the Yanks. Powell and Green and some of them begged me to let them go after the Yanks, but of course I couldn't do that. They just sat around and talked about how grand it was, and about that damn fool officer that came riding at us with that feather in his hat. Naturally Powell thought he had shot him, but who was to say?

"Well, we had to lie there behind the logs the rest of the day, with the boys wanting to charge the Yanks. Guess it was more of the general's play-acting. He knew we didn't have enough to take on the whole Union army, but the Yanks didn't know that.

"It looked for a long time like that was all the war we were going to see. The weeks went by, and it got colder. We built log huts all around Yorktown, and the boys had to go out and lie in the trenches for six hours at a time. Huddle in those log huts, play cards, spin yarns. Spent a lot of time gathering firewood when the weather got colder. Up there it looks sometimes like there never will be an end to winter, that God has gone and changed all the rules of nature and decided to let the earth smother and die forever under the snow."

Moses Duncan tilted his head down and looked at the gray head bent over the whittling.

"After that winter, the war started for us. In the spring, they pulled us back to Williamsburg. That's where the Yanks started coming at us. We never saw another outfit like that one that we sent running at Yorktown. Must have been green. What they put against us after that—well, they were different. But in time we were different, too.

"You see, we had not seen any Yanks much through the winter. Maybe a picket here and there, with a few musket shots back and forth to relieve the boredom and let each other know we were there. Their artillery would fire off a few shots at us, too. But sometimes we even forgot they were still there. Then all of a sudden one afternoon, on a kind of rainy, blustery spring day, their artillery started tearing up the ground ahead of us, and we were ordered into ranks. Couldn't see any Yanks anywhere until they started coming out of the woods in front of us. Lord, I didn't know there were that many Yanks in the whole world. And when we commenced to firing, these didn't turn tail. They just kept on coming. At least we found out later that they were coming on, because there was so much smoke and dust in the air that we didn't know what was coming at us. The men would load and fire and load and fire. I don't even know when I realized what was happening, but— whether there was an order to retreat, or not—we were moving back. I rallied what I could find of the company, but by then a regiment had come in from our right, and the next thing I knew the Yanks were turning back."

"What about Lewis, Captain? Did he run?"

"There was a lot of confusion, Reverend Powell. I couldn't keep track of all the men all the time."

"You don't have to lie to me, Captain. You think I care about that, but I don't."

Moses Duncan felt the chill again, in spite of a quickening wind that swept hot air ahead of the growling thundercloud. If I could tell him the truth about it, he thought, I would tell him that I ran, just like the boys ran. Maybe I ran first. I don't know. I would tell him that Lewis Powell dragged in after two days, like a whipped dog with his tail between his legs, and looked at me and looked away, sharing the knowledge of what we had both learned about ourselves there at Williamsburg. No need to ask him where he had been. He might have told me, but it would not have made any difference if he had. Maybe that is why they elected me captain that same month of May. Because they knew I had run, too, just like them. Had run, and then come back.

"Go on, Captain."

"What?" Moses Duncan asked. "Oh, I forgot where I was for a minute. Anyway, pretty soon we reorganized the company, and Henry Stewart and his son came back to Jasper. I was the captain then. General Robert E. Lee took command before long. By then, we had marched all over those roads outside of Richmond and stood against the Yanks in so many places that I can't recollect all of them.

"He took us north after that, General Lee did. It's all a blur to me now. Manassas and Sharpsburg—when the day turned into blood and every minute lasted an hour. Fredericksburg. That's where I took sick. I didn't see any of the boys after I got sent to the hospital in Richmond."

George Powell picked up his hat and fanned his face with it.

"Captain, I said that it didn't make any difference whether Lewis run or didn't run. Because I know sooner or later that boy will do whatever he finds out he has to do. Ever since he was a little chap he has reminded me of a mule I had once. You get him started in one direction, it takes God almighty and all his angels to turn him."

He sighed and glanced at the gathering clouds, then back at Duncan. "Are you scared, Captain Duncan? I don't mean were you scared then. I know you had to be. But are you scared now? Scared of facing those boys again in this world or the next, because you know you are not going back. A man over yonder at the livery stable said there was talk of you running for office. County clerk or something like that. Anybody looking at you can tell you are a sick man. But tell me the God's truth. You wouldn't go back to the war even if you were not sick."

Moses Duncan stared at the old man. This one was different from the others who had come to ask about their sons.

"Just like I thought, Captain. It has been near on to two years since you and those boys marched out of this here field full of all those hopes that you were going to lick the whole Yankee nation."

Moses Duncan glanced at the half-withered dogwood tree, with the darkening, grumbling cloud behind it. Soon Mattie would come, bringing her gift of cornbread and cutting off his view of the half-dead tree.

"You marched out of here, expecting to be back in less than a year, with the war won to your satisfaction. There are a good many folks around here who think that is still going to happen. If I was ever among them, I am not among them now. Not with my boy Wash huddled trembling in a corner feeling around for the arm and leg he left in a hole in Tennessee. Left them there with the pieces of his brother Oliver." George Powell tapped the blade of his whittling knife against the stick and peered into Moses Duncan's eyes. "Do you know why this war will not be won?"

Duncan laid his head against the chair back and looked at George Powell from under drooping lids.

"I'll tell you why. I was over to Thomasville a while back and I heard of a widow woman there who was so hard up that she had to hire one of her strongest niggers out. Big black buck, could do the work of a mule. This man she hired him to, Pete McLendon, had a pretty sorry reputation as the sort who would always treat other folks' property worse than he treated his own. You know the sort. Well, one day after the nigger tried to run off to the widow woman to tell her about how he had been beat, McLendon got some of his friends together and they beat him one last time. I heard it said that you could not have told him from a dead hog when those boys got through."

Moses Duncan waved his hand at the gnats and squinted at the old man.

"Captain, some think God is punishing the South for sins like that."

Duncan opened his eyes wider and looked at him.

"Me, I don't know, Captain. Looks to me like God has done more to me than I ever deserved."

Moses Duncan pushed on the arms of his chair and sat forward. "I waded through that sunken road at Sharpsburg, with it as full of blood as Swift Creek is full of water. My feet are so stained with it that I will never walk out of it. So if God ever meant to punish us for anything, he has done it already, with more than enough blood to wash out all the beatings of all the nigger slaves that ever picked a cotton boll."

George Powell stood up and slipped his knife into a sheath hanging from his belt. "Maybe so, maybe not. But, Captain, that is why you would not go back to the war, even if you were made whole again, healed by the touch of the Saviour himself." He bent over, picked up his hat from the ground, and set it on his head. "Looks like it's trying to blow up a storm, and I have got a piece to go. All I can say is that you are one of the smart ones. Maybe my boy will be a smart one, too, when the time comes, as long as he does not learn any mischief in those places the war took him to."

The wind was whipping the branches over them as the old man turned and stalked across the field. Mattie's brother's wagon appeared around the bend in the road. Moses Duncan stayed where he was, watching the black cloud above him taking the shape of a greedy buzzard, with a thick body and crooked wings.

5

GETTYSBURG, PENNSYLVANIA
JULY, 1863

WHEN THE COLUMN STOPPED, Lewis was too tired to look right or left, but kept his eyes fixed on the blanket roll that angled across the back of the man in front of him. A louse was crawling on the blanket toward a hole, and Lewis watched as it rounded the frayed edge and crept under the layer of blanket.

Then they marched again, and Lewis's eyes dropped to the clumps of dry clay that their feet stirred and shifted. He spat. Two years. How many months? days? hours? His first year of enlistment ended, and he was glad to re-enlist for the fifty-dollar bounty. It didn't matter. Everybody had to stay in the army anyway, with the Conscription Act and all. Everybody but some of the officers, like Captain Stewart and his son. Twenty slaves at home, and you didn't have to stay. Rich man's war, poor man's fight. But with the bounty, he and Riley were rich for a while. They had a good time with the money in Richmond — at least with some of it, until he lost the rest. He would always think it was that whore that took it.

Lewis stumbled into the man in front of him when the column stopped again. Rest halt. No one wasted any energy talking. He and Riley threw their sacks and bedrolls onto the ground and laid their heads on them, having learned during two years to catch sleep when they could find it. In his dreams Lewis still marched, climbing stairs toward where a veiled figure waited. He did not know who was behind the veil, but he thought if he could only climb long enough, he would find out. Sometimes the figure—was it a man or a woman?—lifted a hand to the veil and then the dream would end, with the hand poised either to tear the veil aside or to guard it.

Habit woke him at the same time as most of his comrades. He shook Riley by the shoulder. Dim, droop-lidded, feverish eyes, face flushed. How long has he—? Funny I didn't notice, he thought. Shivering, too.

"Riley, we got to start again. You look sick, man."

"Ain't nothing wrong with me, Doc. Just got the trots, is all. Sergeant give me a dose of that there sawgrum tonic he carries."

Lewis helped Riley to his feet, and they fell into the formation. As they started again, he looked at Riley ahead of him, carrying the regimental flag. Never will quit, he thought. Like John Wilkes Booth in that play at Richmond, nearly two years ago. Macbooth? No, Macbeth. Slipping through Yankee lines to put on a tragedy for the Confederate army. He's in for the rest of the war, just like me, just like Riley.

Riley was sick, but you never heard him complaining. But the year of campaigning had taken something out of him. Last year on the Fourth of July, he was still the old Riley, full of brag and song, when they backed the Yankees up to the James River. Then Confederates met Yankees on a hill of blueberries above the James, ate sweet berries, and swapped tobacco for Yankee coffee. By then they had their fill of war—lying in muddy trenches, marching in the rain, cringing at the whine of minié balls out of the mist. Riley danced a jig with a Yankee artilleryman who said he was an Irishman, new in the country. The Feds had recruited him by giving him a uniform and telling him they were giving him a job at the post office. The Irishman, who had rosy cheeks and a short, stubby nose and talked in a way that sounded like singing, laughed and said that it was some post office and he was damn tired of delivering canisters to the Rebs. Riley told him that he was damn tired of receiving them.

"My dogs are killing me," Sam Mitchell groaned to nobody in particular. "Got to get new boots. Where did Sarge say that shoe factory was?"

"Place called Gadsburg or Gittlesburg," Henry Holmes said. "Something like that. Up yonder."

Lewis wished he could get some good boots this time, the new kind, cut for right and left feet. His feet were sliding all around in the ones he was wearing. Lewis felt he could not take many more miles like the ones they had walked on Maryland and Pennsylvania roads and fields. At least they were eating better than any time since marching into Maryland in the fall of last year. Taking over that mill a few miles back gave them a chance to stuff their knapsacks with flour and corn meal, and everybody had a good chicken dinner.

The officers called a halt so that artillery could pass. While they waited beside a creek, the men heard firing ahead, the steady boom of artillery mixed with the crackle of muskets and rifles.

After they filled their canteens at the creek, they sat beside the road and waited, indifferent to the battle ahead. It might mean that they would go into the fighting or it might not. It was late afternoon, and they might get to rest during this one. That was all that mattered, anyhow. Some men were already asleep.

A group of officers came along the road on horseback. It was General Dick Anderson and his staff.

"Hey, General," Henry Holmes yelled, "when we going to hit the Yanks?"

"Which outfit is this?"

"Perry's Brigade, sir."

"It won't be long now."

"Ready when you are, General."

"I know. You always are." The general passed them, riding toward the sound of battle.

They marched again, toward the town on a hill, yellow in the setting sun. Outside the town they were ordered into parade step as they passed General Lee's headquarters. They did not see the general, but the men cheered anyway.

Turning right, they marched past Pender's Division, setting up camp after the battle. Bodies of Union soldiers lay on both sides of the line of march.

Some men yelled at the Floridians. "Where've you been? Now you get here."

"We come to finish the job for you," someone called out.

Marching away from the town beside the ridge, the brigade set up camp, company by company, in a grove of oaks. The men of

Company I built fires and wearily cooked supper. Most of the hundred who had set out from Jasper had not come this far. After Henry Stewart and his son resigned, the men elected Moses Duncan captain, and now Duncan himself was back in Florida, laid up with typhoid. Some had just vanished. You looked up one day and they were gone. Others Lewis had helped to bury near Richmond, at Sharpsburg, at Fredericksburg, at Chancellorsville, or at some of the dozen other places where they had fought. Dysentery, typhoid, pneumonia—they would bring you down if a Yankee bullet failed to. So they had one officer and about two dozen men left.

While they ate their supper, Lewis took his Bible out of his knapsack, and some of the other soldiers sat with him and Riley while he read the Twenty-third Psalm. "Thou preparest a table before me in the presence of mine enemies," he read, as they all looked up at the dark ridge opposite, smoky from fires like their own. When he read the last words, "and I shall dwell in the house of the Lord forever," he closed the Bible slowly, and the men stared into the fire for a long time.

Most of the soldiers sat in groups and talked. Nobody wanted to be alone. When Lewis went to look for Riley, he found him lying on his blanket, feverish and muttering. Lewis brought water, wet his own shirt, and wiped Riley's hot face. They talked about home until Riley fell asleep.

When morning came, Lewis chopped some fat bacon into chunks, built up the meager fire, and stirred the bacon in a tin pot over the fire until it sizzled and let go of its grease. Then he stirred in two handfuls of flour and cornmeal. When the mixture was thick enough, he spooned some of it into a cup for Riley and took it to him. Then he sat down to eat the rest of the greasy cush.

Around mid-morning, they were ordered to the top of the ridge. Lewis went behind Riley, who dragged the butt of his musket as he walked, like a man still trying to wake up. The soldiers formed a single line through the woods, facing the fields, but after nothing happened for a long time, they sprawled on the ground and talked or slept. Lewis had known better than to load his musket. Too many times when he had loaded, he had been ordered to wait, and had to take too much special care to see that his gun did not fire and hit the man next to him. Sam Mitchell carried one of those .52-caliber Sharps like the ones the Yanks had, but Sam's was an imitation made in Richmond, and Sam had twisted it out of the clutch of a dead Virginian. It was easy to unload one of them, because it was a breech-loader, but Lewis did not like the them anyway. They were not as trusty as the real thing. He had seen too many of them blow up in soldiers' faces.

About noon they heard musket fire on their right, but the shooting subsided. Later they were aware of a large force moving behind the ridge, and they watched as a column of thousands of men passed behind them and came into the woods on their right.

Lewis had learned to wait without fearing. The battle would begin when it would begin. At Seven Pines a year before he had shit all the fear out of himself, cowering in the mud of a bloody ditch. He had felt helplessly alone then, the world convulsing around him. He no longer thought that his army would win or that it would lose. He only marched, loaded his musket and fought. and went on to where he would stand and fight again. Second Manassas, Sharpsburg, Chancellorsville—men around him fell and died, their screams splitting the air and their blood soaking the ground, but he had walked through it unscathed. For the past year he had followed General Robert E. Lee, had raised cheers for the general who led the army into victory after victory, had thrilled to the commanding presence of that solemn man in gray as he would pass the troops in review or on a cross-country march. Each day brought a new order, and Lewis did not ask where the orders led. He only obeyed. If someone were to ask him when he thought he would go home or whether the South would win the war, he would not have been able to understand the question. He was part of the great machine of Lee's army, and he decided nothing, asked or answered no questions.

In the late afternoon, the heavy crump of twelve-pounders began on the right, firing onto the opposite ridge, and smoke drifted toward Lewis. For another two hours they waited in the woods; then they began to make themselves ready. It happened among them all at the same time, without any command or even any words being spoken. Lewis stood with the rest of the company to load his musket. He reached into his pouch for a cartridge, bit into the paper, then poured powder down the barrel. Then he dropped the .58-caliber shot down the barrel, whipped out the ramrod, and tamped the shot into the bottom of the barrel. He set a percussion cap under the hammer and eased the hammer onto it, just as Lieutenant Hall relayed the command: "Guide right, on me!" At quick step they moved out of the line of trees, with Riley ahead of them, the regimental flag tilted forward.

When they came into the open, Lewis saw a line of blue uniforms on the far side of the road, turning into puffs of smoke. Before he could hear the rattle of rifle fire, he heard a thug as a man near him was hit.

Through a haze across the field, Lewis saw clods of earth rise toward him lump after lump as twelve-pound shot walked like invisible giants toward his line. Screams of men and horses told where the cannon balls had torn holes. A canister shell burst ahead of them, and he shut his eyes against the blast of sand and rocks that stung his face. When he opened his eyes again he squinted into dust and smoke, and his eyes burned. Out of his dry throat rose the yell that blended with that of his comrades in the line while it answered the booms of artillery and whines of shot hurled at them.

Lewis stumbled on something—a body or a root—but got back to his feet and went on, moving right until he could see the next man in line. A fence loomed in front of him, and he paused long enough to fire for the first time into the dim shadows across the road, shadows lit only by the yellow flashes of musket fire. Then he set a foot on the top rail of the fence, vaulted over, and slid into a sunken road.

Suddenly the blue line broke. While crossing the road, keeping low, Lewis groped with shaking fingers into his ammunition pouch, pulled out a cartridge, and started to reload. Just as he touched the paper to the mouth of the barrel, someone fell against him, and he dropped the cartridge. Huddling against the bank on the side of the road, he pulled out another cartridge, reloaded, groped for the ramrod, drew it, and rammed it down the barrel. He had to set the stock on the ground to hold the musket steady enough to replace the ramrod. Then he went up the embankment on shaking legs, and scraped across the low rock wall at the top.

Stumbling in the smoke over rocky ground and blue-coated bodies, Lewis no longer knew who was on his left or on his right. He yelled again as he ran after the fleeing enemy. Suddenly he found himself in a clear place in the smoke, where officers tried to dress what was left of the line. He could not hear their voices for the screaming and the rifle fire, but he was moving back up to the line when he heard the whit of a minié ball and the crack of rifle fire from his left. Out of the smoke appeared a line of Yanks.

Lewis spun left and fired into the blue line, then threw down his musket and ran with the rest of the brigade back the way they had come. At the sunken road, several men stood firing past him as he clambered over the smashed fence and fell onto the road.

"Doc! Help me!" The voice came from a few yards up the road, and it was Riley's voice. Men lay along the road, groaning or silent. A man slithered to the edge of the bank, away from the steady rifle fire, rolled onto the road, and lay still, blood gushing from his mouth. A riderless horse galloped by, its nostrils streaming blood.

Lewis ran along the road, looking for Riley. He was propped against the bank, moaning and crying out like a child pleading for its mother. "Doc! Where are you?" He clutched his stomach, and blood oozed between his fingers.

"Oh my God!" Lewis groaned. "Riley, I got to get you out of here." Looking up, he saw another soldier climbing up the opposite bank of the road, and Lewis jumped up and grabbed the tail of the man's shirt. "Come here and help me with this man."

The other soldier jerked his arm away and slammed Lewis on the side of the head, growling, "Let go of me, you damn fool."

Another man stood in the road, repeatedly loading his musket, pointing it blindly into the haze ahead of him, and pulling the trigger. "Thompson," Lewis yelled at him, grabbing the hot barrel of the gun. "Quit loading! You done misfired, and you ain't doing nothing but packing shot in!"

"Well, hell fire," Thompson grunted, then seized the barrel in both hands and slung the gun spinning into the smoke, as if he imagined that the overloaded barrel would blast the unseen enemy.

Lewis grabbed Thompson by the sleeve and pulled him toward Riley. Then, with Lewis holding Riley under the shoulders and Thompson holding him under the knees, they climbed the far bank of the road and half dragged the wounded man over the shattered fence. Riley yelled in pain as they stumbled across the furrowed field toward the trees. When they set him down to rest, Lewis looked closely into Riley's face and watched his lips move in a wordless plea.

The sounds of battle were remote and distant, daylight nearly gone, when Lewis and Thompson brought Riley under the shelter of the trees. A field hospital had been set up beyond the creek, and they took Riley there. When they saw a tent with a surgeon working over a man on a table, they went toward it, but a sergeant stopped them.

"Lay him back yonder under that oak tree. Can't you see there's plenty ahead of him?"

"But, Sergeant," Lewis argued, "he's hurt real bad and he's going to die if he don't get help right away."

"Don't dispute with me. Take him over yonder."

"Come on, Powell. Ain't no use disputing."

Thompson began dragging Riley toward the tree, and Lewis helped him lift the inert, moaning body.

A dozen men were lying under the tree, groaning and calling for water. Lewis peeled off his own dark coat and rolled it into a pillow for Riley. Then he sat by his friend while Thompson went to get water.

Riley opened his eyes and looked at Lewis, then shut them again. Lewis widened the rip in Riley's rough homespun trousers to look at the wound. Pink intestine pulsed up through the clotted, torn flesh. When Thompson came back from the creek with water, Lewis tore a strip off the bottom of his shirt, moistened the cloth, and washed around the wound. With his free hand, he tried to wave off the black flies that swarmed over Riley and himself, stinging indiscriminately. Riley groaned and muttered, his face glistening as though smeared with oil in the flickering light of a lantern that somebody had hung from a branch. No help came.

Stretcher-bearers continued to carry in more wounded, laying them in rows along the slope. At the hospital tent, three lanterns hanging from the ridgepole turned the surgeon into a black, faceless machine, his arm a rhythmic lever, cutting away parts of men. Lewis mechanically mopped Riley's face and wondered if there was anything the surgeon could do for him. It looked like something had gotten inside him and ripped its way out. He was going to die.

Riley began to mutter again. "Lewis, remember when we drove them cows to Jasper? Them fellows didn't know what hit them when we got into them, did they?" Then he fell silent, except for his groans. Sometimes he would talk in a way that Lewis could not understand, about the witches that they had seen in Booth's play at Richmond. "It's bad times ahead in the stew pot," he would say. "I see the witches a-stirring it up."

Lewis did not leave Riley's side. Thompson brought him his bedroll, and he lay beside Riley all night, in a fitful sleep that mixed Riley's babble about the witches and the stewpot with the groans of the men being carried to the tent.

In the morning Thompson was back, bringing Lewis a tin cup of hot cornmush. As Lewis drank it, he looked at Riley, whose breath by now was coming in great heaves and pauses. In a pine tree above him a thrush was singing, but beyond the songbird vultures drifted.

The first orange rays of sun pierced the thicket of trees while artillery rumbled behind the opposite ridge. The ground trembled under Lewis even this far away. But only his bones felt it. His ears could take in only the sound of Riley's gasping. Lewis wiped blood and saliva from Riley's lips and mopped the oily face. The thrush rustled a branch above them as it flew away, and some dew sprinkled onto Riley. Riley opened his eyes, and said, "Doc, I've had just about enough of this here war." He frowned and stared at Lewis.

Lewis looked down at him and wiped his face again. "You're going to make it, Riley. I'll get you out of here." He bit his lip and felt his eyes go hot and wet, but he believed what he had said.

Lewis did not know that he had been asleep until he felt a hand heavy on his shoulder.

"He's gone, Powell." It was Sergeant Willis's voice.

"What? What did you say?"

"Green's dead, Powell."

"No, he ain't. He's just gone to sleep. Riley? Riley, wake up." He laid his hand on Riley's shoulder. "Sarge, I was talking to him just now. He ain't dead." Then he looked at Riley's pale face, and he knew.

Riley's shirt was open, and Lewis began to fumble the buttons into the buttonholes, but his eyes blurred and he could not see his hands. He kept on till he had buttoned the top button. He thought about Riley that night in Jacksonville, worried that he might get scared and run, and he smoothed the bloody shirt across his friend's chest. His face looked even leaner now, as if the skull were straining to get out.

"Sarge," Lewis said, "I've got to tell his ma."

"Later, Powell."

Henry Holmes and Thompson came and started to pick Riley up, but Lewis stopped them.

"No, damn it! Wait!" Lewis yelled. "Do you want his guts to spill out?"

He grabbed a threadbare blanket from the ground, ripped a wide strip from it, and wrapped it around Riley's middle, tying a knot with trembling hands. Then he hunched on his knees, his head bowed. He watched an ant crawl toward Riley, and thought that he would let it get almost to him, and then he would crush the ant. When he put out his hand, Riley's body doubled and rose, and Lewis jerked back to see Thompson and Holmes lifting him.

Lewis helped them carry Riley to a clearing where men were already digging a trench. Lewis and Thompson picked up shovels and helped to lengthen the trench. Tangled roots made the digging hard work, as if the earth were doing its best to resist their making room for their dead.

Along the trench small groups of men would gather, talk low, read from the Bible, and go away, while others would come to lay men in the trench. Lewis lifted Riley, then slid into the pit up to his waist. He laid Riley down, crossing his hands on his chest and straightening him so that he was not against the body next to him.

When Lieutenant Hall came with the rest of the company, Lewis climbed out of the trench and looked down at Riley, gaunt and at rest, while the lieutenant read: "How are the mighty fallen in the midst of the battle! O Jonathan, thou wast slain in thine high places." He stopped and closed the Bible, while the men looked at one another, then down at Riley. *Thy love to me was wonderful,* Lewis whispered to himself, *passing the love of women.* Then the lieutenant nodded to Holmes and Thompson, and they started shoveling dirt onto Riley— first onto his feet, then onto his legs.

When the first clod fell onto the piece of blanket wrapped around his belly, Lewis jumped into the trench, pulled off his own coat, lifted Riley's head in a cradling hand, and tucked the coat around his head.

Then he climbed out and walked away and stood with his back to the trench. From ahead of him sounded cannons, hoofbeats, shouts, but behind him were voices hushed as if in church, and the scrape of shovels.

After a while Thompson pressed him on the shoulder as he and Holmes passed on their way back to the woods. Lewis followed them until they came to where Lieutenant Hall sat, leaning against a little oak. The staff of the regimental flag was thrust into the ground beside him, and Lewis turned, lifted the flag, and took it with him.

Hall nodded, closed his eyes, and leaned his head back. Lewis went to a log and sat beside the regimental flag, staring at the opposite ridge, where he could barely make out the flutter of banners and horsemen riding. On the left still rose the clamor of artillery, with smoke and flashes of fire. The wind across the field brought the pungent smell of gunpowder mixed with the stench of rotting flesh. Some men built small fires to cook cornbread.

About noon, when the sun shone straight down on the farms between the armies, suspending the battlefield in a balance, the brigade was ordered into a line at the edge of the woods. Ahead of them, line behind line, a larger force was taking shape. "Virginians. Pickett's Division," somebody said. "Reckon we'll be a-going with them." Then all speech stopped as lightning broke from their own artillery on the right.

The twelve-pounders flamed and the ground trembled until smoke obscured the field near them. Across the valley, on the ridge, beyond farms, fences, stone walls, and scattered trees, dirt and debris burst in dizzy confusion, and the soldiers would have wondered how men could live through it, if each of them had not known that he had lived through furies like this.

Suddenly the Yankee artillery replied, and shells burst in front of them and in the woods to the left where the division waited. Lewis felt sharp pain as splinters showered from high in the pines. Men threw themselves onto the ground, hands over their ears. Lewis thought of Riley in his grave. Was the ground shaking him the way it was shaking the men who lay on it, and would the trembling earth cast Riley out, resurrected, armed again for battle?

For three hours they lay, their officers riding along the edge of the woods between them and the open field where most rounds were falling, shouting that soon they would give the Yankees back some of their own. Then, almost as one man, they rose. No one heard a command, but they spread into charge formation, this time in two lines. Colonel Lang raised his arm and wheeled his horse toward the enemy. Lewis, bearing the regimental flag high, ran to the side of the colonel.

Sometimes a contrary breeze would blow a hole in the thick smoke and dust, showing skirmishers ahead of them, and once the sun reflected off brass trumpets of a band, their absurd harmonies lost amid the scream of artillery. On the left appeared a line of a thousand men, with officers on horseback leading, their battle flag waving its defiant cross, the line closing when a shell burst among them and moving like a wave of gray foam toward the rock wall at the top of the ridge.

Lewis's throat was dry, and losing sight of the army on his left, he kept his eyes on his own officers, when he could see them. Sweat poured into his eyes, and his wool pants were pasted to his legs. Whenever he lost sight of the line behind him, he would wave the flag. A shell exploded, so near that blood and dirt rained on him. At the road, the men dropped into sunken ruts, then groped up the bank on the far side to falter toward an unseen enemy whose guns exploded shells all around. Lewis could not see but felt that fewer men were with him, and he ran toward where he thought the enemy might be. No longer part of a regiment or of any formation, he bore the flag high, squeezing from his parched throat the high-pitched scream that he could have uttered only in battle, could not ever hear without blood speeding through his body, powering his legs forward, always forward, not toward any end that he knew but toward something that he would know when he came to it.

Rifle fire rattled in front of them, and some men stopped to shoot at distant blue coats behind a parapet of logs. Reloading on the run, they kept with Lewis, with the flag.

Yells and shots and screams surrounding him, Lewis turned left to see a smear of blue soldiers firing across a slope and drifting toward him like a fiery beast in a dream. A sharp pain made him loosen his right hand on the flagstaff. He clenched his left hand and swung the staff like a broadsword toward three soldiers. One went down, his cheek bursting red, while the faces of the others seemed frozen in front of him as in a picture, until a heavy weight slammed against his head and the earth rose spinning to crush against him.

6

GETTYSBURG
AUGUST 1863

The hospital was row after row of white tents, like worn hills covered with ashes. When it was not raining, which was seldom, the flaps would be open, and the breeze would bring into each tent the rotten smell of the others. When it was raining, the flaps would be closed, and the smell of lye soap competed with the corrupt smell of death. Stale blood and vomit mingled with the pungent odor of sweat and stale piss from unwashed men, and over it all were the flies, like the plague sent by God to the Egyptians, swarming, buzzing, rising and resettling at every motion of some tormented body.

Lewis took the lamp from the orderly to make the rounds of the cots in one tent. He looked at the man in the third bed. Chest wound. His breathing sounded like a rasp on oak wood. Pale, yellow face, mouth agape drawing in air. The man looked like somebody Lewis knew, and he held the lamp closer. No. He was a stranger, whether a Confederate or Yankee he could not tell. Here it did not make a difference. They were all united in a nation of the dead and dying.

The wound in Lewis's right hand throbbed again, and he raised his forearm, pacing slowly through the tent. He had become accustomed to the involuntary cries of the sick and wounded.

"Oh, Lo-o-rd! Oh, Lo-o-rd!" one man called over and over. Lewis passed him to stop at the next cot and stood gazing at the still figure lying there. He felt the man's forehead and reached for his wrist. No pulse. Lewis held the lamp closer and looked into half-open, unblinking eyes. The slack, open mouth gave the dead man's face a stupid expression. Perkins—Gardiner, Maine. Yesterday morning, when Lewis had scrawled out a letter for him, Perkins had said that he would get well. Kiss Birdie for me. Tell Philip we'll dig clams when I get home. Lewis drew the rough muslin sheet over Perkins's face, then reached into his pocket and pulled out a grimy, colorless tag, which he tied to the end of the cot.

At the back flap of the tent Lewis picked up two slop-buckets and took them outside, where he dumped them into a pit. He squinted his eyes and batted at the flies that swarmed up toward him. When he went back inside the tent a man was waiting for the bucket.

When the surgeon came on duty at dawn, at the end of Lewis's shift, he hastily looked Perkins over, then told Lewis and another prisoner nurse named Crampton to put him on a stretcher and take him out for the burial detail. Just outside the tent, they passed two officers in dress blues escorting two young women. Lewis heard one of the officers tell the surgeon the women were nurses from Baltimore. Crampton, who often bragged of being a ladies' man, stared over the dead man at the girl in front, a brown-haired, rosy-cheeked girl with large breasts. The other woman, taller and leaner, glanced out of deep-set eyes at the dead man, then looked at Lewis with a sympathy that took in all the wounded and dying. Lewis and Crampton passed them and carried the corpse to a wagon.

The hospital began to change after that day. Twice daily a locomotive puffed up to the siding across the road, bringing crates of supplies, and groups of women would alight: women from Baltimore, from Washington, from Philadelphia, to take care of the hundreds of sick and wounded men. Lewis's work became lighter. The plank floors of the tents were washed regularly and there were more clean bedclothes for the men. But the amputations went on as they had ever since the battle, and men died by the score every day.

One day, when Lewis was trying to replace a dressing on a soldier's arm, the man kept jerking the arm away. He was feverish and babbling incoherently. Lewis heard a voice beside him say, "You're not doing it right." He turned to see the slender woman who had looked at him so compassionately a few days before. She wrung out a sponge in a pail of water and bathed the sick man's forehead. Lewis stood back and watched. She turned her brown eyes on him and said, "He's calmer now. I'll hold his arm while you dress it."

This time the soldier did not resist as Lewis unwrapped the bloody dressing, exposing the raw, stinking infection underneath.

"Laudable pus," the woman told him. "It draws out the infection, cleans the wound."

Following her directions, he wrapped the arm again. When the surgeon called him for another errand, Lewis called back, "Be there in a minute." He turned to the woman, who was mopping sweat from the face of the moaning soldier.

"What's your name?" Lewis asked her.

"Maggie Branson. They call you Doc, don't they? But you're not a doctor."

"Powell!" the surgeon called again. "Come here!"

"You'd better go now," Maggie told him.

"Yes'm, but I want to talk to you again." Twisting his body to the side, Lewis crab-walked between the cots to the surgeon.

On Sunday morning, after being on duty all night, Lewis left the hospital and walked toward his tent. The cool air dried the sweat that had soaked his shirt, and carried away the putrid stench of the hospital tents. He walked along a path wet with dew through a mist made silver by the rising sun. Where the path crossed a rutted lane, an apple tree, laden with small green fruit, sheltered a thrush, singing its way into daylight. He felt a new lightness in his feet, and his body seemed drawn upward toward the bright sky above, where a few pink clouds drifted. After hesitating at the gate, he turned left, toward Cemetery Ridge.

Lewis had not been to the battlefield since he had been taken prisoner. From other prisoners and from the Union soldiers he had heard about the charge that General Armistead had led up the hill into the midst of the enemy, of the slaughter by the terrible guns, of the survivors taken prisoner or stumbling wounded back to Confederate lines. He had been part of the charge, and he had make his way as far as he could, bearing the regiment's colors. It was not shame that had kept him from the battlefield; it was the feeling that he had lost more there than he would find if he went back—lost all that was represented by the mighty army that had drawn away in sore defeat, taking Lewis's last link to home. It reminded him of the time that once, as a boy at Live Oak, he had swapped fierce dares with two other boys, dares that had led to a tearing, slashing fight between his dog and two of theirs. Nero, his dog, had put his best into the fight, but Lewis had carried him home, so clawed and torn that he died that night. It was as though the army had turned its dim, fading eyes toward him and crawled away like Nero, in the same way that Riley had looked at him and babbled his life away beyond victory or defeat.

At the crest of the ridge, Lewis looked at the mist-hidden valley, as invisible to him now as it had been under the smoke and confusion of battle. His wounded right hand throbbed again, and he crooked his forearm upward to ease it. Turning left at the Baltimore Pike, he walked toward the cemetery. The townspeople had been filling in shell craters, and already carts drawn by oxen or mules were starting to move along the roads, bearing workmen or bodies dug from shallow graves scattered over the field. Against a fence post grew a blue aster, the only flower in sight.

Lewis paused when he came to the low rock wall that bounded the graveyard. Something rustled at his feet, and he looked down to see a black snake scurry into a hole between two rocks. Meade's army had left the town graveyard an undisturbed island around which the war had raged like a river out of its banks, but one far-ranging shell had smashed into one side of the cemetery, leaving pieces of uprooted cedar lying amid marble fragments. Burial details had been at work enlarging the cemetery helter-skelter across the hillside, laboring against the summer heat to lay the dead in shallow graves. Lewis thought of Riley, lying beyond the battlefield where the earth no longer trembled, finally at peace. "This land is not for me," he whispered to himself. "Not for me." His eyes were hot and wet, and his shoulders trembled. Riley seemed to stand in front of him, and Lewis reached out his hand only to feel the rough bark of a cedar tree. He leaned against the tree, shaking with sobs.

When Lewis looked at the field again, the mist was gone and every rock, every gravestone, every needle of the cedar boughs stood out with brilliant clarity. Near one of the graves, a woman sat on a split-log bench, her back toward him and her head bent over a book that she held open in front of her. A loose brown shawl wrapped around her shoulders, and a gray bonnet covered her head. She sat so still that she seemed part of this place of the dead, a guardian whose permission Lewis would need before he might enter. Then Lewis laughed at the thought. Stepping through the gap where the rock wall had been torn apart, he brushed a loose stone to the ground. The woman turned, startled.

"Why, you're Miss Maggie," he said, snatching his slouch hat off his head. "Remember me?"

"No, I—." She peered into his eyes. "Oh, yes. Doc who is no doctor. I—I didn't hear you coming up."

"I didn't mean to scare you." He reached down to pluck a stalk of grass, then leaned against a cedar while he chewed the stalk. He turned away from her so that she would not see he had been crying.

"This is the first morning I felt like coming up this way. I used to go to the graveyard a lot at home, being as it was close to the church where my pa preached, and it was always peaceful there." He looked down at the book that she had closed already and had laid in her lap. "What is that there book about?"

"It's a book of poems," she told him, "by an English poet named Thomas Gray. I was just reading one called 'Elegy Written in a Country Churchyard.' It's about a graveyard like this, about visiting the grave-yard and thinking about the people buried there who might have been famous if they had lived somewhere else. But they died in a place where the world never heard of them."

"Why, Miss Maggie, that's what I was a-thinking about my friend Riley Green that I buried over on yonder ridge." He sniffed and looked away. "I know he would have been a great man if he had lived."

Maggie looked toward the battlefield, from where the mists had risen, baring the cratered farms, blasted trees, and shattered fences as though lifting a bandage from a raw wound. "Why did you come?" she said. "Oh, why did you come, to do this to this land and to yourselves?"

Lewis looked at her. "Why, I'm a soldier. The army come here, and me and Riley come here with them." He felt that the answer was more than that, but he did not know how to say it. John Wilkes Booth, who knew how to use words and who could utter wonderful speeches that people would listen to and admire, could have said it, could have answered Maggie's "why," but Lewis could not.

"He was the best friend I ever had, Riley was, and it don't seem right just to up and leave him out there. I know they are about to send me to Point Lookout or some other prison camp, and I will never see that his grave gets marked like it ought to be." He stared at the scarred field.

"What are you going to do?"

"I just thought maybe if I was to go over yonder—" He was not sure when he started walking, or what he said to Maggie Branson when he walked away, but a roaring was in his head and suddenly he knew that he was walking on the pike, away from the graveyard toward the bigger graveyard where the battle had been fought. He had to step off the road to dodge mulecarts carrying bodies to be buried for the second time. Along the road shattered artillery caissons blocked his way, and he stumbled over splintered wheels half buried by the rains that had fallen after the battle. Yet the roaring in his head drew him like a summons along a winding path through the debris and over clumps of earth thrown up by the terrible shelling. He felt a sharp, dizzying pressure in his head as a flood of light blotted out the road. He sagged against a caisson axle that seemed to grow aslant out of the ground bearing a broken wheel like a blossom.

A hand touched his arm, and he recoiled.

Maggie Branson stood by him. "Are you all right?" she asked. "All of a sudden you walked away, and I came after you."

Lewis shook his head. "I forgot where I was or where I was going. I heard this noise and seen this light."

"We had better go back now," she said.

Lewis yielded to her light pull on his arm, and stumbled alongside her.

A surrey passed, driven by a gentleman in a black frock coat and tidy hat. A lady in blue satin sat next to him, and two other ladies were in the seat behind them, shielded from the sun by the canopy that stretched over them. Other buggies came behind them, all with four or five people in them, some balancing picnic baskets on their laps. There were children in some of the wagons who would shout at one another, "Look there! Look at the gun!" or "Look at that burned-up house!"

Lewis stopped a black carter who was passing, leading an ox and an empty cart toward the battlefield. "Who are all these people a-coming this way? What they doing?"

"They be from various towns hereabouts, boss," the carter told him. "Comes out every Sunday to look at the battlefield."

At the edge of the graveyard, a man had unhitched his mule and was scattering pieces of metal and cloth on the bed of his wagon.

"What's that man up to?"

"Oh, him. He be a-selling souvenirs—pieces of guns, buttons, haversacks. He be out here near about every day. Some says he makes a lot of money at it."

Two or three buggies had stopped near the huckster's wagon, and the gentlemen and ladies and their children were approaching to look at what he was laying out. Lewis moved closer and watched them pick up buttons, insignia, and pieces of weapons. Maggie stayed close to him, her hand maintaining a slight controlling tug on his arm.

Then Lewis started forward, a growl more animal than human rising from his throat. The tourists retreated, as if battle had suddenly returned to the field, and the face of the huckster loomed nearer, reflecting wide-eyed, stupid fear while the man's arms came up to protect his face. Lewis seized the wagon and rocked it from side to side. With a grunt he shoved it over, spilling onto the ground the shards of brass, braid, cloth, and metal, as the stupefied huckster cowered against a tree, his mouth twisted in impotent fright.

7

BALTIMORE
SEPTEMBER 1863

IT HAD RAINED steadily for the five days that Lewis had been in Baltimore, and there was a chill in the September air. Lewis stepped into the shelter of a shop doorway and pulled out of a pocket the slip of paper with Maggie's address written neatly in a long, bold strokes. A drop of water fell from his cap onto the paper, causing the ink to run, but he could make out "No. 16 Eutaw Street." The rain had soaked through the tight-fitting Union private's tunic he wore, and Lewis shivered.

A horse-drawn streetcar stopped to let off a passenger, then went on its way, its wheels hissing on the wet tracks. Better not get on it, he told himself. The Yank that wore these pants had not left any change in the pockets, and if he depended on the uniform to get him a free ride, some bluebelly might ask for his papers. He had been lucky enough to get away from the hospital. Duty as a prisoner nurse at Gettysburg had been an interlude in the war, but since he had come to Baltimore he had seen other Rebel soldiers sent on to Yankee prisons. His turn would have come soon.

He stepped out of the doorway and trudged along the slick, uneven brick sidewalk. No one else was on the street, and daylight was almost gone. Passing a vegetable stand, Lewis looked around him before he picked up an apple and a carrot, which he dropped into his side pockets. Next door was a hatter's shop, and in the shop window was a picture of Robert E. Lee. Lewis stood at the window and gazed at the sad eyes of the solemn general whom he had once cheered on a dusty road in Maryland. The picture seemed to invite him into the shop, and he opened the door.

A bell tinkled over the door, and a bent, gray little man came out from behind the curtains at the back of the shop. He was chewing and wiping his hands, and Lewis's hunger was sharpened by the smell of corned beef and cabbage.

"Yes?" the old man asked suspiciously, and Lewis remembered that he was in a Yankee uniform and that the man regarded him as neither ally nor customer.

"Mister, can you tell me how to find this here street?" Lewis asked, holding the smudged piece of paper toward the old man.

The shopkeeper swallowed and gazed at the paper as if it held the key to some prophecy.

"Eutaw Street is five streets from here. Follow the streetcar tracks here on Baltimore Street till you come to a brick church, then turn right."

"Much obliged."

The shopkeeper did not reply, and as Lewis went outside and pulled the door shut behind him, he looked back to see the man still watching him.

His feet splashed in puddles, and he hunched his shoulders against the cold rain. He pulled the carrot from his pocket and munched it. A lamplighter was coming toward him, methodically illuminating the misty streets.

At the brick church Lewis turned right into a street of narrow-fronted houses, with high front steps. An empty buggy stood beside the curb, its horse tied to a hitching post. The horse watched in dumb animal indifference as Lewis plodded by, searching the numbers painted on the doors.

Through the door to number 16, silver light shone out of narrow panels of frosted glass etched with a dim bird of paradise. A rotary bell handle projected from the middle of the door, between the glass panels, and Lewis climbed the dozen steps and turned the handle, which set off a whirring ring. A shadow formed on one of the glass panels and slowly took human form. The door opened, and Maggie Branson stood silhouetted against the lamplight of the hallway.

"Miss Maggie," he said. "Surprised to see me?"

"Why, Doc! Come on in out of the rain. Yes, I am surprised to see you," she said as he stepped past her into the hall.

Maggie looked up at him and at the sodden blue uniform.

"No, I ain't signed no parole," Lewis told her, "though by the looks of this here Yankee uniform you might think I done it. And I know you sure tried to talk me into signing. I had to steal the uniform. They was about to send me to the prison camp at Fort Delaware."

"You must be hungry, and you've got to get out of those wet clothes. You can change in the spare room downstairs, and I'll send the girl down with some food."

Maggie led him along the hallway toward a staircase. As they passed a door on the left side of the hall, a young woman came out, followed by a ruddy-faced man with side whiskers.

Maggie turned toward the couple. "Are you going out in this rain?" she asked them.

"It's not raining as hard now," the woman said, "and Mrs. Whitcomb will be expecting us at her recital." She looked at Lewis with disapproval. "But I didn't know you had a caller, and one of our gallant Federal defenders, at that."

Maggie laughed. "Mary, this is Doc Powell, who is not what he appears to be. Doc, this is my sister Mary, who does not care for Yankee soldiers, and this is Mr. Henry Shriver, who seems inclined, for some reason that I cannot fathom, to abandon a warm fireside in order to accompany my sister to a music recital."

Lewis shook the hand that Mr. Shriver held out to him, and he looked at Mary. She was about three or four years younger than Maggie, and her nose had the same upward tilt. Her eyes were a lighter brown than her sister's, with a greenish tint. Like Maggie, she was tall, and brown ringlets showed from under the narrow brim of her bonnet. She looked up at Lewis with eyes that expressed a strong will.

"Good evening, sir," she said to him. Henry Shriver scurried past Mary to open the front door, and the couple went out into the rain.

Lewis turned and followed Maggie down the stairs. "Is that your sister's husband?" he asked her.

"Oh, no. She isn't married."

"She's real pretty."

Maggie opened a door at the foot of the stairs, and he followed her into a small, windowless room with a cot on one side. A washstand with a bowl and pitcher stood beside the cot. A single picture on the wall opposite to the door showed a huntsman on horseback, raising a horn to his lips. Maggie brought a lighted lamp from a table that stood outside the door, and set it on the washstand next to the bowl.

"I will send one of the servants with some clothes that were my father's. They may fit you." She turned at the door and looked at him. "You can stay here till you get rested."

"Might just do that. I'm studying getting me a job soon as I get a chance."

"You ought to sign a parole so they won't send you to prison."

"Reckon so."

"Why didn't you take the oath at the hospital? Lots of soldiers have done it. You endangered yourself by escaping in a Union uniform."

"Miss Maggie, I'm of two minds about what to do. It just don't seem right to quit as long as the army's still fighting." He sat heavily on the bed, his elbows on his knees and his head bowed.

"Well, there will be time to talk about it tomorrow." She left the room and closed the door behind her.

After she left, Lewis took off his wet clothes, then lay down and pulled a blanket over him. He did not know when the servant came with food and dry clothes. Sometime in the night he woke and found them there, a stack of folded clothes and a tray with corned beef and cabbage on a plate, now cold. He ate hungrily, wiping the plate clean with a piece of bread.

He drifted into troubled sleep, the old dreams filling his mind. His father strode toward him but came no nearer. At the top of the stairs stood the veiled figure. Then behind it — as suddenly as a hawk — appeared John Wilkes Booth. Booth laughed mockingly, then jerked away the veil to reveal the anguished face of Riley, tossing his head in a fantastic dance while the flesh fell from his face and holding up a skeletal finger that warned or beckoned. Lewis shouted, but no sound seemed to come from him, although the air was full of screams.

He woke to a soft hand on his arm. Maggie bent over him, her hair falling on his face and her soft breath, sour from sleep, brushing him.

73

"Doc," she said. "You're not there now. You're here, at my house."

"Huh?" He woke to the dim glow of the lamp that she held, to the bare room with its washstand and the picture of a huntsman on horseback. He swallowed and sat up, shaking his head, then resting it between upraised knees.

Maggie left the room and returned with a glass of water. He gulped it down while she drew a straight-backed chair toward the bed and sat beside him. Lewis handed the glass to her and, groaning, lay again on his back. She set the glass on the washstand, next to the lamp.

"I seen Riley again," he said. "His ghost. He thinks I got to go back to the brigade."

She mopped his sweating brow with a damp cloth. "Wait till morning, and then think it over."

He fell asleep again, and when he woke, Maggie was gone. He picked up the clothing neatly stacked on the table by the door and wriggled into the skimpy clothes. He opened the door of the room. He could tell by the light from a window that dawn was breaking, and quick, heavy footsteps sounded from the kitchen above him. Lewis felt his way up the stairs and groped along the dim hall, then slipped out the front door without seeing anyone.

Stumbling along Fayette Street in the morning twilight, Lewis turned toward the wharves, where he could look for a drayman going into western Maryland. He planned to help load barrels and earn a ride into the farmlands. From there he could cross into Virginia and find his way to Lee's army.

The city was waking up. Yesterday's wet gloom became today's gray doubt. Wagons lumbered in from the farms, vendors pushed carts off Fayette into side streets, shopkeepers flung up shutters. Two laborers shouldered past him, jabbering in a foreign tongue, and passed through a gate into a foundry yard. The acrid smell of slops dizzied him and the clattering cartwheels and coarse shouts bewildered him. *This land is not for me.*

When he saw tall masts on his right, he turned into Commerce Street, a lane of taverns. In front of one tavern a fat, aproned saloonkeeper poured water over bricks and began to sweep them. Lewis stopped. Looking past the man into the dim doorway, he thought he recognized a man inside, standing with one foot on a chair and talking to the saloonkeeper like a general explaining a campaign, while the saloonkeeper nodded in agreement.

When the aproned man went inside, Lewis edged closer to the door and stood still. At once he recognized the voice that he had last heard in Richmond two years before, the voice of John Wilkes Booth. As often as Lewis had recollected those clanging scenes in *Macbeth*, he had never expected to meet the player again. Lewis felt relief and pleasure at the coincidence of encountering an old acquaintance in this city of strangers.

Lewis crossed the street and waited in a doorway, leaning against the doorpost with his hands in his pockets and his blue cap pulled forward almost to his eyes. He groped into a pocket of the tight brown coat, pulled out a roll that he had brought from the Branson house, and ate it.

Lewis had waited about a half-hour when Booth appeared in the doorway of the tavern, still talking and looking up and down the lane. He lingered another minute, tossing a few remarks that drew laughter from inside the tavern. Then Booth started up the lane toward Fayette Street.

Lewis stepped out of the doorway and called, "Captain Booth!" Booth turned and looked at him with a smile.

"At your service, my good man."

Lewis walked toward him. "You likely don't recollect me, Captain. Powell? Doc Powell? I seen your play in Richmond two years ago, me and my friend Riley."

Booth wrinkled his brow and peered at Lewis. Then he brightened. "Why, of course. You're the wrestler who won the wager for me that day. But why—what are you doing in Baltimore? Are you out of the army?"

"I was took prisoner at Gettysburg, and I'm trying to get back to my regiment. If I stay here, it's either take the oath or go to prison. They've been sending some of the prisoners out west. I run away when they sent me here."

Booth regarded Lewis for a minute, looking up into his face. A loaded wagon labored up the lane toward them in a methodical clumping of hooves and creaking of wheels. Booth took Lewis by the arm and led him back to the tavern. "We can talk in here."

The tavernkeeper was out of sight, the front room empty of people. The chairs were pushed against dull, heavy oak tables, streaked from recent wiping. Their feet crunched oyster shells imbedded in stale brown sawdust as Booth led Lewis to a corner table where he drew a chair away from the table and sat down. He threw his hat onto the table, pushed his hands into his pockets, and leaned the chair against the wall. Lewis pulled out a chair and sat stiffly, his hands nervously on his knees.

"What has it been like for you, Powell?"

"We been licking them everywhere, Captain, and we could have licked them at Gettysburg, but something went wrong. You recollect Riley Green? He got killed there."

Booth looked at Lewis solemnly. "A hero who dies for his country dies the noblest death, and lives on in his country's heart. Remember that."

"I reckon you're right. My brother Oliver, he got killed in Tennessee—Murfreesboro—and my brother Wash got shot up real bad and sent home. My folks wrote me to come back to Florida, and I got Captain Duncan to give me a leave, but then I decided against going. If I had went, I reckon they might have made me stay and work the farm. Now I'm in for the war. All I want to do is to get to Virginia and find Perry's Brigade."

Booth's lips spread into a broad smile. "By God, Powell," he said, "you're a man after my own heart. With men like you, the Confederacy surely will taste the sweet wine of victory."

"Captain, I have heard tell that a heap of men have deserted the army and gone back home. But that's not for me. I mean to fight on to the end."

Booth stood and paced in front of Lewis, his hands behind his back. "But maybe they will return. Many are the good men rotting in Northern prisons, men who could reinforce the army if they can be freed." He clapped a hand on Lewis's shoulder. "You inspire me, young warrior, to take arms in my country's defense. And I shall! Listen—" He broke off as the tavernkeeper stepped into the room through a curtained doorway.

"Oh, it's you, Johnnie," the tavernkeeper said. "I heard talking out here, but I didn't know you had come back."

"Frawley," Booth said, "I ran into an old friend, and we are renewing auld lang syne. Just serve us a cup of that steaming coffee you brew so well, and bring my friend some ham and eggs."

"Coming right up, Johnnie," Frawley called over his shoulder as he left the room.

Booth jerked his head toward the back room. "A sympathizer with the Cause, a man we can trust."

"Seems to me like there's a lot of folks like that around Baltimore, Captain," Lewis said.

"No wonder. That tyrant, Abraham Lincoln, has kept his troops in this city since the war began. He has closed businesses and thrown some of our leading citizens into prison. Some of my best friends have lost their freedom to that would-be monarch." He leaned forward, his hands on the table, and spoke almost in a whisper. "Listen, Powell. I have something important to tell you, something on which might hinge the future of the Confederacy. But you must swear—on the word of a Confederate soldier—not to speak of this to anyone. Will you?"

A shout from outside and the passing of horses left behind them a silence that gave a solemn, churchlike privacy to the room. Lewis drew his chair to the table. "Yes, Captain Booth, I swear it."

Booth propped a foot on his chair and moved so close that Lewis felt the warmth of his breath and smelled lingering traces of whiskey. Dark shadows encircled his brown eyes with mystery and confidentiality. "I am in contact," Booth told him, "—dare I say *close* contact?—with men highly placed in the government of France. I cannot tell you the particulars now, but I have relayed dispatches to Richmond to inform the government of the Confederacy that the aid of a mighty foreign power stands near at hand. France has sent an army to Mexico. They can maintain power only as long as the Lincoln government is weak. Thus it is to the advantage of France that the Confederate States win their independence. If the army—or if bold men acting in support of the army—can cripple the Lincoln tyranny, then France will recognize the Confederacy and bestow financial aid that will assure the continued life of our government."

Lewis scarcely understood what Booth was talking about, but he was in awe that he, a mere private, should be entrusted with intelligence having to do with affairs between nations.

A clatter signalled the return of Frawley, bringing on a tray a plate of ham and scrambled eggs and two steaming cups of coffee.

As if dropping a mask, Booth blossomed into joviality. "Ah," he exclaimed, rubbing his hands together, "mine host approacheth with tasty viands!"

"Just holler if you need anything else, Johnnie," Frawley said, setting the tray on the table and leaving the room.

Lewis knifed off hunks of ham and stuffed them into his mouth, spooned in the eggs, and gulped down the hot coffee. While Lewis ate, Booth sat, circling his hands around the hot mug of coffee without drinking, and resuming his confidential tone.

"The fate of our country, Powell, hangs in the balance. What if—and listen carefully to this—what if men, strong men, should seize that tyrant in Washington City, spirit him away, and hold him for the release of the Confederate prisoners?"

Lewis set down his spoon and stared at Booth. "What do you mean?" he asked.

"I mean what I said. I intend to take Abraham Lincoln prisoner, and I need you to help me to do it. I offer you the chance to join in the most daring exploit in history. I offer you the chance to save your country in the hour of its direst need."

A passing cart rattled sound through the room and blocked out the light, but Lewis stared above him at the silhouette of Booth, seeing in him again the usurping figure on the stage at Richmond, reaching for a ghostly dagger.

8

WASHINGTON CITY
NOVEMBER 13, 1863

O<small>UT OF NINE</small> blank front windows, the house of Mary Surratt over-looked the pike between Washington City and southern Maryland. A sign in front of the Surratt House announced sustenance and overnight repose to travelers with the money to pay. By day sparrows no bigger than oak leaves skipped through the oaks, and jay-birds and mock-ingbirds quarreled along the rail fence that twisted beside the pike. By night, people said, the house of Mary Surratt was haunted. Haunted by the ghost of John Surratt, who had given his name to a son, to the tavern, and to the town where he had been postmaster, then passed to a world with no names and no outgoing mail, leaving Mary Surratt with two sons and a daughter, a house in Washington City, this inn at Surrattsville, and a burden of debt. Haunted by ghosts of Confederate couriers bound for Richmond or Washington City who used the Surratt Tavern as a safe house and then vanished into the gray certitude of the war. Haunted by ghosts of journeymen and apprentices, of draymen and teamsters, of slaveowners who slept in the big house while their slaves burrowed into straw in the stoveless room off the cowshed. Haunted by a pair of eloping lovers, overtaken at midnight by a shrouded party of three men—whether the party included husband, father, or brothers no one in Surrattsville was ever heard to say—who shot the man and horsewhipped the screaming girl naked in the snow.

The November day was heavy with rain, the earth and sky uni-formly drab, the windows of the Surratt House as bleak as unanswered prayer. A dappled gray mare, hitched to a surrey, was tied to the hitching post in front of the tavern. Lewis Powell, in a black frock coat and a broad-brimmed preacher's hat, came out of the house carrying a carpetbag and a shotgun, and stared along the road at an approaching wagon. The driver of the wagon waved, but Lewis did not return the wave. He set his carpetbag into the surrey and laid the shotgun across the seat before tightening a buckle on the harness. He started to climb to the driver's seat, but hesitated and stood against the horse, feeling the animal's warmth. Lewis blew on his bare hands, rubbed them together, and hugged them under his arms.

Again he looked both ways along the road, then turned toward the door of the tavern, where through the panel window beside the door he could see Mary Surratt kneeling, fingering a rosary, before a statue of the Virgin Mary. She had remarked half a dozen times this morning that it was Friday the thirteenth, as though every lost horseshoe and every broken teacup could be blamed on that coincidence of day and number. Now here she is, thought Lewis, begging God to make a good day out of a bad one.

John Surratt came around the corner of the house, his feet making sucking sounds in the mud. He was a lean, wispy man, with an air of uncertainty about him, as though he were about to turn around and return the way he had come. He chewed on a hangnail on his left thumb.

"Tell your ma to hurry up, John," Lewis said. "We ain't got all day."

"Ma!" John called toward the door of the tavern. "Doc has the surrey harnessed, and we're waiting!" He took hold of a fence post near Lewis and wiggled it. "Another rotten one," he said. "Got to lay out a new fence." He looked at Lewis again. "Don't let on to Ma about that abduction business. The less she knows, the better."

"John, we don't need for nobody to know about it that don't have to know."

John Surratt stamped his feet and swung his arms. "It's cold waiting out here," he said. He looked at the house again. "Anyways, Doc, we might get it all over and done with in the next week. Wilkes will be at Ford's Theater for a week, and he hopes to do it then."

"I can't wait to get in the middle of something again. I never thought I would miss soldiering, but it gets too dull to wait for something to happen. It has been two months now since Captain Booth sent me here, and he told me then that we would capture Lincoln in the middle of November." Lewis walked to the fence and looked south along the pike. He spat onto the mud. "Just the other day I was talking to that courier about Mosby's Confederacy in Virginia and Gilmor's partisan rangers in Maryland. Made me want to head for one of them outfits. No more infantry for me. Hurts my feet too much. Next time I want to do my fighting on horseback."

Mary Surratt came out the door, adjusting her black bonnet. Her black dress and high-buttoned black jacket and the gray shawl over her shoulders made her look more solemn than ever. In two months at Surrattsville, Lewis still looked on her as a stranger. What had Booth called her? "A queen in exile." Something like that. Proud, believing in herself and in the power of the Virgin Mary, and in the Cause. In love with Captain Booth, too, if you could judge from some of the things she said about him. And her twice as old as he is. She was a good-looking woman when she was young, judging from the pictures he had seen of her, and some would call her good-looking now. It almost made him feel sorry for her. But a lot of women were in love with Booth, like that actress that had shot him in New York. Booth still laughed when he told that story.

John came forward to help his mother onto the back seat of the surrey. She handed him her umbrella, looked along the road, and spoke as if Lewis were not present. "I hope we don't have any more trouble from those Tolliver boys, after Lewis getting in that fight. If he had stayed away from that widow over by the river, that Elsie Chalmers, he wouldn't be in trouble with them."

"Miz Surratt," Lewis said, "it was a fair fight between me and Buck Tolliver. It didn't last long neither, before he had to admit he was licked."

"You don't know those Tollivers like I do. They don't forget a grudge."

"That suits me just fine. I wouldn't mind beating Buck Tolliver again. If I had not promised Captain Booth I would come back to Washington City today, I would wait here to find out what they aim to do."

John said, "Ma, the Tollivers are down in Virginia now, and in spite of what the neighbors told you, they are not liable to be back today. Anyway, I have told Doc that it would be better for us if he doesn't come back here. Wilkes has found him a job in Washington City." John helped his mother into the back seat and tucked a blanket around her legs.

Lewis climbed up to the driver's seat, laying the shotgun underneath it, and John climbed up beside him and unwrapped the reins from the post. With one last look in both directions along the road, John tossed the reins, guiding the horse onto the rutted pike toward Washington City.

"I aim to move into the city next fall," Mary Surratt announced. "Mr. Lloyd has been after me to rent the tavern to him, and Anna has to stay there until she finishes school. I don't think your Aunt Gladys is taking good care of her."

"You are right, Ma. Anna needs looking after. I can't understand it. She was always healthy here at Surrattsville. Now she has been down sick ever since she went to stay in the city."

Anna had left Surrattsville barely a week after Lewis's arrival, and her going away had disappointed him. At eighteen, Anna was slim as a boy, still lacking the full-bodied maturity of her mother. Women who knew more about the world, like Elsie Chalmers or Maggie Branson's sister Mary, were more to his liking. Still, his two months at Surrattsville would have been more endurable if Anna or any girl had been there, with rustling petticoats and blushes and perfumes and giggling playfulness.

At Fort Wagner they passed a large camp of Union cavalry, but the sentries waved them on. The infantry camped near the bridge over the Anacostia were more careful, stopping every wagon. Lewis and the Surratts waited in a line while a sergeant and two riflemen questioned some carters. A party of farmers with a load of hay argued with the soldiers while two soldiers plunged bayonets into the bales as if they were attacking a redoubt.

At the bridge, a sergeant and a rifleman came toward them. Lewis gasped, remembering the sergeant from Gettysburg, one of the wounded he had tended. Stay calm, he said to himself. Maybe he won't know me with this preacher's coat and hat on. He whispered to John Surratt, "John, I think I know that there sergeant. He was at Gettysburg when I was there."

John's face went pale. "Oh, God!" he muttered. Lewis felt John shrink away from him.

"What is it?" Mary asked from the seat behind them.

"Keep still, ma," John told her, half-turning. "That sergeant might know Doc."

The sergeant and the private came closer. The sergeant shuffled some papers he was carrying, and one fell. As he turned, the private picked it up, and handed it to him. The sergeant glanced at the paper, added it to the stack, and looked straight at Lewis.

"Sergeant!" called an officer on horseback.

"Yes, sir?"

"Go over yonder to that hay wagon and see what the trouble is about." As the sergeant turned toward the cart, the officer walked his horse nearer to the surrey where Lewis and the Surratts were waiting.

"How do, ma'am?" The officer touched the brim of his hat and bowed to Mary. "You folks headed for Washington City on business?"

John said, "Yes. We've got to see about some property in town, and we're going to the theater to see a play."

"Why, it's Mr. Surratt, isn't it?" the officer asked. "I stopped at your tavern a few weeks ago."

John stirred uneasily. "Yes, sir. And this is my mother, and— uh—Reverend Wood." He nodded his head sideways toward Lewis.

"Pleased to meet you, ma'am. And you, Reverend. Where about's your church?"

Lewis swallowed. "Surrattsville."

"Good place for it. Those Rebels down there need some soul-saving." He laughed, and John chuckled nervously.

"Well, you folks have a good stay in Washington City. Sorry to delay you, but we've had a report that Mosby is trying to slip into the city. Mr. Surratt, I'll stop in for some of those good oysters, next time I'm down your way."

"I'll save a place for you, Lieutenant," John told him. He tossed the reins and the horse moved again, passing the sergeant, who had his back to them and was arguing with the wagoner.

"That there sergeant might not have recollected me no how," Lewis said. "But I would have had a lot of questions to answer if he did."

They rattled across the Anacostia Bridge and along the rutted road leading toward Washington City. At a crossing, they turned left onto Pennsylvania Avenue, following muddy ruts past scattered houses surrounded by broad lawns and gardens. It was starting to rain when they broke out of a patch of woods and came within sight of the Capitol, and Mary opened her umbrella.

"Ma," John said, "I went up in the dome the last time I was in Washington City, and I could see all over the town. It's a beautiful sight. I'd like to take you there sometime, but the steps are so narrow."

"No, thank you," Mary told him. "I prefer to keep my feet closer to the ground. That climbing is all right for you young folks, but I'd sooner climb a scaffold than climb those steps. But is it so that they really have flush toilets in the Capitol?"

"Yes, they have. Some folks say that someday all houses will have them."

"Well, fancy that. I doubt it will be in my time, though."

More soldiers were camped on the grounds around the Capitol, and John had to stop the horse and wait for a troop of cavalry to pass before he could turn onto New Jersey Avenue. They followed the street railway to the Baltimore and Ohio Station, which was almost deserted except for some men unloading hogsheads from a wagon. They turned with the street railway along F Street and followed it to Sixth, where John turned right. At Sixth and H streets he drew rein at a livery stable on the corner.

John helped his mother from the surrey. She waited while Lewis and John unharnessed the mare and led her into a stall. In dumping grain into the nosebag and buckling the bag on the horse, Lewis broke a strap, but he said nothing and left the broken piece dangling.

The rain had turned to snow. Lewis and John tried to walk around the puddles in the street, steadying Mary Surratt between them on the slippery mud. A Negro woman opened the door of the house and smiled when she saw Mary. "We had just about give you all out, Miss Mary," she said. "I've kept supper warming on the stove, and Miss Anna is in the parlor."

They pulled off their coats and hats and gave them to the servant, then went into the parlor. Anna Surratt was in a large wing-backed chair, wrapped in a yellow quilt. "Ma," she said, "I am so glad you

84

are here. Aunt Gladys waited for you, but she just left half an hour ago to go visit a sick friend."

Mary Surratt kissed her daughter and pulled the quilt higher on her shoulders. "Anna, you have lost weight since you came into the city. I need to come live here and look after you." She turned to John. "I can see that I had better not go to the theater with you. I will stay with Anna."

John came to his sister's chair and kissed her on the forehead. "No greeting for your brother?" he said.

Anna hugged him and saw Lewis. "Doc," she said, "how come you to be wearing a preacher's coat and hat? I saw you from the window and thought Ma was bringing a Protestant preacher to the house."

John laughed. "We had to disguise him to get him past the Yankees. As it was, one of them came near to recognizing him."

"Was it just the Yanks you had to get him away from? A little bird told me it was that Elsie Chalmers. Why, she's not good for anything but getting men to fight over her."

"It will take more than Elsie Chalmers to make a preacher out of me," Lewis laughed. "But look who's talking. Is that walleyed widower from Port Tobacco still courting you?"

"He is not walleyed, and besides, I have not seen hide nor hair of him since I left Surrattsville."

"Let's eat," John said. "I can smell that good food all the way from the kitchen. Then Doc and I want to go to Ford's before the play starts."

"I wish that I could see Mr. Booth's performance," Anna said. "Ma says that he always likes to open with Richard III, and I have never seen it."

"Who knows, Miss Anna," Lewis said, "Captain Booth might even find a part on the stage for your brother and me. Wouldn't that be a fine thing?"

John shot him a warning glance and said, "Come on to the table, Doc. Supper is getting cold."

When Lewis and John turned onto Tenth Street, they found a small crowd on the board sidewalk in front of Ford's Theater. Out of car-

riages stepped elegant, richly dressed people in capes and hats—
dignified gentlemen with ladies shapeless under dark capes. The drifting snowflakes spun through the flickering gaslight into the dark and
seemed to have no being outside the pale yellow circles of light. In
front of the door leaned a sign proclaiming in block letters:

FORD'S NEW THEATER Tenth Street, near E
FRIDAY EVENING, NOVEMBER 13, 1863
MR. J. WILKES BOOTH AND THE GRAND COMBINATION
COMPANY PRESENT SHAKESPEARE'S RICHARD III
Richard, King of England   Mr. J. Wilkes Booth
Richmond   Mr. Charles Wheatleigh

When John showed their passes from John Wilkes Booth, he and
Lewis were ushered to the left up a broad staircase, then behind the
balcony seats to a box close to the stage. A short, bald man in a black
suit was talking with an officer in the vestibule outside the boxes, and
Lewis stopped when he overheard the civilian say something about
Gettysburg.

"No, the cemetery dedication won't be till next week. I'll go on
the cars with the President."

"Then he might be here tonight, after all."

"Perhaps he will. Sometimes he decides at the last minute to
come to the theater."

"Well," said a woman standing with them, "better that uncouth
man would come to the theater and stay away from the dedication at
Gettysburg. At least he wouldn't shock everybody with the coarse
stories he told when he went to Antietam."

The gentleman said, "Now, Martha, we don't know what they
say about Mr. Lincoln is so. His enemies have been telling a lot of
lies about him."

Lowering his head, Lewis stepped into the box where John Surratt
was already seated.

"John," he asked, "is Abe Lincoln going to be here tonight?"

"They say he is. Wilkes wants you and me to get a good look at
him." John pointed toward the president's box opposite them, fes-
tooned with red, white, and blue bunting. At that moment a door
opened in the back of the box, and two ladies came in, followed by
an officer and a slender, gray-haired man in a black frock coat.

86

"Is that Old Abe?" Lewis asked.

"That's Seward," John Surratt whispered, "Secretary of State in the Cabinet."

Lewis did not know what a secretary of state was, and he did not care enough to ask. One of the women with Seward was young and uncommonly pretty, wearing a low-cut pink satin dress and her light brown hair done in medium-length ringlets. Once she looked directly at him, and he was sure that she would have liked to know him as well as he would like to know her. What was her name? Polly. She looked like her name must be Polly. And she surely would be interested in Lewis Powell if he were to tell her that he was a friend of the player they were all waiting to see, John Wilkes Booth.

He was jolted from his daydream when John touched his arm and said, "There's Old Abe now."

"Where?"

"In the box underneath the president's box."

Lewis's eyes let go of the girl in pink satin, and he looked at the lower box. A tall, bearded, black-suited man entered after a woman in an expensive dress of brown silk. Abraham Lincoln nodded to some of the people seated in front of the box, and he smiled. When a man walked toward him and shook his hand, Lincoln spoke to the man and laughed. As soon as Lincoln and the woman in brown silk settled into their chairs, other men went to stand in front of the box and talk to the President.

John said, "Do you think you could take him? Sometimes he is in the president's box on the upper level."

Lewis saw himself in the box (maybe even with time to snatch a kiss from Polly) and seizing Lincoln. If they did it right, they might even take Polly with him. She would grow to love him when she understood the heroic service he was rendering his country.

Before the play began, the scene belonged to Abraham Lincoln; after the curtain rose, all attention was claimed by John Wilkes Booth. The lights dimmed until the brass chandelier and the lamps along the balcony flickered, and the curtain rose on a bright display of gaiety, fanfare and gaudy pennants, darkened by one hunchbacked figure— Booth as a cripple voicing his bitter complaints. Lewis looked at Polly in pink satin, jealous that her lovely eyes were focused only on Booth.

The players' words were hard for Lewis to understand, and he was able to apply judgments about right and wrong only to the simple categories of everyday life. Villainy on the stage was beyond him. It seemed to him that because the man wanted to be king, and because he was John Wilkes Booth, the Richard that Booth played was the man who ought to be the king, no matter what or who stood in his way. Any means that he used to become the king were those that would have been used by saint or sinner, by Lewis himself if he had been on the stage instead of Booth. The play called for them. The only thing that went against the right order of things was for Richard to lose his crown along with the head that wore it. But until Lewis knew that it would end like this, he shared in the superior contempt and spite with which Booth speared every other person in the play. Once he even threw that spite beyond the footlights when he balanced on the edge of the stage, glared at Abraham Lincoln, and spat, "The world is grown so bad that wrens make prey where eagles dare not perch."

Lewis waited for Booth's last scene as eagerly as he used to wait behind a palmetto clump on a chill green morning listening for the thrash of a deer. He wanted to be in the box across from him, where he could whisper to Polly, "Watch and see what is coming next. Captain Booth always does a bang-up job on the last scene." "How do you know?" she would ask. "Oh, I know. He's been a good friend of mine for a long time." Then Booth appeared on stage, clad in armor, the sounds of clashing swords behind him as he cried, "A horse! A horse! My kingdom for a horse!" Lewis leaned forward, moistening his lips with his tongue and clenching his fists, glancing from Booth to Polly and again at Booth.

When Richmond challenged him, Booth attacked, his heavy sword resounding against Richmond's shield. Richmond gave way as Booth drove him back and forth across the stage, their swords striking sparks. Booth liked to boast that he could wear down his opponents until they would beg him to give up and die, and now as Richmond appeared to weaken, Lewis thought he saw him plead for Booth to let up on him. Booth backed off, cried out, whirled, and, as ladies screamed, drove Richmond off the stage and up the center aisle. When he had reached the back of the theater with no place further to go, he allowed his adversary to back him onto the stage; then, with a wild shriek of exultant defiance, Booth ran at Richmond with his sword raised for attack, spread both arms, and impaled himself on the exhausted victor's blade. Still Booth did not fall but dragged the scene out as long as he could, circling like a bear surrounded by dogs before he finally fell to jabs from actors rushing in from the wings.

When the final curtain fell, the audience rose in a tumult of applause for Booth. Even Abraham Lincoln stood, but when Booth came out for a second bow, both Lincoln and Seward had left their boxes. And with Seward had gone Polly.

Later, Lewis waited with John Surratt outside Booth's dressing room while admirers came and went. Two young women who looked like sisters lingered, one in a rose-colored dress and the other in pale blue, their plump hands holding their skirts off the floor. With them was a scowling, puffy-jowled man.

When the three went into Booth's dressing room, John whispered to Lewis, "That's Senator Hale, and those are his daughters. Wilkes is engaged to marry the one in the rose dress."

Booth came out of his dressing room, so absorbed in his conversation with one of the senator's daughters that he did not see Lewis and John. Dressed in a silk brocade dressing gown, the make-up wiped from his face, he made a smart contrast with the sinister hunchback he had just played on stage.

"Ah, Senator," Booth was saying, with his hand on Senator Hale's shoulder, "how it grieves me to play my last night in this stately capital and betake me to the cold and heartless North. And Miss Bessie and Miss Eva, I am overcome with sorrow to leave such fair and charming ladies. But the memory of you will draw me back."

Bessie Hale sighed. "I am sorry that you are too tired, Wilkes, to join us for dinner. Next Sunday evening, then?"

"Without fail." He held Bessie Hale's plump, white hand to his moustached lips and kissed it. "Goodnight, sweet lady, and in thy orisons be all my sins remembered."

Booth shook hands with the senator, then made a final bow as the Hales went out the stage door. Closing the door behind them, the doorman told Booth, "Fine performance tonight, Mr. Booth."

"Ah, thank you, Spangler," Booth responded. "Now please see to it that I am not disturbed, for I have business to discuss with these gentlemen."

Booth extended one arm in a sweeping, empty embrace to usher John and Lewis into his dressing room.

As soon as Booth had closed the door, Surratt spoke. "When will it be, Wilkes? I have people waiting, and I must tell them."

Booth motioned for them to sit down and sank into a chair before his dressing table. He looked at his image in the mirror and stroked his moustache. "The time is not right, John. We will be prevented from acting now. As soon as I finish my engagement at Ford's, Lincoln leaves for Gettysburg. We will be unable to take him here."

"When, then?"

Booth looked at him and then at Lewis. "I don't know when. I never know until the day of the performance when he will be in the theater, and it must be at a time when I am not to be on stage. I must give the abduction my undivided attention."

Lewis, leaning forward with his elbows on his knees, twisted his slouch hat and looked up at Booth. "Captain, Miz Surratt don't want me back at Surrattsville, on account of a fight I got into there. Besides, I want to see some action. I am ready to join up with Major Gilmor, if you don't have no use for me here."

John stood. "Well, you settle between you what Doc is going to do. I told a lady I would call on her tonight, and I don't want to keep her waiting."

Booth clapped him on the shoulder. "An important appointment, indeed, John. Kiss her once for me."

Booth closed the door behind Surratt and turned to Lewis. He rubbed his hands together. "So, young warrior, you thirst once more for the wine of battle. But I am not surprised. As soon as I dress, let us go where we can talk."

While Booth dressed, he asked Lewis about his two months with the Surratts. He laughed when Lewis told him about the carriage rolling off the Potomac ferry, with John in it.

"He would have drowned for sure if I had not been there to pull him out," Lewis chuckled. "Then I come to find out that he weren't in no deeper than four feet of water, at most."

Booth reached into an inner pocket of his coat, pulled out a roll of bills, peeled off several, and handed them to Lewis. "Put this money in your pocket, Powell," he said. "You will need it." He laughed again, saying "Four feet of water," then set his hat at an angle on his head, lifted his gold-headed walking stick from his dressing table, and strutted out the door. Lewis pulled on his slouch hat and followed.

"Still on the job, I see," Booth told the doorman. "You're a man to be relied on, Ed Spangler, and I may need you for an important task some day."

Spangler held the door for them. "Good night, Mr. Booth," he said. "Just let me know if I can ever be of service to you, sir."

Lewis followed Booth into a dim alley lit by one lamp opposite the door. The snow had stopped falling, and thin ice cracked under their feet as they started up the alley. They turned left into another alley and walked to F Street. At the end of the alley stood a horse, saddled without a rider near, its reins dragging in the snow. The horse stared at them until they came close, then wheeled and galloped toward Ninth Street, its hooves thudding hollow on the snow-covered mud and cobblestones.

At Tenth Street Booth hailed a hansom cab and told the driver to go to Ohio Avenue. Tired as Lewis was, he was too excited to sleep after they turned onto Pennsylvania Avenue. Through the large windows of the elegant restaurants on the right he saw ladies and gentlemen dining. But the left side of the street teemed with men. Drunken soldiers and laborers reeled in and out of saloons and gambling houses, and here and there a brightly dressed woman would approach a man and walk away with him. Restless pleasure charged the night of this city, and Lewis even forgot Polly.

The hansom turned left onto Fourteenth Street to pass along a darker way, lit by widely separated lamps. Along the street were soldiers in twos and threes. Where Ohio Street angled left, Booth called on the driver to stop, handed him some coins, and leaped from the cab. Lewis followed him into a street full of men in blue uniforms. Lamps shone from the fronts of houses, and feeble lamplight tried to follow men reeling out of saloons, some with their arms around women. Booth and Lewis threaded their way around the men, some laughing, others cursing loudly or calling the names of friends. Lewis stumbled into a soldier and a woman clenched in a tight embrace. Booth stopped for him, and Lewis hurried toward the actor, hopping over a blue-uniformed boy retching in the gutter.

Booth started up the steps of a house where red lamps flickered on either side of the door. The heavy oak door opened as if in response to a magic command, and a black doorman reached for their hats. "Good evening, gentlemen," he greeted them with flashing teeth. "Come right in. Why, it's Mr. Booth! Pleased to see you, sir. Miss Susanna told me to let her know soon's you got here."

A piano clattered above a babble of male voices and shrill female laughter. A haze of tobacco smoke dimmed the edges of the bright reds, yellows, and greens of draperies and wallpaper. Before disappearing down the hall, the black doorman bowed and waved them toward a doorway sparkling with a curtain of hanging glass beads. Booth pushed through the beads and led Lewis into a large parlor where a dozen men, most of them in uniform, sat drinking at tables or at a long bar, while others leaned against the wall talking with women wearing thin, almost transparent nightgowns. Against a wall stood a piano, played feverishly by a black man wearing a shirt striped in bright red and yellow. The piano player bounced on the stool like a man with St. Vitus's dance, mouthing words into the noise. Directly in front of the door, a wide mirror showed another smoky, loud room, with another Booth and another Lewis Powell advancing to meet them across the polished mahogany bar. Lewis gaped at the sparkling gold elegance of the room.

A woman left the bar and came toward them, smiling. She had olive skin and dark eyes, with long black hair that lay on her shoulders and fell onto breasts revealed by a low-cut pink gown.

"Johnnie!" the woman shrieked. She stopped, clasped her hands together in front of her, fluttered her eyelids, and groaned, "Oh, wherefore art thou, Romeo?"

Booth embraced her. "Call me but love, 0 Francine, and I'll be new baptized. Henceforth I never will be Romeo."

"No," she laughed, "you will be the same Johnnie Booth. What will it be, Johnnie, before you rush to the bed of the Duchess?" She spun away from him and turned over two glasses on the bar. "And for your friend?"

"Brandy, as always, for me," Booth told her.

"And I'll take whiskey and water," Lewis said.

From behind them came a throaty woman's voice, strong enough to overcome the commotion of the room. "Johnnie Booth, you cruel man! You have been neglecting us something awful."

Lewis turned to see a plump, blonde woman of about thirty in a bright emerald gown cut deep to show full breasts. She pouted at Booth and glanced playfully at him, with one hand on her large hip and the other wagging a finger at him.

"Ah, my heavenly Susanna," Booth replied, "how can you malign me so when I have carved my way through the entire Federal army to reach your side?" He pulled her against him and patted one ample hip, at the same time claiming the wagging hand, heavy with rings, and pressing it to his lips.

"Johnnie, you handsome devil," Susanna laughed, "I can forgive you anything." She wrapped thick arms around his neck and kissed him.

Lewis picked up the glass that Francine pushed toward him and drank while he looked around the room. Francine came closer and moved against him, her arm around his waist.

"How is business, Susanna?" Booth asked.

"Never been better, Johnnie. It will suit me for the war to go on another two years. Life will be dull again when it's over, with just the congressmen for trade."

"Where are you from?" Francine asked Lewis.

He gulped whiskey. "Florida."

"I've heard they have awful big alligators down there."

"Yes. Lots of them."

Francine squinted and rubbed against him. "Oooh, I am afraid of alligators."

"They don't bother you much if you stay out of the swamps."

She gripped his arm tightly and said, "I'll hold on to you so you can protect me."

When they started out of the room, with Lewis staggering to try to keep from treading on her feet, a soldier called out, "You come on back right away, you hear, Francine!" When he waved and grinned, Lewis stopped at the door, ready to go back and hit the soldier. But she kept walking, drawing him through the doorway where the sparkling beads tinkled. He embraced her tightly as they climbed the stairs, their feet sinking into the red carpet as they passed crystal lamps adorned with winged cupids.

At the head of the stairs, Francine pushed a door open and led Lewis into a sparse pink room with a narrow, high-posted bed covered with a pink comforter. He watched while she unhooked the back of her dress, stepped naked out of it, and turned to throw back the comforter. The springs creaked when she lay on the bed and pulled him toward her. They creaked again when he lay beside her and kissed her.

"How long you known Johnnie?" the woman asked.

"Captain Booth? Oh, about two years, since I seen him in a play, that play with witches in it."

She was at work unfastening the buttons of his breeches while he groped at her breasts.

"He comes here a lot, you know."

"Who?"

"Johnnie. Johnnie Booth. He comes here to see the Duchess. Stuck-up little bitch. That's her sister that's the madam. Susanna Turner. The one you seen down yonder? Well, she keeps her sister, that's Ella Turner—we all call her the Duchess—she keeps her in a real fancy room upstairs for just when Johnnie comes to town."

"I don't want to talk about her. I want to talk about you."

"I bet Johnnie Booth wants to talk about her plenty. I hope he gets a belly-bait of the stuck-up little bitch. She makes me awful tired, I'll tell you that. Francine, fetch this. Francine, honey, fetch that."

Lewis lay on one elbow and moved his hand over her breasts and down to her thigh. He felt her take hold of him. "I'm sure you're an awful sight prettier than she is," he said.

"You're sweet. Come on now," she said, wrapping her arm around his waist and pulling him on top of her.

"He's a real good player," the woman said.

Lewis pulled away from her and looked down. "What?"

"Johnnie. Johnnie Booth. He sure is a good player."

He made a noise in his throat like a wallowing hog, then sighed and pulled away from her to lie on his back.

"I go to see near about every play he's in," she went on, "every time he comes to Washington City. I like it best when he does Shakespeare. Did you ever see *Romeo and Juliet?*"

"No."

"It's real good. It's by William Shakespeare? You know? I cried at the end when I seen it. He taken poison—John Wilkes Booth did. And the girl stabbed herself. It was real sad."

*   *   *

"Mister Doc! Wake up, Mister Doc!"

Lewis looked up into the black face of the doorman, timidly trying to shake him awake.

"What do you want?" Lewis tried to see where he was, but felt that he was in the middle of a dream. He raised his head, and let it fall onto the pillow. He squirmed against the silk sheets and pulled the comforter higher on his body.

"Mister Doc, Mister Johnnie say come on downstairs now. He waiting for you there."

"Is it morning already?"

"No, suh, but he say tell you to come on down now."

Lewis rolled over and sat on the edge of the bed while the Negro left the room. The deep pink of the curtains flowed into a wan color that depressed him, closed him in, made him want to escape from the cramped, lonely room.

Stumbling to one of the chairs, he sat down to pull on his breeches. When he stood to slip his braces over his shoulders, he instinctively felt his pockets. Empty. He knelt on the floor and felt under the chair for the roll of bills that Booth had given him. Then he felt under the bed and on the bed. His heart pounded with fury. That whore had stolen his money! He jerked the door open and tore into the hallway, colliding with a soldier and a girl who were passing. Lewis shoved them aside and rushed headlong down the stairs.

The Negro doorman, startled, stood at the foot of the staircase until Lewis was almost on top of him.

"Get out of my way!" Lewis bellowed. "Where is that woman? I'll kill her!"

At a table in the parlor sat Francine with two other women and three soldiers. "Where is my money?" Lewis yelled. "Give it back!"

Her eyes wide, she cowered in her chair, and one of the soldiers, a big man, jumped up and swung toward Lewis.

"Let me by!" Lewis shouted.

The soldier gripped his shoulders and pushed him back. "What do you think you're trying to do?"

"She took my money. It was right here in my pocket. I want it back, or I'll break her neck!"

95

The other two soldiers also squared off against him, and the big one again shoved Lewis back when he tried to get around him toward Francine, who was trying to crawl under the table.

"What's going on here?" said a woman behind Lewis. He turned his head as Susanna Turner came through the door, followed by the doorman and Booth. "None of my girls stole your money. You lost it somewhere."

"I had it when I come in here. That damn whore took it." Lewis tried to shove past the three soldiers toward Francine, but someone grabbed him from behind, clamping his arms against his body, and a strong forearm wrapped around his throat. He grunted and tried to draw air into his lungs.

The men pulled him from the room and into the hallway. He tried to dig his heels and hold back, but he was being dragged backward, as helpless as a man caught in a flood, until he felt cold air around him. He bumped down the outside steps onto the brick sidewalk.

When Lewis could see again, the door was shut above him. Coughing, rubbing his neck, he pulled himself onto the lowest step and sat, shaking his head back and forth. He heard footsteps and balled his fists while he tried to push himself onto his feet.

"Easy there, young panther," came Booth's voice. "Here is your bankroll. Silas found it on the floor of the room."

Lewis grunted and accepted the money, which he dropped into a side pocket. Then he took the coat and hat that Booth handed him and put them on.

Booth glanced back at the house, took Lewis by the arm, and guided him along the rutted street.

"If you were trying to call attention to yourself, you surely found the best way to do it. One of those soldiers claimed to be in the provost marshal's office. Said he remembered you from somewhere. If they find out you're a Confederate soldier, it could be either prison or parole out West."

Without speaking, Lewis limped beside Booth along the muddy street, now nearly deserted. At the end of the street stood a lone cab, its driver dozing between a pair of lamps that flickered on either side of his box.

When Booth tapped the driver on the arm with his cane, the man stirred and regarded him stupidly.

"Over the Long Bridge," Booth told him. Then he hoisted himself into the cab, and Lewis climbed in behind him. The steady clop-clop of the hooves drummed them out of the dim lamplight and into the gloom at the end of the street, where they turned left. Their way was dark now, lit only by an occasional lantern in the hand of someone walking by. They crossed a canal rotten with excrement and decaying animal carcasses.

"It will be best for you to leave Washington City for a time. If you join Gilmor or Mosby, I can send a message to you when the opportunity presents itself to move ahead with the abduction of Lincoln."

"How can I find Major Gilmor, Captain?"

"Go to Gaithersburg. Ask there. There will be people who will help you find Gilmor."

Lewis fell silent, while Booth talked — of his passion for Southern independence, of life on the stage, of the women who had loved him and those he had loved. Lewis dozed. The ride might have gone on for hours, for all that Lewis knew. He felt himself roughly shaken awake by Booth.

"Follow me, Powell."

Booth sprang from the hansom, and Lewis stumbled after him.

"Stay here till we get back," Booth told the driver, "and let me have a lantern there." He lifted a lantern from its bracket on one side of the driver's box.

Lewis followed Booth as he left the road, and, holding the lantern high, strode along a narrow, snow-filled path between small trees.

Above them on a hill loomed a large mansion, one solitary window high on an upper floor lit by a single lamp. At a bend in the path glowed another lamp a hundred paces ahead of them, near the gate.

"Stop here!" Booth shielded the lantern with his hat. "It's a guard post. Come this way."

He turned and walked past Lewis, backtracking to where another path led to the right along the side of a hill. Still shielding the lamp, Booth went along the path beside a hedge until he paused at an opening, then beckoned Lewis to follow. They stepped through the gap in the hedge and looked at Washington City below them, luminous under a rising moon. The snow had stopped falling, a thousand lamps dotted the city, and through it flowed the Potomac, a curled silver ribbon.

Lewis shivered and turned up the lapels of his coat. Why don't he say something, Lewis thought. Don't see no reason to come all the way up here and just stand and freeze.

"Magnificent sight, isn't it?" Booth finally said. Lewis grunted to show that he agreed, and shoved his hands deeper into his pockets.

"I like to come up here whenever I can, Powell. But it's rare to find a night as clear as this one." He sighed. "Times that try men's souls." He turned to Lewis. "Do you know whose house that is on the hill?"

Lewis turned and squinted behind him, but the house was hidden in the darkness. "No, Captain," he said.

"That is Arlington House, Powell, once the dwelling of General Robert E. Lee."

Lewis turned again and looked, but this disclosure had made the house no more visible than before. He shivered, turned again, and looked with Booth toward Washington City.

Booth said, "I yet will strike at the heart of that city below us. There was a time when the soil on which we stand was Southern soil, but now Yankee officers sleep within the walls of Arlington House yonder while Lee himself lays his head in a tent on the field of battle. The times call for unyielding spirits. When Washington suffered a bleak winter at Valley Forge, one man wrote: 'These are the times that try men's souls. The summer soldier and the sunshine patriot will, in this crisis, shrink from the service of their country; but he that stands it now deserves the love and thanks of man and woman.' The man who wrote those words was Thomas Paine. It is his spirit that we need today, the spirit of the man who remains steadfast in the service of his country, the spirit that will raise the Confederacy out of the dark night of despair and exalt her within the bright sunrise of victory."

Booth turned toward Lewis. "Kneel, O young warrior."

Lewis, confused, fell on his knees, his face away from the glistening city, gazing up at Booth.

Booth lifted his walking stick and rested it on Lewis's shoulder. "The name I proudly bear—that of John Wilkes—is that of a man who defied a tyrannical English government, a man who stood for liberty against tyranny. I have lived my life in an attempt to be worthy of that name. Now I bestow on you the name of the man whose words call us to serve our country." Booth raised the walking stick slightly and let it fall again on Lewis's shoulder, where he held it firmly. "From this moment I rename thee. Thou art no longer Lewis Powell. Thou art Paine. With this name thou bearest the *pain* of the South, of her wasted fields echoing to the tread of a hateful army, the *pain* of weeping mothers and wives who will see their beloved husbands and fathers and lovers no more, the *pain* of orphaned bairns crying unto the night in wails of bereaved anguish. Go forth, bearing that burden of *pain* until thou shalt raise thy arm to avenge it."

The cold in the earth pierced his knees, but Lewis continued to kneel in the silence and darkness, held there by the pressure of Booth's cane on his shoulder. On the hill above them a cannon boomed, its echoes reverberating across the hill at Arlington and on into the wasted fields of the South.

9

MARYLAND AND VIRGINIA
NOVEMBER-DECEMBER 1864

IT DID NOT TAKE Lewis long to find Major Harry Gilmor's Raiders. A talkative old farmer gave him a ride into Maryland, and at the general store in Gaithersburg he asked for Gilmor. Within two hours he was mounted on a chestnut mule behind a brawny young farmer, riding out of town. When they passed through the gate of a farm, three hounds ran from under the house, barking and wagging their tails. A man in his thirties, wearing a green wool shirt with black braces, was sitting on the porch of the farmhouse in a straight-backed chair tilted against the wall, chewing tobacco and spitting it through his bushy brown beard.

"What you got there, Palmer?" he asked the boy who had brought Lewis.

Palmer sat on his mule while Lewis slid to the ground and walked up the steps onto the porch. "Fellow says he wants to join with us," Palmer told the man.

"What outfit you been in, son?"

"Are you Major Gilmor?" Lewis asked.

"Major ain't here now, son, but you can talk to me. I asked you, what outfit you been in."

"Perry's Brigade, Captain."

"Infantry?" The man spat a wad of tobacco. "Think you can stay on a horse?" The man grinned at two young men—one in a red-checked shirt and the other in a faded blue Union tunic—who had come out of the house onto the porch.

"Let me have one, Captain, and I'll show you." The man stood and went into the house, telling Redshirt and Bluecoat, "Find him a horse and fix him up."

"Come on," Bluecoat said, and started down the steps past Lewis. Lewis turned to follow him, when suddenly his feet were kicked from under him, and he sprawled onto the hard clay at the foot of the steps. Stunned, he pulled himself up, but Bluecoat's knee caught him in the chest and sent him onto his back. He flared with anger as he rolled over and pulled himself to one knee. Standing, he became aware of other men gathering in a circle around him. Chin down and fists ready, he charged toward Bluecoat, who backed away laughing. His rush carried him past Bluecoat, who dodged and drove his fist into Lewis's left side. Lewis pivoted and swung his right fist into the man's face. Stepping backward, he felt a body against the backs of his knees, and he tumbled onto his back, his feet thrown high by Redshirt.

A chorus of jeers rose from the circled men as Bluecoat fell on top of Lewis, his thumbs groping for Lewis's eyes. Lewis grabbed the man's wrists and forced his arms apart. As the man's sweaty face fell against his, Lewis bit through the sharp stubble of whiskers into Bluecoat's chin, and he heard a howl. He tasted a hot rush of blood as the man jerked his chin free. Thrusting his right hand up, Lewis gripped the man by the throat while he strained his own body up, throwing Bluecoat onto his back. But his adversary was on his feet first, and before Lewis could stand, a fist smashed into his right eye and he fell again, his ears ringing and bright circles of light spinning in front of him. He threw up his arms to ward off his opponent's blows as the man fell onto him, thudding his fists against Lewis's head. He felt himself slide into a dark whirlpool.

He woke to the shock of water being sloshed over his head, and he sat up slowly, groaning at the ache in his side and his head. An aged Negro man was standing over him, holding a bucket.

"You all right, boss?"

Lewis looked around. It was almost dark, and no other men were in sight. He shook his head and rubbed his swollen jaw. His body weighed heavily on him.

"Don't fret none about it, boss. Them fellows likes to break in the new men. Show them who is the boss, you know? They don't mean nothing by it. Come on in the house. Sam's got some biscuits and coffee for you."

Lewis tried to get onto his feet, but fell back. Then Sam held onto his arm and helped him up. He followed the old man, stopping to lean on the doorpost when a wave of dizziness came over him. He slumped at the table while Sam set a cup of coffee and a plate of biscuits in front of him. It hurt him to swallow, and after a few bites he shoved the plate aside, found a cot in the next room, and slept.

The next day he was given a horse and a pistol, but nobody said anything about the beating. He stayed to himself, and no one spoke to him. On the third night, the band raided a farm that they said belonged to people who sided with the Yanks, posting Lewis as a lookout. He listened to them shooting and yelling, firing the barns and driving away horses and cows. Later, they divided the wagonload of corn, potatoes, and household belongings that they had hauled from the farm. One man was proud of a clock with fancy gold numbers on it, and declared his intentions to give it to a certain lady. They told Lewis that he would get his share after he had been in the company longer.

A week later, when he was on patrol with four raiders, they sent him to take the horses to a creek for water. Leaving the other men's horses at the creek, Lewis rode to the nearest ford on the Potomac, where he crossed into Virginia after dark.

When the sky began to grow light, Lewis left the road, dismounted, and led his horse to a deserted barn. Two walls had been ripped out to become firewood for the armies that had passed through, but there remained a piece of roof overhead and a corner where he could make a bed. He scraped together some moldy hay, heaping it in the corner. Then he took the saddle and bridle off the horse and left the animal in what had been a stall, blocking the entrance with a plank before spreading his blanket and oilcloth on the hay and falling asleep.

"Wake up, Johnny!"

Lewis bolted awake and jackknifed to a sitting position. He blinked and stared up at three soldiers in blue. Boots and spurs. Cavalry.

"Who are you? What are you doing here?"

"Huh? Let me wake up." He shook his head and looked up again. Now he saw their horses outside the barn.

"I work on a farm outside of Flint Hill. I come down here to pick up a team of oxen and take them back."

"Where you going to get them?" The man asking the quesions was a sergeant. He had a thick yellow beard and hard eyes.

"Uh—Middleburg."

"The hell you say. You're one of Mosby's gang. Where is Mosby now?"

"I don't know what you mean."

"You're coming with us." The sergeant jerked him to his feet and made him roll his blanket and oilcloth.

The three soldiers mounted, and one of the privates led Lewis's horse while Lewis stumbled ahead of them toward a clump of trees in the middle of the field. Once he fell when his foot slipped into a hole, and the horsemen waited for him to get back onto his feet.

About a dozen tents were pitched in the trees, but only two men were there, cooking over a fire. His captors tied his hands and led him to the fire, where he sat on a log.

"Found this here straggler over at the barn yonder," the sergeant told the men by the fire. "The captain will want to talk to him. Don't give him nothing to eat."

The two soldiers at the fire were debating whether winters in Michigan were colder than winters in Wisconsin. As soon as the three men who had captured Lewis left the copse of trees and headed back across the field, one of the men left the fire and brought Lewis a steaming cup of stew. "Here, Johnny," he said with a wink, "you look hungry. Never mind what the sergeant says." He was a lean man with a toothy grin and hair that was almost white. A pink scar ran along his left cheek. Lewis took the cup and drank greedily. The two soldiers went back to talking about hard winters they had lived through while Lewis lay against the log and slept.

When he woke up, the soldiers were still talking, and one of them mentioned Mosby. Lewis had heard Gilmor's Raiders talk about Mosby's raids on the Yankee troops and supply trains in this part of Virginia known as "Mosby's Confederacy." So this troop was out to catch Mosby. That was all right with him, as long as he could convince them that he was not a spy. If he could not do that, they would hang him on a tree limb in the nearest town and make the people come out and watch him kick and strangle. He had heard enough about it that just to think of it gave gave him a cold chill. Like the night when Aunt Sarah had said: *You will hang.* He shuddered and slept no more. He stared at the rope that held his wrists and felt his throat tighten.

A chill wind hummed all day through the oak branches, barren against a somber sky. Toward sundown the wind gave way to a distant drumming that came gradually nearer, until it divided into separate hoofbeats. Lewis looked around when he heard horses snorting and saddles creaking. The riders scarcely spoke as some went about building their cooking fires and others fed the horses.

Lewis heard footsteps crunch behind him. The sergeant who had captured him reached down and took him by the arm. "Come on, Johnny," he growled. "Let's talk to the captain."

The captain was a short, stocky man with a black beard, busy pulling off his boots.

"Captain, here's the Reb I told you about. The one that was bedded down in yonder barn."

The captain looked at Lewis. "What are you doing in these parts?" Lewis could tell that he was not interested in asking him questions.

"On my way to Middleburg to bring back a brace of oxen, Captain."

"Seen any Rebel cavalry around here?"

"No, sir."

"Aw, hell, Sergeant, he ain't going to tell us nothing. Just tie him up good and keep him here tonight. I know where Mosby is—found out today—and I got vedettes out watching him. I'm hitting him first thing in the morning before he's done snoring good." He turned to another officer. "Nelson, post the guards and let's eat some of them chickens we brought in."

Lewis slept restlessly against a log outside the fire circle, with his hands and feet tied. He dreamed that he was back on his father's farm with Riley and with a woman who was sometimes Maggie Branson and at other times her pert sister Mary. Then gunshots, shouts, and tramping feet invaded the dream and he woke. Horses galloped through the camp and fire flashed from pistols. A man ran by, cursing. Lewis rolled toward an oak tree and hunkered against it.

A rough hand seized him by the shoulder, and a cold gun muzzle pressed against the side of his head.

"You got a gun?" someone demanded.

"N-no. I'm tied up here. Don't shoot."

A hand moved down to his wrists.

"So you be. Are you a prisoner?"

"Yes. Yes, I am."

Lewis looked up at a gray uniform in the flickering firelight. The Confederate soldier drew a sheath knife and cut the ropes around Lewis's ankles and wrists.

"Stay close to me," he said. Lewis followed him, rubbing his wrists and stumbling in the dark.

Somebody had thrown more wood onto the fire in the middle of the camp, and men converged on it, most of them barefooted and in their underwear but some wearing their blue tunics. One was the Yankee captain, bewildered and absurd in long white underwear, still wearing his blue hat with gold cord. Confederate soldiers came behind them, herding them into a circle and ordering them to sit on the ground. Other Confederate soldiers came out of the tents with carbines, pistols, and sabers that they threw onto a pile.

An officer of average height with a slight blonde moustache leaned against a tree, eating a chicken he had pulled from a spit over the fire. He looked up as Lewis came toward him with the soldier who had freed him.

"Sir," the soldier said, "I found this here man tied up over yonder. Says the Yanks took him prisoner."

"What's your name, son?" the officer asked.

"Lewis Powell, Captain. I'm a private in Perry's Brigade, Lee's army. I was trying to get back to my outfit when they caught me."

"Well, Powell, Meade's whole army is between us and General Lee. It won't be easy to get there." He poured coffee into a tin cup and sipped it, then made a face. "These Yanks do make it strong."

He looked again at Lewis, who stood a head higher. "If you are in Lee's army I know you can shoot. Can you ride?"

"I've rounded up cattle in Florida, Captain."

"Tom, let him pick out one of those horses we just took from the Yanks. We can use him."

The officer went on gnawing the chicken leg. Tom led Lewis around the Yankee soldiers huddled together and shivering on the ground. He squinted and looked for the man from Wisconsin who had shared his stew, but it was too dark for him to tell one man from another.

"Tom, who was that there officer?" Lewis asked.

"That's Colonel John Mosby. You'll be riding with Mosby's Rangers now."

As soon as Lewis found himself in a cabin with some of the rangers, he fell onto a bunk and slept the rest of the day. When he woke, he blinked and tried to recollect where he was. Two men were talking at a table. Above the table hung a single kerosene lantern, its yellow flame flickering in a curtainless window. Lewis rolled to the side of the cot and sat. Then he pushed himself up and stumbled across the room to a washstand. He bent over and ducked his face into the bowl, then shook his head and wiped his eyes.

"Payne."

Lewis turned, thinking that he heard John Wilkes Booth's voice again, the way he had sounded on that night below Arlington House three weeks before, saying the name that Lewis had allowed to slip until now into a neglected corner of his mind. Lewis squinted toward the table and recognized Colonel Mosby with a captain named Will Chapman.

"That will be good," Mosby said. "Have Johnnie Munson take Powell to the Payne farm and billet him there. He might even be some help to the Paynes while he stays."

Lewis rolled his blanket while Chapman and Mosby talked about other things. Hearing them say the name that Booth had given him did not surprise Lewis, because nothing surprised him. Immune to wonder at coincidence, he believed and had always believed that everything that affected his life came directly from the mind of God.

Lewis pulled on his overcoat just as Captain Chapman's voice came out of the shadows at him. "Come on, Powell. I'm sending you with Munson." Chapman went out the door, with Lewis following, and called toward a knot of men standing around a fire. "Munson! Come on here and take Powell over to the Payne farm."

A ranger left the circle and came toward them. Lewis turned to untie his horse's reins from the hitchingpost, and when he looked around he could not see Munson anywhere.

"Watch this, Powell!" said a voice above him, from the bare limbs of an oak tree. "T'clk! T'clk!" A horse, riderless, walked and stood under the tree. Then, with a loud "whoop," a body dropped out of the tree into the horse's saddle. Another yell, and horse and rider were off at a gallop.

Lewis caught up with Johnnie Munson at the edge of the woods. "How did you like that, Powell? Comes in pretty handy when I'm out scouting for Yanks."

"Break your fool neck doing that," Lewis told him.

"Not me. I'm too good at it."

They fell into a trot along the road, side by side. "How old are you, Johnnie?" Lewis asked.

"Fifteen. I heard the Colonel tell somebody one day that I'm the best soldier he's got. Said I ain't got enough sense to know danger when I see it, and I'll fight anything he tells me to. I'll show you how to do that trick sometime, Powell."

"No thanks. Do that with a saber on and you shove it up your ass."

"Saber, hell. Colonel won't let none of us carry one of them damn things. Says they ain't good for nothing but swatting a balky mule on the backside with. Have they issued you a pair of Colt .44's yet?"

"Issued me one. Got it right here under my coat."

"Hell, one ain't no good. You got to have a pair of them. Get you another one tomorrow. Some of the boys carries a extra pair in their saddle-holsters or their boot legs. Me, I'm looking for a pair with ivory handles, and I'm watching to lift them off some Yank. We got to turn here, Powell, up this lane."

They turned their horses off the road and started up a rocky lane between fences. It was still dark, but a streak of silver dawn showed between gray strips of cloud. A light sleet stung Lewis' face.

"Another thing, Powell, is Colonel likes for us to wear our uniforms, to look like soldiers. I sent up to Baltimore for me a special outfit, and I expect to have it back by Christmas. Speaking of uniforms, you got to watch out for Jessie's Scouts."

"Who are Jessie's Scouts?"

"Why they're a bunch of Yanks and renegades and Yankee-lovers that sometimes they dress up in Confederate gray and fool you about who they are. Anyways, you got to watch out for them."

"How will I know them if I see them?"

"You just will. Bet you ain't got no Spencer, neither."

"What's that?"

"A Spencer—a repeating rifle. The Yanks have got them just coming out now, and we can get all we want anytime we raid them. .52 caliber. Hold seven cartridges. They tell me they just started using them at Gettysburg, so they are kind of new."

"Got to get me one, then."

The boy chattered on about Mosby and his capture of a Yank general and about his plans for the uniform he was going to buy.

Enough light had come into the sky for Lewis to see the fields when Johnnie turned his horse onto a curved lane of leafless trees, and they rode toward a house at the crest of a knoll.

Halfway up the lane of trees, Johnnie Munson stopped and whispered, "Wait. Something is wrong."

A shift in the wind brought the smell of burning, and timbers smouldered near the lane.

Johnnie dismounted and handed his reins to Lewis. "Draw your pistol and be ready to come up if I call you." He walked toward the house.

Lewis listened with his pistol growing heavy in his hand. Even above the rattling of the sleet against his hat and coat he thought that he heard footsteps behind him. He turned his horse and looked back toward the road, and then the footsteps seemed to come from his right. Once he thought he heard a party of horsemen.

A shout came from the house.

"Powell! It's all clear up here. Bring my horse." Lewis slipped the pistol back into its holster and rode toward Johnnie's voice. Johnnie stood in the lane about twenty paces from the house. Lewis handed him the reins of the other horse and dismounted.

Johnnie laughed. "Don't get spooked, Powell. Ain't no Yanks around here. I found an old darky at the house, and he told me the fieldhands and house servants run off last night, and they set fire to that corncrib we seen smouldering back yonder. Now come on to the house with me so we can find Mr. Payne."

Something hummed past him, and the crack of a shot came from the house. A woman screamed.

"The devil!" grunted Johnnie, reaching for the shotgun slung on his saddle.

"Uncle, put the gun down!" a woman pleaded. A black man shouted from the house, "Don't shoot, boss! We got his gun!"

Johnnie moved toward the house, and Lewis pulled his pistol and followed. Three shadowy figures struggled on the veranda.

Johnnie leaped up the steps to the veranda and became the fourth figure in the struggle. Then he jerked back, brandishing a musket above his head.

"Let me go!" demanded a white-haired old man held by a woman and an old black man.

"Whew!" said Johnnie. "You near about shot me, Mr. Payne. Did you think I was a Yank?"

The old man sobbed, and his knees bent. The woman and the Negro lowered him gently to the floor.

"Why, it's Johnnie," the woman said. "Thank goodness he didn't shoot you. He can't help himself. He came back from town yesterday evening to find all the darkies run away and the fires started. He managed to save part of the kitchen, but he's been mixed up ever since, always thinking they are coming back to steal and burn again."

"It was them two new ones that done it," said the Negro. "Them that run off last week with the Yanks. Come back yestiddy when Massa was away and talked the other ones into taking whatever they could find and running off with them. Most like they's the ones that set fires, too." He let go of the old white man, who covered his face with his hands and knelt sobbing. "Now just me and my wife and the old and lame ones is left here at Grandville."

"Miz Payne," said Johnnie, "this here is Powell. The Colonel sent us over here to stay." As if wondering what to do next, Johnnie looked down at the old man sitting on the floor of the veranda.

"Johnnie," she said, "please help my uncle into the house. He needs to rest. Henry knows how to take care of him."

Lewis and Johnnie lifted the moaning man and steadied him into the house, with old Henry following, and lowered him into a chair in the parlor. In the sickly light of a "Confederate taper" — a pyramidal lump of grease and tallow — the old man had the pallor of the dead.

Lewis watched the old man sprawled in the chair with Henry loosening his shirt, mopping his brow, and talking to him in soothing tones. When he saw that he could not help them, he went outside to the veranda. The woman leaned against a pillar sobbing quietly, her face indistinct, her black hair long against her pale shawl. She kept her back turned to him, a silhouette against the gray light of the sky.

"Ma'am," Lewis ventured.

She did not reply.

"Lady . . ."

She straightened, turned toward him, and clutched her shawl to her breast. "Private Howell — " she said.

"Powell, ma'am."

"Powell, Cicero will show you where you are to stay, and he will bring you food."

"Can I do anything to help you out, ma'am?"

In the face that she turned toward him, he saw grief, sorrow, self-pity. "No. No one can do anything but end this wretched war and put the world and our Grandville back the way it used to be." She walked past him into the house.

Lewis watched the sky in the east grow light. The sun showed white behind a gray curtain of clouds. A voice behind him came like a whipcrack. "Well, don't go to sleep standin' up, Powell. Get the horses and come on."

Johnnie was behind him with a black dwarf whose face was like one Lewis had seen in a book, one of those shrunken faces on a cathedral in Europe. He took his reins and followed Johnnie and the dwarf.

"Who is that old man that shot at us, Johnnie?" Lewis asked.

"That's old Mr. Scott Payne. We are lucky he's not a better shot. Either that or didn't have sense enough to see what he was shooting at." He laughed. "The lady is his niece. Her husband is Colonel Payne in the Virginia infantry. He got taken prisoner last summer in Pennsylvania, and he's in a Federal prison now."

Lewis looked back at the house and thought of the sobbing woman. He tried to remember the words of John Wilkes Booth. *Pain of the widows and the orphans. Pain.*

"What's keeping you, Powell?" Johnnie called to him. Lewis led the horse toward the barn.

Lewis woke in the hayloft in the afternoon. He slipped down the ladder, leaving Johnnie Munson asleep, saddled his horse, and rode across the fields. He did not see any of the slaves. Must be run off, or hiding, or gone fishing while the old man is sick in bed, he thought. The field was damp after the rain and sleet, and the wet stubble of last season's corn rasped under his horse's hooves.

It was after dark when he rode back to the barn. He dismounted when he passed the house and led his horse up the lane toward the barn, guided by the glimmer of a lamp. The night was almost clear, and a full moon was rising through scattered clouds. A noise from the house made him look to his left. A door opened on an upstairs balcony, and a woman came onto the balcony. He stopped and looked up at her, outlined against the dim lamplight in the room behind her. At first he thought it was Mrs. Payne. But this woman was more slender, and the light behind her showed her hair to be a lighter color. She raised her hands toward the moon and murmured something that sounded like a poem or a hymn. After a moment, she flung a shawl around her shoulders and hugged it to her. Then she turned and went into the room, stopping at the door and looking out again before closing the door.

Lewis turned toward the light flickering from the barn, and followed it till he came to the barn door. Johnnie Munson sat on a hay bale, eating cornbread and ham. "'Bout time you got back here, Powell, before I et up all your supper. A runner was just here from Captain Chapman. He wants us to meet the rest of the company at midnight. Looks like we'll get a little action tonight."

"Johnnie, is there another woman staying up there at the big house, beside Miz Payne?" Lewis asked.

"Not that I know of. Why?"

"Thought I saw a woman just now."

"Probably Miz Payne."

"Probably."

When they rode out an hour later, Lewis looked toward the house, but he saw only a glimmer where the upstairs room was.

They rode to a blacksmith's shop next to a rocky creek, and they waited there until the rest of the company joined them. Johnnie Munson led Lewis to an outbuilding and helped him select a uniform, boots, another Colt .44, and a Spencer repeating rifle, which Lewis thrust into his saddle holster.

An hour later Lewis and Johnnie, with a company of rangers, crouched beside their horses on the edge of a pine forest, looking down into a hollow where two companies of Federal cavalry were camped. The Yanks were slow in settling down, singing and drinking around two campfires. Now and then some drunker ones would whoop and fire their rifles into the air. All the time the rangers on the hill had their eyes on the two sutler's wagons in the middle of the encampment.

Suddenly hooves sounded from their right, and two officers rode into the bivouac. The Federals quieted down when one of the officers shouted hoarsely at them. "Damn it all," he raged. "If I have to come up here one more time to shut you up, it will mean a round of court-martials." Then he rode away.

Johnnie and one of the other rangers snickered and had to stuff their shirtsleeves in their mouths to stay quiet. Soon the camp was still, with only one drowsy sentry by one of the fading campfires.

"All right, boys," Chapman passed the word along in whispers, "it's time to mount."

They lined up on the edge of the pines. Lewis breathed deeply. He felt a nudge in his right side, and passed the signal along.

"Whee-ee-hoop!" Captain Chapman yelled and the line broke down the slope at a gallop. They knocked over the sentry before he could pick up his rifle, and within a minute scattered the horses of the Federal soldiers. Some men ran from their tents, shooting, while the rangers rode back and forth through the camp, firing at the flashes of gunpowder.

Lewis pointed his rifle to his left and then to his right, but he could not see a Yankee in the clear. Then he saw another ranger near him and yelled, "How can you tell which are ours?"

"Damn the difference," growled the other man. "Just pitch in and shoot anything!"

By the time the shooting was over and the Yanks were being rounded up in the middle of the camp, some rangers had capsized the sutler's wagons and were tearing through their treasures.

Above the babble of shouts and commands and quarreling voices came another drum of hoofbeats. Lewis and Tom Ogg ran to the edge of the camp as a Yankee officer rode up.

"Damn it, I told you men to stop all that commotion tonight," he screamed. "What does this mean? What in hell does this mean?"

Tom Ogg poked the barrel of his pistol into the officer's side. "It means that Mosby has got you," he said, as if explaining to a child.

The officer's body sagged forward in his saddle. "Well, that beats hell, don't it?" he said.

The rangers rode away from the scene loaded like a migrating tribe. Tins of sardines and cheese, figs and claret wines, beer and chocolate, brandy, whiskey, champagne, Hostetter's Bitters, cigars—all the stores of the sutler found their way into saddlebags and sacks slung onto captured horses. They ate oysters, pickled onions, and chocolate, and they drank—some for the first time—beer, wine, brandy, and whiskey. They puffed out acrid clouds of cigar smoke. They sang. They raised their voices in all the songs they knew. Their eyes grew hot with tears as they brayed to the cold moon:

> At home bright eyes are sparkling for us.
> We will defend them to the last.

Finally, they were sick. One by one, they tumbled onto the side of the road, puking or jerking their braces loose to let their befouled breeches drop.

Lewis slept the next day in a dry creek bed, and when he woke he joined another ranger who knew two girls on the other side of the ridge. Bearing gifts of food and rolls of wool and silk, they went courting. The girls were willing, their mother not very watchful, and Lewis and the other ranger stayed two days.

10

FAUQUIER COUNTY, VIRGINIA
1863

Lewis made his way back to Grandville in a wet, cold dawn. His sore muscles resisted when he hoisted the saddle onto the rail of his horse's stall. Most of the scoopful of grain that he aimed at the feed trough spilled, and his head throbbed as he climbed the ladder to the loft. He unbuckled his gunbelt and fell onto the hay bale with his clothes on.

Shouts of alarm disrupted his sleep. "The Yanks are coming! It's Sheridan! A thousand of them!"

"We'll stop them, boys!"

"Get those Rebs! Head them off!"

Lewis half stood while still turning over, slamming his head into a rafter as he groped for his pair of Colts. He stumbled toward the ladder and bumped down it, dropping one of the revolvers at the bottom. In the gloom of the barn, he groped in the straw but could not find the pistol. Outside the barn he heard running feet and a piercing Rebel yell.

He flung open a side door and dashed out, colliding with someone and sprawling onto the ground as his revolver fired.

Two boys about ten years old lay on either side of him, their eyes wide open in fright.

"Where are they?" Lewis looked anxiously around him.

"Who?"

"The Yanks, damn it. Where are they?"

"They—they—there aren't any Yanks. We're playing."

A third boy writhed on the ground, about ten feet away, holding his head.

"Oh, God! I shot him!" Lewis moaned. He dropped his smoking revolver and crawled to the child. He cautiously took hold of the boy's shoulder. "Are you hurt bad?"

"My head's busted, I know it is. I bumped into Edward when we fell down."

Lewis felt the boy's forehead. "No blood. Ain't nothing but a lump. Whoosh. You'll be all right." He looked around at the other boys, who had been joined by two younger ones. "You mean to say that with all that yellin' there ain't no Yanks here?"

Each boy looked at the others as if he had been caught fishing in a forbidden pond. "We just play at it," one told him. "Me and Walter and Phillip, it's our turn to be the Rebs, and we were playing like Jamie and Fitz were slipping up on us."

Lewis picked up his Colt and looked at it. "Well, you near about got me to shoot you." He started laughing, and the boys laughed, too. "Well, that is mighty dangerous play. Why don't you play something else?"

"We can't," said one of the smaller ones. "It's Sunday, and our mama won't let us play cards."

"It could be worse," one of the older ones added. "Most Sundays we have to sit through church. But this is our Sunday for the preacher to be at the other end of the county."

"My grandpa," added one of the others, "he says that's just about the only good thing that has come out of the war—not enough preachers to go around means less preachin' to listen to." He gave the others a warning look. "But he says I'm not supposed to let on to Grandma or anybody that he said that."

"Are you one of the rangers that's staying in the barn?" asked one of the boys.

"That's me. I'm Doc. My partner is Johnnie Munson, but I don't know where he's at."

"I'm Edward Payne," said one of the boys. "I live here—me and my brother Jamie do—that's Jamie over yonder. We live here with our uncle."

Lewis went to the barn, the boys following like a flock of geese. He set his hand on Jamie's head. "How old are you, Jamie?"

"Eight," the child said, "and—uh—a half."

"I'm ten," Edward announced.

"My little sister Annie, she was eight when I left home," Lewis said. "I reckon she's ten now. She used to bring me bunches of black-eyed Susans, and she liked to ride on my back."

The boys were full of questions about the war. How many Yankees had he killed? What kind of horse did General Lee ride? Did Lewis have a saber? How long would he stay with them?

Lewis unloaded his revolvers and let the boys take turns strapping on his gunbelt. They ran in and out of the barn, hiding from one another and seeing who could draw the revolvers fastest.

"Edward," Lewis asked, "is there anybody else staying at the house besides you boys and your mother?"

"There's our uncle and there's Clara."

"Who's Clara?"

Edward watched the other boys. "It's my turn next," he said.

"Who's Clara?" Lewis asked again.

"Clara Meredith. She's our cousin, from Warrenton. She came out here to teach us our lessons, and to help our mother and our uncle."

After that day, Edward and Jamie seldom let Lewis out of their sight. They played at being squires to a knight of the olden days. They came to the barn nearly every morning to see if he was up, and they stood guard while he slept. He liked to romp with them, running and playing tag, sledding on the hill behind the house after the first snow.

Johnnie Munson did not come back to Grandville for two weeks, and Lewis ate dinner with the family when he was at the farm. Two days after he first talked with the boys, he met Clara Meredith for the first time. In the daylight she did not seem like the same girl he had seen on the balcony, reciting a poem to the rising moon. Her voice sounded fragile as though she was almost out of breath. She had pale eyes that never looked at him directly. She always blushed when he looked at her, and never spoke to him when she did not have to. Yet he could not get her out of his mind.

The suppers were no more than cornbread and roast pork, or sometimes a roast potato with a bowl of milk. Every meal started with a prayer asking God's mercy on Colonel Payne in prison. After the prayer, Mrs. Payne would have tears in her eyes, and she would not eat, explaining to the boys that she was not hungry or that she had eaten in the afternoon.

Old Mr. Payne was well enough to take his suppers with the family, and Lewis liked sitting at the table, with its white tablecloth and the silver that the family were so proud to have saved from the Yankees, and the clumsy Confederate tapers that melted so fast. He liked hearing Mr. Payne and his nieces talk about the rumors of the war, about the gossip from neighbors—of funerals and births, of illnesses and church-going, of the scarcity of food, of their concern about the needs of Lee's army, of their plans for mending or for the needs to repair this or that at Grandville.

"Good Lord, Elizabeth, what happened to your hands?" Mr. Payne asked one evening.

Mrs. Payne raised her hands and turned them over and over like a person giving some secret signal. "It's dye, Uncle. From the butternut. I have been in Warrenton today helping Mrs. Mason make uniforms for the men in her husband's regiment, and we can no longer get gray dye." She sighed. "Now this butternut is the only color we have. I mixed a vat of it today and have been dyeing what I wove last week."

Clara raised her arms. "Behold, Uncle Scott, the hands of another malefactor. Do you think that our palms will betray us to the enemy?"

"Clara kept us laughing throughout the labor, Uncle. She and Laura Mason made up a song. How did it go, Clara?"

Clara struck a dramatic pose, her stained hands clasped and her eyes closed, and said, "Let's see, it goes . . .

> I am dyeing! Hessie, dyeing!
> Boils the kettle hot and fast,
> With the bark of the plum and walnut,
> Gathered in the days long past.
> Reach a hand: Oh! Hessie, help me!
> Cease thy giggle and look here.
> Notice this great pile of garments
> Thou alone and I would wear.

Oh, fiddle! I can't remember the rest of it, but it was a truly great poem." Her laugh sputtered into a cough.

"So the dyeing was not all for the Cause, I see, young lady. Some of it was for Clara and Laura."

"Surely you don't begrudge us a few moments of feminine vanity, dear Uncle."

He bowed his head. "Oh, Clara, Elizabeth, I wish all your moments could be moments of feminine vanity. You both are working too hard—for your brothers in the army, for this plantation." He was close to tears. "Elizabeth, last week your fingers were so sore and twisted from sewing shoe leather that you could not straighten them for three days. I am worried about your health, my dear. And yours too, Clara."

Clara rose from her chair and went around the table to kiss her uncle on the cheek. "Uncle, here is Private Powell, who goes with our brave Colonel Mosby to raid the Yankees, then comes back to Grandville and helps us with our fences, our fires, our weathered buildings. He and the others like him have to know that we women stand with him." Blushing and looking away, she walked to the fireplace and set another piece of wood on the fire.

Lewis had jumped up to take the piece of wood and put it on the fire for her, but he was too late, and stood dumbly next to her, wondering where to turn next.

She spoke to the fire, not to Lewis. "In every house in Virginia, women are knitting. Socks, caps, sweaters—anything that they can hope to slip through the lines to the soldiers. Their looms and wheels are in constant motion. What few sewing machines there are, they are learning to use. Women tear their dresses to strips to send bandages to the poor men in the field hospitals. There are no shoemakers to be found, and women are making shoes for their children and even for their servants." Her pale eyes, wet and red-rimmed, turned toward him, but looked beyond him, into the heart of the Cause itself. "So, Private Powell, when you ride with Colonel Mosby to fight for all of us, you can go in the knowledge that the women of Virginia stand behind you."

She breathed deeply and coughed. "I was about to say the women are tireless in your support," she laughed. "But I feel too tired right now to say that."

"You had better go to your room and rest, Clara," Mrs. Payne said.

Without any protest, the girl asked her uncle and Lewis to excuse her and left the room, still coughing.

A few days before Christmas, after tending his tack and his horse, Lewis came into the house while the women were in the kitchen. He started up the stairs toward the garret where the boys slept. Misty gray light shone through a window at the first landing, giving him a feeling of stealth. As he passed the hallway on the second floor, he noticed a door ajar, the door into the room that he knew to be Clara's.

He stood for a few heartbeats on the top step, listening to the women's voices downstairs. He stepped to the door and stood as if he were at the door of a chapel. He touched the door, and it yielded, swinging inward with a slight creak. He listened again to the voices, their indistinct, distant rise and fall. Then, his heart pounding in the silence, he stepped into the room.

It was a corner room, with a window in either wall. The windows, hung with lace curtains, gave light onto a high-posted bedstead over-laid with a white, lacy comforter. On a dressing table opposite the windows lay a hair brush, its bristles down and its back painted with a rosebud. He touched the rosebud, feeling the texture of the paint. Then he picked up the brush. Suddenly he heard a noise behind him, but when he turned, no one was there. He turned the brush over and over. A few strands of hair clung to the bristles, and he pulled them loose, twisting them slowly around his finger. He set the brush down and took three steps toward the bed, gazing at the impression on the pillow where her head had lain. He reached toward the lace comforter, then stopped and pulled his hand back. He looked down at the twist of light brown hair glistening against his finger.

All of a sudden the volume of a voice downstairs changed, as if someone were approaching the stairway, and he moved toward the door. With one last glance back at Clara Meredith's room, he half shut the door, slipped into the hallway, and went down the stairs. Encountering no one, he walked back to the barn, and felt along the ledge for his Bible. He opened it and carefully laid the strands of hair in the seam between the pages. Then he closed the Bible and set it back on the ledge.

*   *   *

On Christmas Eve, Edward and Jamie were full of excitement. They roamed the woods, taking Lewis and Johnnie with them, gathering hickory nuts for the Christmas party planned in Warrenton. Lewis helped them cut a Christmas tree and dragged it behind his horse to the house. The boys collected hog bladders to use for balloons and goose quills to blow them up. The smell of baking ham and turkey drifted out of the kitchen.

Near evening, Lewis went back to the barn to put on his uniform. Johnnie was lying on the hay, a blanket over him. "Doc," he said, "I am sick tonight. My stomach feels all tore up. Reckon I won't be going into Warrenton with you. Just tell the Paynes I'm sorry."

"Sure hate to see you stay back here when everybody else is going to be out having fun, Johnnie."

"Don't worry none about me," Johnnie said weakly. "I took a dose of salts, and I reckon I'll be getting all right later."

Lewis dressed and went to meet the Paynes. He rode beside their buggy on the way into town, ready to turn onto a side road if they should meet any Federals.

When they came into town, Lewis dismounted and tied his horse and was helping Mrs. Payne and Clara Meredith from the buggy when a rider galloped down the main street. Lewis put his hand on one of his revolvers as the rider, who wore a full gray cape with a high collar that concealed his face, passed them and reined in his horse a few yards away. As Lewis escorted Mrs. Payne and Clara Meredith toward the door, with Mr. Payne and the two boys behind them, he suspiciously watched the rider.

The door was opened by a skinny lady of about fifty with a toothy, coquettish smile. She nodded as she greeted them, shaking the ringlets of gray hair that touched her shoulders. "Merry Christmas! Merry Christmas to all the Paynes!" she squealed.

"Flora!" exclaimed Mr. Payne, kissing the woman's hand. "And Dora, too!" he said, when another woman with the same toothy, coquettish smile appeared. "What a delight to see you both again, and how kind of you to invite us."

"Why, Miss Ferston, what a lovely gown!" exclaimed Mrs. Payne to the woman who held the door.

Who is that rider? thought Lewis to himself.

"Do you really like it? See? It's made out of all the lavender parasols I could find in Warrenton," replied the woman at the door.

He couldn't be one of Jessie's Scouts, Lewis tried to tell himself. They don't travel by themselves.

Suddenly Lewis heard his own name called. "Private Powell," said the woman at the door, extending her hand to him and wriggling a curtsy, "I am so pleased to meet you."

Lewis took the hand that was stretched out to him while he glanced back at the mysterious rider, drawing toward the house. He tried to drop the hand, but it held on to him in a tight, bony grip, and its owner spoke again. "I," she declared, "am the First Miss Ferston, and this is my sister, the Second Miss Ferston."

She who had been named as the second then seized Lewis's hand when the other let it go. "How d'ye do?" she asked with another coquettish smile. "Our names are really Flora and Dora, but everybody calls us the First Miss Ferston and the Second Miss Ferston because they cannot remember which of us is which. One of us is older, but we refuse to tell which one." She put a finger to her lips and rolled her eyes.

"Long live the Confederacy!" The voice behind Lewis was Johnnie Munson's voice, and Lewis looked around to see Johnnie slinging the broad cape from his shoulders and stepping forward to greet the Misses Ferston.

"Why, it's Cousin Johnnie!" exclaimed the First Miss Ferston.

"How splendid you look!" squealed the Second Miss Ferston.

Johnnie strutted to the door, showing off his splendid new uniform. His boots came halfway up his thighs, and his spurs were handmade with silver rowels. His entire suit was gray corduroy trimmed with buff and gold lace, and he carried a pair of high, gold-trimmed gauntlets carelessly in his left hand. Over his right forearm he draped his cape, and with his right hand he toyed with a gray enamelled belt and a pair of ivory-handled Colt revolvers. Tossing the cape to his left arm, he swept off his hat, with its double gold cord and ostrich plume, and bowed to the Misses Ferston and to Mrs. Payne. Edward and Jamie gaped in wonder and envy.

"So you were just pretending to be sick," Mrs. Payne said. "You wanted to surprise us and show off your new uniform."

"It just came yesterday," Johnnie said. "How do you like it?"

"It's so—so martial, Johnnie," said the First Miss Ferston.

"Yes, martial," agreed the Second Miss Ferston.

"But," continued the First Miss Ferston, "we are keeping our guests in the cold, and you must all come in for Christmas cheer."

Other guests were arriving. Clara Meredith's parents came with her two sisters and a brother. Major Meredith was a skinny, gray man who walked with a cane. His wife, a squinty-smiling, nervous woman, was always cautioning her son about his behavior, while the son was always trying to pick a fight with Edward. Clara's sisters huddled together, as shy as Clara.

Other women brought children. Some sat as though heeding parental warnings, while others squirmed until Clara went to the piano and started tunes that they could dance to. Before long, the boys were blowing up the hog bladders and popping them. Screams and laughter became louder, as the mothers, busy between the table and the kitchen, finally ran out of the will to scold.

Weeks of hoarding had gone to load the table with chicken, ham, turkey, cider, corn, peas, and baked apples. The guests, after months of doing without, had learned the etiquette of how to limit what they took, how to make even as exceptional a dinner as this one seem more abundant than it was.

"My stars, Cousin Elizabeth," rejoiced the First Miss Ferston, "this delicious ham reminds me of Richmond so many years ago."

"Oh, so many years, Sister," added the Second Miss Ferston. "How regal were the banquets that we had in Papa's house in those days now gone forever."

The First Miss Ferston, passing around a bowl of corn, smirked at Lewis. "Private Powell," she said, "you are indeed privileged to serve under such a fine officer as Colonel Mosby. Why, he comes from one of the finest families in Virginia."

"Oh, yes," agreed the Second Miss Ferston, "one of the very finest."

"Colonel Mosby is a scholar and an attorney," went on the First Miss Ferston.

"A brilliant attorney," added her sister. "But there is that scandal"—here she pursed her lips—"that scandal in his youth which it will not do to mention."

"An affair of honor, Private Powell," said the First Miss Ferston, casting a warning glance at her sister.

"It does nòt matter," broke in Mrs. Meredith, "so long as he continues to punish the thieving Yankees."

"Amen to that," said another woman at the table, a long-faced lady in faded black. "Hardly a home in Fauquier County has been free of their depredations."

"I shan't forget their invasion of Warrenton," said the First Miss Ferston, "and the beastly behavior that they exhibited."

"Absolutely beastly behavior," nodded the Second Miss Ferston.

The First Miss Ferston laughed. "It was great sport to deceive the rascals," she said. "When we heard the news that General What-chaname and his bandits were on the way, we hid everything. Sister and I were so burdened with all the silver under our skirts that we could scarcely walk." Both sisters clapped their hands and hooted in laughter. "My silver cream pitcher was constantly clanking against the sugar bowl in a most disagreeable manner, and when Sister fell down, it took me and our sister-in-law nearly five minutes to raise her to her feet again, we were all three laughing so hard."

"Yes, that's true, nearly five minutes," chuckled the Second Miss Ferston.

"Of course the pickles and the preserves had to be put away."

"By all means," spoke up Major Meredith. "Save the pickles and the preserves at all costs."

The First Miss Ferston nodded gravely. "We thought that we had them safe behind a panel in the second-floor hallway when not two hours later my sister-in-law's youngest—that's little Custis over there by the tree—came in wailing and holding his tummy. The little scamp had followed his brothers and sisters and raided the whole lot."

Laughter went around the table as the Second Miss Ferston giggled, covering her mouth with her fan. "Yes, the whole lot," she affirmed. "They ate all the damson preserves."

"Not a one escaped the stomachache," roared the First Miss Ferston.

"Not a one," the Second Miss Ferston assured everyone.

"Well, Flora," said Mrs. Payne, "your preserves were safe at least from the Yankee marauders—in the safest hiding-place, the young one's tummies."

"But that was not the end of it, Cousin Elizabeth," said the First Miss Ferston. "There was the"—she looked slowly around the table and rolled her eyes—"the po-o-o-i-son."

"Yes, Sister, tell about the poison," urged the Second Miss Ferston.

"Well, the Yankees came, they saw, and they were *thoroughly* conquered by it."

"Thoroughly," said the Second Miss Ferston, with a deep nod and a knowing glance around the table.

"Three ugly louts appeared at the door, claiming that they had orders to search the premises. Well, I told them that they were impertinent intruders in my state, my county, and my home, and I would thank them to go back where they came from and raid their own families' homes, and to leave a lady alone."

"Leave a lady alone. That is exactly what Sister told them," the Second Miss Ferston assured everyone that the First Miss Ferston had said.

"Do you think that such a plea could reach within the stony recesses of the cruel Yankee heart?" asked the First Miss Ferston, looking around as if for an answer. Johnnie Munson, helping himself to more ham, seemed not to notice. Lewis started to say no, but stopped himself. Edward Payne, however, answered with a loud "No!" His mother turned toward him and put her finger on her lips.

"That is true, Edward," said the First Miss Ferston. "But the best was yet to come." She sipped from her water glass. "Oh, yes," she nodded, "they had their comeuppance."

The Second Miss Ferston giggled behind her fan. "Yes, and what a comeuppance it was."

"This way and that they went, plundering our house, taking things that it grieved me to lose. All the time they climbed higher and higher, throwing clothing from the chifforobes, flinging blankets out the windows for their fellow miscreants to seize and carry off. Even the lovely quilt our Grannie brought from England—probably a Yankee horse-blanket by now."

The long-faced lady in black sighed. "I know," she said.

"Finally they reached the closet on the third floor," said the First Miss Ferston, "and saw the row of wine bottles." She looked slowly around the table. "You should have heard the vulgar chortling that came from the first brigand who opened that door and saw them. I had just come up the stairs in time to watch him struggle to pry the cork from the bottle. Then he turned it up for a deep drink."

"Sister was there and saw him," affirmed the Second Miss Ferston.

"Well, sir, no sooner did he gulp that liquid than did he spew it onto the wall, grab his throat, and scream, 'I'm pizened! I'm pizened!' Then the like of all the yelling for water you never heard. He nearly flattened his partners in crime in his headlong rush down the stairs and out the front door."

"Pizened!" repeated the Second Miss Ferston.

"What did he drink, Flora?" Major Meredith asked.

"Why, he had gotten into my tonic," replied the First Miss Ferston.

"Sister's tonic—that was the 'pizen,'" said the Second Miss Ferston.

"And a right good tonic it was—iron filings steeped in vinegar," said the First Miss Ferston.

"Iron filings?" laughed Major Meredith. "Steeped in vinegar?"

"The best of tonics, Cousin Charles," giggled the First Miss Ferston, joining in the merriment.

The children shouted above the racket, "I'm pizened! I'm pizened!"

The First Miss Ferston raised a forefinger and shook it, like a furious prophet, toward the candles in the chandelier. "And let me tell you this: not a single Yankee marauder has dared to step across the Ferston threshold since that memorable day."

"Not a one," punctuated the Second Miss Ferston.

A round of chuckles followed.

"But we have a richer brew to serve you," said the First Miss Ferston, rising from her chair and signaling to her sister, who also rose. "Clara, will you help me to serve the coffee that Johnnie Munson and Private Powell brought us? You have a special treat ahead of you— coffee from Yankee stores."

While Clara was pouring the coffee, the Misses Ferston brought out their Confederate fruitcake, full of apples and heavy with molasses and pepper, and served it all around.

"What a treat to have cake," said the long-faced lady in black. "I have attended dinners where guests have had to resort to reading recipes aloud in lieu of dessert."

"Yes," said Mrs. Meredith, "it always makes for a lively evening when the ladies vie to see who can bring the most delicious-sounding recipe."

"I've never tasted better coffee," said Major Meredith, savoring the steam from his cup.

"Yes, Cousin Charles," said the First Miss Ferston, "I am forced to say that I have tired of Sister's rye coffee."

"Sister has tired of it," giggled the Second Miss Ferston. "Truly I have tried every mixture that has been recommended to me—wheat, ground chestnuts—but now I have developed a blend of parched sweet potatoes and dandelion roots, mixed with the rye, that some have thought tasted almost like the real thing. Until now." She sipped her coffee.

"The worst brew that I have tasted," said the long-faced lady in black, "was the one made out of parched brown peas that my cook served. It cured me of wanting coffee for a long time, but this makes up for the waiting."

"I remember your cook, Martha," said Mrs. Meredith. "Is she still with you?"

The lady in black shook her head. "Alas, she has left me like all the others. She has found a harder life, I know, among the Yankees. There's hardly a darky left in Fauquier County," she moaned. "They say that some of the darky women have even thrown their babies in ditches."

"Good heavens, Martha!" exclaimed the First Miss Ferston. "Have you seen such a thing?"

"No. I have not seen it, but I have heard that it is so."

Mr. Payne said, "Freedom is too heavy a burden for them. Too heavy. I cannot believe that it is worth it to them, but they will seek it." He cleared his throat and looked around him.

"Tell them about Isaiah's letter, Uncle Scott," Mrs. Payne said.

"You all recollect Isaiah," he said. "He was my coachman, like my own son. Closer to me than anyone. I taught him to read and write, despite the law against it, and I gave him liberties that made him the envy of every servant in the county." He looked down and swallowed hard, and when he looked up again his eyes were wet.

"He repaid me," he said hoarsely, "he repaid me by fleeing from me when those rebellious servants encouraged him to." Again he cleared his throat. "Last week I had a letter from him. He wrote it in that neat script that I remember him practicing late at night when he was a little boy. He said, 'Master Scott'—the old man stopped and wiped his eyes—'Master Scott, I love you and you have been good to me, but you taught me—taught me about Patrick Henry and what he said—Give me liberty or give me death—and that is the choice—the choice—that I had to make.'" Drained now of words, old Mr. Payne sat still, his head down.

Lewis stared at Mr. Payne, and at the others around the table. The old man's words hung heavily over them all. A woman in front of Mr. Payne broke the silence.

"As ye sow," she said, "so shall ye reap. If you had not taught your servant to read, he would not have got such ideas into his head. He will not be happy in his freedom. He will not be happy."

Others murmured their agreement. Yes, their servants would see what an elusive will-o'-the-wisp freedom was, and they would only end up as wage-slaves of the Yankee.

"Cousin Amelia!" The First Miss Ferston summoned Clara Meredith's sister. "Your mother has been telling me what a piano virtuoso you have become. You must play for us."

Amelia blushed and hung her head, then glanced at her younger sister and giggled self-consciously.

"Yes, do, Amelia," pleaded the lady in black, and others added their entreaties. "Yes, Amelia, play for us."

The First Miss Ferston rose, followed by the Second Miss Ferston, and both beckoned to Amelia, who looked around like a cornered doe until, with her head down and her eyes fixed on the floor, she pushed back her chair and went to the piano. The men stood as the other ladies and children left the table to stand around the piano behind her.

Clara Meredith followed her sister to the piano, and Johnnie Munson, who had devoted his full attention to eating all during the supper, was on his feet right away. Lewis jumped up and stood between Clara and Johnnie. Clara whispered something into her sister's ear, and her sister smiled and started to play. When she made a mistake, she blushed, begged everybody's pardon, and started over. Lewis stayed between Johnnie and Clara, admiring her slender figure in the black and white checked dress, her white hands on her sister's shoulders, the bouncing of her curls as she nodded in time with the music.

When Amelia played "Pop Goes the Weasel," the children sang, then danced in a ring, reaching out to pull Clara and then Lewis and Johnnie into the dance.

The Second Miss Ferston gave the children some playing cards and they sat on the floor near the fire to play. Lewis and Clara took chairs to the corner where the elders were sitting, while Johnnie played cards with the children.

"Tell me, Charles," Mr. Payne was saying to Major Meredith. "What do you think of this talk about negotiating a settlement to the war?"

Major Meredith squinted into the fire and thought before replying. "Well, I spoke with James Randolph last week after he came back from Richmond. There's little talk of negotiation there. As a matter of fact, President Davis spoke this month, and said that our only reliable hope is in the most vigorous resistance."

"There is some talk," said Mr. Payne, "that little Alec Stephens, the Laodicean Vice President, tried to meet Lincoln several months ago, but failed to do so."

"Yes, I have heard that said. Stephens appeared to favor negotiating for peace. There are a few others besides who think that if we hold on until after next November's elections, a Democrat will be elected to succeed Lincoln, and we can then negotiate a more acceptable peace, one that will preserve the Confederacy intact."

The First Miss Ferston, who had been listening with her brows quivering and her lips twitching, hooted. "Hold on, do they say! It's not a matter of holding on. It's a matter of driving the Yankee upstarts off Virginia soil. Let us hear no talk of negotiation. The only thing for us is to back our brave General Lee and his men all the way to victory. There must be no talk of surrender!" She sat more stiffly and glared down at Major Meredith.

"None whatsoever!" exclaimed the Second Miss Ferston. "No talk of surrender!"

Major Meredith looked wearily at both of them.

"As for that tyrant Abraham Lincoln," went on the First Miss Ferston, "why should we give any thought to that backwoods buffoon at all? His arrogant Proclamation makes it impossible for us to think of anything but fighting on to victory. His obstinacy holds our prisoners, like our poor gallant cousin William Payne, fast in his loathsome prisons. Lincoln!" She sneered the name. "Lincoln! The best treatment for him is not political defeat. It is a bullet."

"Yes, that is right," agreed the Second Miss Ferston, "a bullet through the heart."

The First Miss Ferston turned to Lewis. "Surely, Private Powell, you are prepared to wage war until the last Yankee leaves Virginia soil."

Lewis looked at the tears welling on the wrinkled lower eyelids and felt the gravity of her plea. "Yes, ma'am," he told her, "I don't see how we have any choice."

"See there, Cousin Charles?" the First Miss Ferston gloated. "Here is a young man who will go so far as to shoot Abe Lincoln himself, whenever his orders tell him to. God bless you, Private Powell." Impulsively, she seized Lewis's hand in her clawlike grip, pulled it to her lips, and kissed it. She closed her eyes, and held his hand against her cheek, while her tears ran onto his imprisoned fingers.

Riding alongside the buggy where Clara Meredith sat with Jamie asleep in her lap, Lewis resolved to talk to her the next day. Lewis thought about holding her when he had swung her in the dance, listening to the high sweet tone of her voice when they sang.

Dismounting, he went to Clara's side of the buggy and, before lifting Jamie from her lap, put his arms around her waist and kissed her. She twitched in surprise, and shoved him back. Then he carried Jamie from the buggy, holding him on his left shoulder while with his right hand he reached to help Clara to step down. In the lamplight, he could tell how confused she was as she twisted away from him and stepped to the ground without his help. She walked past him onto the veranda. Mr. Payne, busy helping Mrs. Payne down, had not seen. Lewis handed Jamie, still asleep, to his mother, tipped his cap, and watched them all go into the house. Clara did not turn around when Mrs. Payne told Lewis good night and thanked him for escorting them.

Whistling softly, Lewis led his horse to the barn. As he was reaching to lift the latch on the barn door, a voice came out of the shadows.

"That's far enough, Reb. Stop right there."

Lewis froze, then moved his hand toward his Colt revolver, only to feel a strong hand grab his right arm. A laugh sounded close to his ear.

"Tom?" Lewis asked.

"Sure enough." Tom Ogg laughed again.

"Sure could get yourself killed doing that." He felt a sharp, hot flush of anger.

"Shucks. And you can get yourself shot or captured, you don't look out no better than you done just now." He relaxed his grip on Lewis's arm. "Cab Maddux is here with me. Get your gear. Captain Chapman wants us for a raid."

Lewis looked toward the big house, where a single lantern shone in an upstairs window. He turned and unlatched the barn door. He brought his gear down from the loft and tied it to his saddle. Then he followed Tom and Cab to the road. When he looked at the house again, he could see no light there.

11

FAUQUIER COUNTY, VIRGINIA
EARLY 1864

ON NEW YEAR'S DAY, Mosby sent Chapman's company through a snowstorm on a patrol, and when they rejoined the regiment, they found that they had missed a raid on a Yankee camp at Harpers Ferry. To make matters worse, Lewis had to spend most of the winter with Tom Ogg, Cab Maddux, and Johnnie Munson on a windswept little farm in Loudoun County, with an old bachelor who told the same stories over and over. The few times they came across any Yanks, they would amuse themselves by shooting at them out of the woods, just to make the Yanks chase them.

Several times, Lewis started a letter to Clara Meredith, but he did not think it was as good a letter as he wanted to send her, and he would throw it away. Lewis would play cards with Cab and Tom and listen to Johnnie Munson trying to play the Jew's harp until he got sick of listening and they all threw Johnnie out into the snow. Sometimes Cab would bring a jug of whiskey and all four of them would get drunk and run through the woods, chasing one another and shooting. When Washington's Birthday came, Lewis and Tom celebrated in Harpers Ferry at a whorehouse. Lewis found a photographer's shop and had a picture made of himself, which Tom told him was a good likeness. He looked at it and decided to give it to Clara Meredith, and the next time he was alone in the cabin, he wrote another letter to her.

Dear Miss Clara,

   I reckon you are supprised to recieve a letter from yours truly
Doc Powell. One of our runners promissed me that he would take
this to you. There is not much to do here but just play cards and
shoot at the Yanks. We got in a scrap not long ago and I run into a
wire that the Yanks streched accross a rode and got bunged up pretty
bad, but I am much better now.

   I have a picture of me that was took in Harpers Ferry, and I will
bring it the next time I come to Grandville. I often remember the
party we went to at Christmas and how we danced and sung there.
I hope you are not mad about what I done when you were getting
out of the buggy. I have not forgot that neither.

   I have had a lot of time to think this winter, and I am thinking
that you are a very special and very pretty lady and I am in love with
you. I have thought about how much you are doing for the Cause
and doing to help the soldiers who are fighting for the South.

   I want to talk some more with you about this when I get back
to Grandville.

Yours very truly,
L. Powell

                    *   *   *

Lewis rode back to Grandville in late March, just after Easter. The
woods were white with dogwood, and wildflowers bloomed out of the
wetness left by the melting of the last snow. He cut across a field still
littered with the stubble of last year's corn, where brown earth took
from the white dogwoods and blue wildflowers and gave bleakness
back to the land.

   Jamie saw him first. He stared, then rubbed his eyes. "Edward!
Edward! It's Doc! He's come back!" the boy shouted, running toward
Lewis.

   Lewis reached down, picked Jamie up, and swung him onto the
saddle in front of him. As they rode toward the house, Jamie said,
"Do you know what Edward said, Doc? He said that you would not
come back." He turned a broad smile up toward Lewis.

   Edward came out of the house, followed by his mother and his
uncle. Lewis handed Jamie down to Mr. Payne, and opened his arms
for Edward to run to him with an embrace.

   "Where is Miss Meredith?" Lewis asked.

"She left last month for her cousin's home in Lexington," Mr. Payne told him. "Her cousin has been ill and needs help with her children."

Mrs. Payne said, "She left a letter for me to give to you. Edward, go and fetch it from the bureau drawer where I keep the letters."

Impatient to read Clara's letter, Lewis had to listen instead to Mr. Payne's troubles with the farm. Finally able to get away from the old man, Lewis led his horse to the barn, with the boys running along to help him unsaddle, curry the horse, and pour the grain into the trough.

At last alone, he tore open the envelope. He held the letter up to a sunbeam slipping through a chink in the barn wall and read:

> Dear Private Powell,
>
> What trying times you have been through during this terrible winter. I pray that God will protect you and bring you safely through the battles that you are enduring.
>
> All of us are well at Grandville, but my cousin has been very ill in Lexington, and I must go there to help her and her little ones. I will be back in the latter part of July. I look forward to receiving the photograph that you wrote of. I am making something special that I hope you will like. As for your kind compliments, I thank you for them, although I am unworthy of them. Beyond that, I can say no more until we meet again.
>
> My prayers go with you.
>
> Your devoted friend,
> Clara Meredith

Lewis took the Bible from his saddlebag and opened it to the page where he had hid the strands of brown hair three months before. After reading the letter three more times, he set it gently on the same page. Then he closed the Bible slowly and lay back, watching the pattern that the sun's reflection from a water trough made on the ceiling. It danced there while a mockingbird sang in rhythm with the glowing light from the sun.

The captain did not send for him, and Lewis spent mornings plowing a garden for Mrs. Payne and helping Mr. Payne mend fences. In the afternoons he went with the boys to fish and catch frogs, which they brought back to the house for the cook to fry. The cook hacked the legs off the frogs and skinned them. Then Lewis laughed with the boys by the stove while they took turns lifting the pot lid to watch the legs twitch in the sputtering grease.

One late afternoon Lewis and the boys were sitting on a log, watching their fishing corks on the top of a little pond, when Jamie asked, "Doc, do the Yanks kill children?"

"What are you talking about, Jamie?"

"Don't worry, Jamie," Edward said. "The Confederacy will win the war, so that man will not kill us."

"What man?" Lewis asked.

"He's talking about the Yankee officer that came to see us last month when we were at our house in Warrenton," Edward told him. "He told our mother that he was a friend of our father when they were at the university in Charlottesville, and he came to pay his respects. Mama told him that he could go pay his respects to Papa in that dreadful prison at Johnson's Island, if he wanted to see him.

"The Yankee officer told her that he was sorry to hear about Papa being in the prison and all, and that he hoped that some day, after the North won, the North and the South would live in peace. Mama looked at him with that look she has when she gets so very angry, and she said to him, 'Sir, we will remain enemies as long as I live.' She said she could never forgive the terrible things the Yanks have done to us and to our land. Then she told him, 'If the worst should happen and you should win this war, you may return, not to live here in peace, but to kill me and my children. But we shall never live in peace.'"

Jamie said, "And that's why I want to know if the Yanks kill children. I don't want them to k-k-kill me—and to kill my b-b-brother—and—and my mama." The little boy broke into sobs, dropped his fishing pole, and buried his face in his hands. Edward put his arms around him and looked helplessly at Lewis.

Lewis squeezed Jamie's thin little arm. "That won't happen, Jamie," he promised. "I won't let that happen."

In a pine tree overhead, two crows started a raucous bickering, then fluttered away, while Lewis and the boys stared at dragonflies moving over the still pond in the waning light.

When Lewis rode to the forge that night, Captain Sam Chapman was playing cards with the blacksmith.

"Take a hand, Powell," Chapman said.

"Not what I want, Captain."

"What do you want?"

"To shoot Yanks."

Chapman looked at the blacksmith, and both of them laughed. The blacksmith dealt Lewis a hand.

For more than three months, Lewis spent nearly every night in the saddle. During the days he slept in barns, in stables, in attics, in graveyards, in country churches, sometimes even in feather beds, and once on a houseboat drifting down the Potomac. Sometimes in small bands, sometimes in company or regimental force, they ambushed Yankee camps and supply trains, picked up stragglers, or raided sutlers. Sometimes, after they had grabbed all that they could carry from sutlers' wagons, they would let their prisoners take what was left.

He wrote another letter to Clara Meredith and tried to send it to her in the Shenandoah Valley by a courier, but he never knew if the letter got to her. Johnnie Munson went to Fauquier County once but came back without news of Clara or the Paynes.

One hot morning, Lewis was riding with the regiment along a road in Loudoun County. The men looked less like soldiers than like revelers bound for home after a masquerade ball. Every man was swathed in a different color of bright calico cloth, and some had wound turbans around their heads or wrapped their horses in the gay colors from ears to tail. Their day had begun when their single Napoleon cannon shelled a frightened, confused Maryland village from across the Potomac. Then, whooping like savages, the rangers had forded the river and galloped through the town, looting it of sacks of flour and grain, of lanterns and liquor, until coming across a splendid find—a warehouse full of calico. Not a man could resist heaping onto his horse's back a treasure that would gladden the heart of his mother or sister or wife or sweetheart. In their retreat across the Potomac they even dropped what they had taken for themselves so that they could hold on to every yard of the precious fabric. Jubilantly they trailed it out by the yard and dragged it through the water and mud.

Lewis, his gray uniform invisible under a toga of red, yellow, and green, was riding beside Tom Ogg. "Tom," he called out, "what day is it?"

"About the fifteenth of July, I think, Powell."

"Tom, I got to head back to Fauquier."

Lewis rode up to Captain Richards at the first watering stop. "Captain," he said, "I want to go back to Warrenton. I'll be back in a few days."

"Is it a girl, Powell?" the captain asked.

"Could be, Captain."

"Tell the sergeant you've got my permission to go. And kiss her once for me."

Johnnie rode up. "Can I go with Powell, Captain? He might could use some help—with the Yanks, I mean."

The captain bit off a plug of tobacco, chewed, and looked at them. "Five days, boys," he said.

At sundown the next day, after Lewis and Johnnie separated at a crossroads, Lewis tied his horse outside the Misses Ferston's stable. When he told them who he was, the sisters opened the door with squeals of welcome. They clucked and crowed over the bolts of calico that he brought. The First Miss Ferston gushed that she had never seen prettier yard goods, and the Second Miss Ferston agreed.

The sisters brewed him some blackberry tea, repeating the story of saving the tea service from the Yankees.

"Where are you going now, Private Powell?" the First Miss Ferston asked.

"I am going to Grandville. Do you know if Miss Clara Meredith is there yet?"

The sisters looked at each other.

"Why, she—" began the Second Miss Ferston.

The First Miss Ferston broke in, "Cousin Clara has been in Warrenton for a month, Private Powell, at her father's house. She—she has not been well."

Lewis set his cup down, spilling most of the tea. "I had not heard that. Is she bad sick?"

"She has been, but we hear that she is better now," said the First Miss Ferston. She stood. "But you must go there now, before it's too late—uh—too late in the night, I mean. So we talkative old ladies shall not detain you any further." She smiled her coquettish smile, picked up a lamp, and led Lewis to the door.

Lewis walked his horse down the road to the Meredith home. Honeysuckle perfumed the night, and a nightingale sang in a thicket. Memory and a rising crescent moon guided him to the house. A light shone in an upstairs room, but he heard no voices and saw no one. He mounted and rode to Grandville to sleep in the barn.

A crowing rooster woke him, and he ate biscuits and eggs in Mrs. Payne's kitchen while Edward and Jamie, full of self-importance, rode their ponies toward town to look for Yankee soldiers. They came back to tell Lewis that they had seen a squadron of Yankees at the edge of town.

"I'll just go in civilian clothes and leave my uniform here," Lewis said, picking up some biscuits and putting them in his coat pockets.

"No, young man," Mr. Payne warned him. "They are on the lookout for Mosby's men, and if they find you without a uniform, they will hang you as a spy. Wait until after dark."

So Lewis spent the day at the farm, mending harness and sharpening tools while the boys drew stories out of him and the sun rolled backward in the sky.

When he knocked on Major Meredith's door an hour after sundown, Clara's sister Amelia was waiting to lead him to Clara's room. The thin-faced girl who lay on the silk pillow was a stranger to him, her hair in the lamplight darker now and her eyes sunk in dim hollows. She smiled and held a hand out toward him.

"Miss Clara," Lewis murmured as he kissed her cold hand.

"Private Powell," she said, "how good of you to come to see me. I feel better already." She raised herself from the pillow, and her sister fluffed the pillow behind her.

"Clara has been much better today," Amelia said. "She took all of the soup that I brought her."

"Why, I shall be back to my gardening any day now," Clara said, smiling. "And it's about time. I have been a slug-a-bed too long now, making cruel demands on my poor sisters."

"Stop saying that," Amelia told her. "Laura and I are all too glad to do whatever we can for you." She looked at Lewis. "Clara, Private Powell brought the most handsome bolts of calico. I am already planning the dress that I intend to make. All of it was destined for the wardrobe of some Yankee lady, he tells me, until Mosby's Rangers intercepted it."

Clara said, "I am sure that you can put it to as good a use as the high-toned Yankee girls can. Amelia, look in the top drawer of my bureau and hand me the parcel there. I made something special for you, Private Powell, while I was in Lexington." She smiled, then began to cough.

Lewis looked around helplessly, picked up a glass of water, and held it toward her. She touched his hand with her cold fingers.

Amelia handed Clara a package wrapped in blue cloth, which Clara held toward Lewis.

Lewis took the parcel, unwrapped the blue cloth, and unfolded a woolen Confederate flag. He held it up, admiring the bright red of its field, the crossed blue bars, and white stars. "It—it's sure a fine flag, Miss Clara," he said. "I had a friend in the Jasper Blues, Riley Green his name was. He was our color-bearer, and this reminds me of him." He folded the flag again and wrapped the blue remnant around it. "I will take this back to the ranger regiment, and we will use it there."

Clara coughed again. Her mother came into the room as her sister supported Clara's head and raised the water glass to her lips. Her mother poured a spoonful of a dark liquid. Clara sipped the spoonful of medicine and lay back.

"Thank you for coming for the flag, Private Powell," Mrs. Meredith said. "Clara has spoken of little else for weeks, and I am sure that she is much better now that you are here and she can give it to you."

Lewis tucked the blue parcel inside his coat and took Clara's hand. "It will get good use," he told her.

"The banner of our country does not wave over as many places as it once did," Clara moaned. "May this one fly over some field or some town where the Yankee flag now flies." She sighed. "People are talking now about our army under siege at Petersburg, and they say that a terrible battle is about to begin at Atlanta."

"Don't think of those things now," her mother said, stroking Clara's shoulder. "Just think about getting well."

"Don't you just hate the Yankees, Private Powell?" Clara asked.

Lewis moistened his lips. "Hate them?" He was quiet for a moment. "No. I don't reckon that I do."

Amelia asked, "Why, you have to hate them to be a soldier, don't you?"

Lewis swallowed and looked at the Confederate taper, its guttering light surrounded by a small cloud of moths. "We had a man in our brigade that hated the Yankees. One time when we caught up with some dead Yanks—least most of them were dead—he done—he done things to them that I can't tell you about. Later on, I happened to be near to him when we was getting shelled real bad. Well, when the shelling come to be over and done with, we could not find this fellow nowhere. Nothing left of him." He looked at Clara and Amelia, who were watching him to see what would come next. "I puzzled about it, and one of the older men told it to me like this. He said that man hated too much. You can kill, but you can't hate. If you hate, you get careless and you die."

"Enough of this talk about hating and killing," Mrs. Meredith said. "You must rest, Clara."

"No, mother," Clara told her. "Let him finish what he was saying."

"There's nothing more to tell, Miss Clara," Lewis said. "I have met all different kinds of Yanks. I have seen more than my share of the mean ones, but some of them at Gettysburg treated me all right, and there was one fellow, a man from Wisconsin, that shared his stew with me when they captured me last November. If I ever get a chance to pay back the kindness, I hope to do so."

Clara smiled again and shut her eyes. "I hope you can."

"Well, that is enough now," her mother said.

"First, Mother," said Clara weakly, "let me ask Private Powell one more thing. It's about General Hunter." She motioned to her sister, who held the glass to her lips. Clara coughed and looked up at Lewis. "Private Powell, when I was at Lexington, there was a general named David Hunter—a Virginian and a traitor to his state—who led his Federal army there, and without any reason he burned the home of Mrs. Lee, a friend of my cousin. General Hunter is a criminal, and if you ever meet him, you must kill him."

Lewis half-smiled at her, not knowing whether she was joking. "Well, Miss Clara, I don't reckon we will ever meet each other, but if we do, I'll remember what you said."

"Now, Clara, you must rest," her mother said. "Private Powell can come back tomorrow."

Clara lay still and closed her eyes. Lewis looked at the bed before he went out the door, seeing not the girl, but the mass of shadows in which she lay buried.

A screech owl split the night with its shriek as Lewis rode from the town. Heat lightning flashed among distant clouds, and the cadence of his horse's hooves sounded amid the trill of crickets along the road. He reached inside his coat for the flag that Clara Meredith had given him. Tomorrow he would have to ride back to the regiment, and he would miss the chance to talk to her, to tell her that he loved her, to ask her to wait for him until the war was over. Why, with a girl like that, there was no telling what a man might be able to do. He thought of how it would be to live on a plantation with a wife like Clara Meredith, with slaves bringing in the cotton crop, with business trips to Richmond, Charleston, Jacksonville.

Lewis's body rocked with the gait of his horse, and he imagined he was riding home. He would ride with the regiment from the depot at Live Oak, and a crowd of people would cheer as the men came home from the war, with pretty ladies in ruffled dresses waving from carriages. His horse would carry him, alone now, past Godwin's farm and past the school, where children would come outside and admire him in his gray uniform, riding his chestnut mare. He would quicken his horse to a trot when he saw the live oak trees on the hill where his father's house was. Martin would be standing at the gate, waiting to take his horse. Lewis would dismount then, and walk up the path to the house where his mother would stand on the top step, her arms reaching out to hug him, and his father proud behind her. Annie, grown to be a young woman, would run past them to greet him. Wash, healed of his wounds, and Susan and the children would gather around him. In the door Aunt Sarah would stand, like a statue. He would tell her, "The signs—see, you read them wrong, Aunt Sarah. I'm back, spite of what you said."

The best part would be his farm. He already knew where it would be, had found it when he was fifteen years old, after Wash had yelled at him for hiding in the hollow back of the south forty and going to sleep. It was the only time he ran away, but he went to the house, filled a poke bag with cornbread, and set off, taking with him the old flint-lock that his uncle had given him in Georgia. He followed a winding road north to the river and walked down the bank of the Suwannee, then slept in a farmer's barn and got a meal in return for sawing a cord of wood. He stayed in the woods for three days, fishing out of the river off a bluff. On the fourth day a leaky boat floated down the river, and he swam out and dragged it ashore. He warmed pine resin in a broken gourd and used it to plug the cracks in the bottom of the boat, enough for it to stay afloat on the river. Then he floated downstream and around the big bend. That night, he slept on a sandbar at a wide curve of the river, and when he woke the next morning a doe, with a fawn beside her, was lapping at the river water not ten paces from where he slept. She looked at him as if she accepted him into the world around her. Then the doe and fawn turned, climbed the gentle slope, and disappeared into the brush. Lewis got up from where he slept, climbed to the higher ground, and thrashed through gallberries to stand on a bluff under blossoming dogwoods. Rays of the rising sun slanted between pines and reflected from the carpet of leaves and pine needles. All was white and gold, and the fallen leaves rustled where wood mice scurried. Walking along the bank, Lewis found a ruined cabin, its roof fallen on one side and a crude rock chimney rising out of the wreck. The cabin was sheltered by an enormous oak, its gnarled trunk reaching twisted limbs over the dark river. He built a fire in the fireplace and spent that night under the leaning roof. The next day he turned toward his father's house.

George Powell punished Lewis by making him sleep in the barn for a week, and after that told him to sing in church. Lewis sang "This land is not my home," and from that time on he would think about that bluff on the Suwannee, which he came to call Hebron, because it seemed like the land that Joshua had given to Caleb in the Bible.

Lewis did not talk to anybody about Hebron until he met Riley. He would tell Riley about it, and they would talk about going home to buy it and farm there. Now Riley was under the ground at Gettysburg, but Lewis still meant to go to Hebron. Jesus had led him to a vision of Hebron, to the neglected land that he would clear and sow with crops bearing a harvest of blessings from God's bounty. He would ask Papa to give Martin to him, and he would take a bride. He wanted that bride to be Clara Meredith.

When he climbed the ladder to the loft above the barn, Lewis pulled the little Bible from the ledge beside his cot and, in the first rays of dawn light, touched the strands of hair he had placed there, remembering the loose hair of Clara Meredith spread on the pillow beside her head. He fell asleep thinking of her.

"Doc!" His name being called lurched him out of a dream, where his sister Annie and Clara Meredith and Edward and Jamie danced in a circle while his father, gaunt and all in black, beckoned to him and pointed to a mountain shrouded in clouds.

"Doc! Doc!" Lewis sat up, fully awake now and aware of the high sunlight beaming onto his cot.

"Who is it?" he asked.

"It's me. Edward. Down here." He heard Edward climbing the ladder.

"What is it, Edward? What do you want?"

"Mama says for you to come to the house. She has something to tell you."

Lewis pulled on his clothes and followed Edward down the ladder. "Do you know what it's about?" he asked.

"No. She just told me to come get you."

Mrs. Payne was in the parlor, sitting in a wing-backed chair, while Mr. Payne stood staring out of a window. Lewis pulled off his hat when he came into the room, and Mr. Payne looked around.

"You may go now, Edward," Mrs. Payne told the boy.

Edward left the room, and Mr. Payne stood at the door, watching him go down the center hallway and outside.

"Please sit down," Mrs. Payne said. Her eyes were red from weeping, and she wiped her nose with a handkerchief that she held balled in a fist.

"Private Powell," she said, "I need your help in telling my sons about something that has happened. They are so fond of you, and I want you to help them bear the news."

Lewis looked from her to Mr. Payne, and then back at her.

"I know, ma'am," Lewis said, clearing his throat. "Colonel Payne, it's been hard for him in that prison."

"It's not Colonel Payne that I mean. It—it's Clara Meredith."

Lewis felt a hot rush of blood to his face. He looked at Mr. Payne, who stared back at him. "What do you mean?" he asked. "What about Miss Clara?"

Mrs. Payne said almost in a whisper, "She is dead."

Lewis steadied himself against a table, then sat down again and stared at Mrs. Payne.

"But somebody has told you wrong," he said. "I saw her last night, and her mother and sister said she was better."

Mrs. Payne looked up. "The message came this morning. She died in the night. Her sister went to wake her, and she was gone."

Lewis listened to the ticking of the clock grow louder. He watched the weights hanging in the case below the clock and felt the same weight pulling his heart toward the earth.

Later he took the boys fishing and talked with them about Clara. Jamie wanted to know if Clara was already in heaven or if she would not go there until after the funeral. Edward flung rocks into the pond while they listened to the lament of mourning doves.

Lewis rode into Warrenton that night with the Paynes. They filed past the bier where Clara Meredith lay in white, her flowing brown hair neatly braided on either shoulder. Lewis thought that she looked older now, with a wisdom that came with death. He reached into his coat pocket, took out the blue parcel that she had given him, and slowly unwrapped it. He let the flag fall loose and draped it across her body. Then he walked past the people in the parlor and out the door. He mounted his horse and rode out of Warrenton.

He was about a mile out of town when he heard a horse galloping after him. He turned off the road, pulled his revolver, and waited under a willow. The horseman behind him slowed to a walk.

"Powell?" It was Johnnie Munson's voice.

Lewis slipped his revolver back into its holster and moved back into the road.

"I saw you leave, Powell, and I came after you." Lewis did not speak, but turned his horse back onto the road beside Johnnie's.

When they stopped to water their horses at a creek, Lewis and Johnnie dismounted, holding their horses' reins. Above the croaking of a hundred bullfrogs Lewis heard hoofbeats. Two horsemen stopped twenty feet from them and stayed in their saddles while the horses drank.

"Evening, boys," one of the horsemen said. Lewis jumped when one rider pulled off his hat and moonlight glinted on his insignia.

"Evening," he said. Then he whispered to Johnnie, "They're Yanks, Johnnie."

Their revolvers came out at the same time, and Lewis and Johnnie fired together. The riders dropped from their horses, and one thrashed in the edge of the stream before lying still. Johnnie swung into his saddle and called to Lewis, "Come on, Powell. Let's get out of here."

Lewis walked toward the bodies. Moonlight shone through the leaves onto the face of one of them, a boy a year or so younger than Lewis himself. Blood spurted from a hole in his neck and was lost in the stream. Lewis bent over, dragged the body out of the water, and laid it straight on the edge. Then his knees gave way, and he sagged to kneel beside the body, sobbing, his eyes blind with tears.

After that, Lewis Powell rode in the vanguard of every attack, and while minié balls whined past him, he stood with less concern than another man might have shown for a swarm of black flies. "The Terrible Powell," Mosby called him after one ambush, and the name stuck to him like pine tar. "Powell is too reckless," Captain Chapman told Mosby, and when Mosby organized a new company with Dolly Richards as captain, he transferred Lewis into it. Lewis went west with the new company to harass supply trains bound for Sheridan in the Shenandoah Valley, and rode east to attack trains aiding Grant in the siege of Petersburg. He mastered the art of "skedaddling," the pride of the rangers, galloping after fleeing Yankees and knocking one sprawling, or grabbing another by the shirt to jerk him off his feet. Yet any man who surrendered to him found a friend in Lewis, who would share his rations with his prisoner and protect him.

12

FAUQUIER COUNTY, VIRGINIA
LATE 1864

IN NOVEMBER, Lewis and Tom Ogg nearly blundered into becoming prisoners of the Yanks. That was the time Lewis saw Colonel Mosby the merriest, and the time he saw him the angriest.

Lewis thought Mosby would choke laughing at Tom's story, and Captain Dolly Richards was laughing so hard he could not mount his horse. "Tom Ogg! Tom Ogg! Don't you know Tom Ogg?" Mosby kept saying. "Chapman," he called out when Captain Chapman rode toward them a puzzled look on his face, "listen to this one. Tell him, Tom."

"Well, Captain," Tom drawled, "the colonel sent me out to scout for Yanks, and I couldn't find none. So just as I was headed back for our troop, with Powell and Berry riding behind me, I come on a picket. When he up and challenged, naturally I thought it was our troop, and I told him, 'It's just me, Tom Ogg.' 'Who?' he wanted to know, kind of suspicious-like. 'Tom Ogg,' I told him again, 'Tom Ogg. Don't you know Tom Ogg?' 'Hell, no,' he said, 'I don't know no Tom Ogg. Get down off your horse and be recognized.'

"Well, I dismounted, cussing him for a damn fool, and I asked him, 'What company you in anyhow?' He told me, 'Company E.' Well I knowed the colonel had just organized that new Company E, so I said, ''You must be that green Company E.' Well, whenever I led my horse towards him, I glimpsed him a little better, and Lord, if it weren't a bluebelly. I'd set slap down in a wh ˙� swarm of 'em. While

I was still in the shadow of a big elm, I says, 'Man, I'm lame. Let me get back on my horse. Ain't you got no respect for an officer?' 'Well, all right, get back on the horse.' So I mounted, and I wheeled my horse and was out of there like a bellow out of a bull, yelling to Powell and Berry, 'Let's go, boys!' And the rifle balls whizzing past us you ain't never seen the like of. Now I know I can outrun anything a Sharps can throw at me."

Captain Chapman chuckled and said he would expect the Yanks to know Tom Ogg the next time. Then he turned to Mosby. "Colonel, I've got bad news. Six of our boys got captured when we attacked that wagon train over by Front Royal, and the Yanks killed them."

Mosby gasped. "Killed them!"

"Hung two of them, and shot Overby and three others. One was a boy named Rhodes that was riding with us. Shot him right in front of his ma, with her begging them to spare him."

"Who ordered it?"

"George Custer."

Mosby walked to a pine tree and leaned against it with one hand over his eyes and face. His head was bowed.

"Seven hundred Yankee prisoners I've taken," he said. "Seven hundred, officers and men, and I've forwarded them to Richmond, every one." He kicked a pine cone and studied it as it rolled down a slope and rested at the bottom. He looked up, scowling at Chapman and Richards. "Find George Custer for me, or bring me the first seven of his men that you take."

Lewis looked at Tom, whose jaw was set in sullen anger, and the two of them led their horses down the hill to the road, where they mounted. As he rode away, Lewis looked back at Mosby alone under the pines.

Two days later, at sunset, Tom Ogg was waiting when Lewis went to the kitchen for a supper of sweet potatoes, pork, biscuits, and buttermilk. Edward Payne told them a Federal patrol had passed by about noon but had not come to the house.

"How many, and which way was they headed?" Tom asked, gulping a mouthful of biscuit.

"About a dozen of them, headed south."

"We'll keep an eye peeled."

.They pushed their chairs back, and Lewis scooped up three biscuits and dropped them into his poke bag before following Tom outside.

About a mile from Grandville, they joined four other rangers, and the six of them fell into single file as they rode through the night. Lewis held his reins slack, knowing his chestnut mare would stop when the leader of the column would signal a halt. They listened on all sides, hearing only night sounds—a hoot of an owl, the song of crickets, the bounding of a deer.

His horse stopped, and Tom Ogg, at the head of the column, passed word back to dismount. The party led their horses off the trail under a cover of oaks and waited, pinching their horses' nostrils to keep them from whinnying. The sky was clear, and Lewis looked through bare branches at scattered stars. It was nearly midnight. From the main road ahead came the sound of a troop of horses moving at a trot, with the clinking of metal and the rhythmic pounding of hooves, too fast to be the main body of Mosby's Rangers. Surely a Yankee patrol. Tom gave the word to mount. "Like as not they're headed for Bristow. We'll cross the road, round west, and meet up with the main troop north of town."

Within an hour they had gathered with the rest of the company, and Captain Richards led them to a railroad line. Mosby posted Chapman's company there and led the main body along the rails into the gap. After a mile they halted near a cut where the rails dipped between high bluffs. Lewis had drawn to the front, near Richards and Mosby. Five of Mosby's men were lounging on the embankment, their horses standing near them, when the first riders approached.

"What's been keeping you, Colonel?" Lewis recognized the voice of a man from Georgia named Daniels. "We had the rail drug aside for an hour now."

"Good work," Mosby told him. "We picked up a telegraph message that the train was half an hour late, but it's started now, and if we move fast, we'll still have time to finish before daylight."

Mosby stayed at the rails with Daniels and his party while the rest of the troop rode to the top of the embankment. Captain Richards sent vedettes a mile in each direction along the rails, and the others dismounted and stretched out on the ground.

Lewis was the first to hear the whistle and the chuffing of the engine laboring up the grade near Manassas, heavy with supplies for Sheridan in the Shenandoah Valley. Soon the locomotive would drop into the gap toward the break in the track where they waited.

The crash was all the louder for the silence of the night. The dislocated track threw the locomotive on one side and it toppled in a belching of sparks and steam. Behind it the cars rolled one into the next with a tearing of wood and a shriek of metal. There was an instant of near silence, broken only by the hissing of steam and the thud of something falling far back within the cut. Then came the shouts of men and the screams of women.

"Come on, boys!" Richards yelled. They galloped along the embankment to the end of the cut and dismounted. Mosby, on horseback, had passed the locomotive, and men ran after him on foot. Daniels rode beside him, holding high a lightwood-knot torch. Flames lit a shattered car with bent bars hanging from a window out of which two Union soldiers were crawling. Mosby pointed a pistol at them. "Get over against the bank and lie on your bellies!" he yelled. "You're prisoners! Who's that? Powell?" Lewis ran toward Mosby. "Go in and get the strongbox out of there."

"Here, Doc." Daniels handed Lewis a crowbar. Men were running past the car when Lewis crawled inside. Other men with torches followed them. Daniels held his torch close to the window while Lewis found the strongbox. He used the crowbar to pry loose the chain holding it to the wall, then handed the box to two other men who had come to the window. They ran along the rails while Lewis scrambled out of the window and ran toward the shattered cars.

"They won't come out, Colonel," a sergeant was saying to Mosby. "Can't but one of them speak English, and he says they paid for their passage and they ain't leaving."

"Herr Kapitan! Herr Kapitan!" a man in a black coat with a gray goatee was screaming at Mosby. "We are Germans, and we have nothing to do with your war. Let us go on our way."

Mosby laughed. "Mein herr, I am going to burn that car, and you had better get your fellow Germans out if you do not want them to burn with it."

A corporal ran to Mosby with a bundle of papers. "Look what I found, Colonel! Newspapers!" He laughed. "New York Herald Tribunes!"

"Give me one of them," Mosby said. "Let me catch up on the news in New York. Then use the rest of them to fire the cars." He grinned at Dolly Richards. "Phil Sheridan will have to find something else to wipe his bum with."

The Germans in the car were shouting at the soldiers and waving frantically. "Fire them, boys!" Mosby ordered. The men scattered the bundles of newspapers into all the cars, and those with torches touched them into flame. Women screamed as the smoke curled through the first car.

All at once the German women and their ashen, frightened children were pushed out of the doors of the leaning car, and baggage was tossed behind them. Then the men followed. The car burst into flame, and the fire spread to the next car and the next after that. Some people stood in anguish as the flames licked along the cars, but one young woman ran toward Mosby. Spreading her arms helplessly, she wailed, "Colonel, how can you do such a thing? Why—why—my father is a Mason."

Mosby touched the brim of his hat. "Ma'am, I can't help it," he replied. He turned then and followed his men, making their way back toward their horses, laden with baggage from the wreck.

"Colonel," yelled a ranger, "there's thousands of dollars in that strongbox."

"Good. Divide it," Mosby told him. "Bugler! Sound retreat! Richards! Cover us while we withdraw."

Richards relayed the order to his company. They rode to the crest of the south embankment while the rest of the troop galloped out of the cut past them.

On a night two weeks later Lewis was sleeping in a barn near Warrenton. A cold wind was throwing rain against the shutters when he woke to hear his name being called.

"Powell! Wake up!"

Lewis rolled over and looked around. In the darkness he heard someone coming up the first rungs of the ladder.

"Who is it?" he asked.

"It's Cab Maddux. Hurry up. The colonel wants us." Lewis pulled on his boots and rolled his blanket, then dropped it through the trap to the barn floor below. He strapped on his pistol holster and groped for the short-barreled shotgun, which lay across one of the beams. When he lowered himself down the ladder, Cab was tightening the girth on his own saddle. Pulling on his heavy uniform coat, Lewis moved to the stall where his own horse waited and felt for the smooth leather of the McClellan saddle. He ran his finger along the groove that a minié ball had left in it weeks before. Then he dropped the saddle onto his horse, cinched it, and fastened the bridle. He led the horse out of the barn into the damp, chill night, its hooves crunching on the icy ground.

As they mounted, Lewis asked Cab, "What's going on? Hope we get another Yankee train. I could use another two thousand dollars."

"Nothing like that this time. Sergeant told us to go to Ashby's Gap."

They did not speak as they rode. Looking down, his hat pulled down to his ears and his collar high on his neck, Lewis imagined that he was standing still and that the world was moving under the horse, rocking him with its motion. Irregular dark patches passed and gave way to wider bands of earth, followed by dark patches again. The sky was getting lighter now, and the low black parapets of stone fences rose on either side.

A dog barked when they rode into a settlement, and a chorus of barks answered. In front of a store a single horse was tethered. A man stood up from where he had been huddled on the porch wrapped in a blanket. He walked into the street toward them, a gray shadow identifiable only by the hat with one turned-up brim.

They reined in and walked their horses toward the man. "That you, Cab? Powell with you?"

"Sure enough."

"Captain Richards says take the right fork up yonder and go to Rectortown. I'll wait here a while longer."

"What's up?" Cab asked.

"Thought you knew. Charlie Whiting took a couple dozen of Custer's boys yesterday over near to Winchester, and he's meeting the colonel with them at Ashby's Gap. Colonel's taking them on to Rectortown, and you fellows got to scout the road between there and here."

"Hope there's lots of rope in Rectortown. Looks like we're going to have us some fun," Cab said.

"Let's go, Cab," Lewis told him.

"Don't you do nothing before I get there, you hear me?" called the lookout as they spurred their horses to a fast trot.

Twenty-seven men shivered in the public square at Rectortown. Their capes and coats had been taken from them, and some hugged their shoulders. Others stood silent, their heads high and their teeth clenched. Facing them, high on his dappled stallion, sat John Mosby, wearing his gray cape edged in scarlet and his hat with the side brim turned up. He had grown a sparse beard since Lewis had seen him last, but it did not obscure the grim line of his jaw or the stern set of his lips. Mosby watched a ranger walk along the line of Federal prisoners, holding his hat toward each in turn as they drew slips of paper from it. A crowd of townspeople had gathered at one edge of the square, mostly men and older boys, some sitting in wagons and others standing, shifting from one foot to the other. One prisoner groaned when he glanced down at the paper he had drawn, then clenched it tightly in a fist and gazed in front of him. Another looked down at his paper and giggled loudly, and he had to cover his mouth. Others would not look at the papers, while one of those who did look sobbed and sagged against the man on his right, who put an arm around him.

Dolly Richards stood next to his horse near the prisoners. As soon as the last man had drawn from the ranger's hat, Richards called out, "Every man who has a blank piece of paper step back two steps." Some men looked for the first time at the papers they had drawn. The man who was holding his trembling comrade let go slowly, then kissed his friend on the cheek. He held his hand on the other man's shoulder as he drew back, then let his arm fall.

One of the remaining seven was a boy about fourteen years old who sobbed and buried his face in the chest of a red-bearded man. The man held his arm around the boy's shoulder and hugged him close. He looked up at Dolly Richards and said, "He ain't nothing but the drummer boy."

Richards turned toward Mosby.

"Draw another one. I want seven," Mosby said.

Richards pulled a piece of paper out of his pocket and began to tear it into twenty pieces. "Come here, Powell," he called. He marked an X on one piece of paper and dropped them all into Lewis's hat.

Lewis passed the red-bearded man, the boy, and the other five hollow-eyed men, and walked to the line of twenty, who had, without a command, come to rigid attention behind their seven comrades. The first man in the line spoke to him. "Cold day, Johnny—but we've got it colder in Wisconsin." Lewis looked at the man's faint smile of recognition and hesitated before holding the hat toward him. The yellow moustache, the scar on the cheek—it was the man from Wisconsin who had shared his stew with him nearly a year before. Still looking at Lewis, he took a piece of paper from the hat without glancing at it. Lewis pulled his eyes away and continued down the line.

When Lewis had finished, Richards cleared his throat and commanded, "Whoever's got the paper with an X on it, step up here."

For the second time, every man looked at the paper in his hand. Lewis tightened his lips and caught his breath when he saw the Wisconsin man step forward and lay his hand on the drummer boy's shoulder. The drummer boy laughed and skipped toward the rank of the men who would live another day. "Did you see that?" he crowed. "Ha! ha! I don't have to go!" Someone slapped him hard in the face and clapped a hand over his mouth.

Richards turned toward Mosby and saluted. Mosby was silent for a full minute. Then he said, "Dolly, you know what to do. Take them as close to Custer's headquarters as you can get." He turned his horse slowly and rode to the edge of the square. The line of farmers parted to let him by. "Good day's work, Colonel," somebody called to him. Mosby did not reply but rode along the rutted street without turning his head.

A wiry, bronzed lieutenant rode toward Richards. "Captain," he said, "I would sure love to lead this detail."

"Puryear," Richards said, "few of us have got any stomach for this business. But there's nobody else that has felt a Yankee noose around his neck and come back to tell about it, like you have. And I know I can count on you to get right under George Custer's crupper. Form a squadron of volunteers and take them to Winchester."

Puryear grinned. "Thank you, Captain." He saluted, and Dolly Richards touched the brim of his hat.

The rangers were scattered around the square, some slouching in their saddles, others standing beside their mounts, talking in low tones. Puryear called for volunteers and several men came toward him.

152

While the officers were talking, Lewis took a pile of blankets from a cart full of confiscated clothing and weapons and went over to the seven condemned men.

"Powell!" Puryear yelled. "You damn Yankee-lover! What the hell do you think you're doing?"

"They're cold, Lieutenant," Lewis told him. He set his feet and faced Puryear, who turned away, sneering.

"The devil will make it hot enough in hell for them by tomorrow dawn. But I'll take you with me so you can lug the blankets back." He turned to the twenty-odd men who had volunteered. "Prepare to mount!"

Lewis took the reins of his horse from Cab Maddux and led the horse to the squadron. He watched as the seven condemned men mounted, their hands tied in front of them. Then Puryear commanded his squadron to mount. "Powell," he said, "I want you in the rear."

With three riders on either flank of the prisoners, the squadron rode slowly out of Rectortown.

They waited all day at a farm outside of Rectortown, and Lewis did not go near the solitary circle of prisoners. After dark, they rode for two hours, with vedettes ahead of them. Lewis could not see the Wisconsin man, who was near the middle of the column. He was surprised to realize that he wanted the man to escape. Several times the column had to narrow to double file to cross bridges, and Lewis thought a prisoner could make a run for it when they were at the far end of a bridge. He was not sure that he would try anything like that himself because he knew how good a shot Puryear was.

· Suddenly, muffled shouts and gunfire came from the front. Puryear rode back. He told the rear guard, "Damn prisoner broke through and got away. We shot, but I don't think we hit him. My vedettes say there's Yanks camped about five mile ahead, so we have got to hang them here."

They rode into a field where a single lantern glowed. Lewis moved forward and saw that the Wisconsin man was still among the prisoners, who were in a cluster surrounded by rangers with drawn pistols.

Puryear was tying a hangman's noose. "All right, who goes first?" he called. "Here, Daniels, throw the end of the rope over yonder limb."

While Puryear tied the free end of the rope to the tree trunk, two rangers came forward, leading a horse and rider between them. The rider reeled in the saddle like a drunk man, and the rangers took hold of either arm. They blindfolded him, and Puryear edged his own horse to where he could drop the noose over his head. Puryear backed up to strike the horse on the crupper with a coil of rope. The horse jerked forward, leaving the rider kicking and grunting in the air. His body kept twitching even when his legs no longer kicked for support. Lewis stared, and his hand came up to rub his own large neck. Behind him a ranger vomited. They waited a long time for the man to die. No one spoke, but finally Puryear jerked the rope loose from the tree, and the body dropped like a hog carcass.

Two rangers led the red-bearded man forward. He shrugged their hands away and rode in front of Puryear. He spat. "Tell Mosby," he said, "that my death is on his conscience. I was not in Custer's command when his men were hanged, and I had nothing to do with it."

"I'll tell him," Puryear said. "Hold him, boys." The man sat erect as Puryear fixed the noose around his neck. Then, with a whoop, Puryear smacked the horse on the rump. He leaned on his saddle horn watching as the red-bearded man kicked against the air.

The Wisconsin man cursed when a ranger took hold of his horse's reins. The horse jerked toward the ranger, and the Wisconsin man struck out with his tied hands in one fist, knocking the ranger off balance. Two others grabbed him and his horse, hauling the cursing man toward the hanging tree.

"Hurry up," Puryear snapped. "This is taking all night." He threw the noose onto the man's neck. "Powell, come here," he said.

Lewis walked his horse to Puryear. The lieutenant looked at him, his eyes glowing in the light of the lantern. He held the coiled rope toward him. "I want to see if a Yankee-lover can use this."

Lewis looked at the sneer on the lieutenant's face, then took the rope. Lewis raised his arm, and releasing pent-up rage at the tedious years of the war, at Puryear's insolence, at the idiocy of Riley Green's death, and at this man come from Wisconsin to lay waste the fields of Virginia, he struck and shouted. The man from Wisconsin thrashed at the space under him, while Lewis slung the used coil at Puryear.

"Let's get this over with!" Lewis shouted, drawing his revolver. Nobody prevented him as he rode at the three surviving prisoners and emptied the revolver at them. One horse bolted with his rider, but the other two men tumbled from their saddles and thudded to the ground. Lewis dropped the pistol back into its holster and looked around at the silent circle of rangers.

"Let's get out of here," Puryear said, as quietly as if he were ending a funeral. "Let that other one go."

Lewis swore to himself that day that he would kill John Puryear. It was not until New Year's Day that he had his chance.

Colonel Mosby had been wounded five days before Christmas in a shoot-out. The rangers did not know if Mosby would live or die, and he had been taken to his mother's house in Lynchburg. Since then, nobody had been able to control John Puryear and those like him.

On New Year's Day, a Federal division was leaving Warrenton, heading back to Washington City, and the rangers were attacking units separated from the main body. That morning, Lewis and Cab Maddux came upon three straggling cavalrymen, whom they disarmed and took prisoner. They made the prisoners ride ahead of them and had set out toward Warrenton when they heard gunfire from the right, beyond a patch of woods.

"Doc," Cab said, "you take these prisoners on to town and leave them while I go see if our boys need some help over yonder. Come on when you can." He spurred his horse off the road and into the woods.

Lewis ordered the prisoners to dismount and hobble their horses while he rested his shotgun on his saddle horn. Then he told the prisoners to remount, and they rode into the deserted, shuttered town.

In front of a store sat a green recruit named Murray standing guard over two other prisoners.

"Murray," Lewis told him, "I've got to go back and help Cab. Look after these here prisoners for me."

"Sure, Powell." Murray gestured with his shotgun for the three prisoners to dismount, and they sat on the ground with Murray's prisoners.

Lewis rode back along the street and turned onto the road leading out of Warrenton. He had reached the lane when he heard shots being fired in the town. Turning, he saw Murray riding toward him, hatless and out of breath.

"Powell! You've got to come back," he yelled. "Puryear and a civilian have taken our prisoners. I've got to have your help."

Lewis spurred his horse hard and galloped with Murray back to the town. As he turned into the street where he had left his prisoners, he saw a body on the ground and two men on horseback. One was John Puryear, wearing a hat like Mosby's and a cape, and the other a bareheaded civilian, reloading a shotgun.

Lewis rode toward them, his revolver in his hand. "Hold it there!" he shouted at the civilian. "What are you doing? Those are my prisoners!"

The startled man looked back at Lewis. He let the shotgun fall to the ground.

Puryear's hand was already on the butt of his revolver when Lewis leveled his gun at him. "Stop right there, Puryear," he warned.

Puryear's voice was calm. "Powell, Mr. Keith has got good reason to shoot these here Yanks. They burned his house and insulted his wife and mother. Leave him be."

"I don't care what they done. I've got good reason to shoot Mr. Keith for killing my prisoner." Lewis glanced at Murray, who sat on his horse watching them, his face pale and eyes wide. The two survivors among Lewis's prisoners stood by their horses, uncertain and scared. Apart from them stood Murray's two prisoners.

"Puryear," Lewis said, "maybe I can't defend all the prisoners, but you are not going to shoot the ones that I took. Maybe you ain't gentleman enough not to kill a prisoner, but I'll keep my word and take these two Yanks to the regiment. Now I have taken all I'm going to take off you, and if you make a move to shoot these men—either you or Mr. Keith here—I'll lay both of you in the road with a hole right through you."

Puryear, his lips tight and his eyes narrow, slowly lifted his hand from the gun and set it on top of his left hand on the saddle horn. When Lewis looked at Keith, the man's head was lifted high and he returned Lewis's glare.

"Boys," Lewis said to the two prisoners who stood by their horses, "mount and cut off the street and take the road out of town. I'll be right behind you." He set his revolver back into its holster and swung his shotgun across the front of his saddle, leveling it at Puryear.

The hate in Puryear's eyes met and mingled with the hate in Lewis's. "Powell," he said, "the next time we meet, you be ready to shoot."

Lewis backed his horse a few paces along the street, the shotgun still pointed at the lieutenant. Then he cut his horse between two buildings and rode onto the pike toward his prisoners. He thought he heard a shot behind him, but he was not sure.

At Grandville that night, Lewis found Johnnie Munson waiting. "Doc," he said, "I came here to warn you. Puryear aims to kill you. He is going to come looking for you, to arrest you for drawing down on an officer, but he plans to shoot you and say you were trying to get away."

"He missed a good chance today in Warrenton."

"Doc, I don't see why you done it to start with. You can't point a gun at Puryear and get away with it."

"Johnnie, I couldn't let him kill my prisoners."

"Here's some grub I got out of Mr. Payne's kitchen. Don't go in, so Mrs. Payne and the boys will not have to tell Puryear they have seen you."

Lewis looked toward the house, then took the bag that Johnnie handed him. "Thanks, Johnnie. I won't forget what you done for me." He clapped Johnnie on the shoulder and got back on his horse. "I'm not afraid of Puryear, Johnnie. But I am tired of shooting and being shot at."

"Where are you going?"

"Baltimore. I know some ladies there. Maybe get me a job."

"We have had some good times together, Doc."

"Sure have, Johnnie. Take care of yourself."

"You, too, Doc."

Lewis rode to Warrenton, following every obscure trail that he knew and stopping often to listen in the windy night for hoofbeats or for the clank of metal on metal. It was snowing when he came to the churchyard, dismounted at the gate, and peered into the gloom of the graveyard. He could see only the nearest gravestones, with snow falling on them, and he thought of Clara Meredith lying under the frozen ground, her brown hair in braids falling over her slim shoulders. *This land is not my home.*

Mounting, he unbuckled his shotgun and dropped it to the ground. He took out his Colt revolvers and let them fall. Then he rode onto the Warrenton Pike. "Are you out there, Puryear?" he called. "Here I am—in the pike." Only the wind answered.

The next day at Alexandria, Lewis went to the Federal provost marshal's office. A soldier took his horse, and he never saw it again. He had to wait all day in a room with three bearded, hungry Rebel soldiers in faded homespun shirts and blue Federal breeches. Two of them slept, while the third swayed back and forth and moaned.

Finally a lieutenant called Lewis into a bare little room furnished with only a table and one chair. Lewis stood in front of the officer.

"Name?" the officer asked.

Thou art Paine.

"Lewis," he answered. "Uh—Lewis Paine."

Something fell to the floor in a nearby room, and a man said, "Damn it."

Lewis told the officer that he was in the Second Florida, and he made up a story about the whereabouts of the brigade. The officer sent him back to the big room, and after that two guards escorted him to a damp stone cell.

Other men would stay in the cell for a day, or two days, and go away. Sometimes there would be as many as six men in the cold cell, where they ate dry, moldy bread or watery oat mush. Two weeks limped by before a guard called him. "Paine!" Lewis had forgotten he had given that name, but then he remembered and followed the guard.

Near the front door of the building a sergeant showed a paper to Lewis. "This here is a parole," the sergeant said. "Are you Lewis Paine?"

Lewis said that he was.

"Raise your right hand."

Lewis raised his hand.

"Do you swear allegiance to the United States of America and swear that you will not again take arms against the Union?"

"Yes."

"Sign here."

Lewis wrote "L. Paine" at the bottom of the paper. It was Friday the thirteenth, and he wondered what Mary Surratt would say if she knew.

13

BALTIMORE
FEBRUARY–MARCH 1865

MAGGIE BRANSON PUT the ledger in the top drawer of her writing desk and eased the drawer shut. She locked the drawer with a key on a large ring, then hung the ring on a hook above her bed. Turning down the flame of the lamp on the center table, she noticed that Annie had neglected to trim the wick or clean the chimney again, and she told herself to speak to her once more about it. Perhaps it was time to let her go.

Maggie gathered her skirt forward and sat in her armchair. Closing her eyes, she rubbed her hands over her temples and sighed. Caesar leaped into her lap and mewed, treading his feet against her thighs. As she stroked him, he lay across her lap and began to purr.

The clock struck nine, but she did not stir. Mary was seldom this late. Their mother had already retired for the night, complaining of a headache. She found some excuse nearly every evening to avoid spending time with Lewis. Sometimes Maggie wished he had never come back. In the month that he had been staying at the house, her mother had never ceased to find fault with him. Not that she ever let on to Lewis himself or to anybody else but her daughters, but she never let a day go by without commenting to Maggie about his "commonness," or his heavy tread, or her uneasiness at having a former member of Gilmor's and Mosby's rangers at her house. "You know very well," she said once, pursing her lips, "that no matter how much we may think of those men as patriots, a lot of people think of them as little better than bandits. And we can have trouble here if some of the boarders tell the military authorities about him."

"But Mother," Maggie reminded her, "he *has* taken an oath and surrendered."

"It's all a trick, you mark my words. He could have been sent here by that Gilmor himself to spy out this town and help him to raid it."

"Mother, Colonel Gilmor was captured last week. His raiding days are over."

"Well, whatever is afoot, I want us to keep clear of it. Some of the boarders have been whispering already about the packages you and Mary have been sending to the Rebel prisoners."

"You know we have permission to do that. And who can find fault with us for sending a little flour and medicine and blankets to those wretched boys? The winter has been dreadful at Point Lookout, and even worse in New York and Ohio, and they need all the help that we can give them. Why, you have even sent some food yourself. Mother, nobody wants this dreadful war to cease more than I do, and sometimes I am so angry with these men and their killing that I could cry. But that doesn't mean that it's not our duty to help ease the suffering of the wounded and the sick."

"It's our duty, Maggie, right enough, but that does not mean we have got to bring them into our home."

There was more that Maggie might have said, but she did not say it because it had to do with what she had seen and where she had been, and she knew there was no way that she could make others see it as she had. She had smelled death at Camp Letterman in Gettysburg, and she had seen many a feverish, thrashing boy clutching at the empty spaces where an arm or a leg had been, an arm that would not lift an ox yoke or hold a girl again, or a leg that would never again take him running across a meadow, and she had known many a boy to smile at her and talk about his farm in Ohio or Alabama, then turn his face to the wall and lapse into the great silence, still holding her hand. These things had changed her forever. One day she had realized what it meant. For her there were no walls. The walls that divided North from South, men from men, free men from slaves, even the dead from the living, had crumbled under the weight of the deaths she had witnessed and even abetted. She lived in a city of Rebel sympathizers occupied by Federal troops, but these absurd distinctions of allegiance to men and laws in Richmond or in Washington meant nothing to her. She knew now that the Confederacy would lose, that the poor, ragged armies would leave their tattered flags in the dust of a Northern victory and limp back to their wives, their sweethearts, their farms and bleak futures and somehow start again. This is what men and women had always done after wars and would always do. There could have been for her no exultation of victory or even the unimportant chagrin of defeated honor. It was all defeat, all pathetic death under a lowering sky or in the heat of a hospital tent. There were no walls, and her house had no walls that would shut out the war's sorrow.

She heard the front door open to Lewis's heavy tread and Mary's quick steps. They stopped in the hall and said a few words to each other before Mary went to her room and Lewis went up the two flights of stairs to his garret. Waiting for her sister, Maggie dozed. She sank into a rhythmic softness measured by the ticking clock and the purring cat. Then she woke to Mary's tapping on her door.

"Come in," she said.

Mary opened the door and stepped into the room. She had changed to her nightgown and robe, but her hair was still pinned.

"I was afraid that you had gone to sleep."

"No, I was waiting for you. I finished the accounts and sat down to think about things."

"What things?"

"Oh, Mother and you and Lewis and the coal bill, and all sorts of things. Where did you go tonight?"

"Unpin my hair and I'll tell you." Mary knelt next to Maggie's armchair and handed Maggie a hairbrush. Maggie pulled the pins from her sister's brown hair and watched it fall over her shoulders. Maggie loved the silken fullness of her sister's hair, as abundant as when she had been a child and lacking the coarseness of her own, which, though she was only thirty-three, was already showing strands of gray. She slowly brushed Mary's hair and listened to her talk, in words as flowing as her hair, full of the joy and spirit that had always pleased Maggie.

"We went to Mrs. Heim's again tonight. Mr. Heim is in Philadelphia on business again, but Mrs. Heim and Edward and William were there. Edward is teaching Doc to play chess, and he says Doc is getting to be good at it. William is so funny. He has pictures of General Lee and General Jeb Stuart in his room, and he always tries to get Doc to talk about the war and the fighting. He tells his mother he wants to join the army and fight."

Maggie shook her head. "Just like a twelve-year-old boy. But there are wretched children in the army not much older than that. Does Doc tell him about the fighting?"

"Not much." Mary stood and walked to the fire, where she poured a few lumps of coal from the bucket and rested her forearm on the mantel. She stared at the flames, her back toward Maggie. "He doesn't like to talk about it. Sometimes he is so silent and brooding that I think he must be seeing the horrors of Chancellorsville and Manassas and Sharpsburg and Gettysburg all over again. I've not forgotten what you told me about him running mad at Gettysburg when the man was selling battlefield souvenirs, and, Maggie, sometimes I fear that I will see that again. I'm almost afraid to look into his eyes.

"But, praise God, I didn't see that look tonight. Just the sweetness, the goodness that he shows when he is at his best. Do you remember when he sang for us last week in the parlor? That Baptist hymn that he used to sing in Florida, 'This land is not for me.' I cried when he sang it, and I cry again whenever I think about it. His home is so far away, and I am thankful that we can make a home here for him, a sanctuary."

She sat on a stool next to Maggie's chair, and Maggie brushed her hair again.

"Maggie, did you know that Doc has been reading Father's old medical books? He wants an education, and he is ashamed that he lacks schooling. He talks often about a surgeon who was at Gettysburg when he was there."

"Dr. Smiley?"

"Yes, that's the one. Doc worked under him, and he says that he wants to be like him, to heal people."

Mary turned. "Maggie, do you know who Doc reminds me of? Enoch Arden, that's who, in Lord Tennyson's poem. I even thought of Doc when I read the poem for the first time, last year. I hadn't met him but one time, but he seemed to be to be what Enoch was—strong and adventurous and homeless."

"Enoch had a home, but he left it, and he was marked for sorrow and death." She handed the hairbrush to Mary. "Mary, Annie in the poem chose wrong, and her best life was with the one that she married at the last, Philip Ray."

Mary stared again into the fire, as if looking there for the words to answer her sister. "But she loved Enoch," she said slowly.

Maggie lifted Caesar from her lap and set him on the floor. Reaching down for her sewing basket, she drew out a folded blouse and laid it in her lap. Then she began to thread a needle, holding the thread and needle high against the light of the lamp and squinting.

"Henry Shriver loves you, Mary," she said, pulling the thread through the eye of the needle. "I can tell by the look on his face when you come into the room. He has a good job with the steamship company, and he is going to make a good living."

Mary uttered a trilling, sad laugh. "Oh, Maggie, you know what I think of Henry. A dull, safe little man. Well, go on, say it. I know you're thinking it. I am ten years older than Doc."

Maggie bit the thread. "I was not thinking such a thing. You said it. I didn't."

Mary got up and went to the fireplace again. She stared at the fire, then turned toward Maggie, her hands clasped behind her. "Maggie, who is John Wilkes Booth? I heard Doc and Charles Heim talking about him. Charles was so excited when he found out that Doc knew him. Doc told me he's a player. It made Doc feel important to tell Charles that he has been to the theater and knows some of the players. Charles said he was going to come—he and Ed Blair—and take Doc to the theater some evening."

"Yes, I remember John Wilkes Booth. His father and his brothers are a famous acting family, and they live somewhere near Baltimore. I saw him play Richard III two years ago, and I fell in love with him that night, like every other woman in the audience. I came home and read the play and memorized some lines. But I had no idea that Doc knew him. Where did he say that Mr. Booth is now?"

"He didn't say, but I think that he saw him in Washington City earlier in the war."

Maggie began to stitch a seam in the sleeve of the blouse. "I need for you to do something for me tomorrow. Lucy quit work today, and that means we need another servant to take care of the upstairs rooms. I need for you to go over to Oldtown in the morning before church if the weather is fair and ask around for somebody to hire for domestic help. If you find anybody, tell them to come here and talk to me. Perhaps Henry Shriver will go with you. I'll ask him at breakfast."

"I'll ask Doc. He will be better company."

"As you will. Mr. Barnett is going to walk to church with me, and we will join you there."

Mary went to the door and opened it. She stood in the half-open door, a figure of light against the darkness of the hallway, and turned back toward Maggie. "Don't fret about me, Maggie. You can be sure that I know what is best for me."

"I wish I *could* be sure."

"Yes, you can. And I will hold on to what I want, even—even if it is something that you want, too."

Maggie looked up suddenly—too suddenly, she later thought— to glimpse the smile that Mary showed her before pulling the door shut behind her.

The sky was overcast on Sunday morning, but there was no rain or snow. Walking along Fayette Street with Charles Barnett, Maggie stifled a sigh as she listened to him say over and over, "It don't look good, Miss Maggie, it don't look good." While he recited the woes of the Confederacy and moaned, "I am afeared the Confederacy will soon have to admit defeat," she could not put out of her thoughts the recollection that he owned a thousand dollars worth of Confederate bonds. Charles Barnett walked slowly, as if to a dirge, his hands behind his back and his eyes drooping toward the sidewalk. Maggie slackened her pace to his and quit listening to what he was saying.

In order to stay on the broad sidewalk, they went all the way to Calvert before turning to go up to St. Paul's Church. At the corner, Maggie, looking across the street toward Barnum's Hotel, saw Lewis and Mary.

"Oh," she said, puzzled. "There are Mary and Lewis now. They didn't go to Oldtown after all. Let's go see what kept them from doing what I had counted on her to do."

"Where are they?" Charles Barnett asked. "Oh, I see them now. That big Paine fellow would stand out in any crowd."

They waited for a tram to pass and started across the wide street. Lewis and Mary, in conversation with a gentleman of medium height attired in a black frock coat and gray trousers, did not seen to notice Maggie and Barnett coming toward them. When the stranger gestured toward them, Lewis looked around and said, "Miss Maggie! Barnett! Here is an old friend we met up with as we was going by. Captain Booth, this here is Miss Maggie Branson and Mr. Charles Barnett. What do you know? I never would have expected to run into John Wilkes Booth here, when the last I seen of him was in Washington City."

"Is it Mr. John Wilkes Booth then?" Charles Barnett asked. He pumped Booth's hand. "I'm mighty proud to meet you, sir, mighty proud. This is a distinct honor. I have seen you on stage, sir, and admired your acting ability."

"Indeed it is a pleasure to meet you all," Booth declared, bestowing on Maggie, Mary, and Charles Barnett the eye of a player surveying his audience. "Paine, how favorable blow the winds that bring you such friends, especially ladies of such grace and loveliness."

"Will you be staying in Baltimore long, Mr. Booth?" Maggie asked.

"No, Miss Branson, pressing matters beckon me to other climes. Would, though, that I might linger in this beloved city, blessed with such beauty as yours and your sister's, but alas, fate will have it otherwise. Even now an appointment draws me away against my will. But, Paine, my young warrior, if you still might be interested in that venture in the oil business that I broached to you once, come back to see me tonight here at Barnum's, and we will have further words on the matter."

"Why, yes, Captain," Lewis said. "I think I would like to talk about that business."

"Splendid. Agreed, then. Tonight at eight. Adieu, ladies. Gentlemen." Both took off his hat and bowed. A hansom cab was parked in front of the hotel, and Booth stepped into it, with a word to the driver.

As the four of them walked up Calvert Street, Charles Barnett began a tedious story about Booth's performances, then remembered that it was his brother, Edwin Booth, whom he had seen. Maggie walked in silence, hearing little of it. There was something haunting and troubling about Booth's eyes, and she shuddered a little even now to think of the steady penetration of his gaze, which awakened a response from the one toward whom it was directed without imparting anything of the one from whom it came. She felt under a spell that might have been a threat to her, yet which she saw little reason to try to escape. Words rose to the surface of her memory, words that she had lodged there long ago, spoken by Queen Margaret about Shakespeare's twisted villain who had waded through slaughter to seize a kingdom:

> Sin, death, and hell have set their marks on him,
> And all their ministers attend on him.

In the church, the full diapason of the organ endeavored to overwhelm those thoughts, but they would not recede. When she knelt, she prayed for protection, but she was not sure for whom she asked it.

"Oh, how grand!" said Mrs. Branson. "My gardenia has some buds." Maggie looked up as her mother bent over the plant, poured water from the little can, and then shifted the flowerpot into the square of morning sun that lay on the brown planks of the kitchen table.

"Maybe we will have an early spring," Maggie said. "Yesterday I saw a lilac bush getting ready to bloom."

Mrs. Branson arched herself backward and rubbed the small of her back. "And how I will welcome spring!" she said. "My rheumatism gets worse every winter, and spring always helps me get over it. What is the day?" She went closer to the clock hanging on the wall and squinted at the circle where the number of the day nestled among pink and white clouds. "March tenth. This is the first day we have seen the sun all month, and I feel like having Daniel spade the garden for me. I will be seeing to that Annie, for I don't think she's doing the rooms proper. Mary, call me before you go to market. I want to look your list over." She left the room, and Maggie and Mary listened to her heavy tread on the stairs.

Mary closed the door. "Maggie," she said, "before Mother interrupted, you asked about Doc," she said. "Doc has not told me anything about where he is going, and I lack the right to insist on knowing. I am fairly sure that he spends time with that player, but that is all I know. I even told him that he is welcome to bring him here, but he says that Mr. Booth—Captain Booth, he calls him—is too busy with other things. He is even mysterious about it. Yesterday he said that it is better for me not to know where he is going, but that it is something important that I will know about someday."

Maggie went to the stove and lifted the lid on the soup pot. She stirred the soup, then sipped it from the spoon. "Joe Thomas says that Mr. Booth is in the oil business. Is he dragging Doc into some kind of get-rich-quick scheme?"

"I don't know. Do you recollect the time he was gone all night, about the end of February? Well, Henry Shriver found out that Doc had gone to Washington City. When I asked him—Doc, I mean—he said that he couldn't tell me, but that it was an important business trip." She picked up a poker, opened the shiny tin-covered fuel door, and stirred the coals. "Another thing is his name. You've known him as Powell since you were at Gettysburg, but he insists on being 'Paine' to everybody else."

"Mary, as much as I hate to admit it, I'm afraid that Mother is right. Doc's hiding something. He seems confused, but it's more than that. He—" She broke off as the cook came into the kitchen carrying a basket of potatoes. Maggie stood. "Well, you had better get on with your marketing while I go down to the pantry and finish that inventory I started yesterday. I'm afraid that the grocer has been sending us a short measure."

Mary left the room, and Maggie crossed the kitchen to the stairs leading down to the pantry. She picked up a lamp at the top of the stairs and lit it, holding it ahead of her as she descended the narrow stairway. At the bottom of the stairs, the hem of her skirt snagged on a nail, and the board of the last step slipped. Another repair that she would have to see about. Since Rufus had become too old to work and Daniel had taken his place, things were not as well cared for. Her father had trained Rufus himself, and the old Negro had been dependable. Now her father had been dead—how long?—seven years, and Rufus, feeble now, sat mumbling by the fire in the little cabin in Oldtown.

Maggie lifted the ring of keys that she carried at her waist and fitted one into the lock of the pantry door. She pushed the door open and set her lamp on a shelf. The pantry harbored spice, ham, and vegetable odors that had long ago given up their freshness. This pantry had always been a favorite place for her. A child of five when her family moved to Eutaw Street, she had even then preferred to be alone. Their father had sealed off the pantry by building a solid wall of oak boards between it and the tool room. Maggie had discovered the place right away, a place where she could come with her dolls and whisper to them while listening secretly to the life around her: to footsteps in the kitchen above, to workmen going and coming in the tool room— their laughter, their coarse jokes, their gossip. The pantry had been her best schoolroom.

Maggie picked up the ledger and took it to the shelves on the right, where she had left off the day before. She had mounted the stepladder to count some crocks on the top shelf when she heard the door open to the tool room. Men's boots sounded there, and the door was pulled shut.

"We can talk in here," came a voice. She recognized it right away as Lewis Powell's.

"What are you bein' so hush-hush about, Paine?" another man asked, in the nasal tones of Joe Thomas, one of the boarders. Joe was a carpenter, a lanky, muscular man who had been told so many times that he looked like Abe Lincoln that he would sometimes put on false whiskers and entertain the other boarders in the evenings by making ridiculous political speeches and singing humorous songs. There was no malice in Joe, the kind of man who seemed to be happiest when he was making other people laugh. He played a banjo, and when he was in a serious mood, he would lead the boarders in singing.

"Joe," Lewis said, "I told Captain Booth about you, and he wants to talk to you hisself. He says we got about eight fellows together already, and he wants to ask you about throwing in with us. You recollect when I went to Washington City about ten days ago? Well, Captain Booth had been planning to snatch old Abe on the day of the inauguration, but he changed his mind, and I had to go to tell a fellow named John Surratt that it was off. Now Captain Booth has got another plan, and he needs strong backs for it. You see, old Abe likes to go to the theater, and Captain Booth expects about next week he will be at Ford's. So what he means to do is to cut off all the lights, then while everybody's running around scared and confused, me and him will grab old Abe out of his box, lower him to the stage with a rope, and be out the door before anybody can figure out what is going on. That's where you come in. You look so much like Lincoln that he wants to put you where you can get folks even more confused."

There was silence, then feet shuffling.

Finally Joe spoke. "I don't know, Paine. Sounds kind of risky to me. I ain't so sure it's going to work."

"You don't have to decide right now, Joe. At least just say you will go with me to Barnum's tonight and talk to Captain Booth. Then you can hear what he has to say."

"Well, Paine, I reckon I could do that. Tonight? Yep, I reckon I could go listen to him. But don't count on me for sure. I ain't saying nothing yet."

"Sure, Joe, I know. But don't tell nobody what we been talking about, because if you do, our goose is cooked. I wouldn't have told you if I didn't think I could trust you."

"You can trust me, Paine, that's for sure."

"Good."

"Well, Paine, I got to go now. I got a job to get to."

As she listened, Maggie had eased herself down the ladder and sunk onto the straight-backed chair that stood by the table. Now, as the door closed behind Lewis and Joe, she sat stiffly, gazing at a dim corner of the pantry. She knew a dangerous serpent lay coiled just beyond her reach. The plot that Lewis had told Joe about was so absurd that she did not see how grown men could believe in it. Yet evidently they did believe in it and intended to act on it. And it was all being talked about here, in her house. Why, it meant danger for them all— for Mary, for herself, for their mother, not to mention for poor Joe Thomas, as harmless a creature as there ever was. She might simply confront Lewis with what she had heard, but she was afraid. She had seen him lose all self-control at Gettysburg and attack that frightened vendor, and she did not have any idea of what he would do if she tried to defy him. Even if he did not lose his temper, she was not sure that he would withdraw from the plot. And it was out of the question to inform the military authorities. She did not want to bring on the very troubles she sought to avoid.

Maggie picked up the lamp and left the pantry, pulling the door shut behind her and locking it. She was setting her foot on the lowest step to go upstairs when a piercing scream resounded through the house. A man shouted and footsteps moved heavily, hurriedly, above her. Maggie ran up to the kitchen. The cook was not there. Crossing the kitchen to the hallway, Maggie heard a woman screaming, "Stop! Help me somebody!" The cook was standing at the foot of the stairs, hesitant, when Maggie passed her and ran up to the first landing. Annie, the maid, was scrambling down the steps, while Lewis rumbled behind her. "Damn nigger! I'll kill you! I'll kill you!" Maggie flattened herself against the wall, grabbed the hysterical girl by the arm, and drew her below on the steps, where Annie crouched, peering around her and pleading, "Oh, don't let him get me, Miss Maggie! Help me!"

"Stop right there, Doc!" Maggie commanded him. "I won't let you hit this girl again." Annie huddled against Maggie, blood trickling from her lip.

Lewis stopped and looked down at her. "I couldn't help it, Miss Maggie. When I come in and told her to clean up my room, she acted smart and called me a damn Rebel and said she wouldn't do anything I said. So I hauled off and hit her."

Before Maggie could answer him, she was distracted by the sound of heavy footsteps in the downstairs hall. She looked down to see two soldiers starting up the steps. Annie pulled away from her and tumbled down the steps toward the soldiers shouting, "That's him! That's the man that beat me up. Don't let him get at me again!"

"Annie! Hush! Let me handle this," Maggie ordered her.

"No ma'am," one of them, a sergeant, said. "We'll take care of it." He walked warily toward Lewis. "You better come with us."

Lewis stood, subdued and sullen, glaring at the soldiers.

"Sergeant," Maggie said, "we'll take care of this right here in this house if you'll let us alone."

"No chance of that, ma'am. Somebody come running out and called us in and said that this here woman was getting beat up, and now she tells us the same thing. So he can do his explaining to the provost marshal. Come on with us, you."

Lewis said nothing but twisted between Maggie and the sergeant, then clumped down the stairs with the soldiers behind him and Annie staring warily at him from a corner of the downstairs hall.

The sergeant turned to Annie. "You come on down to the marshal's office in an hour to give us a statement. Good day, ma'am," he said to Maggie.

Maggie followed them to the bottom of the stairs and watched as they closed the front door behind them. She looked back at Annie, who had fallen sobbing into the cook's arms. Maggie thought suddenly of her mother, and turned to go upstairs to look for her. Just then, her mother appeared on the stairs, her hand clutched at her throat and her face pale.

"Is it over?" she asked. "Have they gone?"

"Yes, Mother, come on to the parlor and sit down."

Maggie put her arms around her mother and led her to a chair in the parlor. The cook went back to the kitchen, and the rattling of pots and pans began again. Maggie listened to her mother hurling accusations against Lewis. All at once Annie stood in the door, glaring at them. Maggie looked into her eyes, braced for the accusation she knew was coming.

"I ain't staying in this house another day," the girl said. "Damn Rebels and Rebel sympathizers all over this house."

"Wait here, and I will bring your pay," Maggie said.

Two hours later, Mary returned and Maggie told her about the arrest.

"How dare they!" she cried. "Just for striking an insolent servant!" She threw her cape again around her shoulders. "I'm going to the marshal's office myself and make them let him go. They have no right."

"Mary, don't go," Maggie pleaded. "You won't do any good, and you will just add to their suspicion of us all."

"Suspicion of what, I'd like to know. I'm going, in spite of what you say."

"Well, you can't go alone."

"Henry will go with me." Mary went into the hall and called up the stairs, "Henry!" In a minute Henry Shriver came down the stairs, pulling on his coat. He looked helplessly at Maggie, then followed Mary out the front door.

It was midafternoon when Mary and Henry came back. "That smart-aleck Yankee, Lieutenant Smith!" she fumed. "He wouldn't let Doc go. Even tried to tell Henry that he shouldn't stay here with us Rebels. He must be afraid that Henry will be corrupted by our evil influence. Have you ever heard of such a thing? He asked me about Doc, but I told him that he had not been here before. If I had told him the truth, he would have sent Doc to one of those dreadful prison camps."

When she was alone again and her sister had gone to her room, Maggie felt relieved. Lewis was in Federal custody, and the military authorities did not know about the plot. As long as they held him, he would not involve Joe Thomas any further, and he could not meet with Booth. So, without her having to do anything, the matter had been settled to everyone's advantage. That night, Maggie went to bed feeling that the coiled serpent had been scotched, its head crushed.

The next morning she was in the parlor when the doorbell rang. Maggie answered the bell herself. Lewis stood in front of her between two private soldiers, each with a rifle slung on his shoulder.

"Morning, Miss Maggie," Lewis said. "I signed a parole, and they're letting me go. I came back to get my things from my room, and then I got to leave for New York. They told me they'd let me go if I'd stay north of Philadelphia."

He walked past her into the hall, while the soldiers waited outside. Maggie walked upstairs with him to the garret, but when Mary appeared, she left them alone. Then she went back to her desk until, about fifteen minutes later, Lewis came downstairs.

He stopped in the door of her room, twisting his black slouch hat in his hands. "You've been real good to me, Miss Maggie, and I'm real sorry about this trouble that I made for you all. Soon's the war is over, I mean to come back here. Me and Mary, we got plans."

Maggie went to the door. She took his right hand and held it in both of hers. "This is your second oath, Doc. Abide by it. Stay where the marshal told you to stay."

Lewis smiled wryly. "Why, Miss Maggie, it was Paine that signed that there oath. It's up to him to keep it. Mary, don't forget to send that wire for me."

Mary stood beside her as the soldiers walked Lewis to a supply wagon that was waiting outside. He heaved himself into the wagon, the soldiers behind him. Lewis waved once as they turned onto Fayette Street and moved toward the President Street Station.

14

WASHINGTON CITY
MARCH 1865

Washington City was dark when Lewis Powell walked out of the B. & 0. Station onto New Jersey Avenue. At the streetcar stop he set down his carpetbag, stretched, and yawned. Mary Branson had wired Booth just as he told her to do, and as a result he had spent only one night at the Revere House in New York before receiving Booth's wire on Sunday morning. Lewis pulled the tightly folded paper from his pocket and read it again. "Go right away to John S., who has work for you." The time had passed so quickly that twice he had to ask the conductor on the cars if this was really only Monday, the thirteenth day of March.

Lewis looked down at his gray pants, black frock coat, and black overcoat, then pressed the false moustache against his lip. Passing through Baltimore, especially during the tram ride from the President Street Station to Camden Street, had given him an anxious two hours, but now he was used to the disguise enough to enjoy the danger of it. This "Reverend Wood" identity had worked for him when he had come to Washington City in February, and Mary Surratt had gone along with it, apparently assuming that it had something to do with spy work for the Confederacy. If she had found out from John about their plans, she had not let on that she knew.

When he swung down from the streetcar at Sixth Street, hefting his carpetbag in front of him, Lewis was still heavy-headed from sleep, his mouth tasting like he had just chewed barnyard dirt. His head felt like a mule had kicked it.

At H Street, Lewis turned left to the Surratt boarding house. Light showed through the curtained parlor window as he rang the doorbell, and he heard somebody playing the piano. Was it Anna? No, she played more melody than that, with those fancy runs up and down the keyboard.

The brass door knocker in front of his eyes vanished and reappeared as a gas lamp on the street behind him reflected unsteadily against it. He lifted the knocker and rapped three times. He waited, listening to the methodical scales of the piano. Then he rapped again, three more times. This time the scales stopped, leaving only the wavering light on the brass to measure time.

A boarder who had been at the house in February opened the door. The man lowered his chin to stare at Lewis over thick eyeglasses, causing his chin to disappear and his face to bottom out in thick, hanging lips. He did not seem to recognize Lewis. "Yes?" he asked.

"I'm Reverend Wood," Lewis told him. "Remember me? I come here about two weeks ago to see Johnnie Surratt."

"Oh, yes." The boarder scanned from Lewis's slouch hat down to the scuffed boots, and his voice carried no note of welcome. "Well, come on in, then, uh, Reverend." He opened the door wider for Lewis to pass him into the hall, then pushed the door shut.

When the boarder went to the back of the house, Lewis walked into the parlor where three young women were playing a card game. The two girls who faced the door—one of them a thin, long-necked girl about Lewis's age with blonde hair that was almost white, the other a redhead about ten years old—looked at him with blank expressions, started to smile, then straightened their lips. Then they began to snicker, covering their mouths. The third woman turned around. A surprised Anna Surratt looked at him. Her eyes widened, and she too broke into a sudden giggle.

Feeling something brush his cheek, Lewis reached up and felt his false moustache askew. Fumbling, he pressed the moustache again into place on his upper lip. The girls gave up pretending to cover their amusement and swayed with laughter, Anna laughing the loudest.

Lewis had forgotten what he had meant to say. "I—I am—" he stammered, "Miss Surratt, I am Reverend Wood, and I come here to see your ma about a room." Just then, he heard something plop onto the floor, and he bent over to pick up the moustache. This mishap made the girls even merrier, and they fell against one another laughing. Anna wiped tears from her eyes while Lewis himself began to chuckle. He stuffed the moustache into the pocket of his coat, dropped his carpetbag, and slumped onto the piano stool, looking at the three girls and joining in the hilarity.

Anna Surratt sprang from her chair and ran out of the room, followed by the towheaded girl and then by the little red-haired one. They stopped in the hall, just out of sight of the doorway, and Lewis heard them choking and sputtering with laughter.

"It—it's so funny," said one voice.

"Th-that preacher won't con-convert many souls," giggled another.

Then he heard the footsteps going away along the hallway. He spun around on the piano stool and struck a few notes with his index finger.

Lewis heard a voice behind him. "Oh, it's you! If you have come here to see John, you will have to wait for him."

He turned to see Mary Surratt standing there in a dark purple dress with a lace collar, every strand of her dark hair neatly pinned in place, looking down at him with cold dignity and disapproval.

Lewis stood, ill at ease with her as he always was. "It's Reverend Wood, Miz Surratt." He gave a push to his voice as if to beg her to go along with the disguise for the sake of a venture that she might know of. "Captain Booth said that Johnnie—that Mr. Surratt would have a job for me."

He had used Booth's name without having intended to, but it worked with her like a password. Her features relaxed almost into a smile.

"Is Wilkes Booth coming here?" she asked.

"I don't know, ma'am. He just said that Johnnie would tell me about the job."

Anna Surratt came back into the room, followed by the boarder. She did not look at Lewis but set about gathering the cards scattered on the table. Lewis glanced at the contours of her waist and bust as she bent over the table.

175

"I can let you sleep with John," Mary Surratt told Lewis. "I don't know when he will be in. He went somewhere with David Herold and that man they call Port Tobacco." She turned to the boarder. "Mr. Weichmann, please show Reverend Wood to my son's room."

Anna, without looking again at Lewis, left the room.

"Don't mind the girls' silliness," Mary Surratt said. "Anna has so enjoyed having Nora Fitzpatrick here, after living so long in a house without any girls her own age. And little Apollonia Dean, the red-haired girl that you saw, is such a dear. We all adore her."

The boarder, Weichmann, was waiting for him by the door, but Lewis turned back toward the piano, ready to take advantage of Mary Surratt's unexpected warmth toward him. "Mrs. Surratt," he asked, "do you mind playing something on the piano, like you done when I was here last month? I would sure like to hear some music."

Mary Surratt looked hesitantly at the piano and reached up to smooth the bun of hair at the back of her neck.

"Yes, Mary," Weichmann said. "I would love to hear you play, too."

Lewis drew the stool from the piano, and Mary sat, striking a few soft chords that turned into the simple, sad tune of "Lorena." Lewis hummed until he came to a place where he could move his lips into the words and sing:

A hundred months 'twas flow'ry May
When up the hilly slope we climbed
To watch the dying of the day
And hear the distant church bells chime.

The singing calmed him, putting him at ease there, even among the three girls who had laughed at him and who were now coming back into the room to sing with him. Even the embarrassment of his absurd, transparent disguise ceased to matter as into that small circle Lewis blended memories of his mother and father, his sisters and brothers, of Mary Branson and Clara Meredith.

After that, Apollonia clamored for "My Old Kentucky Home" until Mary Surratt played it, and when Nora Fitzpatrick insisted on singing "The Bonnie Blue Flag," Anna Surratt teased her, saying that Southern songs like that would bring Union soldiers to arrest them all.

They were still singing when John Surratt came in. "You got here sooner than we thought you would," John told Lewis. "Come on to my room so we can talk."

Leaving the others singing around Mary's piano, Lewis picked up his carpetbag and followed John to his room. He dropped the bag onto a trunk in one corner and pulled off his coat while John lay on the bed.

"It won't be long now," John said. "Wilkes told me tonight that he expects Lincoln to go to see a play later this week, and then we'll get our chance to grab him."

"How many of us are in it?"

"Besides you and me and Wilkes, there's Davy Herold, and a German that I can't say his name, so we call him Port Tobacco, because that's where he's from. Davy calls him Plug Tobacco. And there's two fellows that went to school with Wilkes in Baltimore, name of Sam Arnold and Mike O'Laughlin."

"I can't wait to get going at it. I was getting tired of waiting when the Yanks run me out of Baltimore."

"Well, Wilkes will let us know in a day or two. On this coming Wednesday night I've got to escort Miss Fitzpatrick and the little Dean girl to Ford's Theater. You can go with us, and we will see Wilkes then."

"I don't like plays too much, unless it's something good like seeing Captain Booth, but I'll go." Lewis undressed, humming to himself the songs he had sung in the parlor. He went to sleep with "Lorena" and "My Old Kentucky Home" in his mind, and he did not know when John put out the light.

Ford's Theater was crowded on Wednesday night. Lewis followed John Surratt and the two girls up the curved staircase and along the back of the balcony to the boxes on the right, where Lewis had seen Seward more than a year before. John opened a narrow door and ushered the girls and Lewis into a passage leading to the boxes. They sat in the first box, the same one where the president usually sat, and Lewis began to look around, reviewing the plan to abduct Lincoln. Apollonia Dean chattered away, noticing everything about the audience, peering over the railing to see what the ladies were wearing and turning to ask questions of Nora Fitzpatrick, who kept telling her to be quiet and not be so inquisitive.

We could do it, Lewis thought. He shut his eyes tightly and imagined women screaming, himself and Booth stealing into the box through the door behind him. They would already have been waiting in the passage outside the box, and they would move swiftly. He would grab Lincoln while Booth wrapped a rope around him. Then he could lower old Abe to the stage while Booth jumped down to catch him. Lewis would then jump down and they would hustle their prisoner out the back stage door. They could be into the streets and outside the city before anybody would know what had happened. Lewis was confident that Booth would bring it off, and it was an honor to be offered the chance to play a part with him—like a supporting player on the stage, or a soldier on whom the outcome of a great battle depended.

Lewis was so lost in his thoughts that the fall of the curtain startled him. He had quit paying attention to the play, which was called *Jane Shore* and which he had expected to be about the seacoast. But instead it was about people in costumes from olden times, like in the days of Shakespeare, full of talk that he did not understand. So he was like a man in a trance until he heard John Wilkes Booth's voice behind him and turned to see the actor framed in the door of the box.

John Surratt introduced Booth to Nora Fitzpatrick and the Dean girl, and Booth bent to kiss the girls' hands.

"Welcome, ladies, to Ford's," he greeted them. "Is your box comfortable for you? Are you enjoying the play?"

They assured him that it was and they were.

"Pity that you missed the chance to see Mrs. Clarke in the title role. Moderately successful tonight, but that is all," he confided, drawing them all into the mysteries of the players' world.

Booth looked up at Lewis. "Ah, Reverend Wood. What a pleasure to see a man of the cloth grace this house of players with his presence. I trust that you are finding this evening morally edifying and instructive in every respect."

"It's been a worthwhile evening, Captain."

"Splendid, splendid. By the way, I am gathering several friends at a gentlemen's dinner tonight at Gautier's after the performance. I want to discuss a new venture in the oil business. Will you and Mr. Surratt join me there?"

"We'll be there, Wilkes," John Surratt told him.

Booth nodded and smiled. "Ladies, I bid you adieu." He backed out of the box, and Lewis watched him progress along the back of the balcony, stopping two or three times to exchange words with admirers.

Gautier's Restaurant on Pennsylvania Avenue overwhelmed Lewis with its splendor. John said Gautier, the owner, was the lost dauphin of France. Lewis could believe the story as he looked around him at luxury that would befit a palace. Sparkling chandeliers reflected lavender, blue, green, and gold; on the red wallpaper bloomed a garden of velvet flowers. Large-leafed plants and slender palms grew out of pots placed here and there. On the tables were spotless white cloths, set with gleaming ivory plates and gold knives, forks, and spoons. At the tables, engaged in serious conversation, sat gentlemen in elegant black evening suits; with them were beautiful women, their hair curled, wearing bare-shouldered dresses of blue or green or purple satin. Proud waiters passed back and forth, carrying trays loaded with steaming dishes.

When Lewis and John stood at the door, the headwaiter, a slightly built Frenchman with shiny hair slicked straight back from his forehead and a thin moustache that turned up on the ends, approached them with an inquiring expression. He looked scornfully at Lewis's shabby coat and tousled hair and asked, "May I seat you, gentlemen?"

"We are with Mr. Booth's party," John told him.

"Very well. Go up the stairs and take the third door on your right," the headwaiter said. He pointed them toward the stairs as if glad to dismiss them.

Upstairs, John opened the third door, and they entered a small dining room. A long table was set with seven places, and at opposite ends of the room were paintings of men taming horses. The shining hardwood floor reflected light from the fireplace, and the only other light was from a candelabrum in the middle of the table.

Hunched at the table over a bottle of whiskey and a glass was a swarthy little man with a greasy short beard and tangled hair. He glanced up as Lewis and John came in, then poured whiskey into the glass.

"Plug Tobacco," John said, "Wilkes here yet?"

"I haf not seen him. Who's dis?" He looked at Lewis with a squint in one eye.

"You can call me Paine," Lewis told him.

"Oh, yes, Mosby." The little man scratched his beard. "You vas de vun vit' Mosby." He belched, wiped his right hand on his coat, and offered Lewis the prepared hand, which Lewis shook. "I am Atzerodt. George Atzerodt."

"Plug Tobacco," John Surratt said, "Wilkes won't like it, you getting drunk before he gets everybody here." John inspected a hangnail on his right index finger and began to gnaw on it.

Atzerodt laughed before tilting his head back and tossing down the contents of the glass.

John shrugged, walked to the window, and stood gazing out while he continued to chew on the hangnail.

Lewis pulled off his topcoat and threw it on a chair. On the white sideboard stood three bottles, and he poured whiskey into a glass, thinking about what John had said. Booth would not find him confused and thick-tongued like this dirty little Plug Tobacco. A man would have to keep his wits about him for this meeting, and he remembered how sick he had been when he drank too much bust-head in Richmond. One time, but no more.

He heard laughter in the hall and turned as the door was flung open. John Wilkes Booth strutted into the room; behind him were Davy Herold and two other men.

Booth, still laughing at a joke that the four of them had shared, rubbed his hands and looked around the room. "So," he exulted, "our little band of stout comrades is gathered. Splendid! We can get down to work. But first, let the viands be brought! Where is the waiter?"

As if in response to a summons from a special court, the slick-haired, smiling headwaiter appeared in the door with a napkin over his arm. Booth spoke to him in French.

"Mais oui, M'sieur Boot'," replied the waiter, bowing out of the room.

Booth turned to the other six men in the room, smiled, and walked to the fireplace, where he held his hands above the fire, rubbing them briskly and turning them over and over.

"A raw and bitter March night," Booth said, "suitable for planning mighty deeds."

No one else spoke. Lewis looked at Booth while Davy Herold stood beside John at the window. Port Tobacco drank. The other two men stood together in one corner.

"Sam and Mike," Booth said, "this is the stalwart warrior whom I summoned from New York—Paine, the veteran of Mosby's Rangers."

Sam and Mike were small of stature, one in a coat too small, the other in a coat too big. One had a thin moustache and sparse whiskers, the other a thicker moustache with a brown goatee on his lower lip. They did not speak, but nodded a kind of greeting at Lewis, like men who felt out of their elèment.

"Davy, close the door," Booth ordered.

Davy Herold went to the door, looked both ways down the hall, and pushed the door shut.

"Be seated, gentlemen," Booth directed, pulling off his coat and hat and hanging them on the coat rack in the corner. Sam, Mike, and Davy Herold took off their own coats and hats and hung them on the rack. All sat around the table, Lewis and John with their backs to the window, flanking Port Tobacco. Sam, Mike, and Davy sat opposite. Booth stood behind the chair at the end of the table, his back to the crackling fire. He rested his hands on the back of the chair and leaned forward, peering into each set of eyes in turn.

John Surratt coughed and started to gnaw another hangnail. Port Tobacco grinned and looked around the room. He reached for his bottle, seemed to think better of doing so, and dropped his hand onto the table.

"I have called you all here tonight to tell you that the time has come for us to strike," Booth began. He walked away from the chair and paced in front of the fireplace. "The only thing that can save the South is for Lincoln himself to go up the spout. And I mean to smite the very heart of this tyranny. I mean to smite Abe Lincoln himself." Booth pounded his right fist against his open left hand. Lewis's eyes fused with Booth's dark, piercing eyes, and he felt a summons directly from his leader's brave heart.

Booth quivered with excitement. "Southron independence will be insured if we act now. We shall take Abe Lincoln and hold him in exchange for fifty thousand prisoners—the prisoners that the tyrant himself has left to rot in Yankee dungeons. Then we shall see a renewed Confederate army able to drive the invaders from Southron soil and to establish the independence of our country."

Booth stopped talking when somebody knocked on the door. "That must be our dinner," he said. "Davy, bring it in. Tell the waiter that we won't need him."

They watched Davy Herold get up and open the door. Dismissing the waiter, he pulled a loaded cart into the room, its wheels squeaking softly on the hardwood floor. Davy hefted a pot of steaming oysters onto the sturdy oak table. While Booth stared out the window, the others grabbed pewter plates from the cart and heaped them from steaming dishes of fried hogfish, chunks of boiled beefsteak, slices of ham, and fried eggs. There was a pot of hot coffee, and they poured it into thick crockery mugs. "Let me at them eyesters," Davy Herold said as he dumped a pile of oysters on the table and began to pry them open with a heavy knife he drew from under his coat. Lewis poured coffee into the mug and walked to Booth by the window. He wrapped his fingers around the cup and felt the heat move through his hands.

Booth went to the table and poured brandy into a glass. Port Tobacco, who had dozed off to sleep, stirred as the commotion became louder, sat up, and started to open oysters. Lewis leaned against the window frame and watched them.

"When do we go after Lincoln, Wilkes?" Sam asked.

"Day after tomorrow—Friday. That day he goes out to Campbell Hospital, near the Soldiers' Home, to see a play. We will stop his carriage on the way, get him out, and take him across the Eastern Branch Bridge into southern Maryland. There we will have friends to help us hide him and get through the country to Richmond."

"Wilkes," Davy Herold interrupted, "are we going over to Susanna's tonight?"

Booth looked at him sternly. "Not until I have laid my plan before you, Davy."

Mike leered, his mouth full of eggs, and took a swallow of brandy. "Davy, I think that new girl—what's her name? Belle?—took a real shine to you. Bet you a dollar she's the one you're set on for tonight."

"How about it, John? Ready to go with us?" Herold asked Surratt.

John Surratt attempted a feeble smile. He cracked more oysters. "Hell," Sam said. "You can throw in with us tonight, Johnnie. It might be a mortal sin, but all you need to do is run off to the priest and confess it. Then you won't have a thing to worry about."

Port Tobacco gulped down a mouthful of food and spoke up. "Dat is not vat's bodderin' Chonnie." He held up his right hand with the index finger curved down, and shook it limply. "Dat's vat bodders Chonnie."

Davy joined in the whooping laughter, while John blushed and Booth, leaning against the mantel, swirled his brandy and scowled at the glass.

Davy looked up at Lewis. "Are you with us, Paine?"

Lewis started to nod, but the dark disapproval in Booth's eyes stopped him. At that moment, Mike pushed his chair back and announced, "We're going there now!"

"I'm ready!" exclaimed Davy Herold, jumping up and clattering oyster shells onto the floor.

"Not yet!" Booth roared. Sam, Mike, and Davy stopped, frozen in their movement. Booth dashed a chair violently into the corner of the room and leaned forward on his left hand, his head bowed and his right hand rubbing his eyes. "God almighty! Could Cassius and Brutus have carried out the task they set for themselves had they been hobbled by men so lacking in zeal for their cause? I had the chance to strike Lincoln on the day of his inauguration, and I wish that I had done it then. If I had, I would not be plagued tonight with the faint-heartedness of drunken libertines." He looked up as he spat out the words, his eyes burning into Lewis's eyes.

"Who is still with me?"

No one stirred.

Booth pointed at the clock on the wall. The minute hand was groping toward midnight, and a faint movement whirred deep behind the face.

"Behold! The hour is nigh," Booth intoned in a voice like a prophet's. "You all bear knives. If you still stand with me, ready to defend your country, to act in this bold venture that will save our independence, let me see the gleam of your blades before the last stroke of midnight."

The first note of the deep chime startled Lewis with its reverberation in the still room. He gripped the handle of his knife and took it from its sheath under his coat. He held it forward, his arm thrust straight out toward the candelabrum. His eyes were fixed on those of Booth, and he read relief, pride, and gratitude there.

Gong.

Davy Herold, shocked out of frivolity, glanced from side to side and picked up his knife from the table. *Gong.* His blade jerked forward, almost touching Lewis's.

Gong. Sam and Mike looked at each other, then stepped toward the table together. *Gong.* Their knives were out as if in a single motion, and they held them toward those of Lewis and Herold. *Gong.*

Gong. John Surratt, his eyes unsteady and troubled, fumbled under his coat and brought out his knife, which he hesitantly extended toward the candelabrum. *Gong.*

Gong. Port Tobacco, his jaw slack and his eyes half- open, shoved himself to his feet. He groped under his coat on one side, then on the other. *Gong.* When he drew his knife, it slipped from his hand and clattered onto the table among the spent oyster shells. *Gong.* Lewis reached with his free hand, picked it up, and handed it to him. Port Tobacco held it unsteadily in front of him, squinting at it. *Gong.*

On the last stroke of midnight, Booth brought a gleaming dagger from under his vest, near his heart. He plunged it into the table with a sudden thud. "Then we shall not fail! We are ready to strike for our country!" His head down, peering from under his dark brow slowly around the circle, his chest heaving, he muttered:

> Come, noble gentlemen,
> Let us survey the vantage of the ground.
> Let's lack no discipline, make no delay,
> For, lords, tomorrow is a busy day.

15

WASHINGTON CITY
MARCH 1865

LEWIS POWELL LAY on the bar of the country tavern, half asleep, one forearm across his face. His head felt like a barn door had been slammed on it. He grunted and shifted when the lumpy Whitney revolver slipped out of the band of his breeches and clumped on the bar. Lewis reared his head, contemplated the revolver, slid the weapon closer to him, slept, and dreamed he was still playing cards at the brothel they had left that morning. In the dream he turned over a queen of diamonds just as he had the night before, and the queen became the prostitute Francine, then Clara Meredith, then Mary Branson. The cards led to a brawl as they had the night before, but in the dream the cards—displaying the faces of Abraham Lincoln, of John Wilkes Booth, and of men he had watched die—heaped themselves on Lewis, smothering him while a voice said over and over "Do you see him yet?" until he woke.

"Do you see him yet?" John Surratt was asking.

Sam and Mike leaned against the window frame, watching the road. "Not yet," Mike said.

"Perhaps ol' Abe, he done chanched his plans," Port Tobacco muttered, a little hopefully, from his chair in the corner.

Davy Herold sat at a table in the middle of the room, twirling a revolver on its side. "Well, it's time Wilkes came on. I've been waiting here more than two hours."

"Looks like him now," Sam said. He and Mike left the window and pulled coats and hats from the coat rack. "Let's go."

Herold slipped his revolver into a holster. Lewis swung down from the bar and John Surratt got to their feet and grabbed their hats. Lewis picked up the revolver and tucked it into the band of his breeches again.

The door swung open, and Booth charged into the room. He swept off his hat and dashed it onto a table. "Damn! Of all the infernal luck! Everything works against me!"

"What's the matter, Wilkes?" John Surratt asked.

"He's not there. He's not even going there today. We have been foiled." Booth slumped into a chair beside the table, staring blankly at the floor.

"Not going there today?" Mike asked. "But, goddam it, you said—"

"I know what I said. Don't tell me." He looked up at Sam and Mike. "I swear, the manager of the company told me he would be there."

"Then he was a liar or a blamed fool," Sam said. "And, Wilkes, damned if you weren't a damned fool to have believed him."

Booth looked up sharply and jerked to his feet. Before he could reply a pan clattered to the floor of the back room.

"What was that?" John Surratt burst out. "Davy, I thought you told me there wouldn't be anybody back till tonight."

Herold's face went pale. "Th-that's what they told me. We got to get out of here. Somebody might have heard us all this time."

Lewis started toward the back room. "I'll take care of it."

Booth grabbed his arm. "No, Paine, let's get out of here. We can't let anything happen to get in our way."

Sam and Mike were already out the door, making for their horses. Booth ran after them.

"Wait!" Booth pleaded. "We'll try again. I want to set another time."

Sam and Mike hoisted themselves into their saddles. "Wilkes, we'll be going back to Baltimore," Mike said. "We've already taken enough risks. You can find us there."

Booth turned to Herold, John Surratt, and Lewis, who were standing on the porch of the tavern. Bareheaded and pale, his hair disheveled, he looked at them, his mouth twitching in search of words. Port Tobacco pushed past them and went to his horse.

Booth seized Port Tobacco by both arms and glared into his eyes. "You, George!" he said. "You're still with me, aren't you?"

"Let me go, Vilkes!" Port Tobacco cried, his eyes wild with fright. "I must get avay from here!" He shook himself loose from Booth's grip, untied his horse, and mounted. Without looking back, he followed Sam and Mike toward the city.

Lewis had been so intent on watching Booth and the others that he did not see Davy Herold and John Surratt getting on their horses.

Booth dashed toward them. "When—? God, are you running, too?"

"I know somebody has heard us, Wilkes," John Surratt told him. "If we have been discovered, it means our lives!" He wheeled his horse and rode toward the city, with Herold behind him.

Booth, his body sagging, turned toward Lewis, dropping a hand on Lewis's shoulder. "Paine, I feel like Macbeth when his cohorts have begun to desert him."

"What do you want me to do, Captain?"

"Paine, we will turn this thing around yet. Go to the Surratt house and wait for me there. I must collect my thoughts and give you new orders."

Lewis untethered his horse and mounted. A new awareness flooded him with strength and cleared his head, an awareness that he was even more important to Booth than ever. "You can count on me, Captain," he said to Booth's bowed head, and turned his horse toward Washington City.

Lewis ignored the hostler's curious stare when he rode into the livery stable on H Street. He wasted no time leading his horse into the stall next to John Surratt's lathered mount, lifting off the saddle, and dumping a bucket of grain into the trough. Then he went across the street to the Surratt house, feeling the hostler's gaze on him and trying not to look like he was in a hurry.

As Lewis went up the stairs, one of the women came to the parlor door, but he did not look to see who it was.

In the room at the head of the stairway, John Surratt paced back and forth, mopping his brow and talking excitedly to Weichmann, the boarder.

"I'm ruined, Weichmann! Ruined! All my prospects are up in smoke. Look! You said you could get me a job one time, a job in that government office you work in. Can you get me something now?" Surratt paid no attention to Lewis Powell, who stood in the open doorway watching him.

Weichmann sat half-turned from the writing desk, his right arm resting on the back of the chair. He held a quill pen in his right hand. "Well, it's not all that easy, John," he said. "But I will talk to the boss about it." Weichmann looked up at Lewis.

For the first time, John Surratt looked around at Lewis. His eyes widened, and he paled. "My God, Paine! You ought not to have come back here! What if somebody followed you?"

"Captain Booth told me to come here. He said he would be coming, too."

John started to pace again. "My God! I've got to get out of this business. It will drag me down." He pulled a revolver from his side pocket and tossed it onto the bed. "I'll go to Canada. That's what I'll do." He ran his hands nervously through his thin blond hair, then pulled at his beard.

Weichmann, who seemed bewildered, sat watching John pace to and fro. Lewis wanted to laugh at John's agitation but managed to keep a straight face. Any minute now, he thought, he'll piss all over hisself.

The front door was thrown open, and quick footsteps sounded on the stairs. Lewis backed to the opposite side of the room and faced the door, his hand under his coat gripping the handle of his pistol. He let go of the gun when John Wilkes Booth burst into the room, hatless, waving a riding crop.

"Where is Port Tobacco? Did Herold come here with you?" he demanded of Surratt and Lewis.

"Ain't seen them, Captain," Lewis told him.

"Port Tobacco—damned drunk. Probably find him in some bar. Arnold and O'Laughlin, both gone, lost to us." Booth stopped for breath, all the while slapping the riding crop against the palm of his left hand.

John Surratt, trembling, stared at Booth. "Wilkes," he said, "we've got to be more careful. You could have been followed. We've got to change our plans, find a safer chance to carry out the business."

"Why, you cringing poltroon!" Booth growled. "Will you desert me now, when we have our best chance within our grasp?"

"Within our grasp, did you say? Within our grasp?" John sneered. "The man was nowhere near where you thought he would be, and you say within our grasp. Wilkes, what are you thinking? What kind of fool do you take me for?"

Booth saw Weichmann for the first time. "Damn it all," he said, "what's he doing here? I don't trust him."

Weichmann rolled his eyes nervously from Booth to Surratt and back again to Booth.

"God damn you, get out!" Booth shouted at Weichmann. He jerked Weichmann from his chair, shoved him toward the door, and kicked him in the buttocks. Booth slammed the door and, heaving for breath, turned to glare at John Surratt.

Surratt moistened his lips and squared his shoulders. "If Weichmann can't find me a job at the government office he works in, Wilkes, I'm leaving for Canada. This business has too many risks. What if somebody has already told what they know? The Federal authorities may already be on our trail! Do you realize that we can all hang?" He pulled a handkerchief from his pocket and mopped his sweating brow.

Lewis laughed and looked at Booth, who glared at John Surratt so intensely that John had to drop his eyes, as if he had been staring into a furnace.

"Yes, that's it. Run. Turn tail and run," he sneered. "Just now, when our country calls, when God himself demands that you strike a blow for your country's independence, you turn tail and slink away. God!" He burst forth, slamming the whip against the wall and turning toward Surratt as if he would attack him with it. "God! Would that fate had given me sturdier men, not such lily-livered milksops as you!"

"Wilkes, you're mad," John Surratt said. He looked at Booth before he went out the door. Then, in the hallway, he turned and smiled. "Oh, yes, one more thing, Wilkes. Do you want to know where Abe Lincoln was when we were out in the country seeking him?"

Booth looked at him.

"Do you really want to know, Wilkes? Weichmann told me, because Weichmann was where he was. He was making a speech at the

National Hotel, that's where. At your hotel, Wilkes. And a woman on one of the balconies tried to sp—to sp—to spit on his head!'' He was choking with laughter. "And she missed. Ha-ha! She missed, Wilkes!'' He disappeared along the hallway, leaving behind him only the sound of his laughter receding down the stairs.

Booth rushed toward the window as if he saw an enemy in the other self reflected in the glass. He smashed his fist through one of the panes. Lewis heard the fragments clatter to the hard clay below as Booth held his arm, up to the elbow, through the shattered window. His back was steady, his form still, as though all his anger had poured into that one act.

Then Booth drew his hand back through the opening. He did not seem to notice the gash in his hand as he let his arm fall to his side, while blood dripped onto the dingy rug.

His voice was suddenly calm. "I have failed. It has come to nothing,'' he said to what was left of his reflection in the three remaining window panes. He turned and paced slowly toward the door, leaving a trail of blood on the rug.

Lewis moved toward the door behind Booth. "I'll come with you, Captain,'' he said.

Booth looked at him. "What did you say?''

"I said I would come with you. I'm ready to do what you need for me to do.''

Booth sighed. "Would you serve under a leader whose campaign has failed?''

"I done it after Sharpsburg, Captain. Other times, too.''

Booth looked around him at the room, then toward the door. He sighed again. "I need time, Paine,'' he said. "I must go to New York. Come with me there. No—I don't know. I don't know where you ought to go.''

Lewis thought of Mary Branson. "I could go to Baltimore, Captain,'' he said.

"Yes. Yes, that's it. Baltimore.'' Booth ran his bloody hand through his hair, matting the dark curls. He stared at the floor for a long time, then said slowly, "Go to Baltimore, and I will write to you there.''

"You can send a message through Mary Branson, Captain.''

"Yes. Mary Branson," Booth muttered, almost without moving his lips. "I'll write to you through Mary Branson." Fumbling the buttons of his vest, smearing the vest with blood, Booth walked out of the room. In the hall he stopped, groped into a coat pocket, and pulled out a wallet. He pulled some bills from it and held them toward Lewis. "You will need this," he said.

Lewis took the money and stuffed it into a pocket as Booth went on down the hall. Then he turned back into the room. He pulled his carpetbag from under the bed and fumbled through the cluttered chifforobe, pulling out his clothes.

Lewis picked up his slouch hat from the bed and set it on his head. As he went down the stairs, someone started to play the piano behind the closed parlor door. He stopped on the lowest step to listen in the dying afternoon light that slanted through the frosted glass of the door. It was a sweet, sad melody that sounded like a farewell song, and he let it measure his tread to the door and down the outside steps. Then he listened to the melody fading away as he went along the street.

Doubt and misgiving rode the cars with Lewis all the way to Baltimore. A sudden impulse had made him tell Booth that he would go there, but now he wondered if he ought to stay. He had said Baltimore because he wanted to see Mary Branson again, and because he knew that Mary would want to see him. Maggie did not trust him, had become suspicious of him, but she could not keep him away from her sister. Still, he was uneasy about staying in Baltimore. If he went north, to New York or Canada, he would not be near when Booth needed him. All around him he saw newspaper headlines predicting that Grant would take Petersburg any day, and Richmond soon after. Perhaps the papers were wrong, but it was clear the Confederacy was in peril, and he had to help save it.

Lewis rubbed his left hand over the scar on his right, drilled there by that Yankee minié ball at Gettysburg. Jesus's wounded hands were like that. Sometimes he imagined himself spread out on a cross like Jesus, under a burning sun, staring down at the people who mocked him and spat at him. Did Jesus ever think that it had not been worth it?

It was almost midnight when the engine chuffed into Camden Street Station. Lewis left his bag with the stationmaster and went up

Eutaw Street to Fayette. The lamp outside the Branson house cast a yellow circle on the misty night, but the house was dark. Constipation jabbed at his gut again. He felt heavy, tired, yet he knew he could not sleep, and so he walked. He walked along Calvert to the waterfront, then walked along the docks, where someone was always awake. He passed a row of taverns; and he went into one, ordered a pint of beer, and leaned without drinking against the bar, listening to sailors' and soldiers' yarns. Then he walked again along deserted streets under dim gas lamps, ignored by soldiers on patrol. He wanted them to question him, find out who he was, so that he could fight them, and all of the doubts and the goings and comings would be over. But no one stopped him, and as the early light of the March dawn began to turn the rainy night from black to gray, he lay on a bench under an overhang and slept.

At dawn he forced himself to his feet. Stumbling through puddles and splashed by carts, he wandered back to Eutaw Street. He did not think of caution now, but only of finding Mary Branson and the house that would be his sanctuary.

Lewis was halfway up the steps of the Branson house when the door opened, and Peggy, the skinny Irish maid, came out with a broom in her hand. When she turned from closing the door and saw Lewis, she gasped and pulled back as if she had seen a ghost.

"Faith!" she exclaimed, crossing herself. "Sure and you gave me a start, like a man from the land of the dead." She held the broom in front of her like a lance, ready to ward off demons or men. "Everybody said the Yanks had taken you off to shoot you."

"No, Peggy," Lewis chuckled, "I'm very much alive. Here. Touch me if you don't believe me." He advanced up the steps toward her, holding out his hand.

She shrank back, shoved the door open, and scurried into the safe hallway. The door slammed behind her.

Lewis shook the doorknob, but she had locked the door behind her. He was reaching for the doorbell when rapid footsteps came along the hall. The door opened again and Mary stood there, her eyes wide in surprise and fear.

"Doc!" she said. "It is dangerous for you to come here." She looked over her shoulder. "There are people here who would turn you in."

"I don't care. I had to see you. Let me in."

She kept the door half closed. "No, I daren't." She glanced behind her again. "Lucky thing that Peggy told me about you before she told Maggie. I'll have to pay her to keep quiet. Go to the corner by the girls' school and wait for me." She pushed the door shut and vanished into the house. At Fayette Street Lewis turned left and walked a block to wait under a leafless elm on the corner, out of sight of the Branson house. There he hunched against the chilly rain, pulling his coat collar around his neck. He stood back from the edge of the street to keep from being splashed by drays. Across the street a protective red-brown brick wall bore a metal plate proclaiming the premises to be those of the "Western Female High School." On other days Lewis had found pleasure in being on the street when the spirited, fresh-faced girls, cloaked and mufflered, spilled out of those gates, bound homeward in chattering flocks. Now the forlorn windows were gouged into the bleak morning like half-healed gashes.

Lewis watched the corner by the Branson house, wanting Mary to come around it but almost hoping that she would not come. It was against everything that was right, this drawing a woman into the plan. It was man's work, soldier's work. Maybe she would not come, after all. Perhaps Maggie would keep her back. Maggie would, if she suspected what was going on. "Damn!" he said to the senseless windows of the Western Female High School, and a man who was passing by him jerked around to stare, then crossed the street, glancing back as though a snarling dog were chasing him. "Damn!" Lewis said again. If they could have captured Lincoln in Washington City yesterday, Lewis would not be in Baltimore today to ask a woman for help.

Mary Branson came around the corner, holding an umbrella and clutching a shawl against her throat, clad in somber green. She broke into a run when she caught sight of him, and danced into the circle of his doubt. Her smile betokened the gift of herself to the plot, turning her into an unknowing accomplice. Lewis pitied her for her readiness to be used, and raged at himself for using her. In her rush toward him he thought of the Wisconsin man with the noose around his neck, under that oak in Virginia.

Mary crooked her arm into his and squeezed against him. "Oh, Doc," she said, "I was afraid I would never see you again. That

Yankee officer, Lieutenant Smith, was here last night asking a lot of questions, and he said he would be back today." She looked behind her.

"What questions did he ask?"

"Nothing about you. He just wanted to know about Maggie and me sending blankets and food to Confederate prisoners, and he wanted to know if we had been getting mail from Richmond."

"I went to New York when I left here, but I been in Washington City since then. Something important is going to happen."

Mary pulled from him and looked into his eyes. "Does it have anything to do with that man Booth?"

Lewis turned from her and clutched a lamppost in both hands as if he were trying to crumple the cold metal.

"Mary," he said, "I just don't know what to do sometimes. This business is going to pull me down with it. I come here to ask you for help, and I ought not to be doing it."

"What help? What business are you talking about?"

"I daren't tell you that. But it's—it's dangerous. And real important. It can save the Confederacy."

"Doc, nothing can save the Confederacy. It is a matter of days before Richmond falls."

He spoke to the lamppost as much as to her. "Captain Booth knows a way."

"Doc, please listen to me." Mary laid a hand on his arm. "You are out of the war now. Do you remember what you said about being a surgeon? About living at that place on the Suwannee—the place that you call Hebron? Those are the things that count now. We can't turn the world around."

"Mary, I ain't worthy to go back there if I ain't done what I come to do." He shivered and let go of the lamppost as if its chill were that of a tombstone. "Besides, I made promises. I promised somebody in Virginia a year ago. Somebody who is dead now." He took Mary's warm hand and held it between both of his. "The main thing is that I can't pull out of this business as long as Captain Booth is in it, and as long as he needs my help." Lewis stepped closer, still holding her hand tightly. "Listen. He—Captain Booth—is going to send me a letter here in care of you. You have got to bring that letter to me."

"If I do, will you send back to him that you are going to stay here and not go any further with this business, as you call it?"

Lewis did not say anything.

"Will you, Doc?" Mary asked again.

"I—I ain't certain, Mary. I'll do what I have to do."

"Where will you stay, Doc? If Maggie were not so suspicious, you could stay at the Branson House in spite of everything."

"I've got money, Mary. I'll stay at Miller's Hotel. You can find me there."

Impulsively, Mary flung down her umbrella and embraced him. "Doc," she said, "I don't trust John Wilkes Booth. I'm afraid he doesn't mean any good to you." She backed away from him and picked up the umbrella. "I'm not going to let him take you from me again," she said. "You will see. I'll keep you this time." She squeezed his hand and smiled. "I'm so glad that you came back." Then she pivoted and ran toward the house.

Lewis watched her go to the corner, where she stopped and blew him a kiss before vanishing behind the house.

He went to the Camden Street Station to claim his bag, then took a room at Miller's Hotel, close enough to the Branson House for him to stay in touch with Mary.

He could not sleep. So he went into a restaurant on Baltimore Street, sat on a stool near the door, and ordered oysters and coffee. He looked toward the door just as Sam Arnold and Mike O'Laughlin were coming into the restaurant. Sam stopped when he saw Lewis, and laid his hand on Mike's arm. They glanced at each other and turned to leave.

Lewis jumped from the stool and went after them. "Sam! Mike!" he called. "Wait!" He overtook them in a few strides, and grabbed Mike by the arm.

"Damn it! Let me go!" Mike protested.

"I just want to know if you have heard anything from the Captain."

"How could we have heard anything?" Sam said. "We just left him yesterday."

"You don't want to see me, do you?" Lewis growled at them, tightening his grip. "We have got to stick together in all of this."

"Let me go before I call those soldiers yonder."

Lewis glanced across the street. Three soldiers, rifles slung on their shoulders, were talking on a corner about a hundred feet away. The soldiers were not paying attention to them.

Lewis chuckled and let go of Mike's arm. Mike pulled off his hat and mopped his forehead with a red kerchief.

"I don't reckon you want to talk with those Yanks any more than I do," Lewis told them.

"Let's go out here," Sam said. He led the way, and Lewis and Mike followed him to one corner of the hotel porch.

"We had better tell him," Sam said.

"Look, Paine," said Mike, "we are not going any further with this business. You and Wilkes can do what you want to, but Wilkes made a mistake yesterday that could have cost us all our lives. And for what? The plan won't work, anyway."

"You ran away—both of you—and so did Johnnie Surratt."

"It made good sense to get away, and you ought to do the same thing," said Sam. He beckoned to Mike with a toss of his head. "Come on, let's go."

They twisted past Lewis, who turned to watch them hurry down the steps of the porch and melt into the crowd of men on the sidewalk. In the hotel lobby a clock struck. He started to count the strokes, but then he lost count and did not know if it was eleven or twelve.

Lewis had been asleep all afternoon, and he woke to hear taps on the door. At first he did not know where he was, and listened for the tapping to come again.

"Who is it?" he called.

A thin voice answered, but he did not understand the words. When he groped to the door, he opened it enough to see a boy there, silhouetted in the dim light from a lamp on the opposite wall. The boy was wrapped in a long, loose coat, with a slouch hat shading his face.

"What do you want?" Lewis asked.

"Message from Mary Branson," the boy whispered. Lewis pulled the door fully open to reach for the message, but the boy shoved under his arm, forcing the door away from Lewis's hand, and darted to the middle of the room, where he spun around to face Lewis. Recovering from his surprise, Lewis charged at the boy and swung his arm at his head. When the boy ducked, Lewis' fist caught his hat a glancing blow and sent it spinning across the room. Long hair cascaded from the head of the boy, and Lewis looked into the face of Mary Branson.

He stopped with his hand still at the end of the swing. Then he laughed, and she fell into his arms, hugging him tightly.

"See? I told you I would come," she said.

"But I never expected it would be like this."

Her voice, muffled against his chest, said, "I could not have come here alone any other way." She looked up. "Were you surprised?"

"Surprised? Sure was. And to think, I near about knocked your head off."

"I've heard of women dressing like men and fighting in the army. I always wondered what it would be like."

"And I always wondered what it'd be like to meet up with one of them. Never knew till now."

Mary laughed again, hugging him tighter, swaying with him. Lewis reached behind him and shoved the door closed. Its slam echoed in the nearly bare room, canceling the dim light from the hallway and enveloping them in a private darkness. He brushed his lips against the top of her head and brought his hands up to feel the long, soft hair laving over his fingers like water from a fountain while he breathed the strawlike smell of rain that clung to her. She turned her face up to his, and he bent and kissed her softly, then again, his lips tighter against hers.

Trembling, he groped his hand downward behind her knees, felt them bend at the coaxing of his hand, lifted her, and laid her on the narrow bed. Mary giggled when he pulled at the buttons on her overcoat and pushed awkwardly around her body, touching through the homespun shirt the warm fullness of her breasts with their firm nipples.

They laughed together, squirming so that he could pull the blanket over them. He rolled against her, fumbling at the buttons of her trousers, then tearing at his own to release the stiffness straining against them. "Oh, Doc, I love you, Doc," she whispered as he entered her and lost himself in a flood of forgetting.

*　　*　　*

Mary reveled in her game and came to him every day that week. He never knew how she succeeded in accounting for her absence, or how she contrived to slip out of the busy house wearing boy's clothing. Once she came to him in the afternoon, but all the other times were at dusk. They would lie holding each other while he would tell her about his home in Florida, about the Suwannee, about Hebron.

At the end of the week, Mary came with a letter. She took it from the pocket of her overcoat and handed it to him, hesitating. "What will you do now?" she seemed to ask.

Lewis turned up the gas lamp on the wall and looked first at the address: "L. Paine, c/o Miss Mary Branson, Eutaw Street, Baltimore." On the back was the seal that he knew to be Booth's. He tore the envelope open and pulled out a folded sheet. Holding it close to the lamp, he read it aloud, almost forgetting that Mary was in the room. "Paine," he read softly, "I will be in Baltimore on Saturday, the 25th, on my way back from New York. Meet me at Barnum's, and bring Joe Thomas. JWB."

"What day is today?" he asked Mary.

"Why, it's Saturday."

Lewis held the note to the flame of the lamp and, as the paper caught fire, dropped it onto the floor. He pressed the heel of his boot onto the flaming paper and ground it into a mess of charred flakes.

"I have got to see Joe Thomas," Lewis said. "Is he at the Branson House?"

"Doc, no!" Mary begged. "Please don't go any further in this. You don't even have to send a message. Don't even tell that man Booth anything."

Lewis drew her into his arms and held her close against his chest, stroking her hair. "Mary, hush," he said. "You won't change my mind. I love you, and I want to stay, but I have to do what a soldier has to do. Them's my orders that I just burned, and I can't disobey my orders." He held her at arm's length and looked down at her. "So I am telling you now. Don't say no more. It will be over in a few days, and I will be back."

He took his coat and hat from the rack by the door. He pulled the coat on and set the hat on his head. Then he opened the door and stood looking back at her. "Are you coming?" he asked.

She stared at him.

"Come on if you are coming."

Mary's disappointment showed in her face, but Lewis shrugged and started out the door. "I ain't got time to waste here," he said.

He strode through the darkness toward Eutaw Street, with Mary hurrying to keep up. It excited him to think that there was a chance for action again. He waited several times for Mary, out of breath from nearly running in her ungainly boy's outfit, to catch up with him, and he hurried her along impatiently.

The rain had begun in a light mist, and he waited outside the Branson house for Mary to do whatever she had to do to get rid of the boy's clothing and fetch Joe Thomas. He paced along Eutaw Street opposite the house, watching the door. His head was starting to ache, and he rubbed his temples. After about ten minutes, a man and a woman came out of the Branson house and started toward Fayette. He walked toward them until he realized they were strangers to him. They glanced at him and quickened their steps away from him.

It was another ten minutes before Mary came back alone and crossed the street.

Although he could not see her face in the dark, he thought she sounded glad when she said, "He won't come."

"Won't come? Why won't he come? Bet you didn't even try to talk him into it."

"I think he is afraid of whatever it is."

"Afraid? Let me talk to him."

She laid her hand on his arm. "No, Doc. If one of the servants sees you, they might tell the army you are here."

"You don't mean servants. You mean Henry Shriver."

"All right. Henry, too. You've got to be careful."

He could tell what she was thinking. Maybe if Joe did not come with him, Lewis would change his mind, pull out of the plot, and stay with her. That was how little she knew him, how little she understood what a soldier had to do. Just like a woman, to think that she could twist him around like she wanted to, make him go the way she wanted him to go, like a steer being led with an ear of corn.

He pulled his arm away from her and put his hand to his brow, where the ache seemed to center. "Don't care nohow. We can get along without him. We got enough to do the job without him." He moved past her to the middle of the street and shouted toward the house: "Joe! Hear me, Joe? Who needs you? Who needs you nohow? Tied to a woman's apron strings, Joe! Just stay here, then! We ain't never needed you, and we ain't never going to need you!" Then he started to laugh, standing there in the empty street, as he thought of awkward, lanky Joe behind a window curtain listening to him, as he thought of that lily-livered John Surratt calling Booth mad and turning tail to run to Canada, of Port Tobacco swaying drunk in the room at Gautier's, of Sam and Mike huddled together like a two-headed man on the road to the Campbell Hospital. He laughed even louder, almost hysterically, when he looked around to see Mary hesitating on the edge of the street.

When he turned to her, her hesitation ended and she ran toward him, seizing one of his arms in both her hands. "Oh, Doc! Don't go! Stay here! The war is nearly over! That man Booth is the devil himself! He will get you killed! I hate him! I hate him!" She sobbed and pulled on his arm.

Lewis jerked his arm away, sending Mary stumbling backward. "Let me be, damn you, woman!" he barked. She fell onto the stones of the street, and he jumped forward to help her up. But she dragged away from him, the fear in her eyes showing in the lamplight. Suddenly Lewis's eyes blurred with tears, and his hands fell helplessly to his sides.

"Oh, Mary, I am sorry. For—forgive me," he moaned. He looked at the Branson house where, silhouetted against the open door, stood Maggie Branson, silent, her right arm raised toward him, either beckoning or accusing. Lewis spun around and, without looking back, ran into Fayette Street toward Barnum's Hotel to meet John Wilkes Booth.

16

WASHINGTON CITY
APRIL 14, 1865

WASHINGTON CITY WAS a spring of joy for the many who supported the Union, a well of hopelessness for the few who sympathized with the Confederacy. On the first Sunday in April, a week after Lewis came back to the capital with Booth, a week that had seen them again hope for a time to strike at Lincoln and again be disappointed, the Confederate cabinet fled Richmond. Another week, and there followed the stunning news that Lee had surrendered.

On the Thursday night after Lee's surrender, Washington City had staged a great illumination. The city was ablaze with torches, and flambeaux spelled out the name of GRANT on the facade of the War Department building. Lewis walked with Booth and Davy Herold through the teeming city streets, shouldering in glum fury through throngs of drunken revelers. Then they went back to Booth's room at the National Hotel and drank themselves into insensibility. "Aye, a bright and splendid spectacle," Booth groaned. "More so in my eyes were it a display in a nobler cause. But so goes the world. Might makes right." He laughed and downed another drink.

Lewis woke the next day alone in the room. His head plagued him, and he went to the washbasin and dunked it under the water. He came up bubbling and shaking his head. He dried his face and was pulling on his boots when the door opened and Booth came in.

Booth's eyes glowed with excitement. Gone was the sullen gloom of the night before, and he paced into the room with the confidence that had shone from the old Booth. "Paine! Paine, my young warrior! Where is Davy? Good news! The best of news!"

Lewis looked at him in wonder.

"Ha! Our time has come!" He flipped his hat from his head and caught it on the end of his walking stick. "Just now I went to Ford's for my mail, and what did I learn?" His mouth spread into a broad grin as he peered up into Lewis's eyes, and he gripped Lewis by the shoulder. "Abe Lincoln will be at Ford's tonight! And not only Abe! Grant will be there as well!" He struck a swordsman's pose and drove his walking stick straight ahead of him into the unresisting air. "By God! If I don't strike them both down—! You'll see! They'll all see! That Henry Clay Ford, damn him, sneering at me because I am not in uniform, as much as calling me a coward! He'll see! By God, he'll see what John Wilkes Booth will do for his country!" Laughing, he whirled around the room, flourishing his cape in front of him, thrusting and parrying with his walking stick. Lewis's mouth dropped open in wonder, and he was caught completely off guard when Booth poked the walking stick so quickly into his stomach that he jerked back against the wall and stood as if impaled.

Booth backed away and tossed the walking stick onto the bed. He shook a fist toward the window and said, "Now, Abe Lincoln, now I shall avenge my country's slaughter." His arms fell to his sides, and he stared out of the window. "Paine, do you know what I dreamt the night that Richmond first lay unprotected before the ravages of the barbarian Yankee? I dreamt that I stood in that old city, that I felt the bricks of Broad Street under my feet, that I walked toward the ruined Capitol, its shattered walls no longer bearing that majestic roof, its marble floors lying open to the elements, and that I walked inside to the sound of weeping women. And there, shrouded in her finest robes, pale in death, lay a lady of such beauty that my heart shook within me, a lady whose hair flowed like bitter tears and covered the floor beside her bier. I asked one of the doleful ladies who she was, and the lady said, 'Alas, she is the corpse of our country, our ruined South, and we shall never behold her like again.'" His head sank, and his shoulders shook. "And I woke with words ringing in my ears that I have spoken a hundred times as Richard III: 'A bard of Ireland told me once I should not live long after I saw Richmond.'"

Lewis remained where Booth's exuberant mock attack had left him, standing with his back pressed to the wall.

Booth turned to face Lewis. "I hear that John Surratt is in Canada. Sam Arnold and Mike O'Laughlin have not answered my messages. I am afraid that your Joe Thomas was a will-o'-the-wisp. Can I still count on you?"

"You know you can, Captain."

"Yet on Tuesday, only three days ago, Paine," Booth sneered, "when we stood outside the Executive Mansion and heard that abolitionist tyrant call for giving the vote to nigger soldiers in Louisiana, I called on you to shoot him then, and you would not do it. Will you strike now?"

"Captain, you know that wasn't the time then. I couldn't even have got off a good shot."

"The next time he gets in front of me, I'll get a good shot. I would have put him through last week when I went to the Executive Mansion with a party of players. 'It is a pleasuah,' the coarse clown said, 'to meet the son of the illustrious Booth.' Pah! Had he not invoked my father when he shook my hand, I'd have done it then. But, like Richard in the play, it gives me greatest satisfaction to 'seem a saint, when most I play the devil.'" He chuckled and sank into a chair, his legs sprawled to either side.

Lewis pulled on his shirt and buttoned it. He stuffed his shirttail into his trousers and pulled up his braces. "I'm a soldier, Captain, and I'm ready to do what you tell me."

"All the world's a stage, O Paine, and all the men and women merely players. You are a man who goes by many names: Powell, Paine, Mosby, Wood. Perhaps more. Which are you? Perhaps all, perhaps none. I offer you now the greatest role of your career. It is the role that will transform you into your true self. You will win yourself back from the roles you have played. Now go find Davy Herold, and tell him to bring Atzerodt, that drunken oaf, to your room at the Herndon."

Lewis pulled on his boots, stood up, and lifted his coat and hat from the rack. He opened the door and started out.

"Paine."

Lewis looked back.

Booth was pouring whiskey into a glass. He set the bottle back on the table beside his armchair, then extended the glass toward Lewis as he remained sprawled in the chair. He pursed his lips and said, "Paine, I have the sharpest play laid out ever done in America." He smiled, tossed his head back, and drained the glass.

On Pennsylvania Avenue Lewis waded through torn bunting, scattered newspapers, and broken jugs—debris from the illumination of the night before. Not knowing where to find Herold, he decided to start in the nearest place. He went across the street to the Palace of Fortune, where a small knot of men stood outside talking. Inside, the gambling tables were empty, and two workmen were replacing lamp covers and mirrors broken in the illumination. He went along Pennsylvania to Sixth Street, then toward the Surratt house. At Sixth and F Streets, he saw two women in black step from the street railway car, and he recognized them as Mary and Anna Surratt. Before he caught up to them Mary got into a buggy driven by Weichmann. The buggy was clattering away when Lewis overtook Anna Surratt, who had continued alone up Sixth Street.

"Miss Surratt! Miss Anna!" he called.

Anna Surratt turned and looked back at him. "Oh—it's you," she said.

"Yes, ma'am. Wasn't that your mother I just seen with you?"

"Yes, it was. We just came from Good Friday services at St. Patrick's, and now Mr. Weichmann is driving her out to Surrattsville to see about some business there."

"Why, I plumb forgot it was Good Friday. I reckon all this celebrating last night made a lot of folks forget it."

"Yes, last night's illumination didn't seem fitting, did it? There's surely been little cause for celebration at our house, with one brother off in the Confederate army, we don't know where, and my brother John gone to Canada."

"Miss Anna, it would pleasure me to see you to your door."

"That won't be necessary. It's only two streets over."

"Oh, it won't be no trouble. Why, I—"

She turned and started up the street again. "That's quite all right. I said that it won't be necessary."

Lewis caught up with her. "Have you seen Davy Herold, Miss Surratt?"

She walked faster, and did not look at him again. "No, I am not in the habit of keeping track of Mr. Herold's whereabouts."

"Yes, ma'am." Lewis stopped abruptly and watched her walk away. Well, she's a cool one, he thought. No point in keeping on when I know I'm not welcome. Besides, I've got to find Davy Herold. He appraised the movement of her hips as she did her best to put more distance between herself and him.

Lewis turned back to F Street and walked past the Patent Office. Herold had told him once that he knew a poet named Whitman who worked there. Davy liked to read poetry. Lewis could not see anything in it, or even understand it. Give him a good, rousing hymn any day. Anyway, no need to look for Davy there.

People were still coming out of churches. The Catholics make a lot of Good Friday, he thought. All that bloody crucifix business, with that pained expression on Jesus's face. He remembered hearing a preacher say one time at a funeral that if you died on Good Friday you would get to heaven quicker. What if you were killed, like Jesus? Then you must get there even quicker. If that was so, then you ought not kill your enemy on Good Friday, because you would be doing him a favor. But do some people go to heaven fast, and some go there slow? *This land is not for me.*

At Tenth Street he turned left and passed Ford's Theater before looking into the Star Saloon next door, where Davy sometimes went with Booth. Four drowsy patrons sat at tables, while one man, an actor Lewis had seen at Ford's, stood at the bar talking with the bartender. The bartender, wiping the bar, nodded and grunted agreement while the actor talked.

Pennsylvania Avenue seemed like a land of the dead. An almost empty horse trolley passed and here and there a buggy went by, but no people were on the dusty sidewalks. He crossed the avenue, slipping once on a broken cobblestone, and went to look in Harvey's Oyster Saloon. A small, midafternoon crowd was there, talking in subdued tones, drinking beer, and cracking oyster shells. Lewis left and walked up the street, intending to go to the Kirkwood House, where Port Tobacco was staying, to see if Herold might be there.

He shuffled through pieces of glass along the brick walkway. It looked like every street lamp had been smashed in the excitement of the illumination. At Eleventh Street, he was about to cross over when his eye caught the headlines on the paper outside the *Star* newspaper office. "REBEL SOLDIERS START HOMEWARD" read one head-line. He read the news story under it, which said that General Grant had given food to the starving soldiers of Lee's command, and that the officers and men had started to return to their homes in Virginia. Lee himself had reached Richmond. Lewis wondered where the Jasper Blues were. There were no railway cars to take them home, whatever was left of them. It seemed to him that it was his duty to be with them. But he was not with them, and he was not part of Lee's surrender. He was still a soldier, and Johnston's army was still in the field in North Carolina, though it was expected to surrender soon to Sherman. So the *Star* said. But newspapers were often wrong. Perhaps Booth was right. Perhaps the war could still be won by those who acted swiftly enough.

He kept on the same side of the street and did not cross to the Kirkwood. Now he came to the row of saloons and small gambling houses across the avenue from Gautier's where Booth had gathered them a month before to scheme their bold seizure of Lincoln. Lewis stopped at each door and looked inside for Davy. Once he saw a snoring drunk sprawled on his belly, his head resting on his arm. Lewis grabbed the man by the shoulder and turned him over roughly. But the man was a stranger. His eyes fluttered open and he laid his forearm across them, snorted, and relapsed into honking snores.

He stopped at a shabby canterbury to read the sign outside, which proclaimed that Vanessa LeGrand, late of the Paris stage, would ap-pear that night in "Lola's Lament." As he read it, he heard a woman's loud laughter inside the lobby and looked in to see a buxom, rouged woman talking to a man whose back was toward him. Lewis went inside, and the woman stopped talking and looked up and down at him. The man turned, and it was Herold, his eyes puffy from the sleeplessness of last night.

"Huh? Paine? What do you want?" Herold asked.

"Captain wants you to meet us at my room, Davy. Says to bring Port Tobacco with you."

"Who's your handsome friend, Davy?" the woman asked.

"They call me Paine, ma'am. Who are you?"

She held a dimpled, bejeweled hand toward him. "I am Vanessa LeGrand. I perform tonight." When Lewis took her hand, she forced it to his lips, and he felt the hard raking of the rings that covered every finger, reflecting gaudy light.

Davy laughed. "Paine, you can see I am seriously engaged."

"I hope you boys won't miss the performance. The curtain goes up at eight o'clock."

"I'm more interested in when the petticoats go up," Davy said.

She shook a fat finger. "Naughty, naughty."

"Come on, Davy," Lewis said. "We got to go."

Herold looked at Vanessa LeGrand and then again at Lewis. "Well, all right, if we have to."

"Eight o'clock tonight," Vanessa said, following them to the door. "Don't forget."

"You can count on me," Davy said as Lewis pulled him by his coat sleeve toward the avenue.

"Davy, unless I'm wrong, you're going to be plenty busy tonight without messing around with that woman."

"Why? Something up?"

"The captain says so. Where's Port Tobacco?"

"Don't know. But I can find him. I was just going down to one of the saloons to collect some money a fellow owes me."

"See that you find him. I'm going over to Cleaver's stable to see if they got my horse shod yet. Then I'll meet you about six o'clock at my room at the Herndon House."

"Don't worry, I'll be there with Port Tobacco."

Lewis had started across the avenue toward the stable when he heard a commotion coming down the street toward him. With three black soldiers on either side of them and a white officer on horseback behind, ten ragged Confederate prisoners staggered along the middle of the avenue. All were hatless, and five stumbled on bare feet. They were lean and brown, and they walked as erectly as they could, in spite of the weariness that showed in every step. One limped on a single crutch. There was hardly a single uniform among the band. One tall man walked in front, without shoes, his feet bloody. His left arm was in a dingy sling, and an unkempt brown beard covered his lower jaw. His gray eyes peered straight ahead, and his jaw was tightly set against the pain that moved through his body with every step. The others seemed to take strength from him.

Lewis wanted to turn away, but he fell into step beside them. He could not take his eyes from them, and he stumbled on the uneven brick walkway. Out of the saloons came men who had been drinking. They stared in silence. The black soldiers kept their eyes straight ahead.

When the prisoners and guards came to the Center Market, the white officer ordered a halt. They let the prisoners sit under one corner of the roof that covered the market, while the soldiers stacked arms.

Lewis stood at the edge of the market, watching the exhausted men. He looked to see if there was anyone he knew. One prisoner went to a pump in the middle of the market, carrying a canteen a soldier had given him. Seeing an empty jug against a pillar, Lewis picked it up and walked to the pump. He and the prisoner exchanged glances as they passed at the pump. Then, after filling the jug with water, Lewis followed the man to where his comrades sat or lay on the rough stone of the market floor. He handed the jug to a man who took a long drink before leaning to lift the head of a muttering, pale man lying next to him with his eyes closed, a bloody bandage around his forehead. Tenderly, the first man lifted his head and laid it on his own knee. The jug shook as he tried to raise it to his friend's lips, and Lewis bent over to steady it and tilt it slowly.

"Thanks, friend," the man told Lewis. "Old Jake ain't been able to do much besides walk since he caught a minié ball aside the head a week ago. Don't know what keeps him going."

All at once a murmuring arose behind them and grew louder. Lewis turned to see a crowd of black men and women moving toward them. Some of them started to jeer at the prisoners, who listened with patience wrought from weariness and defeat to the catcalls from the approaching crowd. Lewis rose to his feet as the officer moved in front of the prisoners, his hand on his saber, and the soldiers went toward their weapons and started to unstack them.

At the threatening movement of the guards, the mob paused. About a dozen men were in front, with some twenty men and women scattered behind them. Another man came forward, carrying a piece of colored cloth. Announcing "Here it be," he let the crumpled cloth fall loose to reveal a tattered, soiled Confederate battle flag, its red field faded almost to pink and its blue washed almost to the grayness of the stars set in it. Swapped or stolen from some soldier who had brought it out of battle, the flag hung from the man's hands, dragging on the market stones.

The holder of the flag called out, "Now the Rebels is beat, and let their flag burn!" His eyes glowed with hatred as he ran to a brazier that stood against the pillar and touched the cloth to the coals. Flames licked up the cloth toward the cross and dishonored stars, and the stars became sparks, rising in smoke. The black man held on until flame seared his hand, and gloating at the sullen prisoners, he dropped the charred flag onto the pavement.

In Lewis's eyes the blaze filled the marketplace, and he could hear its feeble crackle above the triumphant shouts of the former slaves. He rushed forward past the officer and crashed into the black man who stood over the blacker piece of cloth. The man was borne backward by the force of Lewis's charge, and they slammed together into a wall of people. Wildly, blindly, Lewis pounded at the black face. Suddenly he felt himself gripped from behind by either arm, and two soldiers dragged him back, away from the man he had attacked. Lewis was thrown against a pillar and held there by two soldiers with rifles crossed on his chest while the officer, his pistol drawn, and the other four soldiers faced the crowd.

The women were most shrill in taunting the black soldiers. "Look at you," one sneered, "holding us back from getting at them Rebs."

"Yeah," said another. "Let's get them up yonder on the block where they used to sell slaves, and sell them off."

"If we rush them soldiers right now, we can get them."

The soldiers braced themselves and held their guns tighter. The two men who held Lewis against the post glanced back. Lewis could see the sweat on their brows, their eyes wide with fright.

"Brothers, no!" came a shout from the far end of the market. Lewis jerked his head around to stare at a black man who was as big as one of the pillars of the market. He wore a gray shirt and flannel trousers, and the hair on his massive head was closely cropped. His large neck and square jaw gave his face great strength, and he moved forward swiftly, almost at a run, his hands clasped at chest level.

The white officer turned to face the approaching man, his pistol pointed upward. The men and women in the mob watched the black giant, as if they were waiting for him to command them.

"Brothers! Sisters! No!" the man shouted again. "Do not commit this sin against God and against man. Forbear to strike these poor men."

"Aw, Prince," one of the men said, "we wasn't doing nobody no harm. We was just celebrating the illumination."

"Yeah!"

"That's right!"

"Just illuminating a little."

The big man frowned deeper than ever. "Don't lie to Prince David," he said. "God knows a lie, and I does, too. The 'lumination was last night, and all the celebratin' be's over and done with." He looked over the crowd and laid his hand on the shoulder of the man whom Lewis had attacked. "Looky heah, brothers and sisters! The time for warrin' and killin' an' the time for celebratin' the warrin' an' killin' is over and done with. Listen to Prince David, now! Turn your ears to my words, and turn from your evil ways and intentions! The time for warrin' an' killin' is over, and the time for peace, for brotherhood, for forgiveness done come upon the land!"

He swept his eye along the row of men nearest him, still holding tightly to the one man's shoulder, and then slowly moved his gaze toward the back of the crowd until he seemed to have taken everyone into his sweep. Then he turned and looked at the weary prisoners, at the officer and the soldiers, who had not changed position since he came toward them, and at Lewis himself, still held between the pillar and the crossed rifles.

Lewis felt his rage leave him, driven out by the power the man exerted. He returned the black man's steady gaze, reading in it a mixture of compassion and authority, of a hatred that had long been spent and laid aside, of certainty and self-possession. that he had never before seen in any black face. Even as he felt the soldiers holding him release their pressure and turn, uncertainly, to face the interloper, he felt his own wavering between what his rage and his oath as a Confederate soldier demanded of him, and what the silent command and appeal in those eyes demanded of him.

The white officer with raised revolver stayed motionless. At the officer's feet sat the scattered band of prisoners, beaten beyond indifference, like men looking from the outside upon the events on which their lives depended.

The man who called himself Prince David broke the spell. He leaped onto a raised stone platform beside the water pump. Almost with the same movement, he peeled his homespun work shirt over his head and dropped it at his feet.

"Look, brothers and sisters! Behold Prince David! Three times have I stood on this block and watched the faces of men raising their voices to bid for my freedom! The first time I stood as a child and seen my mammy and my brothers and sisters sold away from me. Twice more, full of hate and spite, I stood there while men bid for my muscle, for to own me as a field slave. Look, brothers and sisters, at the stripes where those owners tried to beat the spirit out of me." Lewis looked up at the broad back scarred by whips, and he looked down at the beaten Confederate prisoners at his feet, and the men on the floor merged in his mind with the man on the block. For the first time, he did not see a difference in skin but only a sameness in defeat and suffering.

"Yes, brothers! Yes, sisters!" Prince David was saying, as he faced the mob again. "They beat me and tried to break me. I run away and they come after me, and they beat me again. And my heart filled with hate! I killed then, brothers, and I hid, like Cain from his evil killin', and the Lawd left these marks on me jes like He lef' the mark on Cain. Then one day the Lawd called to me and said, 'Prince David,' He said, 'hearken unto my word. That hate in your heart is like a poison eatin' into you. Spit it out and cleanse your heart, and go forth to forgive, and to love your fellow man.' And he sent me here to tell you to forget your hate, to look to the Lawd, to love your enemies, to leave vengeance to the Lawd who said, 'Vengeance is mine.' " He paused and stared down at them.

The man who had burned the flag looked away from Prince David and toward Lewis. Then, without a word, he turned away and walked back through the marketplace, past the block where Prince David stood. The other men followed him while the women looked one more time at the prisoners, then followed the men. All at once, Lewis's body was free of the rifles pressed against him, and he stepped away from the pillar. At the sound of hooves, he turned to see a squad of cavalry riding at a trot into the market. The infantry officer saluted the captain.

"What's the matter, Lieutenant?" the cavalry captain asked. "Somebody waved us down and said there was trouble here."

The lieutenant dropped the revolver back into its holster. "Had a little commotion here, sir, but I've got it under control now."

Prince David, with a faint smile, stepped down from the block and moved in the direction where the crowd of black people had gone.

"Hey, you," the captain called out to Prince David. "Wait there. Lieutenant, do you want anybody arrested?"

"No, sir. We can let him go. Everything's calmed down now."

"Good. Let's go then, boys." He reined his horse to the right, and his squad followed him out of the marketplace.

When Prince David disappeared behind some stalls, Lewis stood for a moment, then walked toward Pennsylvania Avenue, his brain busy with unfamiliar thoughts. When he crossed Pennsylvania to go up to Ninth Street, a drayman with a load of barrels yelled at him to get out of the way, and he dodged aside so late that he felt the heat of the horses as the wagon passed him. The driver swore at him, but Lewis barely heard him as he walked into Ninth Street.

He thought about the prisoners. If it had not been for that Prince David, it would have gone bad for everyone. He wondered why the words of a slave could have such an effect on him. It did not feel right to him to owe his life to a slave.

But the words of the man who called himself Prince David still haunted him. It had something to do with seeing the defeated Confederate prisoners led through the streets by black soldiers. It had something to do with the story in the paper about Lee making his way back to Richmond, nearly alone, and with the army that he had surrendered trying to find their way back to their homes. He thought again of what Mary had said that night standing in Eutaw Street outside her house. She told him that it was a waste to keep going with the war, that it was over, and now here was this deep-voiced, scarred slave bringing him the same words. Maybe it was over. Maybe it was time to go back home, to build, to plant a crop. *They shall beat their swords into plowshares and their spears into pruning-hooks.* Was that the word he was meant to hear? And what of Booth and his plan? Booth wanted revenge, yet only a few minutes before, those former slaves would have had their vengeance—avenged their hatred, their stripes, their slavery on helpless prisoners. It seemed as though God had stepped in to save them, had sent this ignorant, powerful black man to deliver a word that would spare them. And Lewis, too. What if God had meant that word for Lewis Powell, too?

He walked into the Herndon House without having seen the street he had passed along. Trudging up the stairway, he opened the door of his room and sagged onto the bed.

Whose orders was he supposed to obey? Mosby's? Mosby had not surrendered yet, according to the newspapers. The army was still looking for him, and the partisan rangers had not been included in the surrender. Lee's? He still could not believe that Lee had surrendered his army in Virginia. But he was sure they had done all they could. Booth's? Booth was his captain now. He had sworn to follow him, to take orders from him like a loyal soldier, that night in Gautier's when they had drawn their knives and pledged themselves to fight to the end on behalf of the Cause.

He got up and paced the room. He went to the window, which looked out onto the alley in back of Ford's Theater. Bricks, crumbled mortar, stacks of boards, and a heap of roof tiles lined the walls of the building. A horse stood patiently tied to a hitching post, and a mangy dog sniffed among broken plaster and boards.

Lewis thought of Mary, how he had left her in the misty night outside her house on Eutaw Street. She had wanted him to stay. When she had shown him her father's old medical books in the library, it seemed that he had found something he had been looking for. It had satisfied him to read through the books, to find words coming easier to him, to learn ways to heal, to mix medicine that would bring people back from illness, to set broken bones, to sew up wounds. Stopping Puryear from killing the Yankee prisoners at Warrenton had taught him that it was more powerful to save a life than to take one. Seeing the Wisconsin man jerking on the rope had brought him shame, sleepless nights with a gnawing in his gut. But the gratitude and relief in the eyes of the men he had saved had stayed with him. He sighed and turned from the window, weary of a world where men had to kill one another, where their orders took them into nights of haunted dreams. *This land is not for me.*

Now he knew what he would do. He would go to Baltimore again, and he and Mary could make plans. He would go to Florida, to Hebron, build a cabin there and plant a crop, and Mary Branson would go with him. But first he would have to tell Booth, tell him that he had enough of killing, that the war was over for him, that what Booth was going to do tonight would have to be done without his help. He would be Powell again, and the name of Paine would be gone forever.

Resolved, he grabbed his extra shirt and underwear and dropped them into his carpetbag. When he came to the pistol, he picked it up and turned it over, looking at it. Then he dropped it onto the bed, strapped his bag closed, and set his hat on his head. He cast one look behind him before he closed the door and walked along the hall to the stairway.

As he stepped onto the top step, a door slammed downstairs. He was in the middle of the stairway when Booth came up the stairs toward him.

Booth stopped. "Where are you going?" he demanded.

"Back to Baltimore, Captain."

"Baltimore! What for?"

"It's all over, Captain. The war is over and done with. Lee is back in Richmond. Jeff Davis is gone. There ain't no Confederacy no more. I'm going back to Baltimore to see Mary, and then I'm going to Florida." He started past Booth.

Booth's fingers dug into Lewis's arm. "So you throw down your weapon and retreat when the battle turns against us. I offered you a place in history, the place of a man who stood by his country in its darkest hour. I offered the chance to turn defeat into victory. But now I will do my work alone, if need be."

Lewis looked down into Booth's dark eyes and glanced away. Booth's grip on his arm relaxed, and Lewis went down the stairs hesitantly.

"Paine," Booth said, almost in a whisper.

Lewis stopped, but did not turn around.

"Paine, what about the Jasper Blues?"

Lewis did not move.

"What about them, Paine? You are the only man left. You bear their charge on your shoulders alone."

Lewis pretended not to hear. He went down the stairs, through the lobby, and out the door. But Booth's appeal gnawed at him. Lewis leaned against a pillar on the porch and thought of Sergeant Willis, of Lieutenant Hall, of Sam Mitchell and Henry Holmes and the other men of the Jasper Blues. He thought of Riley Green, too. After Riley died, could the war end this way? Four years of war had left him knowing only this: One last battle had to happen; war had set in motion a fury in each soldier's blood that could not be laid to rest except at some bloody battleground.

Lewis had not been with them in that last fight.

His hand throbbed and he held it in front of him, as if he expected to see on it, overlying the scar from Gettysburg, the burning mark of Miss Ferston's kiss and her tears, set there the night she said, "Here is a young man who will go so far as to shoot Abe Lincoln himself, whenever his orders tell him to," the night that Clara Meredith smiled approval.

Lewis looked across F Street at the windows of the Patent Office, illumined the night before by six thousand candles alight for the crushing of the Southern Cause. He turned. When he passed through the lobby again, a clock whirred and struck, breaking the afternoon stillness.

Lewis walked back up to his room and tossed his bag onto the bed. Booth was at the window, silhouetted against the dying light of day, his hands clasped behind him. Lewis stood in the middle of the room and waited, but Booth did not turn from the window.

"Seward, Lincoln's Secretary of State," Booth said. "Seward was hurt in an accident last week and is in his bed at home. Tonight you are to kill him while I silence Lincoln forever." Not until he had said this did Booth turn and look at Lewis, his face dark, indecipherable, with the light behind it.

Footsteps sounded on the stairs, and they waited. Davy Herold, hatless, appeared in the door, followed by Port Tobacco.

Booth struck a match and applied it to the wick of the candle on the bedside table. Then he brought it over to the table in the center of the room, shading the flame with his hand.

Davy and Port Tobacco sat on opposite sides of the bed while Lewis remained standing. "What's going on?" Davy asked.

Booth set the candle down and leaned over it, his hands resting on the table. The guttering light flickered on his chin and moustache, making his eyes and brow look as if they were moving in an effort to escape the shadows.

"Davy, tonight Lincoln goes to Ford's Theater, and I will kill him there. I have jobs for each of you to do, and if you do them, we can still save our country." He looked at Lewis, who turned his eyes down.

"There are some who say that our nation has been conquered," Booth went on. "I refuse to believe it. Out there," he said, sweeping his arm toward the window, "out there lies the salvation of the Confederacy. What though Granny Lee has surrendered and returned to Richmond in defeat? Kirby Smith holds the west, secure with fresh troops. And—now listen to this," he said, dropping his voice almost to a whisper. "I have secret promises that Kirby Smith can count on the aid of Maximilian's French army in Mexico. Two years ago my secret mission to Paris led me into the very sanctum sanctorum of the French government, and I saw men in very high places who assured me. Today I have renewed assurances from agents now in Washington City. Have no fear. Even now Jefferson Davis makes his way to a new capital west of the Mississippi, and outside the city—outside these very gates—lies Mosby with ten thousand men, ready to take this capital."

He stood and waited for his words to sink in. Lewis thrilled to the recitation of Booth's hopes. Together they would defy, they would carry the desperate fight into the enemy capital, strike at the heart of the tyranny itself.

Booth said, "Here is what you are to do. Davy, you are to guide Paine to Lafayette Square and Seward's house, then meet me at the Navy Yard Bridge. Paine will follow. Atzerodt, you have been at the Kirkwood House, where you can watch the comings and goings of the Vice President. Kill him tonight! Then cross into Maryland to meet

Davy and me at Surrattsville. You and Davy know the roads and you know the Potomac, and we will escape together."

Davy Herold looked at Booth dumbly, while Port Tobacco grunted. His eyes shifted to Lewis and back to Booth.

Booth walked to the bed, where Lewis's pistol still lay. He picked it up and handed it to Lewis, handle first. Lewis hesitated for less than one tick of the clock, then reached out and took it from him. He looked down at the gun, then tucked it into his waistband.

Booth looked into Lewis's eyes. "Paine, my young warrior," he said, "you are my supporting player, the player on whom the success of our drama depends. It falls to you, because our band has shrunk to four, to slay two of the arch-enemies of our country. First, you will go to Seward's house in Lafayette Square and kill him. Davy will guide you there. Then you will go to K Street, to the home of Stanton, the Secretary of War, and kill him. It is a demanding task, but I know that you have carried out desperate exploits, and I know that you can do this one."

He turned back to the table and cast his eyes toward Port Tobacco and Herold. "As for me, I shall make my way into Ford's and to the box of the President. There I shall find not just Lincoln but Grant as well. I have devised a way to shut off the door leading from the dress circle into the hallway behind the president's box, and I will be at my leisure to shoot them both. Then I will mount the horse that I will have tied in yonder alley and make my way into Maryland to meet Davy and Atzerodt."

He looked around in the candlelight at Lewis, at Davy, at Port Tobacco in turn, in the candlelight, smiling his satisfied, confident smile.

"Good. We shall strike at ten o'clock. By midnight the city will be in total confusion. But before we go, one more thing." He turned and lifted from the floor in one corner the leather valise that Lewis had seen him bringing up the stairs. Booth set it on the table and lifted out a bottle of wine, which he set beside the valise. Then he reached again into the bag and drew out a round white object. Not until he held it toward the candle and turned it over did Lewis see that it was a skull, ivory-colored and highly polished. Booth turned it so that the candlelight flickered into the eye and nose cavities and wavered into the shadow that had once held a brain. The irregular upper teeth grinned a macabre grin.

Setting the skull on the table, Booth produced a corkscrew from his pocket. "Here, Davy," he said, "pull the cork."

While Herold uncorked the wine, Port Tobacco sat down again on the bed. Lewis fixed his eyes on what Davy was doing. His throat felt dry, his palms moist. He wiped his hands on his coat. He felt Booth's eyes on him, but he did not look up.

The aroma of the wine drifted from the open bottle. Booth picked up the skull and cupped it upside down in his left hand. With his right, he took the wine bottle from Davy and, glancing around at the other three, began to pour it into the skull.

Setting the bottle back onto the table, he said, "Now! This seals our bargain." He lifted the skull to his lips and drank. Then he called to Port Tobacco, "Come here, Atzerodt."

Port Tobacco stood, the springs of the bed creaking under him, and stepped toward Booth. "Can I count on you, George?" Booth asked.

"I'll do vat I can, Vilkes."

"Be sure that you do. Drink!"

Port Tobacco looked at the skull, then at Booth. He raised both hands to take the skull and lift it to his lips. He drank and handed it to Booth.

"Davy?"

Davy Herold stepped forward, took the skull, and drank.

"Paine," Booth said, "after this drink, and after this night, you will know yourself more clearly than ever before. Drink!"

Lewis took the skull and looked into it. Nothing was there but blackness. As he raised the skull toward his mouth, a movement beyond the rim of the skull caught his eye. Hesitant, he looked at the fireplace. In front of it sat Aunt Sarah, stirring the coals and twisting slowly up to look at him. "You will hang." He shivered and the skull fell from his hands, clattering onto the table and then onto the floor, spilling wine onto his boots.

Booth bent over and picked up the skull, which had rolled at his feet.

"You will need a steadier hand than that, Paine," he said, pouring more wine into the skull. He extended it toward Lewis again.

His fingers shaking, Lewis looked again toward the fireplace while stretching out an unsteady hand. Aunt Sarah was gone. He took the skull and raised it to his lips. The wine was bitter and hot, and he had to swallow hard to take it down.

Booth smiled and lifted the skull from Lewis's hands. He poured the remainder of the wine down his own throat.

Booth lowered the skull and gazed at Herold, at Atzerodt, at Lewis, in turn. "God has made me the instrument of his retribution," he said quietly. Then he raised his right fist and shouted as if to an audience spread over all the world, "Sic semper tyrannis!"

17

WASHINGTON CITY
APRIL 14-17, 1865

THE GATE INTO Lafayette Square had been left open, and Lewis walked around the statue of Andrew Jackson until he lost count of the times that he had circled it. Then he walked in the opposite direction. Tired of walking, he sat on the base of the statue where he could watch the lights of the Executive Mansion and the lights at the Seward house on one side of the square. He laid his hand on the left side pocket of his coat, on the lump that was the medicine bottle that Davy Herold had wrapped and given him. "That's the best way to get in," Davy had said. "Dr. Verdi is his doctor." Dr. Verdi, Dr. Verdi, Lewis said over and over. Dr. Verdi sent this medicine. Well, it might work. But if it won't work, this will. He put his other hand on the grip of the heavy Whitney Navy revolver in his other coat pocket.

Lewis stood when his one-eyed horse snorted and jerked at the halter tied to a tree limb. A carriage was drawing up in front of the Seward house. A man stepped down from the driver's seat, and a servant came from the house and tied the reins to the hitching post. The servant followed the man inside. Lewis looked again toward the Executive Mansion, where a light detached itself from the far side of the house and moved along Pennsylvania Avenue. Lincoln and his wife, on their way to the theater. The lamp was soon out of sight, but Lewis could imagine the carriage being drawn slowly up the avenue, past Gautier's, where they had raised their knives and sworn to follow Booth's orders. Well, Lewis had kept his promise, even if John Surratt had let him down. And Sam and Mike, too. Lewis could not remember their last names, and he had never learned to tell them apart, but they ran together in his mind as people who would not keep their word. And they both claimed to be soldiers, too.

Lincoln's carriage would be nearing the Kirkwood House, where Vice President Andrew Johnson lived. If Port Tobacco could be trusted, he would be waiting to kill Johnson there. But Lewis doubted that Port Tobacco would go through with it. Certainly Booth doubted it, he could tell. And he would not go through with it if he passed a saloon before he got back to the Kirkwood. He would be there drinking and forget all about what he was supposed to do.

The carriage would pass Grover's Theater, but would not stop there. Better this way. Booth knew Ford's better, and he would find it easier to get into the president's box and get away. That was a good trick he had: to use a stick to block the door leading into the hallway behind the box. Then he would have time to work, and not be disturbed.

Lincoln would be turning onto Tenth Street, and the carriage would take him to the theater. It must be after nine o'clock now, and all the playgoers would be inside the theater. Would Booth be there? Maybe he would be in the lobby to see Lincoln go in. Or maybe he would go over to the Star Saloon next door and have a drink. Booth was a cool one. That is what he would be doing. Lewis thought, I could do with a drink now, but no chance. It won't be long before I have to cross to Seward's house, and I will need a steady hand there. My knife and pistol will have to serve me well tonight. Seward and Stanton. Lean, shrewd Seward, and fat, angry, scowling Stanton, the man who leads all of Lincoln's armies—the man Grant takes orders from. He went over in his mind the streets he would take, the way Davy Herold had shown him, to go from Seward's house to Stanton's.

He looked at the other side of the square, where Grant's name had glowed in red, white, and blue transparency the night before. The boxes with their glass letters were still there, but he could see only the *G* lit by a street lamp. Booth would kill Grant tonight, as well as Lincoln. They had had some bad luck in the last month, but tonight their luck would change.

Look at Old Hickory up there, waving his hat toward the President's House. Now, Lewis thought, my own hat is off to you, old

Andrew Jackson. Lewis could not see the statue's face, but in his mind Old Hickory looked like his father in the saddle of that upreared horse, staring beyond Lewis.

"Son," a voice called.

Lewis looked up. "What, Pa?"

There was no further sound. His father had no word for him, no commands. Now his only commands came from Booth. His father had tried to keep him from joining the army, and if he had listened to the old man, he would not be here now. But it is Now, not Then. It is always Now. Sometimes when he would fear a battle, it would come, and then it would not be the thing in the Time-to-Come that he had feared, but it would be the roaring fire and confusion and smoke of the thing that was happening Now. His father belonged to the Then, to old words that gave him no direction anymore. Booth is the Now, he thought, and I will listen to him direct me toward the Will-be, which the Now will become. But a soldier always lives in the Now.

The visitor came out of the Seward house and got back into his carriage. The clopping hooves passed up the street and died away. Now is the time. Lincoln sits in his box at the theater, and Booth leaves the Star and climbs the curved stairway to the dress circle. He passes behind the audience, goes to the passage behind the president's box, and closes the door. Better act Now. Soon it will be Then, and time will go by, and the chance will be gone.

Untying his horse, Lewis led him out of the gate on the Executive Mansion side of the square, then along the iron fence facing Seward's house. At the corner, he stood a few seconds, taking a deep breath, and with his free left hand felt again for the medicine bottle, for the pistol in his pocket, for the bowie knife tucked in the waist of his breeches.

He looked toward the Executive Mansion, where two windows showed light on this side. Then he stiffened when he heard hoofbeats on his left. His horse stomped a forefoot. A lone rider passed along H Street north of the square and then out of earshot. Lewis stepped onto the rutted, hard-packed street, his eyes fixed on the Seward house. The houses on either side were dark now, except for single lamps by the doorways. He crossed Madison Place and tied his horse's reins to the hitching post.

At the foot of the steps, he stopped and drew out the medicine bottle. Lewis mounted the steps slowly, holding the bottle in both hands. At the landing he paused before turning the doorbell, gripping the bottle in his right hand like a pistol.

The bell whirred deep in the house. He waited, but no one came. He was reaching to turn the handle again when a faint shadow appeared on the frosted glass. It grew until it became distinct, and the door was pulled open. A small, black man, spectacles on his nose, looked up at him out of a deeply wrinkled face.

"What do you want?"

"I brought some medicine from Dr. Verdi. He said that Mr. Seward was to take it tonight."

"Dr. Verdi? Why, he just left here not ten minutes ago. What for is he sending medicine now?"

"He just said to bring it here and give it to Mr. Seward."

The servant looked at him suspiciously, and pushed the door partly shut, so that he stood half behind it.

"Well, give it here, and I'll take it up to him."

"My orders is to hand it to him myself, and to show him how to take it."

"He be asleep now. I can't disturb him."

"It won't take long. He will sleep better after he gets the medicine I brought."

When the servant hesitated again, Lewis pushed through the narrow gap, shoved him aside, and started along the hall. The stairway began about halfway down the hall, and a single lamp glowed at the foot of the stairs. He made for the stairs with quick, long strides.

"Wait, sir! Excuse me!" the servant called behind him. "I'll go in front of you and show you the way."

Lewis paused at the foot of the stairs, and the servant passed him. Lewis fell in behind him.

"Sh-h-h! Not so loud. You making too much noise." The man turned around and held up his hand.

They went up the stairs, Lewis moving so fast that he bumped into the servant twice and had to stop. The pounding of his own heart seemed so loud to Lewis that he could not hear his footsteps. They reached the second floor and turned back along a dim hallway, which they followed to a second flight of stairs.

The servant turned toward Lewis again, their faces so close that the man shrank back. "Please walk more quiet. He be asleep on the third floor."

Lewis crowded close behind, impatient to get to Seward's room. He felt all the frightening expectation of an infantry charge, was not conscious of where he was treading, but he was as anxious to get to the top of the house as if it were an enemy bulwark.

"What is it, William? Who's that with you?"

On the landing above them, barring the way, appeared a young man with dark hair and a moustache, wearing a purple dressing gown.

"He say he brought some medicine from Dr. Verdi, Mr. Frederick." The black man stepped up to the landing and stood beside the young man, looking down at Lewis.

"I am Mr. Seward's son, and I will take the medicine to him. He can't be disturbed now." He held out his hand for the bottle.

"Can't do it, Captain," Lewis said. "Doctor says to give it to Mr. Seward myself."

Young Seward laughed. "Surely you can trust me to give it to my father. If you cannot leave it with me, you cannot leave it at all."

"Well, look and see if he's awake now. I've got to see him."

Turning away and sighing, young Seward walked up the steps and along the hall to the last door, which he opened, and looked in. Lewis stepped up to the landing and watched him pull the door to, then come back.

"He is asleep. You cannot see him."

"But I got my orders from the doctor to see him."

"No. Either give me the medicine or leave now. William, show this man to the door."

William started down the stairs, and Lewis followed him for two or three steps. Then he acted. He wheeled on the steps, leaped back to the landing, and rushed toward Frederick Seward, pulling the Whitney revolver from his pocket and dropping the medicine bottle as he moved. Young Seward's face was frozen in surprise as Lewis raised the revolver and aimed it at his chest.

Lewis pulled the trigger, but the hammer only fell with a loud click. The force of his charge carried him toward Seward, who had backed to the top of the stairs. Lewis gripped Seward's shoulder, raised the pistol, and brought it down on his head. With the bloody Seward clinging to his coat, Lewis struggled along the corridor toward old Seward's room.

Lewis tried again to fire the revolver, but the trigger was jammed, and he grabbed the revolver in his left hand while he drew his knife with his right. Just then Frederick Seward's grip loosened, and he collapsed. Lewis raised the knife and reached for the doorknob. Suddenly the door jerked open, and his rush carried him into the room, past a screaming young woman. Her white, horrified face blended with the white lace cap that she wore, a blur of whiteness above a yellow dress.

A man in uniform sprang from a chair and stared wide-eyed. When he moved forward, Lewis stabbed downward, slashing the man's face. Lewis lunged left toward the bed, where he saw only a pile of bedclothes. He raised the knife and stabbed, hammering, not knowing how many times the knife came down. His hand touched a solid body, which slid toward the other side of the bed. He heard a thud and a groan as the body landed on the floor, and again he raised the knife, but strong arms wrapped around his body, pulling him away from the bed. Twisting, he saw that it was the soldier who held him. He wrapped his right arm around the soldier's neck and tried to hit him with the revolver in his left hand.

The thud of their bodies onto the floor mingled with a woman's screams. Lewis dropped the revolver and tried to raise the knife to strike again at the soldier, but his strength had left him, and he gulped air. The soldier, covered with blood, held Lewis's hands back from striking.

Suddenly another man appeared in the room, shoving Lewis toward the door, and the soldier's grip fell away. At the same time Lewis's hand fell on a bottle on a bedside table, and he hit the newcomer over the head. There was no force in the blow, like the weakness in a dream, and he raised the bottle again, his muscles seeming to restrain him as much as help him, and wild cries, "I'm mad! I'm mad!" burst from his lips. In spite of the pounding, the man pushed Lewis toward the door and into the hallway. Lewis tried again to raise the bottle in his left hand, but his arm was too heavy.

"Oh, God! I'm mad!" Lewis shrieked again, as he spun around and started down the stairs, dropping the bottle.

He almost tumbled down the stairs, unable to slow his descent. Near the bottom of the last flight, he overtook a man who looked back startled over his shoulder as Lewis slashed at him with the bloody knife. Then he flung the man against the banister, plodded through the open door, and sagged down the front steps. He collapsed onto his knees, but found his footing again and staggered toward his horse. At first he could not mount, but leaned against the horse's side, gasping for air. The sharp night cold brought him back to his senses, and the distant screams from behind him seemed part of another world.

With trembling fingers he untied the loose knot that had held his horse to the hitching post. Twice he raised his left foot to the stirrup, and twice it slipped back to the ground. On the third try it stayed in the stirrup, and he heaved his lead-heavy body into the saddle.

When he took the reins in his shaking fingers, Lewis realized for the first time that he had lost both the revolver and the knife. With his free hand he pushed his matted hair out of his eyes. The horse moved along the street at a slow walk, and to Lewis it did not seem strange that this was so. Nighttime had become no time.

"There he is!" he heard behind him. "That's the man!" It was the black servant William's voice.

Lewis did not turn around until after he rode slowly out of Madison Place and turned up 15½ Street. Then he looked back once and saw William following him, alone, passing under a street lamp. He did not quicken his horse's pace.

When he looked back again, no one was following. He wanted to find Stanton's house on K Street. There he could finish his job. But he did not have a weapon now. Yet at once he was surrounded by Mosby's Rangers, and he knew that he would get a weapon. "Cab!" he called. "Cab Maddux!" His voice echoed in the empty street. "Give me a shooting iron, Cab!" The only other sound was his horse's hooves echoing in the street.

Where am I? he thought. I must have passed K Street. Better turn around and go back. He rode back and squinted at a street marker on a lamppost. This is it. But do I go right or left? He turned right. Four riders were coming closer to him. Ours or theirs? He felt for his holster, but it was not there. He felt for the ranger's shotgun that ought to be slung at his side, but it was not there.

The four riders drew nearer. They wore blue uniforms, and sabers rattled at their sides. They rode slowly, spread out across the street, and he held his horse to a slow walk. Then he could see their faces in the flickering light from a street lamp. Bare, fleshless skull-faces, grinning wide skull-grins. A scream pierced the air around him, coming from in front of him, from behind him, from both sides of him, and the riders vanished. He was alone.

Lewis shrieked and turned his horse. He did not try to hold the animal back, but let it gallop through the streets. The night tore at his face, at his hair, and he hunched lower in the saddle, almost hugging the horse's neck.

Sometimes he would slow his horse to a walk while searching for some landmark. He looked for the river but never found it. Sometimes he found himself between rows of houses on empty streets, or he would face tangled woods or open fields with no light. And always he tugged with one hand at his shirt, sticky with sweat and blood. The stench of hot blood drifted from it. Finally his horse could run no more and slowed to a limping walk, gasping and lathered.

Lewis woke on a thick cushion of grass, seeing around him in dawn twilight the black shapes of trees. He sat up and shook his head slowly from side to side. Drumming sounded in his head, and an ache radiated from it and flashed light from inside into his eyes. He thought of the night of blood, of screams, of wild rides through deserted streets, and told himself that it had been a dream.

He rose to his feet and stood swaying, hugging his arms around himself against the chill of the damp morning. His horse was gone. He did not know if he had left the horse and walked away or if the horse had left him. He stumbled over uneven ground and started to look for a road. His foot struck something hard, and he fell across it. He rubbed his shin where it had scraped against the thing that had caused him to stumble, and squinted in the dim light. A tombstone.

On his feet again, he saw more tombstones around him. He was in a graveyard, with scattered, irregular markers and cedar trees. He faltered toward a clump of cedars and a low building in the middle of the graveyard, where he found a vase against one wall of the little wooden shed half full of stale water, with moldy dead leaves on top.

Lewis raised the vase to his lips and drank, and then spat out the soggy, foul leaves. Leaning against the shed was a pickax, and he seized it.

He threaded among a thicker maze of headstones, making for a rail fence that appeared through the mist about a hundred yards away. His foot slipped into a shallow hole, and he fell forward, catching himself against a headstone. As he pushed himself up, he glanced at the name on the stone. He blinked, rubbed his eyes, and looked again. The worn letters seemed to read "Lewis Paine." He gasped, backed off, and let out a shrill, long howl. He wheeled and ran, stumbling over headstones, roots, and shrubs, sometimes falling flat in his terror and getting up and running again. Finally he lost all sense of where he was and where he had been going, and lay exhausted and panting at the base of a large cedar, his face buried in the wet mold of earth.

A bird sang above him, and Lewis lifted his face from the earth. He turned over and lay on his back, looking through the branches of the cedar at the gray sky. A robin stirred in the branches and flitted to another tree. His head throbbed again and he tried to swallow, but he felt only dryness in his throat.

He heard hoofbeats and sat up. Four riders passed along a road on the other side of a low stone wall. Crouching, he peered around the trunk of the tree, watching them until they stopped and dismounted. The pickax had fallen beside him, and he armed himself with it again. He looked up into the tree, then hoisted himself to the lowest branch. He clambered up several more feet and settled himself in thick foliage, hanging the pick on a branch above his head.

The men spread out and walked through the graveyard, each carrying a rifle or a shotgun. They were civilians. Three of them passed close to the tree where Lewis sat, and he picked up enough of their conversation to know that Lincoln was dead and that there was a reward offered for John Wilkes Booth. He gripped the handle of the pick.

The men lingered for more than an hour and then went away. Lewis stayed in the tree all day because other people were passing on the road and carriages came into the graveyard.

He slept and woke again a hundred times that night, shifting from limb to limb to ease the numbness in his body. The tingling of a leg, then the cramping of an arm, made him forget thirst.

At dawn he woke to the distant sound of bells. Other bells joined in, and high, quick tones mingled with low, slower ones to toll a somber symphony out of Washington City. Easter morning, and the bells were ringing in the resurrection of Jesus. *O death where is thy sting? O grave where is thy victory?* In the mocking joy of those bells, Lewis felt that the tolling was for someone else, that he was confined by death. Death had won its victory, and there was no resurrection. But he wished that it could be so, and thought that if he would sit perfectly still Jesus would come forth out of one of the low, vine-covered vaults, take him by the hand, and lead him forth to life. Then his shoulders began to shake, and he sobbed again until he fell into a fitful sleep.

He woke a hundred times to voices, as mourners poured through the graveyard bringing vases of bright red and yellow and white flowers, laying them at headstones and going away. There were other searchers, who brought guns instead of flowers and who stalked in grim silence.

Night came, and morning came again. It rained all the third day, and Lewis shivered, huddled and cramped on the limb. By nightfall the rain had slowed to a heavy, blowing mist, and he stirred out of half-sleep to an awareness that he was alone, that the graveyard had been barren of living people for a long time. He shifted his weight to a lower branch, and his muscles responded to the ache of movement after long denial. Remembering the pickax, he reached up, lifted it from the limb where he had hung it, and dropped it to the ground. His numb legs and arms shot bolts of pain through him as they came awake, and he felt his way down the tree to stand on the ground, trembling.

He leaned against the tree and thought, where can I go? It was night, and maybe under the cover of darkness he could pass through the streets to the Surratt house, where he could find shelter and food and rest. But he would need a disguise. He peeled off his coat and dropped it on the ground. Then he tore a sleeve from his undershirt, rolled it, and slipped it onto his head as a kind of cap. Pulling on his coat again, he lifted the pick and laid it on his shoulder. Shuffling and slow, he groped among low shrubs to the rail fence, climbed over it, and walked along the road.

It took him an hour to find Seventh Street, but when he did, he followed it into the city. At H Street he dodged into the shadow of a barn as two riders passed him, and he turned and walked over to Sixth Street. The Surratt house was the only one where any lights burned, and he was able to find it easily. He did not know what time it was, and it did not seem strange to him that the parlor light would be burning when the other houses on the street were dark.

He walked up the steps and lifted the knocker. It fell, echoing in the empty street. He looked around him, then knocked again. The door opened, and Lewis faced a Union officer. Behind him stood another officer, the yellow light from the hallway reflecting on the broad gold-rimmed lieutenant's stripe on his shoulder and on the bright row of brass buttons on his blue tunic.

"I—I stopped by to do some work for Mrs. Surratt." The words piped shrill from his throat, and his voice cracked after three days of disuse.

"Who are you?" the officer holding the door asked suspiciously.

"I'm a poor—a poor—man—that—I live in the neigh—the neighborhood—and Mrs. Surratt said she would give me work."

"In the middle of the night? You had better come inside."

As if in surrender, Lewis stepped through the door. He felt his arms growing numb and cold.

A third officer came out of the parlor, holding Mary Surratt by the arm. Her eyes were the eyes of despair.

The first officer turned to Mary Surratt. "Did you hire this man? Do you know him?"

"As God is my witness, sir, I never saw this man before."

The second officer asked Lewis, "What's your name?"

Lewis stared at him. Then he looked into the parlor, where Anna Surratt stood regarding him, her hands clasped in prayer in front of a crucifix bearing the twisted, bleeding body of Jesus, while beside her the red mahogany piano sounded a palpable silence.

18

THE PENITENTIARY, WASHINGTON CITY
MAY 21–JULY 7, 1865

W<small>ILL</small> D<small>OSTER</small> <small>WATCHED</small> the sergeant lock Lewis Powell into his chains, drop the canvas hood over his head, and lead him out the door. Doster's mind swirled with pity and self-condemnation. God have mercy on Lewis Powell, he was thinking, and God have mercy on me for thinking that I was glad for the sergeant shutting the boy under that pitiful sailcloth sack, shielding me from that look in his eyes. Three, four hours of talking today, and he has left all hope behind him in the telling. He has ranged beyond me, out to where my pretensions as Will Doster, counselor-at-law, can never reach. I remain behind, exposed to this tribunal of dubious judgment in a vengeful city. The worst of it is that whatever wisdom and confidence I wrapped myself in has been stripped away by the dread in a young soldier's eyes. It shames me and it weakens me, that unplumbed anguish of a man standing at the gateway to death and God's judgment.

Dubious judgment in a vengeful city—man's judgment—is what my job requires me to defend Powell against, and I must still do my best to perform that task. Where did I put that paper with the names? Here it is. George Powell, Live Oak Station, East Florida. Margaret Branson, Baltimore. Captain Dolly Richards, Mosby's Gang. Witnesses at Warrenton. It could hurt Powell to call up the Mosby connection, but I might offset the damage if I can prove that the boy saved the Union soldiers at Warrenton.

Doster paced around his table, then crossed to the witness box in the center of the room. He faced the table which separated him from the nine empty chairs where the nine generals and colonels of the court-martial sat every day. Doster squinted and stared at the chairs, as if by doing so he could conjure the nine judges into the room. He raised his right hand and said, "Nothing but the truth, so help me God. And the truth is that not all of you nine judges are field veterans, but I wish you were, instead of sheltered staff officers from the District, hand-picked to wreak vengeance on behalf of the carrion who must have their pound of flesh.

"Gentlemen of the court, you have decided your verdict beforehand, and the task left for me is to temper your opinion as to the degree of guilt. The funeral of the President with its million illuminations, its crowds of mourners, its solemn catafalque and processions has passed through Washington City. The armies of the Republic are being assembled for a triumphal march through the Capital. Feelings run high in the city, and they bear hard against the accused. They cannot help but inflame your minds. The prisoners have no friends, and we who attempt to defend them are vilified every day in the popular press. One thing is certain: Somebody must be hanged for example's sake.

"Who must hang? All eight? Not likely. Then who? The two that I represent—Paine and Atzerodt? You on the far right, General David Hunter, leave me scant room for hope. As president of the court, you continually sustain the prosecution and deny defense motions. I have been a trial lawyer long enough to read the signs when a judge will sympathize with an objection or when he resents a defendant. Those signs are in your eyes, General Hunter, even in the tilt of your chin, and they tell against me. The same goes for General Allison Howe and General James Ekin. Colonel Tompkins and Colonel Clendenin, you will follow the lead of your superior officers. That gives five against me, with six needed for a conviction. Colonel Robert Foster, I am not sure about you. General Lew Wallace and General August Kautz—I might find some faint hope in either or both. General Thomas Harris. Made your play early, with disquieting results for the defense. You took on a formidable foe when you challenged Senator Reverdy Johnson's fitness to appear as counsel for Mary Surratt. Johnson met the challenge grandly, for sure. 'I,' quoth the Senator, 'am a member of that Senate that creates armies and navies, and makes major generals.' A palpable hit. But perhaps you had the last word, Major General Harris, because Reverdy Johnson has not seen fit to reappear in this courtroom. Nevertheless, I am in your debt because you, the only physician on the panel, suggested an insanity defense for Paine. I don't know if prolonged constipation is a symptom of madness, but if you think it is, I will argue it to win your vote for Paine's innocence.

"Gentlemen, I beg you to regard the fifteen chairs on your right, along the west wall, where the eight defendants and their guards will sit again tomorrow—prisoner, guard, prisoner. The Surratt woman and Davy Herold. The Federal government has not hanged a woman yet, and as for Herold, he is no more than an accomplice after the fact, a mere tool useful in Booth's escape. O'Laughlin and Arnold, childhood friends of Booth from Baltimore, pulled out of the stew before it boiled over. Spangler, stagehand at Ford's Theater, might have made it easy for Booth to escape through the stage door. Mudd, that Maryland doctor, guilty of no greater crime than setting Booth's broken leg and waiting too long to report a suspicious patient. Knew who Booth was, of course, and that's why he is here. That leaves the pair I am defending—Lewis Paine and George Atzerodt. Atzerodt. Plug Tobacco, they call him. Booth sent him to kill the Vice President, but he did nothing. Nevertheless, he is the reason I am here, in recompense for the favors Plug Tobacco's brother on the provost marshal staff in Baltimore did me when I was marshal for the District of Columbia. Once I was in, Burnett, the one prosecutor who will all but acknowledge the injustice of this irregular military trial, twisted my arm into taking Paine's case—'temporarily,' as he put it. It will be temporary, all right, until he hangs."

Doster shrugged and backed out of the witness box. He walked to his table and gathered his papers. They will owe me for this, he thought. A bench, perhaps. Paine will die anyway. I will do the best that I can, of course, but it's a damn shame about the boy. Guilty of assault, but he didn't kill anybody. Someone might as well get some good out of this. Closing remarks to the court ought to show that I know my classics. Faust and Mephistopheles will be good. Quote from Shakespeare. That always impresses. Brutus, elements so mixed in him. Without Reverdy Johnson here to steal my thunder, my remarks can be the most eloquent. Might even turn this into a book. Lincoln's name in the title.

Time to write the letters at home before the guests come for dinner. Good to see the regimental staff again. Not since Gettysburg, and God's miracle that nearly all of them are still alive. Cranston lost an arm in the Wilderness fighting, but he will be there, too. What I would give to have field veterans like them on this commission. They have all had enough of blood. No revenge in them now, after days, weeks of saddle-weary Reb chasing. They know their battle laurels will not be any greener for being sprinkled with a woman's blood. Why could God not have granted me a court made up of men who stood with Grant at Petersburg?

Will Doster, counselor-at-law, dropped the papers into his briefcase, buckled the strap, and left the courtroom.

In the afternoons in the exercise yard, Lewis would talk through his canvas hood with the guards or lean against a wall and try to guess which way the river was. At night he would lie on his pallet and listen to the guards' measured steps, muffled by the canvas bag. He tried to remember what had happened after the night he stabbed Seward, but he could never recollect it. The graveyard came into his memory and then gave way to the scene of Booth's body lying on the deck of a ship. Was it a dream, or had he really seen it? He seemed to remember the clothes with blood still on them, the matted hair and week's growth of sparse beard, the shrunken features of Booth's face. Sometimes he thought Booth could not be dead but would come again. Then he would tell himself this was a foolish thought, that Booth was dead and he might as well die himself.

On that day in the trial when they had put the coat and hat on him, enabling him to move his hands and arms, free of the manacles, he had suddenly remembered who he was. The few minutes of freedom had jolted him so that he laughed out loud. And it had dawned on him that he was on trial for his life and that the evidence against him was all they needed to hang him. He did not know what had been going on at the trial before that day, and he did not even know how many days he had been sitting in the courtroom. His mind had been a windy cornfield under boiling storm clouds. But when he put on the coat and hat he also put on something like his former self. He looked around him and saw other people sitting beside him facing the court: Davy Herold, rubbing his hands together, his face sweaty; shifty-eyed Port Tobacco squirming in his chair; Sam and Mike, whom he still could not tell apart; and Mary Surratt, huddled in black with her shawl pulled over her head. There were two others he did not know, but a guard told him that one was a doctor from Maryland, the other a stagehand from Ford's Theater.

In the days after telling his story to the lawyer, he started to notice people massed at the other end of the long room, all staring at him. They would point and ask one another, "Which one is Paine?" Now and then a man in the crowd would gape at him, as if he were gawking at the devil, and Lewis made a game of staring down each of them. He would count while he stared, and one time he had to go as far as twenty-five before the man looked away. Then Lewis would smile, satisfied, and stare at someone else.

But what amused him most was the officer at the head of the court. Lewis heard guards call him General Hunter, and he tried to remember where he had heard the name before. Hunter. And then one day he remembered and laughed out loud while the spectators looked at him. General David Hunter was the man Clara Meredith had said he was to kill.

Nora Fitzpatrick told about going to Ford's Theater with him and John Surratt and the little Dean girl. She called him "Mister Wood," and for a while he wondered if that was who he was. Then other people would call him "Paine," and he remembered that he was both of them, and that he was Lewis Powell, too.

A doctor told how he had hurt old Seward, his sons, and two other men in the house. Lewis listened and wondered if he could really have done all that, when all that he recalled was being worn out and confused. He felt sorry for young Seward when the doctor said: "I examined the wound and found that his skull was broken; and I said to him, 'You want to know whether your skull is broken or not?' and he said 'Yes.' " Lewis shifted in his chair and wanted to cover his ears, but he dared not.

There were hours of talk about Port Tobacco, but Lewis could understand only enough to know that Port Tobacco had not done what

Booth had told him to do, had got drunk instead of killing the Vice President.

One day Lewis learned that Colonel Doster planned to try to prove he was mad and had sent to Florida for his father. "If the Court please," Doster said to the judges, "in order to go on with the defense, I shall be obliged to call some of the witnesses for Paine. I had intended to present them in a certain order to the court, and I therefore desire that all should be here before I present any. To explain why I wish to proceed with Paine's witnesses in a certain order, I will state that I intend to set up the plea of insanity, and in setting up that plea, I desire to commence with his disposition from youth; and I was therefore compelled to summon friends and relations of his living several hundred miles away from here. They have not yet arrived, and I cannot therefore now present them to the Court."

Lewis seldom thought about his parents. Now he pitied them in that little house in Florida, and he was sorry for what he had brought on them. If he could go back home, he would make it up to them, but he knew he could never go back home and the best way for him to unburden their lives of shame was to die.

Two days after Colonel Doster told the court about sending for the witnesses, Maggie Branson came to the court. She was tired, thinner than he remembered, and she would not look at him.

When Colonel Doster first started asking Maggie questions, Lewis leaned forward, hoping to catch her eye.

"Where did you first meet him?" Doster asked.

"At Gettysburg."

"What was the condition of Paine, and under what circumstances did you meet him?"

"He was in my ward, and he was very kind to the sick and wounded."

Perkins—Gardiner, Maine—flies buzzing against white canvas.

"About what time did you leave the hospital?"

"The first week in September."

"What time did you meet the prisoner Paine again?"

Maggie paused. She was scared, and Lewis wanted to reach out and tell her not to be afraid for him.

"Sometime—" she began, "sometime that fall or winter. I do not remember."

"Where did you meet him the next time?"

"At—at my own home."

Rain, and brown hair catching light like a halo.

"How long did he stay?"

"A few hours—a short time. I do not know exactly the length of time."

"Did you have any conversation with him?"

"Very little."

"Did he say to you where he was going?"

The little lawyer who looked like a rat butted in and said he did not like the question. Then the two lawyers got into a long argument about what kind of question Colonel Doster could ask. And while they argued, Lewis watched the frightened Maggie. Was she shivering? He looked among the crowd for Mary.

Finally Colonel Doster started asking questions again. "When did you see him the third time?"

"In January of this year."

"Where?"

"At my own home."

"Describe how he was dressed at the time."

"He was dressed in black clothing—citizen's dress."

"What did he represent himself to be, or say he was, at the time he came there?"

"A refugee."

"From where?"

"From Fauquier County, Virginia."

"What did he give his name to be then?"

"Paine."

"How long did he stay at your house then?"

"Six weeks, I think, and a few days. I cannot remember the exact time."

Her voice was quieter. Doster leaned closer and asked, "Do you remember the date when he came in January?"

"No, sir."

"But he stayed about six weeks?"

"Yes, sir. About that."

"Did he ever see any company while there?"

"Never, to my knowledge."

"Did you ever see Wilkes Booth?"

Maggie hesitated again, and Lewis thought of that Sunday in front of Barnum's Hotel.

"No, sir."

She must be sure that Charles Barnett won't tell on her, Lewis told himself. He will do whatever she says.

"What were his habits? Was he quiet, or did he go out a great deal?"

"He did not go out a great deal. He was remarkably quiet."

"In what way did his quietness show itself? Did he stay in his room?"

"He was a great deal in his room. His quietness sometimes amounted to forgetfulness. He seemed to be absorbed."

She is keeping Mary out of it, Lewis realized. Mary, standing by him, loving to hear him sing when they were around the piano. Mary, lying beside him at Miller's. *This land is not my home.*

"Did he seem depressed in spirits?"

"I think he did."

"Was he or not exceedingly taciturn and reticent?"

"No, sir. I think not."

Doster paused, backed up a step, and seemed to try to think of another way to ask the question.

"Was he not remarkable for not saying anything?"

For the first time she glanced at Lewis, then quickly back at Doster.

"Yes, sir. He was very remarkable for not saying anything."

"Have you or not a medical library in your father's house?"

"We have a great many old books."

"Did he not give himself up to the reading of medical works there?"

"He did."

"Do you not know whether Paine was exceedingly poor, or whether he had enough to pay his board?"

"He had enough to pay his board."

"Do you know how the prisoner happened to leave your house? In what way did it come about that he left the house?"

238

"He was arrested by the authorities of the city and sent north of Philadelphia."

One of the lawyers for the government, the one they called Burnett, stood then and asked Maggie questions.

"What time did I understand you to say that he left your house?"

"Sometime in March, I think."

"Do you know whether he came directly to Washington then?"

"I do not know." She was looking at her hands, twisting them.

"Was he absent at any time while he was boarding at your house?"

"One night, to my knowledge."

"You do not know where he was then?"

"No, sir."

Then Burnett asked some more questions about the hospital at Gettysburg, and they let Maggie go. She held her head high when she passed the dock where the prisoners sat. But she looked at Lewis as if to say "I tried to do my best for you." He would not see her again, and he thought that she smiled at him. Shadows darkened her eyes, and her hair was thinner now.

When Maggie went out the door that led to the cells, a girl passed her coming in. It was Peggy, the Irish kitchen maid at the Bransons'. Lewis looked at Doster. Why was this woman here?

The girl swore to tell the truth, and Doster crossed to the other side of her so that he was looking at Lewis while he talked to her.

"State whether or not you are a servant at the house of Mrs. Branson," Doster began.

"Yes, sir."

"State whether you ever saw the prisoner, Paine, there."

Peggy looked at Lewis only because she had to, but she quickly looked away. "I did," she replied.

"Do you remember the time when he came there?"

"Yes, sir. Either January or February."

"Do you remember how long he stayed?"

"He stayed there until the middle of March."

"What fixes that date in your memory? Are you sure it was the middle of March?"

"Yes, sir. I am sure of it."

"Do you remember at any time a controversy that Paine had with a Negro servant there?"

Lewis felt a hot rush of blood and clenched his fists. That Annie. Hang me for Seward, but not for Annie.

"Yes, sir. He asked her to clean up his room, and she gave him some impudence and said she would not do it. She called him some names, and then he slapped her and struck her."

"Did he or not throw her down and stamp on her body?"

"Yes, sir."

"And say he would kill her?"

"Yes, sir."

"What did this girl do in consequence of that?"

"She went to have him arrested."

"Did or did not the prisoner, at the time of this beating," and here Doster turned and looked Lewis in the eyes, "say he was going to kill her?"

"He did, while he was striking her."

Through blurred vision Lewis watched Peggy leave the witness stand and make her way past the prisoners' dock to leave the room. He lowered his head and shook it slowly. What a fool he had for a so-called defender! He had been prepared to die for stabbing Seward, but why would Doster bring in this business with Annie, which would hang him for something else?

When the prisoners shuffled out at the end of the day, Lewis told one of the guards at the door, "Tell Colonel Doster I've got to talk to him." The guard nodded before dropping the canvas sack onto Lewis's head. But half an hour later the guard came to his cell to tell him that the colonel was too busy to see him. Lewis shut his eyes against the blackness inside the sack.

That night, for the first time since he had been in the prison, Lewis knew relief from his constipation and from the headaches and weakness it had given him. Then he lay awake in the middle of the night, listening to the guards' boots in the courtyard and their calls every hour. Other sounds were muffled by the heavy sailcloth that cut his senses off from the world.

Staring into his sack of blackness, he found a pinpoint of light that did not move when he moved his eyes. He turned his eyes from side to side, but came back to find the point of light still there. Then he felt that he could float toward the light, and he floated toward it, and when he came to it the light drew him inside. From inside the light he could see darkness all around him, and everybody else was outside, in the darkness. Only he was inside the light. Maggie, Mary, Clara Meredith, his mother and father, his sister Annie, Wash and Susan and the children, Riley, Mosby—even Booth was outside it. He was alone in the pinpoint of light that was a part of the mind of God.

The next morning, after Lewis had stumbled to the door leading into the courtroom and a guard had lifted the heavy canvas bag from his head, Lewis squared his shoulders, breathed deeply, and stepped into the room. When his eyes grew used to the light, he looked toward the crowd gathered at the other end of the room.

The judges sat at their table on his left, writing or whispering to one another, and the attorneys were in a group on the right side of the room.

The lawyers went to their tables as the gavel rapped the court to order. The next time Lewis looked at the witness box, one of the guards was there. Doster started to ask him questions.

"Have you had any conversation with the prisoner during his confinement?"

"I have, occasionally."

"Please state what the substance of that conversation was."

Lewis sat forward, wondering what kind of story the guard was going to tell about him. But then that scrawny lawyer who did all the objecting and protesting, Bingham, started an argument with Colonel Doster. Lewis found it confusing, but he could tell that Doster still thought he was crazy. Finally they let the guard answer the question.

"I was taking him out of the courtroom," the guard said, "about the third or fourth day of the trial, and he said he wished they would make haste and hang him; he was tired of life. He would rather be hung than come back here in the courtroom."

Well, that is for sure what I said, Lewis thought, shifting his weight and smiling. The guard had it right. They might as well hang me. Now they want to talk about me being constipated. Will they hang a man because he can't shit?

When the guard left the box, Lewis looked around to see John Roberts going to the stand. What is he doing here? Of all the guards, he hates me the worst. Likes to spit when I walk by, to see how close he can get to my boot. He sure would like to hang me, if anybody would.

Doster asked John Roberts, "Does your duty call you to have charge of the prisoner Paine?"

"I am not in charge of him more than the others. I am around the prison. I have no orders to be in charge of him."

And a good thing it is, Lewis thought. If he was to be put in charge of me, he would shoot me and claim self-defense.

"Have you ever spoken to him on the subject of his own death?"

"The day that Major Seward was examined here? When the clothes were put on him—the coat and the hat? I had to put the irons back on him, and he told me then that they were tracking him pretty close and that he wanted to die."

For the first time that morning, Doster looked like he could not think of what to say. Well, Lewis thought, if he wants to prove that I do not give a damn if I live or die, he is going about proving it pretty well. But I could have told them that, without all this trouble.

Doster went to his table, looked down, and started shuffling papers, leaving Bingham to take his turn with John Roberts. Bingham made John repeat what he had said about Lewis, and both of them looked straight at the judges, like a couple of foxes slinking out of a henhouse. When John Roberts passed on the way out the door, Lewis met his glance and laughed, and John had to look away.

For the rest of the day, witnesses came and went, talking about the other people who were on trial. Lewis tried to listen to them for a while, then began staring at the spectators or gazing out of the window. When he was looking at the oak tree by the window, a hawk swept down and seized a sparrow. Then the hawk perched on a high branch and tore at the bird with its beak, the feathers floating past the window, a few fluffs drifting into the window and swimming through the steamy air of the courtroom.

When he heard the name "Paine" again, Lewis turned back to the courtroom and saw Doster talking to the judges. It was something about waiting longer for his father to come from Florida. But the general who was the head judge said that he would not wait any longer, would not give Doster more time. Lewis listened, but did not care.

Later, he started to ask the guard to let him talk to Doster, but instead he kept silent and walked outside behind the other prisoners, then waited while they dropped the hood over his head.

Another week in the steaming courtroom went by, and Lewis let himself drift into a daze in which he did not hear what was being said but stared alternately at the crowd and out the window. Then one day he heard the name "Paine" again and sat forward to listen to Doster talking about him.

"I am about to call two witnesses," Doster was saying, "and, to prevent any objections being made, I will state the reason for calling them. My purpose is to show that the prisoner Paine, three months before the alleged attempted assassination of Mr. Seward, saved the lives of two Union soldiers. The connection that has with the plea of insanity is this: It is the very essence of insanity that one violates the 'even tenor' of his previous life; and therefore, if I can show that three months before the alleged attempted assassination, this person exercised a degree of honor and benevolence which he afterwards violated and turned into ferocity and malignity, it will give a high degree of probability to the plea, and his subsequent conduct can only be explained by his being under the control of fury or madness."

When a woman came into the room and stood in the witness box, Lewis tried to remember, while she was taking the oath, if he had ever seen her before. He did not know who she was, and he wondered if Doster was going to bring in somebody like the guard John Roberts again to turn the court against him.

"Please state your name," Doster asked the woman.

"Lucy Grant."

"State where you live."

"In Warrenton, Virginia, on the Waterloo Pike."

"Look at the prisoners at the bar, and see whether you recognize any of them."

"I recognize the gentleman that they said was Mr. Powell."

Lewis looked more closely at the woman. It was the first time that any witness had used his real name.

"Which is that?"

"That one with the gray shirt."

"Where did you see him before?"

243

"In front of our house in the road."

"Was he not at that time in charge of soldiers, prisoners?"

"Three Union prisoners."

"Did, or did not, somebody attempt to kill those prisoners?"

Puryear's hard-glinting eye, his hand poised frozen above his gun butt.

"Yes. Somebody tried to kill them. I do not know who it was. They had on soldiers' uniforms."

"Where did these prisoners belong? Do you know what command they had been captured from?"

"I do not know."

"What time was this? Was there or not a raid at the time?"

"It was after General Torbert passed through Warrenton, around Christmas. I do not recollect the day; but it was about Christmastime."

"Did or did not these soldiers try to kill those Union prisoners?"

"Yes, sir, they did. And the gentleman whom they called Powell tried to prevent it."

"What did he say on that occasion?"

"I saw him in his stirrups; and he told them that whilst he was a gentleman and wished to be treated as one, though he could not defend all, if they killed or captured the ones he had in charge, they would do it at the peril of their lives, as well as I recollect the words. That was the meaning anyhow."

"Did he succeed in getting the prisoners away?"

"They left our house. I do not know what came of them afterwards. They left the road."

"Was one of those men killed by the soldiers?"

"Yes, sir. One was killed. I did not see him fall off the horse, but one of the Confederate soldiers rapped at my door and wanted to bring him into my house. My husband was not at home, and I was scared nearly to death. There was nobody there but me and my small children."

"The man who was called Powell, you say, saved the lives of the two." Doster looked at Lewis.

"Yes, sir. They left there. I do not know what became of them." She looked at Lewis and said directly to him, "Those prisoners ought to be here to answer for themselves, I should think."

With a smile and a nod toward Bingham, Doster returned to his table.

Bingham stood, scraping his chair on the floor. He cleared his throat and walked to the witness box, where he stood for a moment, his hands clasped behind him and his eyes fixed on the ceiling. He rocked up and down on his toes several times before he spoke.

"What name do you say he bore when there?"

"I know nothing about his name. I never heard of him, nor saw him before or since, that I know of."

"You did not hear his name?"

"No, sir. I was speaking of his trying to save those Union soldiers to a citizen; and he said he was Powell. That is all I know of him."

"You feel certain that is the same person?"

"That is the same person. I would know him anywhere, I think."

"You had never seen him before?"

"Never that I know of."

Bingham leaned on the railing of the box and looked into the woman's eyes.

"Or since?" he asked.

"Nor since that I know of."

"Was he dressed as a Confederate soldier?"

"Yes, sir."

Bingham strutted away from the witness like a little gamecock.

One of the generals at the long table asked the woman, "Did he seem to be a Confederate soldier?"

"Yes, sir. He wore a dark gray Confederate uniform."

"Had he any marks of an officer?"

"None at all. He looked rather more genteel than the common soldier."

The woman was allowed to leave the box, and Lewis followed her with his eyes. She was kind of pretty, and she had got most of it right, just a few details wrong, and he was grateful. But she did not look at him again.

The next witness was a tall, bony man, with unruly black hair and a prominent Adam's apple that rose and fell as he swallowed. He glanced around nervously as he held his left hand on the Bible and raised his right hand to swear.

Doster stepped forward and asked the man, "Are you the husband of Mrs. Grant, who has just left the stand?"

"I am."

"Were you or not present at a certain affray that occurred in front of your house last Christmas?"

"I happened there a few minutes after it occurred. I was not at home at the time but arrived a very few minutes afterwards. I was three hundred yards from my house, I suppose, when the pistol firing commenced; and I rushed home as quick as I could."

"Could you see the firing?"

"I could at that time."

"Do you know whether or not the prisoner at the bar saved the lives of two Union soldiers?"

"That is what was said there when I got to the house."

"What name did the prisoner go by?"

"I understood his name was Powell."

"Was he an officer, do you know?"

"Not that I am aware of."

"When was it?"

"On the first day of January last."

While the man talked, Lewis saw in front of him the scared face of the boy in Union blue, the sweat gleaming on his upper lip, his teeth chattering out of cold and fear. The face became the face of the Wisconsin man Puryear had made him hang, and then of Riley moaning and tossing in the lantern light at Gettysburg. He became lost in that swirling memory of all those faces, those deaths and pleadings, and he did not know when the farmer with the wild shock of black hair left the witness box.

Maggie Branson's name jolted him back to the courtroom. "Miss Branson and her mother," Doster was telling the judges, "were brought here as witnesses, and I have learned that they have been held for more than a week in the Old Capitol prison. There is no reason to hold them in custody."

Maggie in prison—and her mother? Lewis shook his head. Canvas bags too? Maggie, protecting the old woman and standing up to her guards. They can't break her.

When the noon recess came, Lewis told a guard that he wanted to talk to Doster. This time he was allowed to wait while the other prisoners filed out the door toward the cells. Mary Surratt passed him, her gaze fixed on the floor.

Lewis stood by the lawyers' table until Doster looked up from his writing. "Colonel Doster," he asked, "you said something about Miss Maggie Branson and her ma being kept in prison. Are they going to get out?"

"Yes, Powell, I will see to it that they get to go back home. They were in custody in Baltimore, so the court thought they had to be kept in custody here."

"They weren't mixed up in none of this."

"I know. There are no charges against them."

"Did they say anything about a fellow name of Joe Thomas?"

Doster glanced at the guard, then moved closer to Lewis and whispered, "Joe Thomas is dead. He killed himself about ten days after the assassination."

"Do you think—?"

"That it had anything to do with this business? There are rumors. But we won't talk any more about that."

He gathered some papers and stuffed them into his briefcase.

Lewis felt the guard's hand on his arm, but he pulled the arm away without looking at the guard.

"One more thing, Colonel," Lewis said. "When you talked to Miss Maggie Branson, did she tell you anything about her sister Mary?"

"Powell, I have to go now." Doster turned away.

Lewis lifted his manacled hands toward Doster. "Tell me, Colonel. I want to know."

Doster looked at Lewis's hands, held apart by the iron bar. Lewis thought that he saw a tear in the lawyer's eye, and he quivered to think that Doster might not answer him.

"Powell—son—" he began. Then he said to the guard, "Soldier, wait over by the door yonder." The guard hesitated, looking from Doster to Lewis, then obediently walked to the door and stood watching them. Doster looked toward the center of the courtroom where some officers were talking, now and then holding their hands close to their faces and laughing. He turned toward Lewis and stepped closer, laying a hand on Lewis's shoulder. "Son," he whispered, "Mary

247

Branson is very sick. She conceived a child but has miscarried. They are afraid for her life."

Lewis dropped his hands and looked away from Doster. He stood still for a minute, and the table in front of him blurred. "Tell her—" he began hoarsely. He cleared his throat and said, "Tell her I'm mighty sorry things turned out the way they done."

The guard was beside him then, a reminder of where he was. Lewis turned toward Doster and said, "We had plans, Colonel—Mary and me did." He yielded to the tug of the guard on his arm and went out. When the sack was dropped over his head, he shuffled back toward his cell, guided by the guards on either side, feeling tears running down his cheeks, and biting his lip hard so that the guards would not hear him crying.

At the morning sound of tin cup and plate clattering to the floor through the bars, the swoosh of mealy mush being ladled onto the plate, and the gurgle of coffee, Lewis did not move but lay on his side, knees drawn almost to his chin, lost in the sack of blackness. He heard the lone guard pacing wordlessly in front of the cell, waiting for him to grope to the bars, to feel for the plate and cup and take hold of them, to hunch on his cot spooning the steaming mush through the mouth-hole in his hood. On other mornings there were two guards, yawning and stretching and bragging about the women they had tumbled the night before. He was glad that this one was silent. Once the guard coughed and spat, the spittle slapping against the floor like a poker player's winning hand being slapped onto a table.

Lewis lay curled in private darkness, not knowing the passage of time because time had long ceased to have duration. There was only This and then That. He had stopped being conscious of a time between.

When someone unlocked his cell door and he heard the plate and cup being lifted away and their contents poured into a slop bucket, he twisted so that he could sit on the side of his cot, then reached down and pulled on his soft leather boots. Then he stood and turned his body toward the door.

"This way, Paine," the sergeant said.

Lewis shuffled toward the door and held his manacled hands forward while the sergeant inserted the chain, strung it, and padlocked it. Then he stumbled between two guards along the corridor, down the stairway, and out to the exercise yard.

Outside, Lewis leaned against the brick wall. Rough lumps of mortar dug into his shoulder and still he stayed there, hearing the other prisoners talking and bargemen shouting on the river beyond the wall. By tilting his head he could see his shoes, brown against the gray dust. When a spot of color appeared, he moved his head until he could see, through the gap at the bottom of his hood, a blue larkspur like those his mother had grown outside her kitchen. It was the first flower that he had seen in the prison, and he wondered how it had managed to struggle to life in that hard-packed gray dirt. He sagged onto his knees and found that by resting the stiff canvas on his shoulders, he could tilt his face down and look more closely at the flower, at its series of small blossoms climbing the stem, each a copy of the one below it but diminished in size. He groped his hand toward the flower and plucked it. At the same time, he noticed a cluster of white flowers near it, and he had to twist his body and throw his head far back to see under the hood a profusion of morning glories hanging far up on the wall. He broke one of the snowy blossoms with his left hand and held the two flowers, rolling the tender stems between his fingers.

Lewis swayed onto his haunches, pushed himself up from his knees, and sagged against the wall. When he felt a guard's hand on his arm and heard a voice say, "Time to go, Paine," he went with a freedom that he had not felt in a long time, as if he had retrieved part of that outside world that he could know only by the feelings in his fingertips.

In his cell, Lewis fell on his knees again and groped under the cot for his Bible. He had stopped reading it long before, but he opened it now this time to give something to it instead of take something out of it. He laid the flowers in the open Bible and touched once more the soft petals before closing the Bible and laying it back under the cot. Then he sat on the cot and hung his head.

"Jesus, Jesus, Jesus," he said.

19

WASHINGTON CITY
JUNE AND JULY 1865

WILL DOSTER STROKED his chin with the wooden shaft of his pen, then sketched trees and cannons on the foolscap sheets until the pen scratched. He changed steel nibs for the third time that morning and squirmed to keep from dozing while the other defense attorneys presented their arguments. But it was hard to stay awake, especially when young Clampitt read Reverdy Johnson's defense of Mary Surratt in that sing-song voice of his.

They have left me in the saddle without a bridle, he thought. No word from old Reverend Powell in Florida, and they deny me more time. That captain in Mosby's gang—Dolly Richards—no reply from him, either. Likely expects to get his neck stretched if he shows up in the District. Then Dr. Norris's wife dying just when I needed Norris to testify that the boy is insane. Seward's wife, too—dying out of shock at what Powell did to her husband and her sons—that dashed whatever hope I might have had that he would intervene to save the boy's neck. To cap it off, four government doctors have come in to testify that Powell is as sane as those epauletted generals yonder. My God! If he had been as sane as they are, he would have stayed with that Branson girl in Baltimore, and not let John Wilkes Booth pull him into that mad plot of his. A Mephistopheles, that Booth. And the boy a poor, confused, ignorant Faust. The irony of it was that he thought he was doing his duty to the South. Some duty. These mad acts have stirred a desire for retribution that even the deaths of all

eight will not assuage. There are those who will not rest until they
have humbled the South and drained it of all hope. Paine did more
than just stab Seward. He plunged that knife into his own people's
heart.

Today is my last chance. I could have done as well by staying
home, like Reverdy Johnson and Fred Stone. The generals and colonels
have their minds set on hanging both my clients. If I had not known
it already, I learned it for sure yesterday at lunch.

"Well, Paine seems to want to hang, so we might as well hang
him." It was General Ekin staring at me when I looked around to see
who said it. Could have been any one of them, anyway. Likely they
all think that.

Doster glanced left along the line of defendants, each flanked by
a guard. Lewis Powell sat with his manacled hands resting on his
knees — hands out of place here, slender as an artist's or a surgeon's.
His legs were stretched in front of him, his head tilted back, his large
square jaw relaxed as he seemed lost in some sight at the other end of
the room. Doster, in response, glanced toward the distant corner, but
saw only shadows and scattered dust motes suspended in summer heat.

He was jolted back to himself when Thomas Ewing nudged him
and he heard the word "adjourn." Mechanically, Doster rose. So they
would give him a reprieve until tomorrow to present his argument. A
reprieve from a charade.

Near about six weeks, the guard said. Lewis never thought of the time
that the trial had been going on, and now it did not matter to him how
long it had been. He came to the court nearly every morning, and he
went back to his cell when the guards told him to go, and he knew no
more of the passing of time than a hog penned for the slaughter. But
today he sensed that it was nearing the end. For two days the lawyers
had been talking about laws and courts and such that had nothing to
do with John Wilkes Booth defying his enemies on the stage and in
Washington City, nothing to do with a soldier obeying the orders that
Booth, his captain, gave him, nothing to do with the blood and
screams and the flight in the darkness, nothing to do with the dreams
that had tormented him in the long, hot nights, nor with that dream
that brought him peace and left him inside the mind of God, leaving
outside everything that he had known.

So when he saw Doster stand, a stack of papers in his hand, clear his throat, and approach the generals, it was with a distant feeling of only mild interest, as though he knew that Doster was going to talk about someone else, not Lewis Powell—about somebody called Paine who had done things for which Lewis Powell would have to die.

The lawyer started by talking about Lewis's life in Florida, about his joining the Jasper Blues, about the war. Most of it was true, but he left a lot untold. Even when he told things that were not the way that Lewis remembered them, it did not matter, because in the telling they came to be so for Lewis. He agreed silently that the man that the lawyer was talking about, the man called Lewis Paine Powell, was the "poor creature, overcome by destiny," that Doster said that he was. And, though he did not know what the word meant, he silently agreed with Doster when he said that John Wilkes Booth held his power over Powell by means of some kind of influence called "mesmerism." And most of all he agreed, even nodded, when Doster told the judges, "I asked him why he carried out such a violent attack on Secretary Seward and the others in his household, and his only answer was: 'Because I believed it my duty.'"

Doster's closing words came in a loud, clear voice, addressed to all the spectators as well as to the officers of the military court. Laying his handful of papers on the table in front of Lewis and stepping to the middle of the room, Doster pointed toward Lewis and said: "This man desires to die in order to gain the full crown of martyrdom; and therefore, if we gratify him, he will triumph over us; but if we spare him, we will triumph over him. If he is suffered to live, he will receive the worst punishment—obscurity—and the public will have nothing to admire. He has killed no man, and if he be put to death we shall have the anomaly of the victim surviving the murderer. Under the laws, this man can be punished only for assault and battery with intent to kill, and, therefore, imprisoned. If we put this man to death, he will live forever in the hearts of his comrades, and his memory will forever keep our brethren from us. If we put him to death, we will show that war is still in our hearts, and that we are only content to live with them because we have subdued them.

"Before I close, one word from myself. I have heretofore spoken of the prisoner as his counsel, I may also speak of him in my character as a man; and I can testify that in the four weeks' acquaintance I have had, hearing him converse with freedom and explain all his secret thoughts, in spite of the odious crime with which he is charged, I have formed an estimate of him little short of admiration, for his honesty of purpose, freedom from deception and malice, and courageous resolution to abide by the principles to which he was reared. I find in him none of that obstinacy which perseveres in crime because it is committed, and hopes to secure admiration in a feigned consistency. Neither is there about him a false desire of notoriety, nor a cowardly effort to screen himself from punishment; only one prominent anxiety—that is, lest people should think him a hired assassin, or a brute, an aversion to being made a public spectacle of, and a desire to be tried at the hands of his fellow citizens.

"Altogether, I think we may safely apply to him, without spurious sympathy or exaggeration, the words which were said of Brutus—

> This was the noblest Roman of them all;
> All the conspirators, save only he,
> Did that they did in envy of great Caesar;
> He only, in a general honest thought,
> And common good to all, made one of them.
> His life was gentle, and the elements
> So mixed in him, that nature might stand up
> And say to all the world, 'This was a man!'

"I commit him, then, without hesitation, to your charge. You have fought on the same fields, and as you have never been wanting in mercy to the defeated, so I know you will not be wanting in mercy to him. You have all commanded private soldiers, and as you could estimate the enthusiasm of your own men, so you will know how to estimate the enthusiasm of those who fought against you. The lives of all of you have shown that you were guided in all perplexities by the stern and infallible dictates of conscience and duty, and I know that you will understand and weigh in your judgment of the prisoner, dictates and duties so kindred to your own."

Lewis looked at Doster and nodded as the attorney gathered his papers and went back to his chair. Doster had done well by him, and he almost believed that he might change the minds of the Union officers sitting on the court.

*   *   *

LIVE OAK, EAST FLORIDA: JULY 1865

Patience Powell did not sleep at night. Tonight she sat in the dark, the shotgun across the arms of her chair. A person could not be too careful, now that the word had gone around that her son was the "Paine" who was on trial. She shuddered when she recalled the dog she had found two mornings ago hanging by its neck from the tree by her front gate. If Lewis had listened to his ma and pa, she thought, he would be here helping on the farm, not in a courtroom in Washington City, with more harm than good coming out of him. It was a shame, but she could not help him now. She had to take care of what family she had left.

When she heard a mule in the yard, she got up from the chair and went to the door, holding the shotgun across her body.

"Missy! It's Martin."

Patience lifted the bar and leaned it against the door frame. She pulled the door open and went onto the porch.

"Is he coming back home now?" she asked.

"Yes, ma'am. Mr. Wash, he bringing Mr. George in the wagon. He wanted me to come on and tell you."

"Is he still drunk?"

"I picked up a lot of jugs and th'owed them in the wagon. I don't know how he got them, but he got them somehow. Saw some ladies that stays over yonder by the church, and they say to tell you don't let him come back there no more, that they ain't going to have him for a preacher, that they don't like it one bit that he been there drinking in their church for five days, and he done run them off when they tried to come to meeting."

Patience Powell laughed and leaned the gun against a post on the porch. "I'll go in and stir up some grits. You go draw some water and heat it for his bath. Might as well make it complete. The niggers is trying to run us out on account of our son, and the whites is trying to run us out on account of Mr. Powell being the way he is. Did Mr. Powell say, after wrestling with the angel for five days in that there church, that he had made up his mind to stay here and look after his family?"

"He don't say nothin' but just that he wants to go to Jacksonville, and then on to Washington City, to see about his boy."

Patience Powell sighed, picked up the shotgun, and walked into the house. Her feet led her by their own memory through the dark room toward the square of dim light that was the window. She dipped her hands in the water of the wash basin below the window sill and splashed the cool water onto her face. She paused, a recollection flickering in her mind. She dipped her hands again into the water and raised them cupped to her face, letting the water pour over her closed lids and then opening her fingers, brushing them along her cheekbones and sunken cheeks covering toothless gums. Her cheeks felt warm above her hands as tears mixed with the water, and she ran her wet hands down her thin, wrinkled neck and over the flattened breasts. Her eyes still closed, she felt again the waters of a spring in the hills of Alabama on a summer morning twenty years before. Stopping berry-picking, she had lifted the baby Lewis, her last-born son, and carried him to the edge of the spring to wash him. Spots of sunlight skipped under the trees and vines, and two redbirds sang among the leaves. A sudden wave of joy poured over her, and caught and lifted her, and looking around, she slipped out of her cotton dress, picked up the baby, who was babbling and waving his arms, and waded into the spring. She felt cautiously for her footing on the rough limerock bottom and held her breath, her heart pounding. Carefully holding the baby with one hand, she laved water over him as he kicked his feet, splashing the water over her face, her breasts. She laughed as a stream of water flowed out of his little stem and hugged him tightly, warmly against her cool bare breasts. Now she raised her hands again to her face and wept softly, for the time that was gone and for her lost son, unaware of the wagon carrying her son Wash and George Powell, drawing like a hearse through the gate in a reluctant gray dawn.

WASHINGTON CITY: JULY 1865

For days Lewis Powell sat on his cot, stroking the dried petals of the flowers lying on the pages of his Bible. They were like the dried-out memory of the day when, after hearing the rat-faced lawyer talking about laws and courts, and not about what "Paine" had done, what Booth had done—when, after all of that, Lewis had heard strange words that might have something to do with him, but he could not remember the words. Perhaps someone would come and tell him what they were.

One evening after the prisoners had been taken for a walk in the exercise yard, he asked a guard. Lewis heard thunder in the distance and felt a wind rise, presaging a storm. "Are they going to hang me, Billy?" Lewis asked.

"Yep, Paine, looks like they aim to," was all Billy told him. But when it would come he did not know. All that he could do was to sit on the cot and touch the dry, dead flowers. He would think about Mary Branson and the life that had grown in her, the child now dead, and his throat would tighten.

At last came a day when the guards did not take him to the exercise yard, but told him to wait in his cell for General Hancock to come to tell him something important. Then the guard lifted the hood from Lewis's head and left him sitting on the cot.

A beam of light slanted along the corridor, and Lewis watched flies dart into and out of the light, swarming over a puddle of mush spilled close to the bars. They were large, green flies, buzzing in a steady monotone. Through the buzzing of the flies stabbed the clang of the metal door and Lewis heard footsteps coming along the corridor—two or three men wearing boots, one tapping with a walking stick. Lewis sat back and leaned against the wall, watching the cell door. The guard at the door came to attention and saluted as two officers in generals' uniforms appeared in front of his cell, followed by Colonel Doster. The generals returned the guard's salute, and the one leaning on the walking stick told him, "As you were. Unlock the door."

Lewis stood. The general with the walking stick entered first, his head tilted high as he gazed at Lewis out of bold gray eyes. His light brown beard was flecked with gray, and his face showed no expression. The other general was General Hartranft, who commanded the prison, and who carried a leather portfolio. Doster followed them into the cell and stood behind them.

The first general said, "Paine, I am General Hancock, and it is my duty to read to you a statement from the court, followed by one from the President. After I have read them, you may ask me about them."

General Hartranft took a paper out of the leather portfolio and handed it to General Hancock, who began to read in a steady tone that reminded Lewis of the priest who had visited Mary Surratt at Surrattsville: "To Major-General Winfield Scott Hancock, United States Volunteers, commanding the Middle Military Division, Washington, D. C.

"Whereas, by the military commission appointed in Special Orders Number 211, May 6, 1865, and of which Major-General David Hunter, United States Volunteers, was president, the following persons were tried, and, after mature consideration of evidence adduced in their cases, were found and sentenced as hereinafter stated, as follows:—

"*Lewis Paine.* Finding of the specification, guilty. Of the charge, guilty.

"*Sentence:* And the commission does therefore sentence him, the said Lewis Paine, to be hanged by the neck until he be dead, at such time and place as the President of the United States shall direct, two-thirds of the commission concurring therein."

Feeling himself sway, Lewis stiffened his knees. Those were the words that he had heard days before in the courtroom, the words that he had been trying to remember. *This land is not for me. To be hanged by the neck until he be dead.*

General Hancock read on, in a voice that sliced words from the paper and dropped them into the solitary cell: "And whereas the President of the United States has approved the foregoing sentences, in the following order—" Here the general cleared his throat and glanced at Lewis before lowering his eyes again to the paper. "Executive Mansion, July 5, 1865. The foregoing sentences in the cases of David E. Herold, G. A. Atzerodt, Lewis Paine, and Mary E. Surratt, are hereby approved; and it is ordered that the sentences in the cases of David E. Herold, G. A. Atzerodt, Lewis Paine, and Mary E. Surratt be carried into execution by the proper military authority, under the direction of the Secretary of War, on the 7th day of July, 1865, between the hours of ten o'clock A.M. and two o'clock P.M. of that day. Signed, Andrew Johnson, President." Hancock stopped and shifted the papers. He squinted at the next sheet and started again. "Therefore, you are hereby commanded to cause the foregoing sentences to be duly executed, in accordance with the President's order. By command of the President of the United States, E. D. Townsend, Assistant Adjutant-General."

General Hancock handed the paper to General Hartranft, who slid it into his portfolio, then looked at Lewis. "Do you know of a clergyman you want to see, Paine?" His voice was quiet, almost friendly.

Lewis's lips moved, but no sound came out. He paused and swallowed. He did not want to sit alone. "Only my pa," Lewis said. "If you can't bring him here, it don't make no difference to me."

"The Reverend Gillette, here in Washington City, has offered to spend the time with you," General Hartranft said. "I will send for him."

Lewis stared at him, hardly realizing what he had said. "General," Lewis said, "you read something there about Mary Surratt. I done what I done because it was my duty as a soldier. But I hope you will tell the President that she did not have anything to do with any of this."

The generals glanced at each other, then passed through the cell door.

Will Doster reached out as though he was going to lay his hand on Lewis's shoulder, but Lewis turned away and faced the door, and Doster let his hand fall to his side. "I am sorry it turned out this way, Paine," he said.

"Colonel," Lewis said, "there's a heap of things bigger than me that I don't understand." He sank onto his cot and looked up at the lawyer. "You done your best for me, and I thank you."

"God be with you, Paine." Doster turned and followed the generals down the corridor.

Lewis stared again at the flies, still buzzing around the spilled mush. There was a cry from down the row where Atzerodt's cell was. Then he shut his eyes as the generals and Doster passed his cell. From somewhere came a low moaning like the lonely sound of a mourning dove on a hot Sunday afternoon.

The guards let Lewis go out to the courtyard, but now they left the hood off. Mary Surratt, clutching a rosary and leaning on Anna's arm, walked there, but neither she nor Anna spoke to him. Atzerodt and Davy Herold paced nervously without speaking. Sam and Mike stayed by themselves, talking in low tones, as if they did not want to be with the condemned ones. With the stagehand and the doctor, they would go to prison, not to death, and that knowledge set them apart.

Guards brought supper to his cell, but Lewis did not look at the food, and after a while they took it away. The yellow light in his cell had surrendered to darkness by the time that Lewis heard two men approaching. Were they coming for him now? Maybe coming to say that he would not die, that there had been a change in orders? He sat on the edge of his cot and waited, his head bowed over the elbows-on-knees posture that the bar between his wrists allowed him.

A sergeant came first and hung a lantern on a peg in the wall. Then he briskly unlocked the cell door and ushered in a tall man wearing a black suit and a high-collared white shirt with a string bow tie. He was a big man, wearing little gold-rimmed glasses that seemed made for someone else, and he cradled in the crook of one arm a Bible, its gold-edged pages reflecting light from the lantern.

"Here's Paine, Reverend," said the sergeant. "He's all yours. He ain't going nowhere—for a while, that is." He set a chair inside the cell, then locked the man into the cell with Lewis. "There's a guard at the end of the corridor," he said. "Holler if you need him."

"I won't need him," the man said.

The sergeant walked away, saying something to the guard before his tread dropped down the stairway and softened into silence.

The man in the black suit stood looking at Lewis. "I am the Reverend Gillette," he said. "General Hartranft sent me."

Lewis stared at the ceiling, waiting for him to say more.

"What do I call you? Paine? Mr. Doster tells me that your real name is Powell."

"You might as well sit down, Reverend, if you have come to stay. You might as well call me Paine, too. I was Powell in the Confederate Army, but now there ain't no more army, and no more Confederacy, neither. So when they hang me, they will hang me as Paine."

Gillette pulled the chair in front of Lewis's cot and sat. He opened the Bible and took out an envelope. "Brother Paine, this letter came for you, and the general gave it to me to bring to you."

Lewis took the envelope and turned it over. The seal had been broken, and on the loose flap was written "M. Branson, Baltimore, Md." His hands trembled as he took out the letter and unfolded it. He leaned against the bars of the cell door so that the lantern light would fall on the page. The script was the bold, self-assured hand that he knew as Maggie's. It read:

Dear Doc,

I am writing this before knowing the outcome of your trial, but I pray that the court will be lenient on you as a person who was doing what he thought to be his duty.

It is my own sad duty to tell you about my poor sister Mary. On the night after she learned of your arrest, she collapsed in a state of acute mental and physical distress. She lingered in this condition for several weeks, under the care of our family physician. The details of her illness are not those that I can mention in this letter, but I understand that Attorney Doster has made you acquainted with them. It was a few days after my mother and I returned home from Washington City, where I testified at your trial and where we were subjected to a summary and unjust imprisonment, that she succumbed. I cannot without tears speak of the sweetness of her nature throughout her long illness, of the warm gratitude that she expressed for every attention, no matter how small, and especially of her solicitude for you. She spoke continually of her affection for you, and of her sorrow at the events that have led to your misfortunes, and to the sufferings of innocent parties.

Sincerely imploring that you will ponder my beloved sister's last wishes for you,

I remain your grieving

Margaret Branson

Lewis wiped his eyes with his hand and sank onto the cot. When he looked at the corner of the cell, he fancied that he saw, lying in the shadows, Mary on a black-draped bier, her brown hair flowing on either side of her head, until she became Clara Meredith, and he could not tell one from the other.

"She is at peace with God, Paine," Gillette said.

Lewis stared at the corner, but he could see no longer the figure there, only the shadows of the wall's angle. He shuddered and went to the water bucket, took the wooden dipper from it, and drank. "I don't want to die," he said. "Nobody does. I want to go back to the Suwannee River and farm the land I found there a long time ago. Of a morning you can see the deer walk across that farm and go down to the river to drink. I want to be there. I don't want to die. But they have made up their mind to hang me."

There was a splash as he dropped the dipper back into the bucket, and he stood by Gillette's right side, stretching out his hands with the iron bar between them. "Do you know what is the only thing I hope for out of it? That is that I won't die just like a rabbit dies when you catch it in a trap. I am a man, and I have lived for twenty-one years, and I want my life to count for something. Maybe I will be the last soldier that will die. And the Yanks can hate me instead of hating my country and the people in it. Maybe their hate will get all used up on me and there won't be no more hate left over for anybody else."

Gillette moistened his lips and held the Bible tighter. "Paine, you will soon be called before a higher bar of justice than that which you have confronted in this land. The judgment of God is swift and sure, but the mercy and forgiveness of God are boundless as the sea. Are you prepared to face God?"

"You want me to beg God for mercy."

"He will forgive. You were like a poor, helpless fly caught in the web of that spider, John Wilkes Booth. That man was to blame for all of this evil, not you."

"If that is so, then God knows it without me telling him. Captain Booth was a great man, and one time I would have followed him into any battle. But Mary did something for me by dying. She opened my eyes to all the wrong we done." Lewis paced back and forth, impatient with the walls that hemmed him in. Suddenly John Wilkes Booth had become part of his past. His last scene had been played, and the curtain had fallen. What Booth believed in was still there, buried under the ashes of what had been the South. It was what Booth did about it that was wrong. "After four years of war," Lewis said, "we could not help doing what we done. There had to be the last fight, and that was what the war brought us to, brought Captain Booth to Ford's Theater and me to Seward's house. A man has to believe in something, the way Captain Booth believed in the Cause. But there has to be a place to stop. That is what Mary was telling me the last time I seen her there in Baltimore, and that is what that black man, Prince David, was saying in the marketplace in Washington City. Everything stops somewhere, and Captain Booth and me, we did not know where to stop. That's what war does to you. It just keeps on until everybody is dead or so wore out that they can't keep going on."

Maggie Branson's clear way of seeing had made him see himself clearer. He had been holding on to John Wilkes Booth the way a dying miser holds on to his gold. Mary, by dying, had set him free from that. Maggie's letter had been like lights going up in the theater after the play. Booth and his world of playacting were out of sight now, behind the fallen curtain, leaving Lewis in the theater to walk out into the dark with Mary Branson.

"Christ died to set you free," Gillette said.

"No, it was Mary Branson that set me free," Lewis told him.

Gillette said nothing.

In the steamy July night, while moths circled and flapped against the smutty lantern, Lewis talked to Gillette about Riley, and Clara Meredith, and Mary, and Hebron on the Suwannee. A new calm settled over him, and the world that never would be came to be the same as the world that had been. He knew one from the other, but the line between them had vanished into a dark wood.

Near dawn Lewis stared at the lantern until the guard came and took it away. When he heard the sergeant and guards coming again, he looked at Gillette, thinking that they were coming for him, but the guards brought him a breakfast of boiled beef and potatoes, with a tin cup of coffee. He ate and drank and set the plate and cup on the floor next to the door.

The door clanged downstairs, and another sergeant appeared with two soldiers, all in starched dress blues. Lewis felt less alone when he saw the soldiers. Gillette, looking in every direction but at Lewis, went to stand by the door. Lewis sat on his cot, pulled off his shoes, and set them side by side near the wall. Then he stood and faced the sergeant. The sergeant took a key from his belt, unlocked the wrist bands, and lifted off the manacles and bar. Lewis rubbed first one red, raw wrist and then the other, until the sergeant unrolled a leather strap, pulled Lewis's hands behind him, wrapped the strap around Lewis's wrists, and tied it with a leather thong. Gillette laid his hand firmly on Lewis's shoulder, and Lewis stepped through the door for the last time and started along the corridor between the two riflemen, with Gillette and the sergeant behind him.

Coming down the stairway, Lewis saw Herold, then Port Tobacco, pass out the door into the courtyard, with Mary Surratt behind them, leaning on a priest's arm. He continued down the stairs and followed them into the bright sunlight. A multitude of faces, some under black umbrellas against the heat, stared at him. Gillette moved around in front of him, a sailor hat in his hand, and set the hat on Lewis's head. The hat toppled off, and another man stepped from the crowd and put the hat on Lewis's head again. Lewis thanked him with a movement of his lips, but with no voice.

His legs moved him toward the gallows, as if with a motion of their own. He even stopped them once, but they trembled into movement again. He heard someone weeping as the procession went by four open graves. Lewis glanced at the graves, then stared at Mary Surratt's bonnet in front of him.

Lewis did not look at anyone in the crowd, but he knew that they were watching him. He wanted them to watch him. He felt less alone now, and the act of the man who had set the cap back onto his head said to him that he was not alone, that someone felt what he was ready to do: to die like a soldier. *This land is not my home.*

Davy Herold, Port Tobacco, and Mary Surratt waited like pillars at the top of the scaffold, and he mounted behind them. A man in a black suit said something, but Lewis could not tell whether it was a prayer or a condemnation. Port Tobacco said in a voice that surprised Lewis with its calmness, "Gentlemen, take care. I am going to eternity now."

Behind him Lewis felt quick hands knotting cloths around his knees and his feet. Then an officer brought a black hood toward him, holding it ahead of him like a gift, and took daylight from him. "I want you to die quick, Paine," Lewis heard, as he felt the rope laid onto his shoulders.

"You know best, Captain," Lewis said.

A sharp command startled him, and he tried to push up, away from time and earth, tried to shout against the hammering of space and the roaring of time.

JACKSONVILLE, EAST FLORIDA: JULY 1865

George Powell came out of the newspaper office of the Florida *Union* into the dusty set of ruts that Jacksonville called a street. Dizziness crowded light from his eyes, and he stumbled out of the way of a supply wagon driven by a Negro soldier in blue. The soldier swore at him and cracked a whip over his horse's head.

"Mister George!"

George Powell stopped and half-turned until Martin caught up with him.

"What did you find out, Mister George?"

"It's no use to go on, Martin. They—It was two weeks ago, about the same day I got the letter from the lawyer. Soon as I found out, they had already gone through with it."

"What we going to do now?"

"Ain't no use in going on up yonder. It's all over. We got to go back home and take care of everything there. Just go on back to the depot and wait for me there."

He shuffled along the dusty street, now almost deserted, except for a wagon here and there that lumbered past. Three old men in black hats sat in a circle, leaning on canes and chewing tobacco. They stopped talking when he came by, and one said "Howdy" to him. George Powell nodded. He passed a saloon and paused, reaching out to touch the door. But instead of going inside, he crossed the street and moved along the shady side.

The street ended, and George Powell came to the river, the murky St. Johns, bearing husks and fetid mold out of moss-shadowed swamps, twisting contrarily northward toward the sea. On a high bank, under an oak, a low wall of crumbling bricks was all that remained of a house. He knelt beside it and shuddered into tears. A rustle in the dissolving bricks made him look around, and he stared into the eyes of a lizard that poked its narrow tongue at him before slithering under the wall.

The stammering son of Amoz knelt before an altar in the year that King Uzziah died, and was vouchsafed a vision. Today God sent no vision to George Powell, settling back on his haunches heedless of the stiffness in his old legs, his head bowed.

"Lord," he prayed, "I am old and weary. Thou gavest me sons, but hast taken them from me, leaving me only my poor crippled son as comfort in my old age. Now thou hast left this land a habitation of dragons and a court for owls, withholding thy blessing in spite of the blood sacrifice of the best of her sons. In thy time, O Lord, heal this desolate land."

Out of the heavy July stillness rolled distant thunder, and a mockingbird in the oak above him started into random song.

AUTHOR'S POSTSCRIPT

Aʙᴏᴜᴛ 1867 Gᴇᴏʀɢᴇ ᴀɴᴅ Pᴀᴛɪᴇɴᴄᴇ Pᴏᴡᴇʟʟ left Live Oak to home-
stead land in central Florida. (Family tradition says they paddled up
the St. Johns River in a hand-hewn canoe.) With them came two of
their daughters, their son George W. Powell—"Wash" in this novel—
his wife and children, and the freedman Martin Powell with his mother
Sarah. They settled near Lake Jesup at a place later called Oviedo.
There twelve years ago I learned about them while doing research for
a local history.

A Court for Owls is historical fiction, not history. Although we
know many facts about Lewis Powell, he remains a shadowy figure.
Most contemporary journalists characterized Lewis as a dull-witted
brute, and later historians such as Osborn Oldroyd and Carl Sandburg
followed their lead. Yet the Reverend Gillette said he had a "cultivated
mind," and General William Payne called him a "chivalrous, gener-
ous, gallant fellow." From the beginning, as far as I was concerned,
Lewis Powell's involvement in events of mythic dimension—Lee's
campaigns, Gettysburg, Mosby's raids, the assassination—called for
telling not in biography but in the informed supposing of fiction.

The novel revealed itself to me as gradually as a pine cone opens.
Fiction has let me into the spaces between scattered, contradictory,
baffling facts. By using fiction instead of history or biography, I can
explore motivation and inner conflict. From behind the "mask" of
fiction, I can guess at things and make believe the guesswork is fact.
The final result is not truth as the historian would define it, but another
kind of truth. Some historians look on novelists as compromising
truth. Yet there is a kind of truth that historiography can seldom

267

reach—truth to human motives and to the waywardness of the human heart.

Scholarship on the assassination flourishes. Especially helpful to me have been such recent studies as William Hanchett's *The Lincoln Murder Conspiracies* and Thomas Turner's *Beware the People Weeping*. James O. Hall, Betty Ownsbey Gregory, Michael Kauffman, Father Alfred Isaacson and others have published illuminating articles in the *Surratt Courier* and elsewhere. Two classic, definitive studies can help the reader feel the texture of life during the war: Bell Irvin Wiley's *The Story of Johnny Reb and the Story of Billy Yank,* on soldiers' lives in camp and field, and Margaret Leech's *Reveille in Washington,* on the capital in wartime.

The story I have told in Chapters 2 through 6 about the Jasper Blues from Florida to Gettysburg is as authentic in its outlines as I can make it. Regimental histories and rosters in *Soldiers of Florida,* Seton Fleming's first-hand narrative of the Second Florida Infantry, Edwin Coddington's *Gettysburg Campaign,* Douglas Southall Freeman's biography of Robert E. Lee, my own meandering across a hauntingly silent, snow-covered Gettysburg battlefield—all made it possible for me to follow the Jasper Blues, ultimately part of Perry's Brigade, as far as Lewis's capture at the lower end of Cemetery Ridge.

We know little about Lewis Powell's service with Mosby. Yet John Munson's *Reminiscences of a Mosby Guerrilla,* John Scott's *Partisan Life with Colonel John S. Mosby,* Harry Gilmor's *Four Years in the Saddle,* and Mosby's *Memoirs* tell much about guerrilla bands and about specific escapades in which Powell was probably involved. In the same chapters the yarns, chatter, recipes, and verses about "dyeing" were originally told in a series of first-person narratives, *Our Women in the War.*

For the trial and prison episodes, I have drawn on Benn Pitman's transcripts, augmented by William Doster's experience as told in his *Lincoln and Episodes of the Civil War.* Hartranft's letterbook faithfully records matter-of-fact details of imprisonment. Documents now in the Library of Congress, including George Powell's letters to the Reverend Gillette and depositions by the Bransons, complement official records.

Much has been written about John Wilkes Booth. Some of what he says in the novel is what he has been reported to have said, but most is what he *could* have said. Reading Gordon Samples' *Lust for Fame* and other accounts has convinced me that Booth was always on stage, calculating whatever he did or said for its effect on an audience, even when that audience consisted of only one person.

I have shifted some events in place and time, and invented others. For example, there is no firm evidence that Lewis Powell met Booth as early as 1861, or that he met John and Mary Surratt before 1865, but I have invented the earlier encounters in order to present the relationships among some of the most important people in the story. Booth apparently hatched the kidnapping plot in 1864, probably in connivance with the Confederate secret service, as William A. Tidwell and James O. Hall have recently shown in *Come Retribution*. Yet he might have mentioned it to Lewis Powell in 1863. As for the night of the assassination, I do not know if Booth ordered Lewis to kill Stanton. I include this order in the plot because I think Booth would have wanted to make a clean sweep of high officials, and because I want to distance myself from the theory of Stanton's complicity, which I consider absurd. All events in the novel could have happened as I describe them, and I took probability and consistency with known facts as controlling limits.

Questions linger about Lewis Powell's relationship with the Branson sisters and with Joe Thomas. Mary Branson was so stirred by Lewis's arrest that she hurried to the provost marshal's headquarters to demand his release, yet oddly she was not called as a witness at the trial. Indeed, her name never came up in testimony. Perhaps this omission is minor in a trial where so many avenues of information were left unexplored, but the facts leave room for the novelist to use his imagination. Joe Thomas's suicide looked so suspicious in the wake of the assassination that Lieutenant H. B. Smith dug up his body in the middle of the night, but apparently without finding evidence that would lead him to deduce that Thomas killed himself for reasons other than domestic and financial.

Of course, it goes without saying that I have used the novelist's license in order to put myself and the reader into the minds of Lewis Powell and other supporting players in what John Wilkes Booth called "the sharpest play ever done in America."